THE
RED ABBEY
CHRONICLES

NAONDEL

THE
RED ABBEY CHRONICLES

O
NAONDEL

AMULET BOOKS
NEW YORK

Library of Congress Cataloging-in-Publication Data

Names: Turtschaninoff, Maria, 1977- author. | Prime, A. A., translator. Title: Naondel / Maria Turtschaninoff ; translated by A.A. Prime. Other titles: Naondel. English Description: New York : Amulet Books, 2018. | Series: The Red Abbey chronicles ; book 2 | Originally published in Sweden by Berghs in 2016 under title: Naondel : kronikor fran Roda klostret. | Summary: Told in alternating points of view, Kabira, Garai, and the other First Sisters share a history of years of sexual violence, oppression, and exploitation at the hands of the vizier Iskan, whose dark powers originate from his control of the sacred spring at his palace at Ohaddin, before the women are able to escape and establish the female haven of Red Abbey on the island of Menos. Identifiers: LCCN 2017011854 (print) | LCCN 2017039110 (ebook) | ISBN 9781683351412 (ebook) | ISBN 9781419725555 (hardback : alk. paper) Subjects: | CYAC: Abused women—Fiction. | Sexual abuse—Fiction. | Escapes—Fiction. | Fantasy. Classification: LCC PZ7.T8824 (ebook) | LCC PZ7.T8824 Nao 2018 (print) | DDC [Fic]—dc23

Text copyright © 2018 Maria Turtschaninoff
Illustrations copyright © 2018 Miranda Meeks
Maps by Sara Corbett
Book design by Siobhán Gallagher

Published in 2018 by Amulet Books, an imprint of ABRAMS. English-language edition published by agreement with Maria Turtschaninoff and Elina Ahlback Literary Agency, Helsinki, Finland. English-language edition first published in Great Britain by Pushkin Press. All rights reserved. No portion of this book may be reproduced, stored in a retrieval system, or transmitted in any form or by any means, mechanical, electronic, photocopying, recording, or otherwise, without written permission from the publisher.

Printed and bound in U. S. A.
10 9 8 7 6 5 4 3 2 1

ABRAMS The Art of Books
195 Broadway, New York, NY 10007
abramsbooks.com

FOR HANNA,
MY FRIEND

Map of

KARENOKOI

AND SURROUNDINGS

Drawn by His humble servant
LANTE AK MAKA-CHEE
BASED ON THE ORIGINAL BY MASTER
HAONG AK SISHE-CHU.

ANJI

Serenity
House

Sovereign
House

Beauty's
House

Glory's
Abode

Tranquillity
Palace

THE
SOVEREIGN
PALACE

The Temple
of Learning

STABLES

THRONE
ROOM

MIRROR
OF TRUTH

ARENA

House of Death

burial mound

ZOO

OHADDIN

under the reign of Raikan ak Ondal-chann

WITH ADDITIONS BY
Garai of the Blood

*T*hese scriptures constitute the innermost archives of the Red Abbey. They contain the history of Naondel and the long journey undertaken by the first sisters to reach the island of Menos. Our journey. It has all been penned by our own hands. Some sections were written before we came to Menos, others after the founding of the Red Abbey. Much of what is written in these accounts must never be disclosed beyond the guardian walls of the Abbey. The knowledge contained herein is far too dangerous. Though neither must the chronicles be forgotten entirely. The Abbey must never forget what was endured to create this refuge for our successors, a place where women can work and learn side by side. May our legacy live on as long as these walls remain standing: Kabira, the First Mother; Clarás, who led our flight; Garai the High Priestess; Estegi, the servant and Second Mother; Orseola the Dreamweaver; Sulani the Brave; Daera, the first Rose; and Iona, who was lost.

KABIRA

There are few whom I have loved in my overlong life. Two of them I have betrayed. One I have killed. One has turned her back on me. And one has held my death in his hand. There is no beauty in my past. No goodness. Yet I am forcing myself to look back and recall Ohaddin, the palace, and all that came to pass therein.

There was no palace in Ohaddin, not to begin with. There was only my father's house.

Our family was wealthy; our ancestral estate was of long standing and comprised a spice plantation, several orchards and extensive fields of okahara, poppies and wheat. The house itself was beautifully situated in a sloping dip at the foot of a hill that gave shade in the worst of the summer's midday heat, and protection from the harshest of the winter's rainstorms. The ancient walls were of thick stone and clay, and from the roof terrace there spanned a far-ranging view over our grounds and those of our neighbors, all the estates and plantations, and the Sakanui River snaking down to the sea. In the east one could see the pillars of smoke rising from Areko, the capital city of the realm of Karenokoi. The city of the Sovereign Prince. On clear days one might glimpse the ocean like a silvery mirage on the southwest horizon.

ᛟ

I met Iskan at the spice market in my nineteenth year. As daughters of a wealthy family, it was certainly not the responsibility of my sisters, Agin and Lehan, and me to sell the estate's yields of cinnamon bark, etse and bao spice. This was undertaken by the overseer and his little pack of laborers, under the supervision of Father and our brother, Tihe. I recall the procession of carts laden with sacks of bark and bundles of bao and gleaming red heaps of etse pods. Father and Tihe rode up front on well-groomed horses. Each cart was flanked by two laborers, on foot, at either side of the horses' heads; both a sign of Father's status and as protection against thieves. Mother, my sisters and I traveled in a carriage at the back of the caravan, with a green silk baldachin over our heads as protection from the heat. The gold-embroidered fabric let through a pleasant glow of daylight, and we jostled along on the uneven path and talked. It was Lehan's first journey to the spice market and she was brimming with curiosity and questions. Halfway to the city, Mother produced steamed dumplings of sweet-spiced pork in soft dough, fresh dates and chilled water flavored with oranges. When the carriage drove over one of the larger of the path's potholes, Lehan spilled meat juice down her new yellow-silk coat and received a scolding from Agin. It was Agin who had embroidered the orange blossoms around the cuffs and neckline. But Mother only looked out over the okahara fields, now in bloom, and did not involve herself in the girls' quarrel. Suddenly she turned to me.

"I first met your father when the okahara was in bloom. He gave me a bunch of the white flowers on our second meeting, and I thought that he must be poor. Other young men gave the girls they were courting orchids and precious fabrics, or jewelry of silver and goldenstone. He told me that I reminded him of the silky-soft petals of an okahara flower. A shocking thing for a man to say to a maid!" Mother chuckled. I bit into a succulent date and smiled. Mother had recounted her first meeting with Father many times. It was one of our favorite stories. They had met by the stream where Mother would often go to fetch water, and which Father happened upon as he rode home from Areko, where he had purchased new farming tools. He was his father's only son and heir, but he did not reveal his name to Mother, nor she her own to him, until their third encounter.

"He had already captured my heart," Mother continued with a sigh. "I reconciled myself with the idea of binding my life to a man of modest means, and thought that perhaps it would be just as well to marry a poet. But then I got—"

The three of us joined in: "—both money and poetry!" Mother smacked my knee with the cover of our lunch pack.

"You disrespectful little cackling hens!" But she smiled, still in a daydream.

Perhaps it was the mood she inspired in me that made me notice Iskan as soon as we arrived at the gardens of the Sovereign Prince. At every spice market the Sovereign opened his gardens of unparalleled splendor to the wives and daughters of noble families. The men, their sons and laborers saw to the arduous physical work of auctioning off their batches of spices in the spice square near the port. Merchants came sailing from far and wide to buy of the renowned spice yields of Karenokoi, and paid a high levy to the Sovereign for the privilege. Our spices would fetch dizzying prices overseas, and the farther the merchants sailed, the more the spices sold for. They were the source of the land's prosperity, and of the Sovereign Prince's fortune.

When we came to Whisperers' Gate, the entrance to the Sovereign's gardens, we had to wait a short while for passengers from other carriages to disembark. Lehan leaned out of the carriage, curious to scrutinize the other women, but Agin pulled her back abruptly.

"That is not any way for a well-born girl to behave!"

Lehan sat back in the carriage with crossed arms and a furrowed brow, provoking an immediate response from Mother: "Scowls destroy beauty." It was something she had said throughout Lehan's life, for she was the beauty of the three of us. Her skin was always fresh as rose petals, even after spending all day out in the sun without a proper wide-brimmed straw hat for protection, or after crying herself sick, as she did if Mother and Father ever denied her something that she wanted. Her hair was thick, and black as coal, and framed her heart-shaped face and big brown eyes in a way that my flimsy hair never could. Agin had the hardest face of the three of us, and large hands and feet. Father sometimes joked that she was his second son. I know he meant no harm, but Agin took great offense. She was the good daughter, the one who looked after me—though I was her elder—and Lehan and Tihe. She was the one who performed offerings to the ancestors, even though that was my duty as eldest daughter. I would always forget, and then Agin would be the one to undertake the tiresome passage up the burial mound, and burn the incense and tobacco to appease the spirits of the ancestors. The only responsibility that I did not shirk was the spring. I made sure to keep it clean, to sweep around it and fish out dead leaves and insects with a net. Yet that was because my siblings knew nothing of the secrets of the spring.

I could already see a great deal from my seat in the carriage

5

without leaning out as Lehan had done. Women and girls, dressed in costly jewel-colored silk coats, stepped down from the carriages, their heads heavy with hairpieces of silver chains and coins. Some handsome young men of the court, with well-kept beards and royal-blue shirts over loose white trousers, helped the ladies down, while little girls, presumably daughters of the Sovereign's concubines, hung flower garlands around their necks in greeting. One of the young men was a head taller than the others. From the silver stitching on his collar I deduced that he must hold a high position in court, close to the Sovereign himself. He wore his hair very short and his eyes were uncommonly dark. When our carriage rolled up to the gate, it was he who stepped forward and offered his hand to help Mother down. She gave a dignified nod and accepted flower garlands from the little girls, and the young man bowed to her before turning back to the carriage once more—to me. I offered my hand and he took it. His hand was dry and warm and perfectly soft. He smiled at me with plump red lips.

"Welcome, Kabira ak Malik-cho." He was well informed also, though it was not difficult to guess that the eldest daughter of the family would step out of the carriage directly after her mother, and from Mother's nine silver chains one could surmise that we were of the house of Cho. I stepped down with care, but did not return his smile. It would hardly be seemly. He still held my hand in his. "My name is Iskan ak Honta-che, at your service. There are refreshments provided by the pond. You must be warm after your long journey." I bowed, and he released my hand. He helped Agin down without a word, but when Lehan stepped out, I saw his gaze linger on her hair, her skin. Her eyes.

6

"Come, Lehan." I took her hand. "The pond is this way." I did not wish to be impolite, so I bowed to Iskan once more. "Che."

He continued to smile, as though he saw straight through me.

I pulled Agin and Lehan along with me. Lehan's eyes were drinking everything in. The beautifully dressed women. The garden paths dotted with crushed seashells. The flower beds of sweet-smelling blossoms with butterflies as big as your hand fluttering hither and thither between. There were many fountains trickling crystal-clear water, and the pendant branches of a parasol tree stretched out above us, offering shade. Mother followed us through the garden, nodding graciously at other harika ladies who were herding their daughters along the paths, and I mused that we too resembled butterflies in our brightly colored silk jackets.

Then the park opened up to reveal the palace, fronted by its huge pearl-like pond. Lehan stopped still, wide-eyed. "I never knew it was so big," she whispered, enraptured.

The royal palace was the largest building in Karenokoi, and it was impossible to conceive of anything more majestic. It was built on two stories and spanned the entire north section of the garden. Its red marble came from inland Karenokoi, which gave the building a color unlike any other in all the realm. The roof tiles were black, and the entrance to the palace from the garden was formed of wide, arched double doors of beautiful gold filigree. The palace housed the Sovereign Prince, his wives, his concubines and all his hundred children, as well as the royal court, which also comprised around a hundred persons. The palace was not at all visible from the city; and consequently few citizens had ever seen more than the roof.

The palace is still standing, or so I heard. Though, naturally, no longer in use.

7

Around the pond were several long tables dressed with gold-embroidered damask and covered with dishes overflowing with chilled fruits, pitchers of iced green tea, candied flowers and pastries glistening with honey. Lehan had eyes only for the palace and its magnificent grounds, and expressed no interest in eating, but Agin and I enjoyed sampling the many delicacies. Mother had found some acquaintances to talk to, and was sitting with them on a bench beneath a jacaranda tree while young girls fetched them refreshing beverages. Suddenly I saw a tall figure in white and blue approaching Lehan where she stood gazing up at the palace. It was Iskan, the man who had been so forthcoming at the entrance gate. He pointed something out to her and she giggled in delight. Mother frowned, and Agin and I sighed as one.

"I'll take care of this," I said and hastened over to Lehan.

"Look Kabira, that's the residence of the Lady Sovereign!" said Lehan as I reached her side. "Iskan resides in the palace. He meets with the Sovereign Prince almost every day!"

Iskan smiled at her exuberant expression. Did this man never stop smiling?

"Perhaps you will permit me to show you the palace? Unfortunately, the second floor is out of bounds to anyone other than the Sovereign Prince and his family, but there are many splendid chambers on the ground floor as well."

"Please Kabira, may we?" Lehan was practically jumping up and down with glee. I laid a calming hand on her shoulder and it seemed to remind her of befitting harika conduct. She stilled and lowered her gaze.

"That is most kind of you, che. But two unmarried young women . . ." I let the sentence hang in the air, unfinished. It was most unbecoming that I should need to remind him of the rules of propriety.

His big brown eyes opened wide and he looked quite appalled. "I should never dream of escorting you alone! My nurse will accompany us as chaperone, naturally."

Lehan peered up at me through her thick eyelashes. I pursed my lips and looked at Iskan, and saw a sort of mischief sparkle in his eyes. He was poking fun at me!

"Very well. Come along, Lehan."

I started hastily toward the steps leading up to the gilded doors, and Lehan squealed and scurried after. We waited a moment in the shade of the bloodsnail-red baldachin hanging above the doors, and Iskan soon joined us with an old woman, dressed in white, leaning on his arm. She nodded at us sternly, but Iskan did not present her. Instead he threw open the doors and showed us in with a grandiose gesture.

"As if the palace were his own," I whispered to Lehan, but she was already gaping at the entrance hall's marble floor and the stunning painted screens dressing every wall. The nurse sat down on a stool in a corner, trying to catch her breath, and Iskan smiled at me.

"As you can see, cho. Everything is most decent."

I scoffed, because I did not know how to respond. He walked over to Lehan, who had stopped before a screen that depicted a ship in front of a green island in the midst of a storm.

"This piece is by Master Liau ak Tiwe-chi."

Lehan's eyes grew wide. "That means it's over four hundred years old!"

"The Sovereign has much older treasures in his collections,"

9

said Iskan genially, and Lehan blushed. She rushed over to the next screen.

"Is she a devotee of fine art, your sister?" Iskan asked, appearing at my side. I was standing with arms crossed and my hands tucked into my sleeves. Mother would have shuddered to see me so, and I noticed the old nurse scowl.

"No, she is not. She simply likes anything that is pretty, golden or expensive." I softened. "Though our father has seen to it that all of his children receive an education in the classics."

"Let me see, your father is Malik ak Sangui-cho. And your estate lies in the northwest, toward the Halim mountains?"

I nodded to hide the fact that I was impressed. "Though not so far as the mountains. Several estates lie between." I glanced at the silver stitching on his collar. "What is your position at the court?"

"I am son, the right hand, of our esteemed Vizier, Honta ak Lien-che."

Walking along the screens of the southern wall, I stumbled and came to a sudden halt. The son of the Vizier! The man I had scolded and snubbed! I removed my hands from my sleeves and bowed low. "My lord. My apologies. I . . ."

He waved away my words. "I prefer not to reveal my parentage immediately. All the better to learn what people truly think of me." I looked up quickly and saw that sparkle in his eyes again. I pursed my lips.

"Better to learn who is silly enough not to realize at once who you are." I was displeased at him for having exposed me so. Yet he appeared to find the situation most amusing, and throughout the rest of our brief tour of the reception rooms and their artistic treasures he paid me at least as much attention as he did Lehan.

10

He was an unfailing source of information on all the beautiful paintings, sculptures and ceremonial objects and furnishings that there were to see. Unlike my sister, I truly was fascinated by art history, and found myself listening with great interest, quite against my will. Iskan had a pleasant manner, though he was clearly poking fun at me. He spoke with ease and animation, and the only thing that irritated me somewhat was his tendency to do so with a certain sense of entitlement. But when he was facing me, and losing himself in the detailed description of a jade statue with its fascinating history of wartime plunder, he focused all of his attention on me. As though I were someone important. Someone he truly wanted to speak with. It was difficult to tear myself away from his dark eyes. When he finally led us back out into the light, he held open the golden door, and his bare hand brushed against mine.

It took a long time after that for my heartbeat to return to its normal pace.

ᚥ

We journeyed home at dusk. Tihe accompanied us, while Father would remain another day to finalize the last trade agreements. Tihe rode out in front together with some of the laborers in their carts, and two hired guards followed behind our carriage. We were as quiet on the homeward journey as we had been talkative on the outbound. Lehan was asleep with her head on Mother's lap before we had even left the city walls, while Agin and I were each wrapped up in our own silence. What she was thinking I do not know, perhaps about the rolls of silk cloth jostling along on one of the carts ahead. My head was filled with the classical paintings I had read about but never before seen with my own eyes, with thoughts of the great echoing halls and gilded ceilings, the throne room of Supreme Serenity and its three-hundred-year-old solemnity. But in every recollection was also the image of intense eyes and a flashing smile. I leaned back on a cushion and looked out into the darkness that had descended upon the district.

Iskan has not left my thoughts for a single day since.

ᚹ

Father came home the following day, laden with purses heavy with coins and full of stories from the spice square, of all the merchants he had met and talked to there, and of how happy he was with how business had fared. Later, when we were sitting in the courtyard, gathered around the supper Mother had laid out under the shade of a baldachin, Father licked oil from his fingers, leaned back against the cushions strewn on the ground and took a glug of wine from his bowl.

"And what about my little girls? Did you have an enjoyable day?"

I let Lehan blather on about the garden and the palace and the nice young man who had showed us around. I stayed quiet. Father watched Lehan closely as she spoke, and when she had finally exhausted the topic, he gazed down pensively into his bowl. "I met a young man before I left for home. He asked if he may visit my daughters with whom he had spent such a pleasant day in the palace."

I looked up at once. Father met my gaze.

"That is precisely what he said—my daughters. Did one of you take a liking to him?"

Lehan blushed and looked down. "Father, I . . ."

"It is quite clear that he is referring to Lehan," I said quietly. "He is only being polite."

"I cannot say that I understand it as polite," Father answered. "It is customary for a suitor to make it known which of the daughters of a household he is courting."

"I was mostly interested in the palace," admitted Lehan. "Though he certainly was pleasant."

"Lehan is still young, husband," Mother said, pouring more wine into Father's bowl. "Only fourteen years."

"What did you say to him?" I tried to sound as though the answer was of little consequence.

"That he is welcome." Mother gave him a sharp look, and he shrugged his shoulders. "He is the son of the Vizier. It is not my place to deny him anything."

"I believe," I said bitterly, "that Iskan is not accustomed to being denied anything. Ever."

I reached for a date to hide my reddened cheeks. Agin, ever keen-eyed, noticed, and I looked away. She turned to Father.

"I cannot wait to set my needle in that saffron-yellow raw silk, Father. Where did you say it came from?"

"Herak. There were many who envied the deal, daughter, you should know! But I have done business with the same tradesman for several years. He buys a great deal of our yield for a very favorable price. In exchange, I buy raw Heraki silk from him. It is most coveted and little goes to export. The Lady Sovereign herself probably does not have as much rare cloth to set her needle in as you do, Agin!"

Agin laughed. "As if the Lady Sovereign would do her own sewing, Father! You are too funny!"

13

I flashed her a secret grateful smile. Now everybody was talking about cloth and not about Iskan.

ᛠ

During the following weeks, there were two hearts that I studied especially closely: Lehan's and my own. Mine perplexed me entirely. I had met a young man who was irritating and self-important, and who had showed interest in my sister. So why did he recur in my thoughts? Why were my daydreams filled with his eyes and smile, and my night dreams filled with his hands and lips? I had never been in love before. Agin and I had giggled about some of the boys in the district, but only in fun. Like children making sand cakes as practice before baking real cakes with flour, honey and cinnamon.

However I tried to deny it, I eventually had to concede that I now had honey and cinnamon on my hands.

Lehan was harder to read. She did not speak of Iskan—but then neither did I. She mentioned our visit to the palace once, but spoke only of the jade throne and not of the man who had shown it to us.

I was quite convinced that her heart was still making sand cakes. Yet this afforded me no comfort. A man such as Iskan would have whatever he desired, and my sister was the most beautiful girl in the whole of the Renka district.

ᛠ

One evening during the hottest of the summer moons, he paid an entirely unexpected visit. Mother and Father welcomed him as an old friend, as if a visitation from the Vizier's son were a commonplace occurrence. The servants rushed back and forth

14

carrying silver trays laden with dates, candied almonds, sweet rice cakes flavored with rose water, chilled tea and vinegar-soaked plums, prepared according to our grandmother's recipe.

I used to love those plums when I was a girl. Grandmother had taught me how to prepare them before she passed away. You must soak a ripening plum in vinegar and sugar with masses of spices. It is eaten during the hottest moons because, according to traditional wisdom, vinegar has a cooling effect on the body. We always had access to fresh spices: cinnamon bark direct from the tree and etse pods still moist with fruit pulp. When you eat the plum, the sharpness of the vinegar makes your eyes water, but the sweetness also tickles your tongue, and the spices caress your palate.

It has been a long time since I tasted a plum.

We daughters were not called into the shaderoom, where Father, Mother and Tihe entertained our guest. The shaderoom ran along the north side of the house, where the hill behind the house afforded a certain protection from the sun, and it was the coolest place to be during the worst of the summer heat. Lehan, Agin and I sat with our needlework and tried not to let our curiosity get the better of us. We could not hear what they were doing, but sometimes Father's hearty laughter resounded across the courtyard to where we were sitting. As darkness began to fall, Father summoned his musicians, and soon the crisp strings of the cinna and the mellow tones of the tilan floated out to us. I smiled down at my embroidery. Not all harika employed their own musicians. We were most worthy of entertaining even the Vizier's son.

The evening was already velvet black, and the air full of the coos of night doves and the violins of cicadas, when Father's most favored servant, Aikon, summoned us. We set our needlework down by the oil lamps and I straightened Lehan's collar. When we stood up, Agin smoothed down the stray hairs on my temple.

"I am glad you chose your sky-blue jacket, Kabira. It makes you look like a blossom."

I pushed Lehan in front of me. "What does it matter," I mumbled, grateful that the dim light veiled my blushes.

Mother, Father, Tihe and Iskan were seated around a low rosewood table in the shaderoom, encircled by flaming lamps. The windows and doors were open to let the cool evening breeze flow through the room, which smelled of lamp oil and food, though the table had been cleared and only a few bowls of iced tea remained. We daughters knelt down on a woolen mat, at a respectful distance.

"You have met my daughters, of course, my most honored guest." Father gestured at us each in turn. "Kabira, my eldest. Agin, my helper. And Lehan, my youngest."

I held my head down-bent but peeked up through my eyelashes. Iskan's gaze swept over us all, and lingered on Lehan. It came as no surprise, yet I had to swallow hard several times. Next to me Agin sighed, ever so quietly.

"Girls, the evening is late and our guest can no longer ride home to the capital. He is to stay with us tonight. Kabira."

I looked up. Father was scratching his beard. "Tihe and I have arranged a meeting with our neighbors in the north early tomorrow. Keep your mother company until our return as she gives Iskan-che a tour of the grounds."

"Yes, Father," I replied, and bowed. Iskan looked at me, and there was that irritating little smile again. I lifted my chin and brazenly met his gaze. I could never let him know of the effect he had on me.

ω

Agin did not want to leave her needlework the following day. "I am the only one with nothing to gain from this meeting," she said mischievously. "You and Lehan are more than capable of entertaining our most lauded guest."

I could not think of a good response, so I scoffed and pulled Lehan along with me down the stairs. Mother and Iskan were already waiting in the courtyard in quiet conversation.

"My ladies." Iskan bowed elegantly as we approached and then straightened to reveal another of his characteristic smiles. That morning he was dressed in a deep-blue jacket and trousers of brilliant white silk. "I could barely sleep last night for excitement about our little excursion."

I immediately blushed and bit my cheeks hard. Could he read my mind? I had not been able to sleep at all. Just knowing that he was in the same house was enough to set my heart aflutter.

"My lord." I bowed, and Lehan did the same. We were both dressed in green garments that morning, hers as light as young grass, mine as deep as moss. I had shown extra care in fixing her hair that morning, as had Agin in fixing mine.

"I should be honored to present our modest grounds." Mother took the lead. We went out through the door in the low north wall of the courtyard. The ground was still moist with dew and the air fresh and fragrant. Iskan walked beside me, with Lehan a few steps behind.

We had a pleasant morning. Iskan was attentive and asked intelligent questions about the estate and everything Father grew, about the number of servants and laborers, and our ancestry and traditions. I had rarely seen Mother so animated and verbose— by Father's side she usually let him steer the conversation, and with her children she was full of warnings and sober advice. Yet now she was proving herself to be full of knowledge about flowers and the maintenance of the grounds. Iskan praised Mother's herb garden and her flower pots, which put her in very good humor, and when he promised to bring her plants from the Sovereign Prince's personal gardens, she hardly knew how to express her gratitude.

Iskan listened politely to everything Mother had to say. At times he asked me questions and kept me entertained with amusing side commentaries. His eyes lingered longest on Lehan. I realized that the same had been true in the palace. Lehan was only fourteen years old and did not have much to say. I was more interesting to talk to, but she was more beautiful, and my heart was aching, yet I was already growing accustomed to the ache. I was not the first girl to suffer so. One day my turn would come and a young man would visit our home for my sake, and perhaps he would not inspire in me scents of cinnamon and honey, but I could live with that.

When Father and Tihe returned, we girls were sent back to our diversions, and Iskan ate a light meal with the men before riding back to Areko. Tihe came looking for us and found us sitting in the courtyard practicing our calligraphy under the baldachin.

"A remarkable man, Iskan ak Honta-che," he said, and sat

down by Agin's feet. He bumped into her arm, as if by accident, so that her brush stroke went askew. She sighed as he grinned.

"Did you know that he has already ridden into battle once? He accompanied the Sovereign Prince's eldest son when they quashed the Nernai uprising. It was Iskan's strategy that won the battle."

"I can imagine," I said sourly, and quickly set down my brush pen before Tihe could ruin my scroll as well. He loved to tease his sisters, yet always took our side against anyone else.

"What do you mean?" Tihe stretched his tall frame out on some cushions and looked up at the bright summer sky. He had grown at an incredible rate over the past year and was now taller than Father. He was over a year younger than me and at least as self-important as Iskan.

"I only mean that Iskan seems convinced that all success is his earning and all failure is the fault of another."

Agin laughed as Tihe threw a cushion at me, and I was glad to have set down my brush pen.

"Girls understand nothing," he said snidely. "Iskan has been schooled in leadership since he was a boy. He is his father's right hand, and there is nothing that happens in the palace that he does not know about, or have involvement in. He gets to be where the *action* is. Not forgotten on a dusty herb farm like me. Next time there is war, I want to be a part of it!"

"Do you really think Iskan has been in actual battle? He and the Sovereign's son were probably sitting in a tent far from the battlefield drinking wine and playing pochasi."

Agin gave me a look of concern. "You are certainly not singing his praises."

19

"Why should I? One egotistical young man is much like another, whether he be the son of the Vizier or the son of a spice merchant." I got up. "I am tired of writing. Can we not begin designing our new jackets? I want one made of the saffron silk."

As soon as we began talking about clothes and needlework, Tihe left us alone, and nobody mentioned Iskan again that day. Yet still his name rang in my ears. Every beat of my heart was singing it, again and again. Iskan. Iskan.

Iskan.

ᚹ

Iskan began to visit regularly after that, and his visits soon took on a familiar routine. He would ride over in the evening once he had fulfilled his day's duties at the palace and spend the evening with Father, Mother and Tihe. The next day, when Father and Tihe were busy with jobs on the plantation, it was up to Mother and us girls to entertain him. Sometimes we would walk through the gardens or adjacent spice plantations. If the heat was too intense, we sat indoors and Iskan would watch as we did our sewing or other appropriate tasks. The ache in my heart became a familiar and constant companion to these visits. I learned to live with it. Agin ceased her little taunts. Even she could see the way Iskan looked at our youngest sister. The only one who appeared not to notice or particularly care was Lehan herself. She enjoyed the attention, that was clear, but I think that she saw Iskan similarly to how she saw Tihe—with sisterly affection. And I think that despite his pride, or perhaps because of it, he was not satisfied with this. So he continued to visit us without taking the decisive step and asking for Lehan's hand.

"He is like a dithering tradesman who pinches at packets and sniffs at cinnamon bark but cannot resolve to make an offer," said Father one evening after Iskan had ridden back to the district capital. He liked Iskan and looked forward to his visits, but at the same time he was irritated that Iskan never spoke his mind.

We sat in the shaderoom and talked while moths of varying sizes danced around the oil lamps and singed their wings. Lehan blushed and went to refill the lamps on the other side of the room. She knew Father was talking about her and could never feel comfortable while others were discussing her future.

"You know how it usually turns out for those tradesmen," Mother replied, and cut a thread from her sewing. "They miss out on the best deals."

Father lit his pipe and took a pensive puff. "Right you are, Esiko. But so far there have been no other offers."

"No, but she is still young. I believe that many of our friends consider it inappropriate to allow their sons to court the youngest daughter with two older sisters still at home."

Agin and I exchanged glances. What could we say? Agin was only sixteen, so just old enough for marriage, whereas I was almost twenty, and Father had not yet received an offer for my hand.

"I suppose there is no hurry. It will give Lehan a chance to grow up a little. It is probably only the spice merchant in me that wants deals to be settled as quickly as possible."

Mother and Father asked Lehan many times what she thought of Iskan, but all they could get out of the girl was that she thought he was "pleasant." They did not want to marry her off against her will, but neither did she seem unwilling. So they let the matter rest. And I resolved that I must rid my heart of this folly.

Ten days later Iskan visited again, but this time he arrived to a near-empty house. Father and Tihe had traveled eastward to buy new bao plants after an entire crop had been destroyed by the harsh summer drought. The worst of the heat was over, and in another half-moon or so the autumn rains would come. It was the best time to renew the spice tree crop. Agin had gone to stay with our aunt to help her sew a bridal gown for her eldest daughter, our cousin Neika. She was to marry as soon as the autumn rains had passed. Lehan had contracted a bad summer cold and lay in bed, while all the maidservants of the household competed to pamper her with hot and cold drinks, compresses and home remedies. That evening Mother and I were sitting alone in the sunroom. Mother was embroidering a collar for Lehan (I could not help but think that it too resembled a bridal outfit), and I read out loud from the teachings of Haong ak Sishe-chu. He has always been my favorite of the nine master teachers, because he mixes philosophy with history. We had come to the third scroll when Aikon opened the door and showed Iskan in. I began to roll up the scroll, but Iskan gestured for me to stop.

"Please, do not let me disturb." He smiled. Mother bowed over her needlework and I hesitated, with the scroll in my hand. It sounded as if he were teasing me, as usual, but would he really do so with Mother nearby? He sat down on his usual cushion, crossed his legs and looked at me encouragingly. My heart was pounding wildly, but I just frowned, unrolled Haong and started reading again.

Iskan listened attentively throughout the whole third scroll and half of the fourth before inquiring as to the whereabouts of the rest of family, when I had stopped for a sip of iced tea. I let

Mother answer. When she told him that Lehan was sick in bed, I studied his face carefully. He asked politely how she was feeling and if there was anything he might do, but I could not find any semblance of concern in his eyes or facial expression. My heart skipped a beat. Though a summer cold was naturally nothing to worry about.

Then Iskan turned to me. "So I suppose you and I will have to amuse ourselves alone tomorrow, Kabira-cho. What shall we do?"

I lowered my head and attempted to look busy rolling up the scrolls.

"You could show Iskan-che the spring, Kabira." Mother set down her needlework.

"A spring? I do not think you have mentioned one, cho."

I had never shown Iskan the spring. It was not oaki—forbidden—but it was sacred. All districts in the realm of Karenokoi were built around a sacred place: a mountain, river, lake or, as in the district of Renka, a spring.

"Our family are guardians of Anji, the sacred spring of Renka," I replied reluctantly. Just as I had expected, Iskan chuckled with amusement.

"I have heard of Anji. In my nurse's tales when I was a boy."

"The spring is absolutely real," I said indignantly.

"I do not doubt it." Iskan leaned back, visibly amused by my reaction. "Though few remain who would call it sacred."

"The old beliefs have disappeared in most of Karenokoi," Mother said. "But in many parts the traditions live on. My mother-in-law took great care to cherish and honor the spring, as my husband's family has always done. She taught my eldest daughter to uphold the tradition."

23

I squirmed. It did not feel proper that Mother should speak of this with an outsider, though neither the spring nor my role as its guardian were secret. However, the true wisdom Father's mother had imparted was something nobody knew but me. Hence why they could make light of Anji's significance. Mother especially had always thought that Grandmother was stuck in the past and was annoyed that she occupied so much of my time with her lessons and visits to the spring, especially at night. It was inappropriate. It was old superstition. Mother was a practical woman. She understood that which she could see and touch, and did not assign value to anything else.

She did not know that much of what she could see and touch in her own home, of her own wealth, was thanks to Anji. She did not know that the spring affected our harvests, our health and our fortune.

"I would consider it an honor to visit your sacred site," said Iskan, and bowed low to me. "Tomorrow, at dawn?"

He knew that I rose early in the mornings. I deliberated. The moon was waxing and it was only a few nights before full moon. Anji was good and strong. Why not? Perhaps I could teach this arrogant man a little humility. Make him swallow his haughty skepticism!

I slammed shut the lid to the box of scrolls.

"As you wish, che." I smiled sweetly at him, and when he raised his eyebrows, I realized that it was perhaps the first time he had seen me smile.

ω

We met the next morning on the path leading to the spring. I

24

brought with me the broom, a drinking bowl, a small clay pot filled with water and Aikon, Father's faithful servant, because I could not be unchaperoned with a man who was not my kin. Iskan gazed in the direction of Areko, which could be glimpsed in the early morning mist like a flickering mirage of shining roofs and smoking plumes. He was clearly restless. Wasting his time here with me, an old maid, when he could be back in the palace in the capital and ... well, doing whatever it was he did there. Enchanting beautiful girls, shining the Sovereign's shoes. He never said exactly what his responsibilities were at the court, but he happily hinted that he was incredibly important and highly praised. I sailed straight past him.

"Follow me," I said as my only greeting. It was more than inexcusably discourteous, especially to such a high-ranking guest. Yet there was something about Iskan that always got my hackles up.

He hurried after me along the path that snaked up the hill behind our grounds. It was late summer now, and all the grass had dried. The hill was brown and dead, and dust covered our shoes as we walked. The autumn rains would come soon. I found myself hoping they did not come too soon. Not before I could teach Iskan a lesson.

We came to the point where the path curved to the left and continued up to the tomb on the crown of the hill. There I turned right, onto a barely discernible trail that led around the hill through the rustling dried grass. My shoes darkened with dew.

"So much haste, cho," panted Iskan. It occurred to me that he was not like the young men on the plantations, used to long rides and hard work. A palace lapdog, that was all he was, used to treats and caresses and no more. I knew that. So why did my heart still race at the sound of his voice so close behind me? Why did the thought of a morning alone with him send delight surging through me, as though I were flying on swallows' wings?

When we rounded the hill and had nearly reached the crevice, I turned around.

"Aikon, you wait here."

Aikon frowned his already wrinkled forehead, but said nothing. I gave him a reassuring smile. "We are only by the spring. I shall call for you if need be."

Iskan held out his hands. "Cho, I beg of you. You needn't fear anything in my company."

I pursed my lips and gave him a look. He smiled broadly. "This is a sacred site. A little respect, che."

He put on an appropriately humble expression and nodded. We walked the last part together in silence. The crevice is scarcely visible until you stand before it, and the spring makes no sound at all. The rift opens to a dark, narrow recess in the side of the hill, with its foot to the east. I continued toward its opening with Iskan, the Vizier's son, close on my heels.

When I was met by the cool air of the chamber inside and the smell of spring water, I felt a sense of calm run through me. All the vexation and the pounding of my heart drained away. No matter what Mother said, this was a sacred place—an ancient site for worship of the divine: the balance of nature. I could feel it every time I came to the spring, and I could not imagine how others did not perceive the same thing. I took a deep breath and let peace wash over me. Then I stepped inside.

Anji was deep inside the hollow chamber. The walls were bare

26

rock and nothing grew in the gloom, nothing except the velvety moss, which was still green and healthy even after our long period of drought. The spring water formed a small mirror by the rock face, no larger than two silk shawls spread out to dry in the sun. It was framed by smooth white stones set around it by someone many generations ago. Some dead leaves had blown up onto the stones, and I swept them away carefully with the broom I had brought. A leaf was floating in the dark water, and I whispered the words that Father's mother had taught me before I picked it out. Nothing dead could taint the sacred water. As always, I was surprised by the coldness of the water on my fingertips. I leaned forward and saw my own face reflected in its untroubled surface. Sometimes other things could be seen in the spring. Things to come. Events from the past.

A face appeared next to mine and gave me a start. For a moment I had completely forgotten Iskan's presence.

"Very pretty. And I truly appreciate the coolness."

I stood bolt upright. My cheeks flushed hot.

"Anji has more than just cooling powers." I took the clay pot and showed him. "This is ordinary water from a normal estate well." I removed the stopper and took a sip. "No poison, see?"

Iskan raised his eyebrows in amusement but said nothing. I bowed down, whispered thanks to Anji and filled the bowl with her icy water. Then I walked to the mouth of the chamber. I looked down at the two thistles growing by the entrance, quite dry and dead. I held up the bowl so that Iskan could see what I was doing, and then poured the spring water over the one to the west, slowly and carefully so the dry ground had time to swallow every drop. Then I poured water from the clay pot over the eastern plant in the same way. Iskan stood leaning against the rock wall with his arms crossed over his chest.

"There. Meet me here three nights from now, at the full moon." I pushed the stopper firmly back in the clay pot, turned on my heel and rounded the hill before Iskan had to time to react. Aikon was waiting for me by the bend with a grim expression. My hands were sweaty and I felt as though I could barely breathe. What had I just done? I stumbled on a stone and Aikon had to catch me to keep me from falling. I had invited a man—a man my parents saw as suitor to my own sister—to meet me at night. Alone. For I knew I would have no chaperone. I knew I would meet Iskan alone, and my cheeks blazed with shame. Yet I was not sorry.

ᛒ

During the three days that followed, I was an exemplary sister and daughter. I took care of Lehan, whose fever had lessened but who was still exhausted and weak. I helped Mother with all of her errands. I made offerings to the spirits of the ancestors up on the burial mound. I waited on Father and Tihe when they arrived home, weary from their long journey and troubled over the rise in the price of bao plants. All to avoid thinking about what I had done. What I was intending to do.

The night of the full moon was cloudless and bright. I sat in my bedchamber and waited until the whole household had fallen into a deep sleep. Midnight had long passed before I dared sneak out.

Unknown birds were singing in the surrounding bushes as I walked the familiar path around the foot of the hill. The colors, smells, sounds—everything was different. I, too, was changed by the night. I had become someone else. A woman who sneaks out to meet the man she loves, with no regard for propriety, family, consequence. My shame, my reservations, I left them all behind. In that moment I was free. Freer than I have ever been since. I often dream about that walk to the hill. In my dreams it is never-ending. Sometimes I am floating above the ground. The shadows are blue, the moon enormous and the air cool against my skin. It smells of dew and soil and etse. Everything in the dream feels real, razor sharp. Freedom and joy swell through me as though my heart might burst.

The dream always ends in the same way. My dream-self becomes aware of something approaching. Something large and black that eclipses the moon and stars. Something about to devour everything. I try to scream. Then I wake up, in my own bed, with the night sky on the other side of the window. My heart pounds and I know it is too late.

Too late to scream.

 barrel

Iskan was there waiting for me when I arrived. He was sitting with his back to the dark mouth of the chamber. Next to him were the silhouettes of the two dead thistles. The eastern one, which I had watered with ordinary well water, looked the same as it had three days previously. The western one, however, to which I had given Anji's water, had a new shoot at its root, the length of a hand.

"It might be a coincidence," came Iskan's voice from the shadows. "You might have come here and watered it every day since we saw each other last."

Yet I heard doubt in his voice. I came to sit down on the

ground next to him. I could not see his facial expression in the dark.

"Anji can bestow life and wealth, if you drink of her water at the right time. And she can bring death and destruction if you drink at the wrong time. The power of the spring is primeval. My father's mother said that all the sacred sites of the different districts had powers once, but that many have been depleted by human greed, or simply forgotten." As I turned to face Iskan the silver chains jangled in my hair. "The spring is the source of our ancestral wealth. It has been used, guarded and cared for by the eldest daughter for many generations."

My father's mother would not have approved of me discussing Anji's secrets with an outsider in this way. But the night and the moonlight had swept away all my reservations and I felt not a tinge of a bad conscience. I was sitting beside Iskan—he and I alone—and I was prepared to say anything to make him believe me. To make him see me.

"So no one but you knows about this?" His voice was full of disbelief. Mocking.

I took his hand, as if it were the most natural thing in the world. As if I had a right to touch him so. His hand was warm and soft in mine.

"Come," I said, and pulled him to his feet. I led him inside the crevice, his hand in mine all the while. My heart was pounding in my throat and my mouth was dry, but my head was clear and my thoughts darted like fish in water. It was dark in the chamber but my feet felt out the way and I led Iskan directly to the spring. She was shining like silver in the moonlight.

"Look down in the water," I whispered. "What do you see?"

30

He leaned forward, callous, disinterested.

"I see myself. And the moon. It's shining. It . . ."

He stopped. Quieted. The disinterest disappeared and his entire body tensed, as though on guard. I did not look into the water. I looked at him.

I was still holding his hand.

Suddenly he turned to me, pulled me close.

"What is this?" His voice was a whisper, a hiss. "What is this I am seeing?"

"Anji shows what has been or what will be. Sometimes she shows your greatest wish."

He stood stock-still. His hands gripped my upper arms so hard it hurt. "Why do you not look yourself?"

"I already know what has happened. I know how my future looks. And I know what I wish for."

The last part I said very quietly. I could hardly believe the words had come out of my mouth. Iskan's face was right before mine now. His eyes were big and dark in his moonlit face. I had never been so close to him before. He smelled of expensive things: the almond oil in his hair, the incense of the palace, the horse that he had ridden to Ohaddin.

A shudder ran through his body. A change—I felt it in his hands, in the grip on my arms. The hardness and tension melted away and he smiled, slow and gentle.

"You do know why I have been coming here all summer, do you not, Kabira?" He leaned forward, and I could feel his breath on my skin. It was sweet with wine. "For you."

Then he kissed me, and it tasted of honey and cinnamon.

From that night on I was a lost cause. A fire blazed inside me, a fire of madness and abandon. There was nothing I would not do to be close to Iskan. Nothing I did not do. I did things I had heard that other girls did for love, forbidden things, things I used to look down on. Now I was the one sneaking out at night to meet my lover in secret. Iskan continued to visit our family just as before, but whenever he spent the night in one of the guest chambers, we always met by the spring. Sometimes he came only at night, just to see me. We would sit by the spring and talk. I asked him about his life in the palace and he was happy to explain. Yet he was not the type of man to speak only of himself. Sooner or later he always led the conversation back to me, and I told him everything I knew about that which most piqued his curiosity: the spring and its powers. I passed on everything that my father's mother had taught me, as well as that which I had discovered myself through experience and intuition. That under the waxing moon the spring water is good and bestows strength, power and vitality, but under the waning moon the water is dangerous, filled with corruption, pestilence and death. Though Anji has greater resources than these alone. For my kin, for generations past, the spring was above all a source of knowledge.

"My mother does not believe in the power of Anji, but my father knows," I told Iskan one night. The autumn rains had begun but it did not rain that night. Swaths of cloud rushed past a waning moon and we had taken shelter from the winds inside the chamber. Iskan had spread a blanket on the wet ground, but the damp seeped through and I was shivering. "We never speak of it directly, but he trusts my advice. I warn him about the coming droughts, floods and pests. I visit Anji and then tell him when to sow and when to harvest. He spreads the word to our neighbors. The wise ones have learned to take heed, then their plantations thrive and their yields grow at the same rate as ours."

"But were you not struck by drought this summer?" Iskan asked. He had taken a lamp with him several meetings ago and hidden it in the chamber between our reunions. Its warm shine illuminated his right cheekbone and almond-shaped eyes. I could barely look at him, he was so beautiful.

"Yes, and Anji foretold it. But what can be done against drought if the channels run dry? Father made preparations to ensure he had enough silver to replace the plants that died."

"How do you see these things? Are they clear images that depict the future?"

I shook my head. "More like feelings that flash through me, pictures in my head and reflections in the water, everything together. They are not always easy to interpret, even for me after years of practice. Sometimes she tells of things that have already happened."

"What use is that?" Iskan stretched out on his back on the blanket, his hands behind his head. The cold and damp did not seem to bother him at all.

"Anji is not for using. The spring is the primordial life force, unfettered and free. What we mortals do with it is up to us."

"Of course, you are not obliged to warn your neighbors," said Iskan slowly. "Your estate could soon be the mightiest in the Renka district."

"Anji forbid!" I drew the sign of the circle on my heart with my fingers. "That would be misuse of the balance. Who knows how it might affect us—or affect Anji herself."

"I might have known you were far too honest for that," said Iskan.

I sat up straight. He glanced at me and saw that I had taken offense. Without a word, he stretched his arm out and pulled me close. His lips fueled the fire that burned in my body and I forgot all about the cold and damp.

ω

The spring became even more significant to me than before. Now it was our place. I would often visit in the daytime as well, to clean away dead leaves and weeds, to refill the oil lamp, and to sit and daydream about Iskan. He did not come to visit the family as often as he had, and my father's irritation was escalating. He had still not made it clear to Father that I was his reason for coming; rather he continued to be amiable and attentive toward all three daughters. Yet he came more often at night, several times per moon. Each time we met he told me when to expect him the next time.

Therefore, I was very surprised when one afternoon I found footprints in the mud around the spring. I had not seen Iskan in five days—had he been here? Had he been waiting for me? Had I misunderstood what he had said? Or was somebody else visiting the spring? I checked the oil in the lamp and found it full, as it had been when I had filled it a few days before. Perhaps not Iskan then, but somebody else.

I could barely sleep the following night, and I got up several times to gaze in the direction of Anji's chamber even though it was not visible from the house. What if he had been waiting at the spring and became angry with me? What if he never came back? My racing mind would give me no peace. When finally the night came that Iskan was expected to arrive, I was hot as though from fever. I dressed myself with trembling hands in the most beautiful jacket I owned, lined my eyes with kohl and fragranced my hair with jasmine-perfumed oil. I did not dare wear my hair chains; their jingling might give me away. I crept barefoot out into the courtyard and waited until I had carefully closed the outer door behind me before putting on my shoes. The whole way up to Anji's chamber I walked as though on needles. My heart sank— there was nobody waiting outside. I groped my way through the dark opening, my feet refusing to find the path by themselves as they usually did. I heard nothing but the beating of my own heart.

Someone was standing bent over the spring. I recognized the broad back and dark hair. I let out a sob, such was my relief, and Iskan turned around.

"It is a full moon tonight," he said. And then: "What is the matter?"

"I thought you had been here," I answered, trying to steady my voice. "I saw tracks around the spring. I was afraid I was mistaken about which night we were meeting."

"No, I have not been here," he answered mildly. "Come, I have brought spiced cakes, prepared by the Sovereign's own master chef."

He walked over to the blanket that he had already spread out in the usual spot, and lit the lamp. In its gentle glow I saw a silver dish of brown cakes, two bowls and a jug of wine. My heart leaped. He had been waiting for me.

We sat and talked as usual, and he told me of his travels with the

Sovereign, and his father the Vizier, to the district of Amdurabi, east of Renka, where the district governor had ordered a great celebration with fireworks in honor of the Sovereign Prince. I drank in every word. Iskan was here once more—with me. Those nights we spent together were like secret jewels I carried with me that no one else could see.

"Speaking of Amdurabi," said Iskan, feeding me another cake, "has the spring shown you happenings in other districts?"

I brushed some crumbs from my lips and swallowed. "No. Anji is the spring of Renka. Her life force is drawn from this soil and these hills. What happens far away is others' concern. In Amdurabi I believe their sacred site is the Mountain of Haran."

"Is that why Anji shows you the future of your family specifically?"

"I do not know. I believe the closer something is, the clearer it can be perceived in Anji's water. But I see what concerns me and mine. You have looked in the spring under the full moon yourself, and you probably saw something entirely different."

Iskan had never wanted to tell me what he had seen in the water. He nodded pensively. "I cannot interpret the visions as well as you. Everything is so disparate and unclear. But I shall practice."

He jumped up and pulled me to my feet. "Come!" He upturned the two bowls and poured out the last drops of wine. "Let us toast with the water of the full moon!"

He filled the bowls with Anji's water and handed one to me. Then he raised his to the heavens and the night. "To us, to the future!"

I lifted my bowl and drank of the cold water, and thought about Iskan and me and the future, and my whole body was singing with joy.

With those little words Iskan gave me hope that he would soon ask my father for my hand. Yet the winter came, bringing cold, dry winds from the northwest, and Iskan's visits to our family grew ever more seldom. We continued to meet at the spring, but also less and less frequently. Iskan excused himself, saying that his father could not afford to spare him too often.

"I am indispensable to my father and his office," he said one night, when we were sitting huddled under a blanket, my teeth chattering from cold. "He cannot manage without me, he says so every day. Father is old and can no longer handle all the intrigues of court as I can. And it is of utmost importance that the Vizier be aware of all happenings at the court of his master. In many ways, I am the most essential person to the Sovereign. More important than those puny sons of his, that is for sure." He scoffed. "You know, the Sovereign gave them new horses—all seven of them. Truly fine horses they are, from Elian in the West. He lavishes gifts on those incompetent oafs, though it is only I who am of any use to him!"

"You were given a new sword last autumn by the Sovereign himself," I reminded him cautiously. "How many can say that they have received the like? He considers you his right hand, as indispensable as his own sword."

Iskan chewed on the inside of his cheek. The storm cloud passed and his face gradually lightened. "Yes, of course. He would be a fool not to realize it."

I swallowed. The Sovereign Prince was sacred. It felt dangerous to speak of him in this way. Like blasphemy. Yet Iskan did so often, and I thought that he must speak very differently at the royal court from when he was with normal citizens.

"But Kabira, you must understand that this means I cannot return for a while now. Perhaps until springtime, when it is warmer." He pulled the blanket tighter around us. "It is so cold that I can never fully warm up again until the following day once I have returned to the palace." He gave me a kiss on the forehead and stood up. "Come, let us toast to springtime and milder winds."

He led me to Anji. He always wanted to drink from her when the moon was new. The water was so cold that it hurt to swallow it. Iskan wiped his mouth with the back of his hand.

"I can feel it endow me with strength—in both body and mind." He took out a clay pot and filled it with spring water. "So I can manage until we see each other again. I will send word, Kabira." He leaned forward and brushed his lips against mine. "Until spring, my little bird."

I stood at the mouth of the chamber and watched him disappear down the hillside, toward the grove where he usually left his horse. The wind was biting at my cheeks but I barely felt it. My heart was even colder.

ᛒ

It was a long and tiresome winter. Gone were my usual high spirits, and nothing brought me joy. The only one who understood the cause of my change was Agin. I often caught her observing me with thoughtfully furrowed brow, which made me even more bad-tempered and off-kilter, so I shrank away from both sisters and spent a great deal of time alone. Mother was concerned. She thought I was bored from the lack of activity in winter. Her solution was to drag me to various neighbors and relatives. I suspect she also believed that what I needed was a husband, but the young men who were hustled into my path were nothing compared to my Iskan. They did not conduct themselves with such dignity. They did not tell such interesting anecdotes as Iskan's from the royal court. Their lips were not as red. Their laughter not as infectious. They did not look at me with the same dark eyes. And they did not make my skin smolder the way Iskan could with his very presence. I am afraid that I met all the polite, honest youths of our district with disdain and disinterest. What could they offer me that the Vizier's son could not offer tenfold?

I would be ashamed now to think of how I behaved, if I were still capable of shame. My reputation was tarnished, and when Mother surrendered and stopped dragging me to all the families of her acquaintance, not a mother remained who would see her son married to the haughty daughter of Malik-cho.

The only thing I did of my own volition was visit the spring, which I did daily, and often several times a day. I kept the surrounding ground free from a single leaf or blade of grass. I adorned Anji with beautiful white stones. I would often sit at the spring's edge in a winter jacket and layered shawls, gazing into the clear water and thinking of Iskan, reliving each encounter we had had there. Sometimes, when I thought about his kisses, I saw in my reflection that my cheeks blazed red. He had kissed me. He had called me his own. He had promised to return.

The spring was altered. Anji and I had always shared a special relationship. Mother would have laughed at me if she had known that I thought so, but it was true. Father's mother found it much more difficult than I ever did to understand Anji and interpret her revelations. Yet now it seemed the spring had turned from me. When I sat at her edge, I could not find that affinity. She was no longer interested in me. Resting with my hand in the ice-cold water, I tried to understand, but Anji did not respond. It felt like both Iskan and Anji had forsaken me, and it broke my heart. I could not endure losing them both.

On the next full moon, I was prepared. I needed to stare into the water to try to understand why Anji had turned from me. Perhaps she could show me Iskan, when he intended to return, what our future held. The worst of the winter winds had settled and a little warmth was returning. Spring would soon come. He had promised to send word by then.

I sat fully clothed on my bed and waited until the household was asleep, just like all the nights I had walked up the hill to Iskan. Yet now it was Anji who filled my thoughts. The full moon hung large and white above my head as I followed the path around the hill, and each blade of grass had a sharp moon shadow. When I approached the chamber, the air was dense with the life force emanating from Anji. She was awake, she was strong! I hurried the last steps, rushed breathless into the chamber to meet her—and stopped dead. Someone was standing in front of the water. I must have emitted a sound, because the person turned around and raised an object that flashed in the moonlight. A sword.

"Who goes?"

I nearly fell to the ground with joy and relief. It was Iskan.

"It is I—Kabira," I said. "You have returned, che!"

He came to me, the sword still in his hand.

"What are you doing here?" He leaned over me, his face in darkness, his voice hard. "Answer me!"

"I came to visit Anji." I outstretched an imploring hand. "Please Iskan, why are you angry?"

"Were you coming to meet another man? Are you going behind my back?" He grabbed my wrist and twisted it.

"No!" I swallowed. I tried to remember how I used to talk to him when he acted this way. "What other man could possibly compare to you, Iskan ak Honta-che, son of the Vizier, the Sovereign's most brilliant jewel? For me there is no other."

He let go and stepped back. The moonbeams played on the sword's edge.

"Have you missed me? Have you thought about me?"

"Every day, che! Every moment! You have kept me waiting so long!"

"I have thought about you also, Kabira. Often, in the lonely nights at the palace." He threw his sword to the ground and stepped toward me. "Are you mine, Kabira? Mine alone?"

"Yes, Iskan, now and forever, I am yours alone."

He leaned into me, his mouth by my ear. "Can you prove it to me? Now, my Kabira?"

I nodded, knowing he could feel the movement against his chest.

"Answer me, Kabira. Say that you want me."

"I want you, Iskan. Please."

I had thought about it many times, when we kissed, when he held me close, when he touched me. However, I had been entirely unprepared for the desire that his hands had roused in my body. My mother had never taught me about such things. I had felt desire in my body that was stronger than reason. I had wanted him. I had wanted him for a long time. Though not here. Not like

41

this. Yet I was afraid. Afraid of his erratic anger, his volatility.

"Then you shall have what you want," he whispered, and kissed my neck. "I shall give it to you. Now."

So Iskan ak Honta-che took my virginity inside Anji's chamber, on the bare ground, and it was not how I had dreamed it would be, but I held on to his shoulders and thought that this meant that he was mine, truly mine. He wanted me. The son of the Vizier who could have anybody he wanted, and he wanted me, Kabira.

It was only later, back in my bedchamber, picking flecks of dirt from my trousers in the handbasin, that I realized I never had asked Iskan what he was doing there at the spring under the full moon. Or what he had seen in Anji's water.

ᴡ

We continued seeing each other, but Iskan no longer visited the house. He met me only at Anji, at night. I suspected that he came alone some nights, like the night I surprised him under the full moon. However, I dared not verify my suspicions, and neither did I ask. I did not want to provoke that cold anger again. That side of Iskan frightened me, so I did everything within my power to keep him in good humor. Asked him about life in the palace. Praised him for the services he had rendered his father or the Sovereign. Took pity on him when he felt he had been unfairly treated, which was often. Iskan saw injustice and insult in almost every deed. Now that we were lovers he revealed more of this side to me. He let his cool composure slip sometimes and exposed his uncertainty, which I took as a sign of his love for me. He was prepared to let me see inside him, and I harbored every confidence in my heart like treasure.

42

Iskan was inordinately jealous of nearly every member of the royal court, despite the fact that he personally held one of the most prestigious positions. Yet this position was principally due to his lineage, and this weighed on him; he wanted a role in his own right.

"There is no one at court with a mind as sharp as mine! They go through life as blind as moles in the earth." Iskan was sitting at Anji's edge and drawing patterns in the water with his fingertips. He seemed to be speaking to the water at least as much as to me. "The Sovereign ought to see it! Yet he is equally blind. He gives his sons all the best appointments. They are mollycoddled layabouts. The eldest, Orlan, cares only for hunting. The others attend parties, take endless amounts of concubines, and are weak and indolent. A man must never let his desires weaken his body or spirit. He should never take so many concubines that they divert his attention from what is truly important." He raised his hand and let the water drip from his fingertips into the spring again, his eyes following every drop, like a lover looking upon his beloved.

"Your time shall come," I said, to remind him of my presence. I sat by his feet with my gaze fixed on his face. "I know it."

"Yes." He smiled, still facing Anji. "I have knowledge they lack, do I not?" His voice softened. "And I am learning more all the time. I am not impatient. I can bide my time, until the moment is right. And when it is, you will tell me, won't you?"

"Does she tell you much?" I asked in a small voice. Perhaps Iskan would soon be able to interpret Anji's revelations as well as I. He would not need me.

"She shows some things," he said slowly, with something like affection. "Not everything I want to know. But she sets me on the

43

right path. Soon I shall learn how to coax it all out of her." He shook the last drops of water from his hand and turned to me, as if awoken from a dream.

"Kabira." He rose to his feet and detached his sword. Pulled on the tie of his trousers. "Now it is your turn."

He took me every time we met. First he drank from Anji, or played with her water, or simply stared into it. I was not to disturb him. When he was ready, it was my turn. It improved after the first time. He kissed me, and caressed me, and sometimes he managed to spark fire and desire in my body. And I wanted him—inside me. In those moments Iskan was mine alone. He was totally and utterly with me, and I competed with no one, not even Anji.

By and by there came to pass that which I had both feared and hoped for. At the peak of spring my bleedings ceased. I was with child. I did not know how to deliver the news to Iskan. I feared he would be angry, though at least then he would have no choice but to finally speak to my father. To ask for my hand. Then we could stop meeting like this, in secret, concealed by night and darkness.

Iskan was in good humor that night. He had brought a thick blanket for us to sit on, and cushions, and rice cakes and sweetened wine. We sat outside the crevice and ate and talked quietly. Iskan talked, and I listened. The Sovereign had praised Iskan's counsel regarding courtiers who had been exposed for taking extra fees from foreign merchants in exchange for better sites at the spice market. All tariffs on spice trade were owed to the Sovereign Prince alone.

"I told the Sovereign that he must make a cautionary example of them. So that nobody would follow in their footsteps. Everyone must show respect for our master, the forefather of all forefathers.

44

The Sovereign prefers not to carry out such dirty work himself, so he delegated it to my father, who passed the task to me. I had them castrated, and all their children, wives and grandchildren slain. Their lineage dies with them, and there shall be no one to honor their spirits when they are dead. They have to live out the rest of their piteous lives in that knowledge." He shook his head when he saw my expression. "Needs must, Kabira. My appointment is to protect the Sovereign Prince, come what may."

I wanted to say that they could have been simply stripped of their property and exiled. Yet I dared not displease Iskan. Not when I had such important news to tell him.

"Iskan-che." My voice must have given me away, because he leaned forward and stroked my cheek.

"There, there, what is it, my little bird?"

"I am with child."

Iskan leaned back on his elbows and studied me. I held my breath, awaiting the explosion.

He smiled. "I have been hoping for this."

I did not know how to respond. My heart leaped with joy, and, for the first time in a long time, I tasted a hint of cinnamon and honey on my lips again. He loved me! He wanted me, and the child I carried! Our child.

He jumped up brusquely and pulled me to my feet. "Come!"

I followed him through the opening into the chamber. Into Anji. She lay dark and quiet in the faint light from the waning moon. Iskan bent down and picked up the bowl he kept at the edge of the spring. He filled it with water.

"Drink!"

"But the moon is waning! Anji's water is bad, oaki!"

"Precisely." He smiled and his teeth gleamed white in the scant light. "Now I can test something I have long wondered about. Drink!"

I could not move. I stood frozen in place and stared at the bowl in Iskan's hand. He made a sound of impatience and took hold of the back of my head in one of his large hands. He pulled back my head and pressed the bowl to my lips. Liquid spilled against my teeth, seeped into my mouth, ran down my throat. I gave up. I gave in. I drank.

I had never tasted Anji's dark water before. It felt cool and soothing in my mouth and throat. Perhaps it was not so dangerous. I had only my grandmother's word for proof that it was filled with death and destruction. I swallowed. Iskan scrutinized me intensely.

"Do you feel anything?"

I slowly shook my head. There was a pulsing, a strange murmur, in my ears. Like blood flowing through my veins, but louder and more forceful. A rush, of a river, of a waterfall. Anji was inside me. I had drunk her water my whole life, her strength was in my body. It mixed with my blood and was a part of me—it was who I was. The figure of Iskan seemed to ripple in the darkness. I saw Iskan as he was standing there, but also all the possible Iskans to come, and those already passed. I saw him as an old man. I saw his death. If I wanted, I could touch it. Move it. Draw it closer. Draw it here.

I stretched out my hand. It was trembling. Iskan was watching; he did not look away from my face for one moment. I brushed my fingers against his death, gently, cautiously. Like playing the cinna. He took a sharp breath.

I let my hand drop and looked him straight in the eye. He knew, right at that moment he knew the power I had over him and what I could have done. He knew what I had refrained from doing.

"I am going home now," I said, and he was taken aback by the force in my voice. I turned around and left.

ω

Over the course of the next three days the child was lost. I remember little from that time. Fever raged through my body and burned away the last remnants of my love for Iskan. I remember blood, vast amounts of blood. I remember the anguished faces of Mother and Agin. I remember whispering voices, chilled water with mint and petals of burnet bloodwort, I remember warm goldenroot compresses, I remember rushing steps.

On the fourth day the fever subsided. I lay in my bed, surrounded by clean new bolsters. Agin sat at my feet looking down at her hands.

"I thought you were going to die. What have you done?"

I turned my face away. "Does Mother know?"

"She has given birth to four children. What do you think?" Agin's voice was hard.

"Do you hate me?" I could not look at her.

She sighed. "No, dear sister. But I am angry with you. Why did you not say anything? You should never have done this to yourself! You should have spoken to Father. He could have forced him to marry you." Yet I could hear in her voice that she did not believe her own words.

"Nobody can force this man. He will never marry me. Ever. I

47

know that now. I am free from him. I will never see him again, I swear."

She stroked my bedcover. "I am glad to hear you say that. He was here."

I felt all the air contract from my lungs. I could not breathe.

"He had the gall to visit Father and Mother, as before. He was very concerned for your well-being. He asked questions. Wanted to know all sorts of things. Father suspects nothing, so he and Tihe welcomed him as an honored guest. Mother did not want to stay longer than necessary, so I had to wait on them. He looked at me . . ." She shuddered. "I had never noticed it before. It was as though he saw straight through me. As though he could affect things with his gaze alone." She shook her head. "I am glad that you are rid of him now. No good could come from it. I saw it, right from the start."

All of a sudden she rose to her feet and came to the head of the bed, bent down and embraced me. I do not know if she had done that since we were little girls and shared a bed. Then, we would often lie with our arms around each other to protect one another from the terrors of the dark. Now she pressed her lips to my hair, which was thick with sweat and dirt.

"Life goes on, you shall see. It will take a while, but one day you will be happy again."

When she got up to leave, I looked at her. "I did not do this to myself." I made a gesture to indicate my body, the bed, everything that had passed. "It was him."

Agin shuddered again. "Then you are well rid of him."

I watched her leave the room. I felt grief, but also relief. I had escaped. I was free.

48

Or so I thought.

The next day I awoke with a murmur in my body. The house was quiet, though the sun was already high in the sky. Spring had almost passed into summer, and I could feel the warmth of the day through the drawn window curtains.

I sat up; my body felt frail and it was difficult to gather the strength to get out of bed. Eventually I stood up, leaning against the wall. The murmur inside me was almost deafening, and I did not know whether it was the house that was deathly silent or I who could not hear. Everything rippled and trembled, as if I could still see into the past and potential futures. The walls did not seem solid. I saw second walls behind them, walls belonging to another house, one much larger and grander than ours. Along those other walls there were people moving about in expensive clothes, their translucent forms gliding soundlessly past in a flash of bloodsnail-red, gold and deepest blue. They were all women. When I reached out to touch a young woman with raven-black hair pinned up with two combs, my fingers passed straight through her arm. For a moment I thought she looked right at me. Then she, and all the others, were gone. The house around me was mine again. I could not breathe evenly and my back was sticky with sweat.

"Agin?" I called cautiously, and my voice thundered in my ears. "Mother?"

No answer came. I waited until my breathing had steadied, then walked slowly over to the door. I had to struggle to stay standing.

The second-floor terrace was empty. The door to Mother

and Father's bedchamber was wide open. I walked toward it, supporting myself against the wall.

On the edge of the bed sat Lehan. She had her back to me and her long, shiny hair tumbled down her slender back in loose curls. The bed was unmade and she was holding something in her hands. The curtains were still drawn over the window, and the chamber was dark.

I took a few shuffling steps inside. She must have heard me, but did not turn around.

"You ought to let some light in," I said. My throat felt dry and sore.

Slowly my eyes grew accustomed to the dim light and I saw what Lehan was holding. A hand. A slender hand that I knew well. Mother's hand. And I saw that the bed was not unmade, but occupied. Mother and Father were lying there. Side by side. The air tremored and I saw a final vision from Anji's water, a vision of Mother as an old woman, and Father as an old man, side by side, surrounded by grandchildren, and with their deaths before them. But that death had been snatched away from them. Drawn nearer by an artful hand. Drawn here. Then the vision was gone.

"They died in the night. All of them."

Lehan's voice was thin and sounded nothing like her own. It came from a place far away, a place she had never been before.

I felt everything collapse at that moment. I knew what she meant. I understood. Yet I still heard myself ask, "All of them?"

"Tihe and Agin lie dead in their beds. Most of our servants too. The ones who are not dead have fled this house of death." There was no sentiment in her voice; it was cold and hard, like steel.

I did not respond. I rushed to Agin's chamber as quickly as I could get my body to move. I found her lying with eyes closed and hands clasped over her bedcover. She looked exactly as though she were sleeping. I sank down on the bed beside her. Held her body against mine, my arm across her chest.

Agin, my sister. Who had always looked after Lehan and me. Who was always thinking of others. Tihe, our proud, beautiful brother. Father and Mother. Dead. And it was I who had brought death to our house. It was my fault they no longer drew breath. I had taught Iskan the secrets of Anji. I had shown him how to use her oaki, her forbidden water. I could not understand why I was still alive. Did he think I would die naturally, because I lay sick and frail?

I wished I had died along with the child I had lost.

I have wished this for more than forty years.

ᚦ

Our neighbors found us. Many servants had fled the house in panic and spread word of the house of death. My parents' oldest friends braved their way over to see if any survivors remained from the terrible sickness that had raged through the household. They took us away with them, tended to us, and helped us bury the dead. Our aunt came, and once Mother, Father, Tihe and Agin had been buried on the crown of the hill, she took us home with her. Lehan and I could not do anything. We barely spoke to each other. We dressed in the mornings, ate what was put in front of us, responded when spoken to, and retired to the same bed when darkness came. Yet Lehan was like a stranger to me. I do not know why we could not find solace in each other. Perhaps my guilt was

51

too great. Her grief too severe. Our aunt and our cousins treated us with utmost respect and sympathy, but deep down, through the mists of my sorrow and anguish, I knew we could not stay with them forever. I simply did not know where we would go.

ϖ

Lehan, our aunt, our cousin Ekhe and I were sitting in the shaderoom one late-summer morning, engaged in embroidery, when one of my aunt's servants entered.

"Iskan ak Honta-che," he announced, and held open the door. Ekhe looked up curiously and Lehan set down her needlework. Auntie rose up to greet her guest with bow after bow and offered him iced tea and cakes. I continued sewing. I dared not look up. He had come to slay me now. He could do it without difficulty. Without remorse. My heart was beating so hard that my hand began to tremble. I heard his gentle voice utter the proper condolences. Maybe he would do it quickly. Then I would not suffer anymore. Not grieve. Not bear all this guilt. I looked up.

He stood before Lehan, his neck down-bent in sorrow, and my sister looked up at him with shining eyes.

"Your mother and father were the finest people I have ever known, Lehan-cho. They were as dear to me as my own parents. I had come to hope that they would indeed become my parents." He raised his voice so the whole room could hear, and took hold of Lehan's hand. "I wished to marry their youngest daughter, Lehan. But after the great tragedy that has befallen the house of Cho, I can no longer bring myself to do so."

My cousin Ekhe let out a little shriek and my aunt rose to her feet at once. "Let me fetch my husband. The head of the family must be present." Iskan nodded, without letting go of Lehan's hand. He looked at me then, straight at me, and I could see a warning in his eyes. A threat.

My aunt returned with her husband, Netomo. They sat down around the low table where the servants had laid out refreshments. I could not move from where I was sitting, and Iskan did not sit down but remained standing with Lehan's hand in his. I could not take my eyes off him, like a sparrow wary of the hawk's imminent swoop.

"No agreement was formalized between me and Malik ak Sangui-cho, nor between he and my father. But my intentions have been clear for a year past. I only waited until I might reach such a role in the palace of the Sovereign Prince that I would be in a position to take a wife. However, now I feel that my actions must be guided by a duty greater than my own desires." He looked tenderly down at Lehan and gave her a sad little smile. "Two girls are the sole survivors of a disease that has struck down their father's entire household. I feel that my responsibility is to take care of them both, in such a way that disrupts their lives and circumstances as little as possible." At that moment he let go of Lehan's hand and turned to me. I could not so much as blink. His gaze bore into me, heavy with the weight of words unsaid. He took a step toward me and I tightened my grip on my embroidery. He must not take my hand. I could not bear to feel his touch.

"Kabira ak Malik-cho. You are your father's sole heir, given that he has no brothers or other male relatives. Marry me and I shall take care of your beloved sister Lehan. Through the marriage she shall become my sister too. We can reside in your father's house, where I shall maintain his estate and your lives can continue as before. You need never be separated, which I am sure you both appreciate. I shall see to it that you want for nothing and that no danger befalls you—either one of you."

As he spoke these final words he locked his eyes onto me, his dark, wrathful eyes. He stood with his back to the others so nobody could see the expression on his face. But I saw. And I understood.

If I did not comply I would not be the only one to suffer. He would kill Lehan. He had done all of this for the sake of the spring. For access to Anji's water. He was willing to do whatever it took to make the spring his own.

I did not make a sound. I knew what my answer must be, but I could not muster the words. My aunt's husband, Netomo, went to Iskan's side. He rubbed his hands together. The son of the Vizier married into the family! It was an opportunity he could not pass up.

"This is all so sudden. You must excuse our young niece's abashment. I am certain that she understands what a generous offer this is and there can be no doubt of her acceptance. Is that not so, Kabira?"

I bowed my head in resignation. Everybody interpreted it as affirmation, and Netomo patted Iskan on the back and congratulated him, and Auntie called for wine and bowls. Soon we were all standing together toasting the health and wealth of the young couple. Iskan raised his red-lacquered drinking bowl to me and leaned forward to whisper in my ear. Everybody giggled and applauded, because it was the most natural thing in the world—a young man whispering secrets to his betrothed.

"You need not fear me, Kabira. Simply do exactly as I say, and both you and your beautiful sister will be safe. Understood?" I nodded. "Good. My first request: speak never more of the spring and its powers to anybody. Never go there again. I will know if you do, Kabira, you know that. Anji is mine now."

His voice was warm and intimate, a tone befitting of secrets between lovers. Nobody could have known of the threat and venom in his words. He turned to Netomo.

"I want the wedding to take place as soon as possible, so that these young women can be returned to their home without delay."

"Of course." My uncle nodded in approval. "Before the next full moon. I have the keys to my late brother-in-law's estate. You will doubtless want to put your new home in order in the meantime."

Iskan smiled. He smiled and smiled all afternoon; he smiled at Lehan and he smiled at me, and only I could see everything his smile was concealing.

ω

I have little memory of the lead-up to the wedding. There must have been a great many preparations, but I was not expected to be involved in any of them. I spent most of the time in the bedchamber Lehan and I were sharing, pacing around like a wild animal in a cage. I racked my brains for a way out of this trap, but saw none. None without risk of incurring Iskan's wrath; none that could ensure Lehan's safety.

I remember one evening when Lehan was readying herself for bed in our chamber. She sat brushing her long hair before the mirror and watched without a word as I paced anxiously. Eventually she sighed and put down the brush.

"What is wrong with you? You are acting as though Netomo

married you off to some toothless old man with scabies. Not the handsome young son of the Vizier who only wants the best for both of us. If anybody should be wringing her hands in sorrow, it is me."

I stopped still and stared at her. She tossed her head, and her perfect skin flushed reddish.

"After all, it is actually he and I who should be getting married."

The words lingered in the space between us like shards of glass.

"But . . . You always said that you did not care for him."

"I didn't." She looked down at her hands, still considerably pink in the face. "But he is the Vizier's son. A man with a fantastic future before him. It would have been a good match. And he is very kind to us. A fine man."

"Lehan, he is wicked!" I fell to my knees beside her and considered my words carefully, to warn her without endangering her. "You must not trust him. He never wanted you. Father himself said that Iskan never uttered a word on the matter. He is wickedness incarnate, oh Lehan, we must run away. Both of us. Perhaps even tonight?" Hope lit up inside me. Run away, yes, why had I never thought of it? Far away, where Anji's visions could not reveal us and Iskan could not reach us.

My sister went completely pale. She looked at me with disgust. "He never wanted me? Was it for your sake that he came, perchance? Is that what you have convinced yourself?"

"Yes, that is the truth, but not in the way you think Lehan. He—"

She interrupted me. "I never thought you would sink so low, Kabira." Her voice was ice-cold and she got up and started rubbing her hands over her arms, as though to brush away my words. "Father and Mother knew. Everybody knew, Iskan said so himself. He wanted to marry me. And now he wants to take care of both of us as best he can. Why should I run away from a man who intends to return me to my family home? I miss it so much I feel I may fall apart, Kabira. I want to walk the halls Mother walked and hold the objects Agin held. I want to be near them again. But you . . ." Her face was full of disgust. "You are struck with madness. You do not deserve such a good man. I am asking Auntie if I can sleep in Ekhe's chamber. The bride-to-be needs solitude."

Before I had time to say anything else, she swept out of the room and left me alone.

ᴃ

Our wedding was performed according to the old rites, at the burial mound outside Areko where Iskan's ancestors lay. There was a small altar for offerings to the spirits of the ancestors, and we stood before it and exchanged the traditional thrice-three gifts between his family and mine. From one of the gift baskets Lehan was holding I took the bottle of fig wine for happiness, the silk thread for constancy and the packet of bao for fertility, and handed them to Iskan. He accepted and passed them on to one of his cousins before turning to Lehan and bowing. She smiled at him, the dimples in her cheeks deepening, and handed him the other basket. Iskan picked out a silver coin for wealth, grapes for abundance, hannam-tree bark for health, vinegar for wisdom and an iron nail to build our life's foundations, and gave them to me. I accepted them. Then Lehan gave us the final gift, a cake of nuts and honey that we divided in half and ate. Then we were married, though the marriage was not yet consummated. This happened after the wedding celebration that was held in what used to be my father's house, now Iskan's. There were a small number of guests eating the delicious food my aunt had prepared, listening to music from my father's musicians, and dancing under lanterns hanging from the trees in the courtyard. Then, when the last song was sung and the last wine was drunk, Iskan led me up to my parents' bedchamber, to our marriage bed. The bed was new—Iskan had had all the furniture and textiles in the house burned, "to dispel the sickness that had claimed so many lives"—but it made no difference. To me it was the bed where my parents had died, where he had murdered them. I could not bring myself to go near it, and hesitated in the doorway.

Iskan looked around and nodded contentedly. "Look here, a genuine Liau ak Tiwe-chi as wedding gift from my father." He pointed to a painted screen that hung by the bed. "It is worth five horses in full combat armor. I have filled the house with valuable art and tasteful furniture. It is truly a home fit for a vizier's son." He sat on the edge of the bed with one foot resting on his other knee. "However, I am thinking of making some improvements. A wall built around the burial mound, for example. And a door to protect the spring, with a lock." He smiled. "That is just the beginning. I have seen magnificent things, Kabira. A glorious future. In a few years you will not recognize your father's estate. I drink of Anji's water every night when it is good, and see her visions every full moon. With each passing moon the pattern becomes clearer. I need only give things a push here, a tweak there, and my shining future will draw nearer and nearer." He lowered his voice. "But drinking of her dark water, the oaki, that is another thing entirely. The force that fills you! Power over life and death. You know, Kabira. You have tasted it. Anji's dark water is the weapon with which I will shape my future, little bird." He smiled with pity and cocked his head to one side. "Though you shall never drink it again, dear wife. And now it is time that you become my wife in the flesh."

He had taken me many times before that night, but this time was different. This time he enjoyed degrading me, inflicting pain on me. He took his time. In the morning, when his female relatives came to check our sheet for the red stain that proved my virginity, they did see fresh red blood. But it had come from more places than one.

He forbade me from going outside. He forbade me from talking to anyone other than himself and Lehan, and Lehan no longer spoke to me. I was not allowed to address the servants and I had nothing to say to Iskan. So my voice faded and I grew quiet. Through my quiet I could hear the din of the laborers building the wall around the hill, and the door in front of Anji. When everything was finished, he showed me the key and laughed. "Now she is truly all mine! Not even the Sovereign Prince himself can get his hands on her secrets. She is like a beautiful woman who gives herself unto one man alone, her only lover. I am the one that she wants. She shows me willingly every pleat and fold of her secrets."

He took me every night.

"Sons, Kabira," he said one night as he sat wiping my blood from his hands. "A man's influence can be gauged by his sons. No one else is as loyal. No one else can act in his name. Alliances made through the marriage of daughters are not to be trusted. I shall have you until I have planted a son in your womb."

I ceased thinking, hoping, resisting. I do not know how much time passed; I no longer concerned myself with counting days and nights. I ceased caring for my hygiene and appearance, yet nothing would discourage him from my bed. It gave me a certain amount of satisfaction to see the disgust on his face as he mounted me; gone was his eternal smile. Still, he did not stop coming to my bedchamber. His superior self-confidence was replaced by furious stubbornness. Each time my moon blood came his perilous wrath grew.

"I haven't the strength for a second woman," he bellowed one night. "Do you think this is a pleasure for me? I must have a son, you damned arid desert of a woman!"

Eventually I fell pregnant. I was young, and my body did not obey my will. He immediately consulted Anji over the sex of the baby. It was a girl.

He drove her out of my body with Anji's dark water.

I would never be able to keep a girl child.

When I finally conceived a son, I had been Iskan's wife for long over a year. Anji showed him that the child inside me was the son he had so yearned for, and he finally left me in peace. I did not see him again for several moons. He spent his time at the palace of the Sovereign Prince, where he did everything to ensure his indispensability. The child gave me terrible nausea but I was grateful for the peace that suddenly descended on the house. I would lie in bed all morning but manage to eat something around midday and then venture into the courtyard. I was still allowed there. I would sit and enjoy the scents of early spring, the dazzling flowers in pots under shady willows, and the birdsong. It was the first time in two years that I had found any pleasure at all. The child inside me had given life meaning again. It was of no importance that it was Iskan's son. It was the dawn of new life, and atonement for all the deaths that plagued my conscience.

I rarely saw Lehan. She was busy taking care of the household that I had neglected, first out of apathy and now because nausea kept me exhausted and passive. Sitting in the courtyard, I heard her voice through open windows, instructing the servants to address various tasks. She moved from chamber to chamber, efficiently ordering all that required order to maintain an estate of this size. I became increasingly aware of how many duties she was taking upon herself. Early in the mornings I heard her instruct the laborers in the day's orders before they dispersed into the fields and groves. This was actually the duty of the head of the household, but Iskan continued to keep his distance. When had my little sister learned how to act this way? Nobody seemed to question her authority and I saw signs of a smoothly run household everywhere: the chambers were kept sparkling clean, the plants in the courtyard were flawlessly pruned and the food served to my bedchamber was varied and delicious with no signs of excess. I attempted conversation with the servants—I was not afraid to do so now that Iskan was away—but the maidservants who waited on me were strangers and unwilling to exchange more than the most superficial of pleasantries.

One afternoon when I was sitting outside with my hands on my belly, enjoying the feeling of the first little kicks, Lehan came scurrying through the courtyard with a roll of green silk in her arms. She stopped when she saw me, as though she wanted to turn around again.

"Lehan." I stretched out a beseeching hand to her. "Come and sit with me awhile." She did not move. I lowered my hand. "Can we not be friends again? I beg your forgiveness for everything I said."

I was so terribly lonely. My pregnancy was a joy but also frightened me greatly. I had nobody to share it with. No mother to ask for advice. Lehan was the only person I had left.

Slowly she approached the bench where I was sitting and perched on the farthest edge. She laid the silk fabric on her lap.

"What do you have there?" I asked amiably. "Sewing yourself a new jacket?"

Lehan ran her fingers over the cloth. At first I thought she would refuse to speak to me at all. Then she took a breath.

"Brother Iskan sent it from Areko this morning. He wants me to sew new chair cushions for the sunroom."

I sat silently a moment, stung by the news.

"It is very beautiful fabric," I finally managed to say. "Unusual color."

Lehan nodded and smiled down at the cloth. "It will go nicely with the green-glazed vases we chose. Iskan had them imported from the Maiko Desert. They are fired from desert sand."

"Have you . . . have you helped him choose many things for the house?"

She did not meet my gaze. "Yes. We have the same taste," she said defensively. "And he spares no expense. He says I am to decorate precisely as I wish."

I did not know what to say. Iskan was treating Lehan like his wife. And she had adopted the roles of a wife. I was a mere necessary evil: heiress and breeding mare. Yet I could not blame

Lehan. It was what she had been raised for: to be wife and lady of the house, and to run the home and household. We were all trained for it from childhood. Yet I had not assumed the role.

Lehan interpreted my silence as judgment. She stood up suddenly and turned to me, her face blazing crimson.

"Just look at yourself! When did you last bathe? When did you last change your garments? The stench coming from you is revolting. You are a stain on our family! It is no wonder Iskan avoids you now that you are finally expecting his child. He could barely bring himself to see you the last few times. He had to come to me to prepare. I helped him."

She smacked her hand over her mouth, in disbelief of what she had just admitted out loud. Her eyes were wide with horror.

"Be careful, dear sister," I said slowly. "You know not what you play with." I was not angry, only filled with unspeakable sorrow. I did not know how to save Lehan from Iskan's clutches.

She turned and ran into the house. I sat still for a long time, watching the open door as if I could will her back with my gaze. It was I who had led her here to Iskan's house. It was my fault she was in danger. Anji's oaki clung to me, ran through my veins. During my childhood I had often felt fortified after drinking water from the spring, even many moons later. Now it was as though I could not rid myself of the impurity; the filth pulsing in my very blood. I would drag everybody down with me into the mire. Even my unborn child.

ᚹ

I felt very little joy over my imminent son. Equally, my fears about the pregnancy and delivery subsided. If I died, I could be free from all this guilt and suffering. The birth was creeping ever nearer and no ill befell either me or the child. Iskan returned home late one full-moon night. He could not keep away from Anji any longer, I guessed. He needed the spring's powers and visions. I heard Iskan's voice move through the house, checking that all was as it should be. He was accompanied everywhere by Lehan's sweet voice as she explained everything she had done in his absence. Then the tones of the cinna and tilan drifted through the open window and into my chamber. They were dining and drinking in the shaderoom. I could go down to join them. Nothing was stopping me. They were surely eating tasty morsels Iskan had brought back from Areko.

I lay in my bed, stroking my taut belly with one hand and humming along with the music. It was an old melody, a favorite of my mother's. I did not wish to dine with her murderer.

I was woken after midnight by Iskan coming into my chamber. In his hand he held a lamp, which he set down on the table by my bed. I propped myself up among the pillows.

"What a sight." He wrinkled his nose. "And a smell. Just as Lehan said. Do you no longer take care of yourself? Remember that you are the mother of my soon-to-be son."

"He does not care how I look," I said. Iskan sneered and approached the bed. He looked at me with those intense dark eyes.

"Is all well with the child?"

I nodded reluctantly.

"Is it time soon?"

"I believe so. Of course, you do not allow me to speak with any woman from whom I can ask advice, but it cannot be long now."

"You need a doula. Of course. It shall be arranged." He said it with disinterest, as though it were yet another irksome necessity to ensure the safety of his heir. He stretched out, languid as a house cat. "Anji's strength flows through my veins. How I have missed the spring water! How I have missed her power and visions. So much has needed building in Areko and the palace. Anji had to wait. But now the time is ripe, Kabira." He smiled and sat down on the edge of the bed. Did he want to take me? I laid my hands protectively over my belly.

"I have many allies now. And it is in their interest that I come to power. It is time for me to become Vizier."

"And your father?" I said, bringing to mind the friendly old white-haired man who had attended the wedding.

"He is old." Iskan grinned. "I imagine that his death is close at hand. You might even say that I have seen it." He chuckled at his joke but I gasped. He spoke of the greatest oaki of all. Patricide. He saw that I understood and nodded as if we shared an amusing secret. "I only have to wait until Anji's oaki is at its strongest. Then I will drink, and visit my father, and when he is found dead the next day, nobody will suspect anything other than that it was an old man's time to depart." He scoffed. "I have seen his real death, of course. You cannot imagine how far in the future it is! What a tenacious tortoise of a man he is. I will have to heave and haul his death closer." He leaned back idly against the bedposts and clasped his hands behind his head. The lamp light flickered on his shiny hair and well-polished buttons. He was the very picture of a carefree young man, used to getting what he wanted. "When I am Vizier, my real work shall begin. I shall be the most powerful man in all of Karenokoi. More powerful than anyone can imagine. Greater than the Sovereign Prince himself."

Only then did he catch sight of my hands pressed against my belly and my defensive posture. He grimaced in disgust.

"Do not flatter yourself. Why would I befoul myself with you now that you have fulfilled the task required of you?" He jumped down from the bed and stomped out of the room as hastily as he had entered. He left the lamp behind him, and the scent of leather and wine. I extinguished the lamp immediately. I did not even want to see the place where he had sat on the bed: the impression, the wrinkled covers. I sank down in the pile of pillows and my heartbeat gradually began to slow. I no longer cared what he did, nor whether I lived or died. Yet I feared him still. Moreover, a small part of me was ashamed. Ashamed that he now looked upon me with disgust, he whose gaze had once made me feel like the most beautiful woman in all the realm.

Through my open window I could hear the horses' whinnies from the stable. Frogs croaked in the velvety night. A cricket was chirping. I let the sounds of the night caress and soothe me.

Then I heard another sound, one I recognized all too well. It came from him. In the chamber beside mine. Lehan's bedchamber. I sat up to listen, and there it was again, a deep moan of lust. He was taking her! My sister, he had forced himself upon her, it could not be true, it must not be true, I had to do something, I had to save her! I looked around for a weapon but found nothing and so rushed into the hall, empty-handed and heavy with the child in my belly. There must be something I could do! If nothing else I could scream, call the servants. It was oaki to lie with one's sister-in-law; it was considered incest.

Outside Lehan's door I heard another sound. A whimper. Heavy breathing. Sounds from her. Not of struggle or fear, but of lasciviousness. Sounds he never got from me. She was enjoying it. She wanted it.

I pressed a clenched fist to my mouth to stop a scream from surging forth. I slowly backed up to my door, with Lehan's pleasure ringing in my ears.

ω

I heard Lehan and Iskan nearly every night after that. Even the night I gave birth to my first son. It was as though they were trying to drown out my screams with their own. It was morning, after many hours of agony, when Iskan finally called for the doula. The ordeal continued until the following night. When Korin finally lay at my breast, through my exhaustion I felt the first seed of happiness. He was totally and utterly mine, this beautiful little boy with his long, dark eyelashes and determined little furrowed brow. Despite the long and arduous birth, he was strong and healthy. His soft little hands, his eyes . . .

No. I do not want to write any more about this.

Iskan let me keep Korin for ten days. Ten short days I could hold him, and give him my milk, and breathe in his scent, and be his mother, his whole world. On the tenth day Iskan had his mother and a wet nurse move into our house to take care of Korin. Iskan personally tore the boy from my arms, and I do not want to write any more about this either. I will never forget my first proper encounter with his mother, Izani, and how she held my son to her bosom as though he belonged to her, as though he had come out of her own body, and how proudly she told her son that she would raise her grandchild to be exactly like his father. She did not give me so much as a glance.

Lehan was the only one who came to visit me, a few days after they had taken Korin away. I had not left my chamber; Iskan had locked the door behind Izani when she carried Korin away. The maidservants came in and emptied my chamber pot and brought me food that I did not touch. My sister stood in the doorway and looked at me a long while. I was sitting huddled up against the wall, where I had spent most of my time. That bed was the place where I had given birth to Korin. I could not lie in it again. I was barely conscious of Lehan's presence until she started speaking.

"He would let you meet Korin if you only composed yourself." Her voice was a mixture of pity and scorn. I looked up but she avoided my gaze. She fingered a ring on her left hand, a large green stone set in gold, evidently a gift from Iskan. Until that moment I had felt nothing but despair and boundless sorrow, but suddenly a violent hatred blazed inside me. It was so powerful that I began to shake. I wanted to speak, but all these overwhelming sensations were crammed in my throat and I could not squeeze out a word.

"You have been behaving like a madwoman, Kabira. Do you not understand that he is thinking only of what is best for his son? An unbalanced mother could hurt her child, or worse." But she did not fully believe her own words. If she did, she would have looked me in the eye.

"Do you know who it is you lie with each night?" The words tore at my throat, raw from days and nights of screaming and raging. I did not take my eyes off Lehan as I clambered to my feet. The skin on my knuckles split open again and the wounds I had incurred from beating the walls with my fists started to bleed. "Do you know whose member is making you pant like a bitch in heat?" Lehan edged out of the door and tried to close it behind her, but I was too fast and darted like a snake to wedge my foot in front of the door before she could close it fully. At that moment I realized that she had come to see me without anybody knowing. No servants were waiting outside. I easily pushed open the door; I have always been stronger than Lehan. Delicate little Lehan with her shiny hair and shimmering skin. "Not only have you taken your sister's husband into your bed, which is already oaki. You sleep with our mother's murderer. You welcome our father's killer into your bed. You spread your legs for the man who slew our brother and sister."

Lehan was staring at me, finally meeting my gaze, her eyes wide with horror. I grabbed hold of her arm and dragged her back into the chamber and closed the door behind us. I leaned my face close in to hers. "Listen now, little Lehan, little harlot Lehan, listen carefully! Iskan made me reveal to him the secrets of Anji, and he found a new use for her forbidden water. It allows him to kill without leaving a trace." I saw my saliva spray on her face, but she made no attempt to wipe it away.

"You are crazy," she whispered, but could not take her eyes off my face, like a vole transfixed by a venomous snake, unable to move.

"Am I? Am I really? Tell me, little Lehan, Iskan's little plaything, does the Vizier yet live? Or has Iskan implemented his plan to kill his own father as well? Perhaps the Vizier passed away in his sleep?"

She went pale. "He . . . he received word yesterday that the Honorable Vizier had passed away in his sleep." She tried to back away. "But he was old. You could have guessed." I did not let go of her arm.

"I could have. But tell me, did Iskan visit his father the day before he died? And was it perchance the day after the full moon?"

Her silence was answer enough. I smiled and opened my eyes wide. I must have appeared out of my mind. "That's right. That's right, little Lehan. Think back. Was the moon waning when our family died? You know it was—I can see it in your eyes. When I lay sick in bed, Lehan, when Iskan forced our first child from my body. You think you are the only one with whom he slakes his lust, but he had me first, you little harlot, many times. And then he murdered our child, and my family, and all the baby girls I have carried before Korin. Why do you think I have been behaving this way?"

She was crying now, with deep sobs that made her body convulse, and mucus and tears were streaming down her perfect face and, oh, how I wished that Iskan could see her at that moment! I was so far removed from my mind and senses that I reached out a forefinger to catch a tear from her cheek, and licked it.

"But . . . but why did you marry him?" she asked between sobs. "Nobody forced you! Kabira, why did you walk into his trap?" She clutched at my free arm with hers and grasped tight, heartbroken.

I studied her contorted facial features, fascinated, because for once she did not look beautiful, but red and bloated and ugly—ugly!

"It was your fault, do you not see?" I cocked my head to one side. "He was threatening your life. If I did as he said, he would spare you. I did it for your sake, you little bitch. And as thanks I have to listen to him making you moan, night after night. As thanks, you have turned your back on me. As thanks, you have helped him take my child from me. Tell me, will you get as much pleasure when he enters you tonight? Will you enjoy him licking your tender young breasts as before? The spirits of the dead walk these halls. They are watching you. They have seen your every deed, heard every moan. Mother and Father, Agin and Tihe. Can you picture them before you? Good. Then think about how you are honoring their memory. I tried to warn you, so do not plead ignorance." I shook her hand off my arm and pushed her away. Spat on the floor by her feet. "One thing you knew without doubt. That he was my husband. Nothing can change that."

I drove her out of the chamber. She offered no resistance. I slammed the door and fell to the floor. All of my energy drained away in an instant. I crept back into my corner and folded my arms over my head. I felt a brief sense of satisfaction from seeing Lehan's whole world fall apart around her. Vengeance flowed through my body like sweetest honey. But soon I was left with a bitter burning in my mouth and throat, and the chamber was empty, and nothing, nothing could give me respite.

ᚹ

Iskan found her that night. She had hanged herself with the belt from Agin's old jacket. He immediately understood the cause, fetched me and forced me to take down her body, and wash and dress it for the burial. I will never forget the way she looked. I will never forget who is to blame for her death.

"Do you not realize that you have only made things worse for yourself?" said Iskan, shaking his head. "Now you have nobody at all. Come Kabira, it is time to stop with this willfulness. If you start behaving like the submissive wife I expected from the start, I will let you see Korin, and give you fine clothes and jewelry.

You are the Vizier's wife now. My great plan is about to be set in motion. I shall extend the house, there is so much to do. I will need several sons. If you do as I say you may meet with them frequently, and they shall call you mother."

There was nothing else left for me. There was nothing to fight for. So I became Kabira, First Wife of the Vizier, and that was my life for the forty years that followed.

GARAI

The other slaves in the Harrera night camp gave me one piece of advice: "Scream and scratch him and you'll only make it worse for yourself. Pretend to enjoy it and you'll become his favorite. Then you might get special privileges. It's the best the likes of us can hope for now."

I am hoping for better. But I have followed their advice. It has already served me well.

I was afraid, of course. I have been afraid ever since my capture. I have not dared offer any resistance. Not even when the men came in the night to abduct me and my sisters while we were sleeping. They must have been tracking us for a long time. They struck when we had diverted our course from the clan for a few days, to gather healing herbs south of the Meirem Desert. No settler dares set foot in the desert itself. We would have been safe there. But we did not imagine any threat, and were not on our guard. I curse myself still. I am the eldest. I should have been more vigilant.

The men feared us. They believed we were powerful priestesses who could kill them with an utterance. They are the sort of folk who fear anything they do not understand. So they gagged our mouths and bound our hands. We were driven southward in haste, unchangingly southward, often under cover of night. Slave-trading is illegal in the northern lands. We were sold in a village to southern slave merchants with long hair and big beards. We came to a place—Harrera, I heard it called—a terrible place, stinking and foul. I was separated from my sisters. We did not cry. We had no tears left.

At the slave market, I was tethered tight to a stake on a platform alongside other similarly young women. We all came from different lands, which was evident from our differing skin and hair. I was the only one with white hair and gray eyes. The men around the platform spoke to each other and pointed at me. From their gestures and glances, I understood that I was valuable: their finest ware.

The auction began. I was saved until last. They wanted all eyes on me. The sun was merciless in Harrera—I had never experienced such heat before. My lips were dried and cracked. My kirtle clung to my body with sweat.

A man approached the platform. He was clothed in blue and white. Tall and slim, but with broad shoulders and thick, dark hair. His lips were very red. He was the only one who looked me in the eye. He did so for a long time. Then he called over one of my sellers.

"Is this how you take care of your treasures? You are ravaging her beauty with your damned sun." He took out a purse. "Name your price. I will pay." When the men stammered something about the auction, he scoffed impatiently. "Name your price, I said, so that I may remove my property from the blazing heat before it is ruined." He filled his hands with silver and gold, more than I knew existed in all the world. That was my price. That was how valuable I was. Then he gave orders, and a man hastened up to the platform and severed my bondage. I fell to my knees. The beautiful man extended a pitcher of cold water. I did not have the strength to raise it to my lips, so he held it to my mouth as I drank. Then he personally carried me away from the market. To shade. A stable, a stall. He let me rest there, and drink water, and somebody brought balm for my burned skin. The next day he came to see me.

"You already look much better. Now I must find out whether I made a wise investment." He untied his trousers. I immediately spread my legs.

He was careful not to hurt me, and I remembered the other slave girls' advice. I had been with men before, clan men, who had done as much for my pleasure as for their own. This man did not do so. Why should he? I was not his equal: he owned me. It was soon over. Afterward he seemed very pleased.

"A woman who knows her place, who does not fight back, or mutely grimace in disgust. And the most beautiful woman I have seen, besides. You will be a sensation in Areko. Yes, I should say that I made a good investment." He wiped himself off on the hem of my kirtle. "I would have you bathe now, but we must leave this place. I have made a number of business arrangements here and it is wisest not to linger."

"Yes, Master," was my only response. I, Garai of the roaming folk, called him master. We who serve no master. We obey only the earth herself and her decrees. And so we roam, and honor our sacred sites, and keep our distance from the settlers. The ones who keep to their coins and houses, lords and laws. No human laws apply to us. The energy lines in the earth, her veins, lead us true on our treks. The ground bestows upon us the food and shelter we need. We carry our history with us in story and myth. Our cunning guards our spirits and bodies, and guides us through the storm. But now a new me is emerging. And this new self, this new Garai, has a master whom she bows to and spreads her legs for and obeys in all ways.

We left Harrera that same day. I was put farthest back in the caravan, on a pack mule with the rest of my master's purchases. He had brought me shawls and hoods to shelter me from the hot sun, and I had plenty of water to drink, and was given a meal in the morning and another when we stopped for the night. I slept with my master in his personal tent. He never restrained me— because where could I run in this vast desert? I would be dead before I left their sight.

My master had his way with me every night. I continued to be compliant, gentle and placid. Unlike I had ever been before. But I knew I must push my old self down into the innermost recesses of my memory. My old ways must never reemerge. Because though my master treated me well, and better and better the more I complied, I knew the truth. I saw the same thing in him as I had seen in the eyes of the men who stole me and my sisters that night, and in the eyes of the men who had sold me for silver and gold: to them I am a thing. Not a person with feelings or needs of her own. Just something for them to fear, or profit from, or use. The moment I become a burden they will do away with me. And I want to live. That is what the old Garai wants. She wants to return to the Meirem Desert, and hear her mother sing at sundown, and hold hands with her sisters. The new Garai does not believe any of this is possible. But the old Garai refuses to surrender.

Now we are in Areko, the capital city of the district of Renka, the land of my master. We arrived yesterday night, after a journey of many moons. I have bathed and been directed to a small room in my master's residence. He told me that he only intends to stay here until his new palace in Ohaddin is ready. Then he will transfer the Sovereign Prince and his entire royal court to Ohaddin too. The Sovereign knows nothing of this yet. Tomorrow my master intends to present me for everybody to admire and adore. New clothes have been brought to my room, strange garments made of silk with brightly colored embroidery. Ornamental combs to hold my hair up, bands for my arms and fingers—beautiful objects to show off my value. Everybody in this place is obsessed with objects. In the clan, we had only what was needed, and that could be carried on our backs. Knives, rope, herbs, flint, food. Can a ring keep you warm at night? Can you eat an ornamental comb? Does an embroidered jacket heal a festering wound?

I have stolen paper and writing implements from my master's purchases. Mother knows letters and the art of writing. It was one of the things she taught me as she was training me to become her successor and skillswoman of the clan. I have not often had reason to practice. There was never much reason to write anything down. All Mother's knowledge is stored in her head, like seeds in a pod. Whatever I was curious about, she could pluck the necessary information from her memory and answer my questions. What need was there for writing? But she taught me the art simply because it was one of the skills she had acquired, and she wanted me to learn everything she knew.

Now for the first time in my life I have reason to write something down. My progress is slow. My hand lacks the facility that comes with practice. But I must struggle on. I find myself in a foreign land. Everybody around me speaks a foreign tongue. I understand some. In our clan, we spoke Siddhi, the language of the roaming folk, but I know many others as well. One does when one is constantly on the move and encountering different peoples. I do not know how many languages Mother knows; certainly more than she has fingers. The language here in Areko is the same as one I learned when we visited the sacred Mount Omone. It is much farther south than we usually roam and the language spoken in the provinces around the mountain was unlike anything I had heard before. Hard and angry, I thought it sounded, not at all like the many upland tongues. Here in Areko they speak a dialect with a slightly different accent, but most words are the same. I am relieved. It makes it easier for the new Garai. She cannot yet express much, but it is not expected of her. It is enough to understand.

There is comfort in having a language of my own to write in. I know that nobody can read what I have written. Through writing I can keep my native tongue alive. But the words seem lifeless on paper, as though their life seeps away when I bind them with my brush pen. There is so much more to a language than the letters. Melody, tone, rhythm, pauses—everything I have no way of capturing. Perhaps everything dies when captured. Like the jalapo, the rare bird found only on the slopes of Omone. It is said that its song can heal sickened spirits, those trapped in grief or fear. The jalapo draws its power from Omone itself, and if ever a bird is captured and taken from the mountain it will die before long. Perhaps the same is true for the soul of a language. I do not know—I have never written an extended account before. But now I must try, because I am afraid that otherwise I will forget who I am. And in this golden cage I will wither and die, like the jalapo.

I write at night, and hide my writings in my room. Everything that I, Garai of the Blood, truly am must be concealed and hidden.

I am the sweet meat of the salamander
I am the sunset over the golden rocks of the Meirem
I am the evensong of the life force
I am bare feet on the awakening earth in spring
I am the pointed leaves of the bloodtongue
I am red scars on white skin

ᛒ

I met my master's wife today. I was viewed by many, including the Sovereign Prince himself. His sons had covetous eyes. But the only person I met, the only person who spoke to me, was the wife of my master. She came to my little room after my master had presented me. She is tall and awkward and lacking all softness and charm. She is with child, around halfway, I should think. She looks old, much older than my master. She must have some great secret that enabled her to ensnare such a man. Perhaps her father was very rich.

I fell to my knees on the floor and bowed low. This new Garai, this weak and submissive girl, she knows what to do. She knows who has the power, who she must bow to and how low. She surprises herself with her knowledge. Where does it come from? But Garai's bow did not please the wife. She marched over to me and snatched the combs from my hair.

"You are slave-sold," she hissed. "Only a wife may wear seven combs in her hair. For you one will suffice."

At that moment I understood my place: nethermost; slave-sold; lower than the lowest. I stayed bowed down as she arranged my hair. My silence and submission seemed to calm her. She took a step back when she was finished.

"Rise." I did as she ordered. She eyed me carefully, turned me around with a rough hand. "I can see the appeal. Your coloring is most unusual. But your garments are absolutely hideous. The yellow color dulls the luster of your hair. You should wear pale blue. Perhaps with silver embroidery to bring out the shimmer of your hair and skin."

I did not say that it was my master who had given me the clothes. I only nodded.

She sighed. "If you keep Iskan satisfied perhaps he will stay away from my bed. I suppose I should see that as a blessing." Suddenly her expression softened and I saw that she was not as old as I had first thought. Actually only a handful of years older than me. I gestured toward her swollen belly.

"Your first?"

The hard expression returned. "No. My third son."

She swept out of the room without another word. Then, later that day, some servants came with beautiful silk coats in pale blue with silver threads and pearl embroidery. They weighed more than my whole pack in the clan. The new Garai dresses up in these impractical clothes every morning. She sets up her hair with an ornamental comb. She covers her scars under long sleeves and heavy silver arm bands. I write so that I do not forget, and I hide these pages under a loose stone panel in the floor of my room. These are the things I must remember:

The true Garai bears symbols on her skin. Three scars from blood offerings. Two for promises made. One for an enemy defeated. The new Garai shall never replace the warrior, the wisdom, the life force.

ळ

Today I asked the wife whether I may go out into the garden. I have seen it from the window.

"That is the garden of the Sovereign Prince," she replied shortly. A little later she came to fetch me and led me to the locked doors that separate the women's residence from the rest of the palace. Two men were standing guard, with blue jackets and sabers by their sides.

"His Highness has given us leave to promenade in his garden this afternoon," she said. One of the guards unlocked the doors and we stepped through the gilded doorway. We descended a small back staircase, with the guards close behind. I wanted to rush, I wanted to run, but the wife's gait was slow and heavy with the child she bore, and I restrained my fervor. We emerged onto a terrace and the garden spanned before us, dazzling and lush. I had not realized how much I had missed living plants until I stood among them again, and a gentle sigh forced its way out before the new Garai could prevent it. The wife gave me a sharp look.

"I will sit here in the shade."

One guard stood behind the bench where she sat, while the other followed me as I took tentative steps out into the garden.

The plants here are very different from anything I have seen in my roaming. Some have thick leaves and fleshy flowers, which I think must make them suited to this climate, enabling them to hold liquid during long periods of drought. Others have enormous flower cups, larger than my face, and emit a wonderful scent. I think they would not survive the dry summers if the Sovereign Prince's master gardener did not water them. I saw some men watering and tidying the flower beds, but they turned from me, and the guard cleared his throat to steer me in another direction. It is clear: I am not to speak to any man but my master, and preferably not be seen by any either. I wonder whether the guards here are eunuchs. They are slender and beardless with boyishly smooth skin, so it is not impossible. A grotesque custom.

At first I was overwhelmed by the floral display and thought I would never find what I was looking for. All the plants were so unfamiliar to me, and between the nectar-dripping flowers fluttered butterflies larger than I could ever have imagined. Beautifully shaped trees offered shade from the harsh sun and I could have happily strolled around in wonder all day. But I supposed my time was limited, and sooner or later the guard would return me to the terrace where the wife was waiting. So I took a deep breath and reached out with my mind, and there, deep within the soil, I could feel the earth's power pulsing. It smacked of something different, against the soles of my feet, from the energy of the mountains back home. It was not as bare and wild, but fertile and voluptuous and full of life. I stopped still and closed my eyes, letting the life force flow through and fill me. When I opened my eyes, my gaze fell on the wall that encloses the palace garden and separates it from the city, whose hustle and hubbub I could hear but could not see. The wall caught the rays of the late-afternoon sun and there, in the cracks and crevices between the stones, a familiar plant was meandering out with long pointed leaves and modest little red flowers. I smiled to myself.

With the guard's attention briefly elsewhere, I picked a clump of the thin leaves. Their tart aroma filled me with an intense feeling of happiness. It smelled like home. I pushed the bunch up into one of my sleeves, and the sharp edges scratched my scars.

The sting made me remember. Other scars. Another place. I closed my eyes and was immediately transported to the edge of the desert, with Mother by my side.

We were walking on the eastern mountain ridge. It was early morning, and the sun's first rays were lighting our path, while night prevailed in the desert farther below. Mother and I both had our spears in hand and her gray hair gleamed in the rosy morning light. The sheer slopes glistened with the moisture of clouds that had descended during the night and were now being lifted by the sun back to the mountain peaks. Mother crouched down to point at something.

"Do you see, Garai? This humble plant is called Goddess Tongue. It needs very little to survive and grows almost everywhere. Put it to memory. It can be a woman's best friend."

"When?" I asked, and crouched to look. Long, pointed leaves stuck to a thin vine woven in and out of the cracks in the mountainside.

"When she wants to keep her moon blood flowing. When she does not want to be with child."

"Children are a gift," I said, and stood up. "That is what you have taught me."

"It is true. I have never used Goddess Tongue myself. But there are women whose lives can be threatened by pregnancy. Or wisewomen who want to let their moon blood flow freely, so that their contact with the life force stays strong."

83

Mother raised her arms to the east, to greet the sun, and when her sleeves slid down I saw all her scars glimmer white in the soft light. So many scars. So many promises, offerings and victories. I hoped that I could bear as many scars one day.

When I looked around, I found myself back on the terrace, lying on the cool marble floor. The wife was sitting on the bench and looking at me.

"You lost consciousness," she said shortly. "The guard carried you here."

I blinked. The vision had been very strong. Or was it only a memory? A memory of my mother from one of our many treks up in the mountains. I closed my eyes to my pain. The new Garai has no memories, no secrets. I took a deep breath and cut myself loose from the life force pulsing in the earth below us. I sat up.

"It must have been the heat. I feel fine now."

We went inside, and the guard escorted me to my room where a meal was awaiting me. I ate in solitude and then swallowed a few of the narrow leaves. I did not want to bear his child. I never ever want that. I want to keep bleeding, and keep my contact with the life force, and not forget who I am.

Garai priestess
Garai daughter
Garai hunter
Garai roamer
Garai.

ᚹ

My master is at Ohaddin overseeing the work on his new palace. Much of what he bought during the journey to Harrera was material for the build. Before he traveled, he told me that the work had already been under way for three years. We were lying in his bed, the one he always calls me to when my services are required. His room is peculiar, with expensive carpets on the floor, large glazed earthenware jugs, pictures painted on screens along the walls, and more silver lamps than I can count. I do not understand why he needs so much silver and gold and paintings. A roof against rain and cold—I understand why settlers want that. They are not hardy as we roamers. But what is the purpose of everything else? What more do they really need than a window out to the sky and wind and sun?

As though he could read my thoughts, my master gestured with contempt at all the decadence. The new palace, he explained, would be completely different. Magnificent. He has sent out a whole fleet of tradesmen to gather logs from Terasu, the jungle-grown island realm in the South, and an army of laborers to the marble quarries in the North. Areko's best architects, stonemasons and carpenters are already at work on the building.

"My palace shall be the center of the world!" he said, and clasped his hands behind his head. I thought he must be jesting. The world has but one center: the bottomless Sea of Semai, the navel of the world, connected by navel string to the body of the Goddess before she gave birth to the earth in a flood of blood and salt water. I thought everybody knew that. I wanted to correct him, but the new Garai shushed me. I ran my fingertips lightly over the scars on the inside of my wrist and said nothing.

"Thrice-three more years before completion. Though I hope to be able to move the entire royal court there beforehand."

"The entire court, Master?"

"Yes, my beautiful savage." He smiled contentedly. "The Sovereign's health is failing. I give him fortifying water from a very special spring on my land in Ohaddin. It helps him, at times." He chortled, as though at a secret of his own. "But I have explained to him that it would benefit him greatly to live nearer to the spring. Many are those who would gain access to the spring's powers, of course, but I have explained to the Sovereign that it is the privilege of the monarch alone." He turned on his side to face me. The soft lamplight made his skin shimmer. He is not muscular, like the men in our clan. Rather he is strong and smooth like the kawol, the great cat that presides over the mountains around the Meirem Desert. He reached out a hand and caressed my breasts.

"There are many who envy me. They have since I was born. My mother knew from the beginning that I was special—chosen. Destined for great things. And now I am proving her right. She sees the same in my sons, Korin and Enon. I am developing a dominion that they shall help me rule. Korin is only four years old but has already mastered horse, bow and brush."

"Does Master have any daughters?" I rarely ask questions. My master enjoys talking anyhow. Yet I was curious. His wife has the face and body of a woman who has gone through pregnancy many times.

"Daughters! What do I need them for? All they do is incur expenses in upbringing and dowry. No, I shall have only sons. Many. I have seen it."

The new Garai forbade me to speak. She swallowed all the words welling up in my mouth.

He lost himself in his thoughts awhile, his hand still fondling my breasts.

"The Sovereign sees the intelligence in my plans too. He has given me access to his gold reserves, but funds are already beginning to dry up. I thought he was a richer man. But there are ways to replenish supplies, of course. Raise taxes. War, and the spoils of war. And I shall see to it that the neighboring cities understand that it is in their interest to support Areko financially. Or else . . ." He yawned. "I have not yet decided the best way to go about it. But when the time comes, the Ohaddin palace shall become legendary in all the known lands." He pulled himself up. "Come to me. Once more, then I will sleep before my journey."

I lay still, and made the sounds he likes, and even though it always takes longer the second time he soon rolled off me and immediately fell asleep. I lay still until he was snoring deeply, then crept quietly out and through the narrow passageway back to my own room. My master does not like me to be in his bed when he wakes. Now I am sitting and writing this by lamplight because I need to let out everything the new Garai prevented me from saying. That daughters are worth so much. My mother saw untold worth in her four daughters. She knew that each one of us was a blessing. Mother said that long ago there were many wisewomen, and that the whole world followed the paths walked by the roaming folk. That everybody knew the earth was born from the womb of the Goddess. But now we who know the truth live our lives persecuted. Though we have knowledge and plants and cures that can help people, we must keep our beliefs and our rites secret.

But Mother initiated me into the lore. She had already

intimated its deepest secrets before I was abducted and sold. To me and my sisters. I wonder where they are now. I wonder whether I will see them again in this life. I do not believe I will. Though perhaps they are thinking the same about me, right now, this very evening.

The weight of the spear in my hand.
The roar of the kawol in the darkness.
The blood of the Goddess below the earth's surface,
throbbing under naked soles.

ᛒ

The time came for the wife to give birth while my master was at Ohaddin. I heard the screams and commotion. Many servant girls were running up and down the corridor outside. I am free to wander in the residence outside my room, where the wife and other women in the Sovereign's household have their quarters. My master has his own rooms here, but they can only be accessed from this residence via the secret passage from my room. I think that other men have similar arrangements with their wives and concubines. But guards abound, and they make sure that nobody strays into the wrong room. My master said it is a sloppy arrangement and that in the new palace it will be entirely different. I rarely leave my room: it is all the same to me.

After an especially drawn-out howl from the wife's quarters I opened my door and peeked out. A servant scurried past with a jug and bowl on a tray. I slipped out and the guard let me in to see the wife. The anteroom was full of people. Some old women dressed in white sat around burning incense and mumbling prayers. They worship spirits of the dead and know nothing of the Goddess. Young wives of high-ranking courtiers were sitting on silk cushions and talking quietly, but every time a scream was heard from inside the room they blanched and had difficulty returning to their conversation. The servants were rushing to and fro with various objects for which I could see no use.

No one stopped me from going in to see the wife. It was warm inside her room and incense was burning in there too. I sniffed at the air, and stretched out my tongue to taste the smoke. It was mainly useless and would do nothing to ease her sufferings, but I also detected aulium. Good, that should afford her a little relief. There were dreary old ladies mumbling prayers in there too. The wife, white as snow and dripping with sweat, was lying in a large bed. A tall, bony servant girl in a gray jacket held a fresh cold compress to her forehead. Yet another contraction shook the laboring woman's body and she bellowed wordlessly with mouth wide open. Her long, dark hair lay tangled on her pillows and her eyes were sunken. There did not seem to be anyone tending to the actual birth, other than through prayers and cold compresses. I walked over to the bed, pulled the covers off the wife and examined her quickly. She glared at me, but then came another pain that made her unable to speak. Her contractions were close together, but I could see that she was not yet very open. The child seemed to be in the right position.

"How long has she been in labor?" I asked the servant.

"Since last night," she replied. She seemed calm and capable. She could help me.

"Get all these women out," I told her. "You and I will manage the birth, but I do not want anyone else in this room."

She looked me in the eye and nodded. I hurried back to my room and searched through my supplies. I had gathered and dried a wide selection of plants from the Sovereign's garden. I did not even hide what I was doing. Nobody but the servants sets foot in my room.

The ideal remedy would have been gamleaf, but it does not grow this far south. They are mostly decorative plants that grow in the Sovereign's garden, so I had not managed to get any brannberry either. But bao, which is used as a condiment here, actually has pain relief qualities in larger doses. And I had thousandroot. It would have to do. I rushed back with my packets and found more white-clad women in the anteroom. They gave me nasty looks as I ran past, and muttered their prayers with even more fervor. There is a time for prayer and a time for action, my mother always said. Now was a time for action. I could thank the Goddess afterward.

When I entered the room, the servant was standing by the door and the wife was lying on her side in bed, panting. Another woman remained: my master's mother, Izani, her gray hair clinking with silver chains and a jacket so laden with pearls and gems that she could barely lift her arms. Her face was dark with anger.

"You! Slave-sold! It is not your place to give orders."

The new Garai fell to her knees and touched her forehead to the floor. I knew that this woman held higher rank than the wife. She had the final word on everything.

"Forgive me, most venerable mother of my master. Where I come from it is a slave's job to deliver babies. Let worms eat my eyes for my wrongdoing."

"Get up."

I did so, and pretended not to notice the wife wail at another contraction. "Permit me at least to deal with the messy part, my lady, so that the blood does not ruin your clothes."

Izani looked over at the wife. I could see that she would much rather leave, but did not want to let it seem as though I had made the decision.

"Get that slave out of here," hissed the wife, which helped Izani make up her mind.

"Slave-sold, do not leave Kabira's side. As soon as the child is born, I want you to bring it to me. If it is a healthy boy."

"Yes, my lady."

Izani left the room.

"Has she gone?" the wife managed to say between two contractions.

"Yes," the servant girl replied and then turned to me. "Do you need anything else?"

I looked at her and realized that, despite her height, she was just a child. Thirteen years at most. But she was calm and collected and seemed unfazed.

"What is your name?" I asked.

"Estegi."

"I need hot water and a drinking vessel, Estegi. And peace and quiet. This baby wants to come out, but it will need a little help along the way."

Estegi nodded and hurried out of the room. I neared the bed. The wife had glassy eyes and her breathing was irregular. I crouched down and looked her in the eye.

"I know that you harbor no love for me. You know nothing about me, so trust is a lot to ask. But you have no one else who seems to know what they are doing. And I do. I have delivered dozens of babies in my clan. In the Meirem Desert." It pained me to have the name on my lips. I had not uttered any of my home names out loud since I was taken as a slave. If only I had had my spear then! I bit my tongue to stop all the other names from flooding out. Names of my sisters, my mother, everybody in our clan, everybody in the other roaming clans.

Her gaze sharpened and she furrowed her brow, untrusting.

"I have not always been a slave. Do you want my help?" I spat in my palm and held out my hand. A contraction made her screw her eyes up in pain and scream. I waited, my hand extended. She kept her eyes shut even once the contraction had passed. Then, all of a sudden, she pulled a hand free from under the cover, licked it and offered it to me. I held it in mine.

"Good. Now first you must sit up."

She did not have the strength left to protest. When I got the wife upright, Estegi came into the room with a jug of hot water and several bowls. I told her to put them down on a table and then had her support the wife while I quickly mixed a large dose of bao and a pinch of thousandroot in one of the bowls and filled it with water.

"Now you should walk," I said, and came to stand by the wife's side. "Lean on me and Estegi. When my concoction has stood awhile, drink it and it will help you."

"Poison," she gasped. I scoffed.

"Why should I poison you? I will drink it first, if you like."

I have since wondered about what she said. That perhaps it was not an accusation, but rather a request.

Once I had gotten the wife up on her feet and calmed her breathing with my herbal concoction, the birth went much quicker.

In the early evening, I laid a well-formed boy at her breast. She looked at him for a very long time. Then she turned away.

"Fetch the wet nurse," was all she said. Never before have I seen such coldness in a new mother. When I did not react, she turned to look at me, her face contorted in pain. Not even in the worst moments of her labor had I seen such agony.

"Do it now!" she ordered. Estegi hurried away without waiting for my say-so. The wife's whole body was shaking, with anger or exhaustion, I do not know which. All of a sudden she cradled her son's hand in hers and kissed his thin eyelids. She whispered something in his ear. Then she looked up at me, and her eyes were enormous.

"Iskan will name him. Please, take him now. Torture me no longer."

I realized at that moment that I had never seen her with her children, even though this was her third son. She did not have the countenance of a woman who had chosen her own lot. This life. This lovelessness.

I reached down and picked up the baby. He was big and felt solid in my arms. He was completely calm, but smacked his lips slowly. He was hungry. I carried him out into the anteroom, where the women all immediately exploded in cries of delight, tears of joy and yet more prayers. Izani took him resolutely from my arms and held him high, as proud as if she had just delivered him from her own womb. The boy whimpered as the old woman's gem-studded sleeves scratched at his tender new skin. Estegi soon returned with the wet nurse, and my master's mother reluctantly gave her grandson over to the nurse's care. I called Estegi over to me.

"Fetch something fortifying for Kabira. A broth, perhaps. And a sage infusion to keep her milk at bay. Make sure she has plenty to drink. But above all, see that she is left in peace. For as long as she wants. Understood?"

Estegi nodded. I knew that it was a lot to place on such a young girl's shoulders, but I trusted that she could manage. Besides, there was nobody else I could ask.

I pushed myself through the mass of chattering women and back to my room, where I slept for a night and a day. I am glad my master is not here at the moment, so I can rest and order my thoughts.

I have been sure to take my dose of Goddess Tongue every day. I shall not bear the seed of a man who would not let me keep my own children—my own flesh and blood.

ო

There is nothing for me to do here. My master uses me daily, but in the spaces between there are oceans of time. Time that just drains away. I pace from window to window in my little room and peer out onto the world. Pick up objects and put them down again. Never before have I been so idle. We used to always be on our way somewhere. Up in the mountains on a hunt. Through the desert to converge with another clan. South to collect plants. Around the Lake of Bodien, in the middle of the Meirem, which takes a roaming clan seven days to circle. By its western shore grows Sanuel, the ancient tree with roots deep in the heart of the earth. We would often trek to the sacred sites, like the Sanuel tree and Mount Omone and the bottomless Sea of Semai. We went there so that Mother could perform her blood offerings. And after

I had passed my eide, I began making offerings too. Sometimes I touch my scars to remind myself. That I am an initiate. That I have communed with the life force of Sanuel and gifted my blood to the tree.

When we were not roaming, we would do things with our hands. Build fires. Mend garments or gear. When Mother was educating me and my sisters, we always had something in our hands, even when we were listening. The old Garai was deft at carving. All I needed was a good knife and a decent piece of timber and I could carve anything: a spoon, a bowl, a flute, a button. A toy for my youngest sister when she was a girl.

She is still not much older than a girl. If she is alive. I wonder where she was sold to.

The new Garai does not think about it. She lets the questions and memories of the old Garai appear less and less often, almost only when I am writing. Yet I have so little to write about. The new Garai is good for nothing. All she does is wait—wait to be seen by her master. Her hands are nervous birds flapping here and there around the room with neither task nor purpose. She tries on different jackets to see which one suits her best. She combs her hair. She listens to the sounds of the palace. She follows the changing of the seasons from her window. Rain sounds different against a roof than it does out on the mountainside. Sometimes she thinks she wants to go out in the rain, feel it on her skin, feel the wind tear through her hair, let the wind believe it can lift her and carry her away. It is not the new Garai who thinks this, but the old. The new holds her head down and turns away from the storm, in toward the pictures of painted storms and mountains and oceans.

The new Garai is betraying everything I held sacred and significant. She is worthless, purposeless. She pleases her master, bows her head, she avoids eye contact with the guards. I hate her.

But she is useful for one thing. She knows how to keep me alive.

ʊ

To pass the time I have started gathering plants. I pick healing herbs from the garden and dry them for future use, but I have also started growing my own. I ask Kabira what the different plants here are called, and write their names down in my most beautiful handwriting. My writing has improved greatly since I began with my secret notes. It soothes me, and gives me something to do. I sketch the plants, and then I press them. I showed some pages to my master, and he gave me a humoring smile. But some days later Estegi, the skinny servant girl, delivered gifts to my room. She laid them on my bed with care. The highest-quality leaves of paper. Ink in three different shades, several quills, brushes and paints.

"Are these from my master?" I asked. Though who else would they be from?

Estegi nodded. "Do you know how to paint?"

"I am practicing. Mostly flowers and plants," I answered, touching the paper.

She backed out of the room, but stopped at the door. Lingered a moment.

"What is it?"

"Could I . . . could I borrow some of the pictures later?"

"For what?" I frowned.

"Embroidery," she whispered, embarrassed. "I should like to

learn how to embroider truly beautiful flowers, but it is difficult. A picture would help."

I put down the paper. "You can do it here, in my room. I do not want you to take the pictures away."

Estegi nodded, taken aback and grateful, and closed the door behind her.

I write less now. I pick and press and paint instead. Estegi sits in a corner, with a finished picture of a flower in front of her, and embroiders with silk thread on thin fabrics. I think she makes things for the wife. Kabira comes by sometimes and looks at us with her cold, superior gaze. Ever since the birth she has been paying me visits. The new Garai makes herself as submissive as possible when she comes, offers her the best sitting cushion, asks Estegi to fetch iced green tea. Kabira usually waves away our servitude and simply sits down. Often it is a long time before she says anything. I begin my painting again, and Estegi picks up her needle and thread. From out in the garden we can hear songbirds, and from the palace come voices and footsteps. I never address her first. The new Garai knows her place.

After a while she speaks. Asks questions about my work, or tells me something about the plant I am working with. Then I can ask questions. About the name or application of the plant. But there are many plants she does not know. Then she turns abruptly to Estegi and asks if the embroidery will be ready soon.

Yesterday, while we were working, she came into my room with her hands full.

"It is not proper for a concubine to be so ignorant," she said, and laid some scrolls down on a table. Estegi moved quickly to light a lamp and bring a sitting cushion to make Kabira comfortable. She let the servant girl putter about. Then she sat down and fixed her judgmental gaze on me.

"You must learn about the great poets. And the history of Areko. The Vizier expects only the best from his household."

I think that my master is more interested in other attributes of mine, and would rather hear himself speak than listen to me. But I stayed quiet, as the new Garai has taught me.

"You can paint while you listen," the wife said graciously, and began to read.

She has a pleasant voice, and I do enjoy poetry, but I have never heard anything of this sort before. The story bores me, because its subjects mean nothing to me. Rulers, men of power, wars and military campaigns, territories won and lost. Nothing about what really matters: the earth itself. Its life force. The lives of people in harmony with the life force. Still, I put her recitations to memory, and when she was finished I put down my brush and recounted the most important parts of the historical scrolls and poetic verses back to Estegi and Kabira. They seemed impressed,;not even the wife could hide it. For me it was nothing noteworthy. Mother had taught all her daughters in this way: through narrating from her memory stores, then demanding that we retell everything back to her. It did not need to be word for word, as long as it was true. I realized that I had lost some of my skill. My memory was not as sharp or able to absorb knowledge. I have decided to work to improve this. Not for the sake of any other but myself.

ᚥ

So our days and evenings pass. It is most often Estegi who waits on us. She is quick, quiet, and has great skill in anticipating Kabira's

98

wishes before she is even aware of them herself. The sun treks across the floor and shows the passing of the day. Darkness falls, Estegi lights our lamps. The cinna players are dismissed. The night birds begin their song, first tentatively, then with more and more surety and force. I speak little. Kabira talks, recounts things. Purposeless things: art; poetry. Some people she calls the old master teachers. I listen and try to understand. But I cannot. How can words describe truth? Everything I bind to paper withers and dies. Even if I wrote a poem about a lizard in the desert, how could I capture the reality of the lizard? And what can a poem tell us of the sun, or the coolness of the night?

Naught.

Yet Kabira talks. And I listen. And the sun glides on and night comes, and then day again, and all we can do is wait.

ꙍ

My master has been away traveling a lot of late. He is overseeing the construction of the palace in Ohaddin and travels around the provinces buying timber, marble and stone. He is obsessed with construction in a way that is difficult for me to understand. Sometimes, when he returns from Ohaddin, he is altered. There is a darkness in him then, one that masks a profound power. There is a difference in the way he takes me. There is a difference in the way he looks at me. His gaze touches something inside, something of myself I do not want to share. It is as if he can see the old Garai, but she does not frighten him. He can see the new Garai as well, and the one to come. After spending time with him I feel completely exposed, inside and out. I want to hide, but there is nowhere to hide from his gaze. I wish I could call forth the old Garai at those times. She was strong. She was fearless. The power of the very earth rushed through her veins; she had spoken with the Sanuel tree, her soles knew every stone of the Meirem Desert, her hands knew how to create and shape. Her scars bore witness—

My scars. They have faded. I tried to count them just now, and I could not find them all.

ꞷ

A long time has passed. Years. I have not written, because there has been nothing to write.

Soon the palace in Ohaddin will be completed. The build has lasted eight years.

My master called on me today. When he had had his way with me, he stood by the window and watched the first luggage carts roll out from Areko on their way to Ohaddin. He stretched. His body is still as smooth and firm as the first time I saw it several years ago. He has hardly aged at all. The same cannot be said about me. I have no opportunity to move around as I want to. I eat too many sweet cakes, honey-soaked chilled fruit and fried weja rolled in sugar. My belly has become bulged and my cheeks round.

My master rubbed his hands against his thighs in delight.

"At last. How I have worked for this! I shall move the Sovereign Prince and his court in at the end of this moon, to coincide with the new moon. Then I will have him where I want him. His obstinate sons are to remain in Areko. They do not understand that they are playing entirely into my hands."

"How is that, Master?" I knew that he wanted my questions.

"When they are not in their father's presence, they have no

influence over him. And when he does not see them, it is much easier for me to dispatch them on missions that appear important, but which serve only to keep them out of the way. Then I and I alone can steer the Sovereign Prince precisely as I wish. Each and every decision he makes, big and small, shall come from me. I will begin by sending his firstborn into battle against Herak. They have refused to submit their tribute payments for three consecutive years now. They shall bow to the power of Ohaddin and Areko. And that power, my little savage, is mine now. All of Karenokoi shall kneel before the Sovereign, and to me."

He turned to me. I was lying naked on the animal hide on his bed and he wrinkled his nose. "You are getting fat. And you are not as young as you once were."

I felt ashamed. Who am I if I have no worth in the eyes of my master? I pulled the hide over me and lowered my gaze. My master cast a last contented look out of the window and then called in a servant to help him dress. I stayed lying where I was until they left the room. Then I got dressed and walked through the secret passage to the great hall of the dairahesi. It was deserted. I rang a bell, and Estegi appeared without a sound and bowed submissively. She has grown over the last few years and is now a head taller than me. Her nose is even larger than before; she is certainly not a beautiful woman. Even if she is thinner than me.

"Fetch my things. I am going to bathe. I want oil of arremin and my own blend of almond oil and rose water. At once."

I lay in the bath for a long time. Massaged my scalp with sweet-scented soap, scrubbed away all the hardened skin with a pumice stone. Shaved in the places I knew my master wanted me to be smooth. Plucked my eyebrows and the moustache that had begun to grow on my upper lip. Rubbed myself down with almond oil until I was smooth as a newborn baby.

What will happen if my master takes a new concubine? Will he leave my bed completely, as he left his wife's when I arrived? My days would become even emptier. I have no worth other than what he bestows on me. His gaze gives caresses, judgment, value. His hands give my body the contours it otherwise lacks. Sometimes he even gives me pleasure. I hate that. But usually he gives me a different sort of gratification: that for a short time I am worth something. If that is taken from me, what will I then have to wait for?

ʊ

Kabira came in as I was writing that last part. My door was not locked—it has no lock. I did not even attempt to conceal my papers. Kabira has seen them before and never given me away.

She sat down on some cushions and waited. After a while Estegi came in carrying a tray of hot tea, which smelled of rose and mint, and a little heap of sugar-dusted cakes. Estegi served the tea, first to the wife, then to me. I picked up several cakes and stuffed them in my mouth. The sweetness filled me with an immediate sense of pleasure. Estegi withdrew toward the door, where she sat down and awaited further orders.

I looked at Kabira. She sat so calmly, collected, sipping her tea. She has as little activity to fill her days as I do—indeed less, because my master does not even visit her bed. I know that she has duties toward Izani, that she appears at public ceremonies with the sons, but those can only be brief respite from this non-life of perpetual expectancy, of idleness and melancholy.

"How do you endure it, First Wife?" I asked her, breaking the silence.

Kabira scoffed. I did not think she would answer. She drank her tea. Eventually she spoke.

"I am no longer concerned with what happens to me. He has already destroyed everything."

Her voice was quiet and rasping. She sat hunched over her tea bowl, her features veiled by the steam.

"Every day I carry the memory of my dead kin. Everyone he has taken from me. My sons who do not even know me, who are ashamed of their mother, and recoil from my touch. Yet he will not allow me to die."

She stayed silent awhile. Sipped her tea.

"Has he visited you?"

I nodded. She put down her bowl. Looked out of the window. "Did you talk to each other?"

We had never discussed my master before. But I had led the conversation here.

"Yes. Some. He is pleased with the building work in Ohaddin. Less pleased with me." I pointed at my belly and thick thighs.

She quickly turned her head and looked at me. She smiled, a twisted sneer. But it was not cruel. More . . . sorrowful. As if she understood what I meant. And it struck me that she, despite everything she had just said, might still feel something for him. Something I have never felt.

That makes her more of a slave than I have ever been.

She whispered something to Estegi, who quickly got up and left the room. Kabira stood up and sighed.

"Come now. Time for you to pack up your things. You do not

want anyone to find your papers." She straightened her jacket.

"Iskan is moving us to Ohaddin along with the Sovereign Prince and his household. Ready yourself for a new home."

ϖ

I have packed my belongings, the things I understand as my own: jackets and trousers he gave me, my hair combs and jewelry. My pressed flowers and writing implements. My dried herbs. I have hidden my secret notes in the back cover of the folder where I keep the pressed flowers.

But none of this is mine. I know that. It all belongs to him. In the desert, everything was free—the flowers, plants and animals—nobody owned them, we took what we needed and carried our tools and utensils with us, nothing more. My master owns everything I see around me. He owns me too.

I do not know when we are moving. I am not allowed to know anything. Neither is Kabira. We are entirely in his hands, objects to handle as he pleases. I find the unpredictability one of the hardest things to bear. I never know when he will summon me and use my body. I never know about anything in advance: things simply happen to me, suddenly and without explanation. One day we will be told to sit on a palanquin and we will be taken to Ohaddin, yet another new place I have never been before. A new cage for me to wait in.

ϖ

Today we arrived at Ohaddin. It is evening and very late and I am tired from the journey, in a rocking, swaying and suffocating palanquin. I felt nauseous and irritable, and Estegi, who was my companion, was afraid of me and by the end did not even dare respond to me. But I must write now, at once—it is so wonderful—I understand why I am still alive, I finally understand! Everything has led me here, my patience is being rewarded, and I thank the new Garai for keeping me alive, praise be to the earth and sky and the spirits of the dead!

I could feel it as soon as we were nearing Ohaddin. It was late afternoon, the sun was low in the sky and our convoy passed tired, sweating laborers on their way home from the spice plantations. The palace emerged from behind a hill, so much bigger than anything I could have imagined, and at that very moment I felt it. The vibration. Faintly at first, like a scent on the breeze, a scent of something delicate and elusive that you recognize and try to name, but cannot. Just then Estegi offered me a piece of watermelon rolled in honey and rose water, but I held up my hand and told her to be quiet. Completely quiet and still. The convoy wound its way farther, and with the bearers' every step we came closer to the palace and the sensation intensified. A humming. A murmur. A rhythm that pulsed through my body. I have never felt the life force so strongly before—it is powerful, more so even than the sensation I got from the stem of Sanuel. I could barely sit still, the urge was overwhelming to jump from the palanquin and run to meet that power, that call.

By the time we were carried into the walls of Ohaddin, dusk had fallen and all the guards held torches in their hands. There is a house especially for the women, called Beauty's House, and I caught glimpses of large rooms and halls and an enormous bathing pool as I was taken to my own room. Everywhere were gold and painted screens, pots and vases, flowers and fountains, and everywhere hummed the murmur, the song that is even now calling to me.

I lie upon silk cushions under the hide of some striped animal and my room smells of rose and incense, and yet I cannot sleep. The old Garai, the wisewoman, cannot sleep. She has awakened now. She is more awake than ever. She runs her fingers over her scars and she yearns to go out and find the sacred site she knows is close. She wants to make an offering to it, and she knows that this is the great offering, the one she has been preparing for her whole life.

Still, she must wait. I shall find the site. The new Garai will keep me alive here too, in this enormous cage, and I will seek out the source of the song, and everything will have been worth it.

Everything.

ᚹ

The old Garai lies in wait. I will not forget her, not again, but life here in Ohaddin is more difficult than before. I can feel the life force, every day it beckons and calls to me, but I am denied access. The great offering, so close and yet so out of reach. My master's inner darkness is ever increasing. He takes possession of my entirety when he enters me. My body and my mind. I cannot defend myself against him, not by any means.

I want to give myself new scars, to cut, to see the blood trickle forth. But I know that it would be wrong. The wounds must mean something. The scars must represent genuine offerings. I cannot cut only to afford myself relief.

ᚹ

My master took his mother, the wife and me on a walk around the garden already today, on our first day here. Naturally, Izani was accompanied by three servant girls carrying parasols, cushions and a basket of chilled drinks. Kabira took Estegi with her so that she could look around, but had her carry a parasol, so that Izani could not complain about a servant being allowed to go idle. We were followed by two guards with curved sabers. It was clear that my master wanted to show off his creation. Bask in the glory of our admiration. And he has cause.

The garden is exquisite. My master made sure it was completed before bringing the Sovereign Prince, he explained, so it was ready before the palace buildings were erected. He wanted to dazzle the Sovereign with as much splendor as possible, in order to ensure that he would move here willingly and spend gold on a palace of his own. In the west are the three buildings of my master's household: Serenity House, where he has his private quarters, his bath and his library; Sovereign House, where he works, gives audience and meets other men of power; and Beauty's House, where we women live together with his mother and servants. The kitchen is also in here. Through the garden, from northwest to southeast, runs a manmade stream with little waterfalls and bridges. In the east, like a mirror image of the houses my master had built for himself, are a further three houses belonging to the Sovereign Prince. But more will be built, for a sovereign must have greater splendor than a vizier.

"Everything is built from the best Karenokoi can provide," my master said as we stood in front of the Sovereign's palace, with Izani on one side and the wife on the other. I stood respectfully some steps behind. It was early morning, but sounds could already be heard from all the houses: there was a lot to arrange, what with the whole household unpacking and putting everything in order. Furniture and servants had been sent in advance, and now the residents could settle in. "I have acquired exotic woods from a great island in the South," said my master. "Terasu, the island is called. Do you see the columns? How black they are? It is an uncommonly hard type of wood that does not grow in these parts. It needs no painting or treating and it is almost as difficult to work as stone." He snickered unpleasantly. "It is not the only exotic thing I brought with me. You will see."

The palace houses are two stories high, built on a platform so they cannot be seen from the ground. The platform is covered in brightly colored tiles, patterned with flowers and leaves that look so real as to compete with the magnificence of the garden. The gilded ceiling shone in the bright morning light and Izani raised a ring-covered hand to shield her eyes. My master saw and smiled. "The brilliance is intentional, so that all beyond these walls cower before the grandeur. Nobody must doubt where all the power in Karenokoi lies. None of the princelings have anything that can compete. Soon they shall all bow, nay grovel, before the power of Ohaddin. My power."

"My son, you have truly created something remarkable," said Izani, and patted her son proudly on the arm. "Would you not agree, Kabira?"

The sharpness in her voice when she spoke to her daughter-in-law was immediately audible.

"There is nothing like it in all the known lands," said Kabira. Her voice was expressionless, formal.

"You cannot recognize your father's old estate, can you?" Izani looked at her son's wife.

"No, none of it, chi. Everything is far more resplendent and wonderful."

I heard the sorrow she hid behind her words but my master was deaf to it. Or he did not care.

We strolled farther below the flowering fruit trees. Birds with shining red and blue feathers were singing in an enormous cage.

"I have had all sorts of songbirds brought here," said my master, indicating the cage. "Many can fly freely in the garden, others I keep in cages. The Lady Sovereign and her daughters are very keen on birds. We have hired young boys with slingshots and bows to patrol the garden and shoot any birds of prey. There is already lively insect and seed trade going on beyond the walls of the palace. Feed for the birds."

The garden was full of laborers busy watering, clearing and cleaning. Everything is perfect, not a leaf out of place. Nothing dead or ugly is allowed.

"Might you show us the herb garden, che?" Kabira asked her husband, in her most respectful voice.

Izani scoffed but my master nodded. "Naturally, cho." With an exaggerated gesture, he took his wife in one arm and his mother in the other, and escorted them along a winding path between fragrant bushes overflowing with pale pink flowers. As they brushed past the branches, petals fluttered down around them that were crushed under my sandal-clad feet as I followed. We crossed the stream over an arched bridge with richly decorated balustrades. Gold-colored fish darted past in the clear water. My master pointed to a pond into which flowed the stream. Willows bent over the still surface of the water and water lily leaves rested like jewels on a dark mirror.

"I have put carp in the water, for my sons to fish. There are several small boats that can be kept cool in the water on the hot summer days. Concerts shall be performed here for the Sovereign's women—over there, on the other bank, a platform can be erected and they can sit facing the sunset, and the musicians can play on floating boats adorned with lanterns and entertain the court. I shall call it the Garden of Eternal Serenity."

"Magnificent, my son." Izani nodded. "You must invite the princelings and their families as well. When they see all this beauty, such costly splendor, they will dare not do anything but kneel before you."

She did not notice that she had revealed too much: that it was the Sovereign Prince they should kneel before. But Iskan noticed and smiled. "And here, I have granted your request, wife. I had a rose garden created, and with it, as a surprise, an herb garden."

We walked past roses of every color, and came eventually to a low wall. My master opened a gate and let us in. His mother stopped outside with furrowed brow, ordered her servants to put up the parasol and fan her. Estegi also stopped outside, at a respectful distance from the Vizier.

In long narrow beds, in spirals and circles, grew all sorts of herbs and spices. I bent down, touched the leaves, took in the scents—sharp, sweet, bitter, fresh. There were all the medicinal plants I knew of, and many more I had never seen or heard of before. This is a place I can walk around and explore, gather, dry, paint. Learn. I walked farther in, and saw that many of the plants were growing in their optimal sites, but that some were wrongly placed, and needed more shade or more space. My fingers were itching to dig, transfer, replant.

I turned around. The wife was standing a few steps behind me looking at a sage plant. My master and his mother were in conversation and Izani looked irritated. I thought it must be because her son had fulfilled Kabira's wish. Izani did not tolerate Kabira getting her own way in any matter.

I knelt before the wife, and it was I who did it—I, Garai—and not the new one who only showed respect as a strategy for survival.

"Most venerable First Wife," I whispered, so that my master could not hear. "I thank you."

"Rise, woman!" the wife burst out, evidently bothered. I did rise, but then bowed deeply.

"Thank you. You have shown me a great kindness. I know what it must have cost you." I looked pointedly at Izani.

"Yes, yes. It was your concoctions that cured me from my severe ill health this winter, after all. And Sonan said that his cough was cured after the infusion you gave him. That was probably what convinced my honorable husband. Not my words. His sons are his greatest asset."

My master has no daughters. He does not visit Kabira's bed, and I have made sure that I do not get pregnant. My master thinks I am barren, and it does not worry him. He has the sons he needs, he says. They are ten, nine and seven years old now. Wild and willful and strong. I can hear them playing outside as I write. I have never spoken to them. It is not my place. The times they visit their mother I keep to my room. They must not be corrupted by the vision of a concubine. I do not know who decided so. My master or his wife. Perhaps it was me.

The boys live with Izani. Not with their mother. They visit her, sometimes, when Izani allows. Afterward Kabira does not show her face for several days. She eventually returns to the sunroom, where I draw flowers and Estegi embroiders and one or two cinna players entertain us, accompanied by the sound of the fountain in its marble basin, but she is always quieter than usual. After a while she participates in conversation again. Gives orders to the servant girls. Criticizes my clothes. Orders fresh cakes and demands that a screen be moved so that the light falls better on the painting. Takes out a scroll to educate me. Then everything is as before.

I did not know what I should say to her. Words do not suffice. She can pretend otherwise but I know the herb garden was a gift to me. I suddenly gained a deeper understanding of Kabira. She did not despise me. Whatever else she might have thought of me, I was her only friend.

I bowed again, and took her hand, and kissed it quickly. Released it before Izani had a chance to see.

"Hurry now, Iskan has something else he wants to show us."

I do not yet know how, but I shall reciprocate this gesture of friendship. This gift Kabira has given me.

Iskan brought us back through the garden, northward. When we reached the snow-white marble steps of Beauty's House, he stopped and kissed his mother lightly on the cheek. "You can stay here, Izani-chi. I see that you are tired. Soon it will be insufferably hot. I have a little surprise to show my wife."

Izani was displeased, yet had no choice but to abide. She swept into the palace with her servant girls in tow. Estegi followed after Kabira and my master. I hesitated a moment,

112

then ran after them. My master's mention of a surprise was not in a benevolent tone. And I sensed a tension in Kabira. She had shown me kindness. I did not want to abandon her. The guards followed behind me.

We walked northward, toward the wall. A grove of zismil trees appeared before us, and my master gestured to the guards to wait for us under the trees. Zismil also grow on the slopes of Omone. I know their scent. They have a stubborn method of growth, with curved, narrow trunks and sparse crowns stretched toward the sky. They are fast-growing trees, and some were already taller than man-height, though they could not have been there for more than a few years. I saw Kabira clench her hands into fists. She quickened her pace. The zismil trees obscured my view. I could not see where they were going, but I could feel it. The song of the life force, which was always present in Ohaddin as an underground hum, intensified further still. I started to pick up my pace too. Soon I would see its source! Soon I would know its origin, and could begin to prepare my offering!

Kabira emerged from the grove before me. She stopped and looked up. Let out a little cry.

We had come to the foot of a small hill situated against the wall surrounding Ohaddin. A path led straight up the hill, lined with night-black stone tiles. The path finished at a door in a high wall that roundly enclosed a section of the hillside. The wall was crowned with a blood-red roof, resting partly on the wall and partly on the hill itself.

Iskan turned to his wife. He smiled his predatory smile.

"The door is made of the strongest metal, dear wife. It cannot be burned. It cannot be destroyed. Anji is mine, and mine alone, and nobody else can access her."

All color had drained from Kabira's face. "The graves. On top of the hill. My family."

She was having difficulty getting the words out.

"I removed them to make space for the roof." My master shrugged his shoulders, unconcerned. He does not even share his people's respect for the dead. They do not worship the earth or other gods here, but they do honor their dead, and even I have started to light beeswax candles on the holy days. One for each of my sisters. One for Mother. I do not know whether they are living or dead. But I want to show that I have not forgotten. I understood that he had committed a terrible transgression by desecrating these graves.

Kabira stood motionless.

"I shall permit the Sovereign entrance at times. To partake of the spring's water. Sometimes when it is good. When I need him to be healthier, for a while. And sometimes when it is bad, if I need a weak ruler to steer as I wish."

My master did not guard his words in the slightest. Not even admission of high treason was dangerous when only disclosed in the presence of women. We were nobody at all. As unimportant as grass on the ground. As interchangeable.

"You cannot imprison Anji like this!" Kabira clutched desperately at his arm. "It is not right!"

Never had I seen her so dismayed. Never seen her willingly touch her husband.

My master shook her off his arm. He continued to smile. Her distress did not bother him in the slightest. He gave no response. Just walked away through the zismil trees and disappeared.

I had to help Kabira back to Beauty's House. The guards followed us a few steps behind. The sun was already hot, and it smelled strongly of soil and zismil resin.

Now I know that Kabira also knows. I have tried to coax her into talking about it today, but she refuses. Turns away, retires to her private quarters, or changes the topic of conversation. But I know that she knows more than she will admit. Maybe we could gain access if we worked together! Because she is right: a source of power cannot be imprisoned and kept to oneself. That is what Iskan has done. That is where his power originates from. I see that now. I see whence the darkness in him comes. I see how he is able to look inside me and touch my many selves. It is a relief to know. It is a power I understand, that I am schooled in. I can protect myself from him better now that I know.

I pull the new Garai over me, and now she is a disguise, nothing more. Inside me, in my true self, hums the power that I cannot yet reach. But one day. One day.

Garai the artful
Garai of the cunning tongue
Garai, concealing
Garai, waiting
Garai, awakening

I am continuing from where I had to stop yesterday, because that evening I discovered that we are not alone in Beauty's House. Izani has the whole upper floor at her disposal, and lives there

115

with my master's sons. Bottommost live the servant folk. In the dairahesi there is only me in my little room, and the wife in her large, opulent quarters. There are sunrooms and shaderooms and several bedrooms, but they are empty. Or so I believed. When I came out of my room, I was confronted with a girl sitting cross-legged on one of the cushions by the fountain in the great hall. I stopped. She was clearly no servant. She did not look like anybody I had ever seen before, and I was reminded of my master's words about exotic things he had brought back with him from Terasu. The girl was tall and dark-skinned and she sat with a very straight back. She turned her face to me and I saw that she was very beautiful, and younger than I was when I became slave-sold. In her curly hair was a single comb. A slave, then. Like me.

"Who are you?" I asked, without etiquette or protocol. Kabira was not there and could not chastise me.

She looked up at me with large black eyes. She seemed to understand my question.

"Orseola," she answered in a deep voice. She was dressed in some sort of exotic golden fabric drawn tightly over her breasts, and I realized that she is my master's new concubine. At last I am free! All day I have been rejoicing internally. I am free!

"My name is Garai," I said, and smiled. And then, as if the palace and garden and everything in them were mine: "Welcome to Ohaddin."

ORSEOLA

We lived in trees. It was by the delta. We could not build houses on the soft, wet earth, so we built them high in the treetops. In Karenokoi they could never dream of such trees as grow in Terasu.

I know, for I have seen their dreams. I tried to weave my trees into their dreams—trees with trunks as great as houses, with canopies that embrace the sky. But it never worked. The people there cannot imagine anything so big. So mighty and eternal, yet living.

In those trees, there was space for several houses. Between the trees were bridges. Our fathers wove them from rushes and reeds. The long bridges were woven with ornate patterns. The patterns told you where the bridge spanned to and from, and bore the sign of the weaver. My father's signature pattern was dark-brown waves.

Rope ladders hung between the branches of the trees. During festivities the children would decorate them with flowers. We could do most everything from the treetops, even fish. But to make fire and pick flowers, we had to touch the ground. We children used to venture to the edge of the city and then down onto the water. We paddled in bulrush boats until we came to the grassy islands where the flowers grew. Pink flowers, and white, like the ones on the lemon trees here. Big as a child's face.

We loved those flowers, and loved to pick them and make

garlands. Our mothers were happy when we returned in boats filled with blossoms, and we loved our mothers then too.

With the rope ladders dressed in flowers the trees themselves appeared as though in bloom.

Goveli was a vaster city than Areko, all high up in the treetops. There was the market tree, and a tree with houses for all the work posts. There were trees for the rich, each with one house on many levels, and trees for the poor with many small shacks crowded among the branches. There were pleasure trees and mourning trees. In the pleasure trees lived the orphaned girls and boys who offered their bodies in exchange for food and clothing. In the mourning trees flower garlands were hung up for the dead, their names etched into the rinds of fruits. They remained there until they rotted away or disappeared into the bellies of animals and insects. The mourning trees had a sickly smell. They stood on the eastern edge of Goveli.

The hometrees were sacred. They must not be harmed—neither with intent nor by accident. The most sacred of all was the Queen's tree in the heart of the city, where the Queen lived with her entourage. The tree was the oldest in Goveli—so old that nobody knew its age.

In the city were jesters and beggars, musicians and witch doctors, seers and sayers. Stargazers and singers, sluggards and fishermen, lawmen and junk-dealers, weavers and tailors, carpenters and whittlers, boat builders and seafarers, healers and jewelry makers, bird tamers and insect gatherers.

There were no smiths. There were no warriors.

My grandfather was a net maker. My father made lutes and harps from hazel wood.

My mother was a dreamweaver.

ʊ

I remember—

The trees only ever died of old age, and suddenly. One day the leaves would begin to fall. Then we knew the trunk was rotten through and it was not safe to remain. The tree dwellers had to gather their houses, plank by plank, and carry them away along the bridges. Lawmen allotted them new trees, and after ceremonies of thanks and naming, the people reassembled their homes. They were never exactly the same as before, for the trees' branches determined the shape. A room shrank here, a floor raised there, an extra veranda was formed.

When a tree died, three days of mourning were declared. Words of thanks were carved into the bark of the deceased tree. That was the only time a blade might touch a hometree. They engraved the names of all who had ever dwelt within its branches, back to the very first. The lawmen had it all written down on their long scrolls. We wore necklaces of dried leaves and could not swim or sing until the three days of mourning were honored. The necklaces were rough and itchy. Crumbs of dead leaves found their way into our clothing. The bridges creaked under the weight of the house parts being carried away.

When the days of mourning were over, the next hometree was celebrated with poetry and dancing. My father was a fine poet. I remember the gleam of his white teeth in darkness while he recited his verse. He sat topmost in the canopy, swinging his feet and mead jug, his poems floating out across city and sea.

119

I remember our breakfasts. Soured goat's milk with nuts, seeds and honey. Our bowls were empty saorse shells that Father painted with his special pattern of waves in red and white. On the nights when Mother was dreamweaving, she came home late and slept until midday. Father had a workshop farther down the tree trunk, where the sawdust produced by his work would not bother anyone, and he worked there from early morning. It was often up to me to give my little siblings their breakfast. We usually sat on the veranda to eat while the city was awaking around us. We could hear conversations in the hometrees, babies crying and goats bleating from where they grazed on the roofs. Birds of every color flew around, or sat singing on the railing of our veranda or tree branches. In summer the drone of the insects was nearly deafening. We children smothered ourselves in clay to avoid being eaten alive. The feeling of the planks beneath my bare feet, cooled by the night air. The crunch of nuts between my teeth.

After breakfast I rinsed out the bowls and put them on their shelf in the main room. Our house had three rooms. One for food and gathering. One where Mother and Father slept and one for us children. We had two verandas, one to the west and one to the north. Our goat, Bark, grazed on the roof and provided us with milk, cheese and souring. When Father had the time, he played for us on the lute and mandolin, and Mother sang songs of myth and mirth and dreams. As the eldest, I was responsible for the little ones. But as soon as Mother was awake I would sneak away, out onto the roof, up through the branches. I had friends whom I played with wherever we found an interesting place, and we sang stories of our own, and made playthings from empty nut shells and cones. When the heat of day became too intense, we went swimming in the sea or the channels, quick like eels, and then climbed up high where there was most breeze.

One of my friends was named Aurelo. He had a wide, smiling face and black hair that he tied up tight in the center of his crown. We used to compete to see who could get around the city the fastest. And who could steal a piece of fruit from the market tree in the midst of all the trade. And who dared jump down into the water from the highest branch. We competed over everything, but when we were tired and hungry we would share the stolen fruits fairly, and if anyone bigger ever challenged us, we always fought together, as a single beast with four raging paws and two biting mouths. Uncle and his wife called us the flying terrors of Goveli, because we hurtled headlong through the trees as if we were flying.

Of course we fell sometimes. There were wounds and scratches and sore ribs. One time Aurelo broke his arm and could not climb for several moons. I went and played with others, because such is the cruelty of children. But when he was better, we were the flying terrors of Goveli once more, and nothing could keep us apart.

Nothing but his dreams.

ᛟ

I remember the first time I entered someone else's dream. It was a hot night. Summer. Everything was clinging to my skin; the very air was dense and intrusive. I was lying between hot little bodies on my sleeping mat and trying to sleep. Not a single breath of wind moved in the hometree to give respite. My brother, Obare, sighed in his sleep. All of a sudden I knew I could fly. I kicked off the floor, hard, and up I rose. I made swimming-like strokes through the air and I flew. Out through the window. I was above our house. Soon I was above Uncle's house, higher up in our hometree. I swam higher, while below me people were running along the tree branches and bridges—earthbound, treebound. I was high among the treetops, flying unhindered between the branches, leaves falling around me; I was a fish-bird. I looked at my hands swimming through the air and saw that they were not my own; they were smaller and darker-skinned. It was easy to land when I wanted to, and I did so among the little children, who were all filled with wonder and awe.

"Orseola," said Mother, shaking me gently. I looked at her. The name she was saying was not mine. I was too hot. I wanted to fly again. When I got up, my limbs felt so heavy. I wanted to be free. To leave everything behind. I did a few strokes and leaped out through the window.

I fell.

ᚹ

I hit the ground badly that time. The healer had to stay with us to take care of me through the worst of it. My left arm has never been the same since; I still cannot straighten it fully. Mother said that I had been delirious with fever and seen visions that led me to jump out of the window. For a long time she wove me cooling, calming dreams, free from pain, and I slept well. Mostly because I knew that she was sitting there, on her stool by my pillow, watching over me. Never have I felt so safe. Never had Mother given me so much attention. Father stayed with me often when Mother had matters to attend to or food to prepare; he told stories and sang and played for me.

Aurelo visited sometimes. He was more loyal than I had been when he was bedridden. He brought me stolen fruits, which tasted so much better than the ones given to me by well-meaning relatives, as well as gossip and news from the city. His skin smelled of adventure and sun and salt water, and the room felt less stifling and airless with him by my mat. One time he asked me why I had jumped. I repeated what Mother had told me. That I had a fever and was dreaming.

But deep down I knew it was something else. Only I did not know what. It had been so vivid. So real. Like a waking dream.

ᚹ

The next time it happened was during my convalescence. I was sitting outside one evening on the western veranda. The worst of the heat had passed and the westerly winds were cool. I was alone—the little ones were already asleep, Mother was preparing a new batch of soured goat's milk in the main room and Father was visiting someone who had commissioned a mandolin.

A gust of wind came rustling through the leaves. I heard its movements long before it reached me. As it glided over me, I found myself standing in the market tree in front of the fruit and sweets stand, and I was allowed to taste everything. Nobody was stopping me; they were all just smiling and nodding. Yet, at the same time, I was still sitting on the bench on our veranda with the westerly wind in my hair. My mouth was stuffed with sweet flavors until I felt like gagging, but still I ate and ate while also sitting entirely motionless on my bench. I could not move, I was about to choke, and eventually I vomited, straight onto my own lap.

Mother rushed to my side; she did not scold me. She carried me inside, cleaned me up and gave me pungent herbs to rub inside my mouth. Yet the sickly taste remained. When she laid me back down on my sleeping mat next to my little siblings, my sister, Oera, smacked her lips in her sleep.

ϖ

I was afraid that I was losing my mind. I did not understand what was happening at all. I did not speak about it to anyone. Not until Aurelo's dream.

ϖ

I was well again, and Aurelo and I were playing in one of our favorite trees. It was a kaora tree by the water's edge, a small one with a canopy so dense that in it you could be completely hidden from sight. We had been swimming all morning—I was relishing having control over my body again—and then ate mussels and kaora fruit. Finally, we each lay in the fork of a bough, full bellied and sleepy, letting the wind cool our hot bodies. Aurelo peered at me from under his thick eyelashes.

"You have grown weak during your sickness. Your arms are no longer strong like mine." He pointed. "Look. They are completely round." He ran his eyes over my body. "All your parts are beginning to become round."

I threw a kaora core at him, and it hit him straight in the middle of his forehead. "I still throw better than you." I turned onto my side and closed my eyes. The sounds around me were comforting, it was warm and I was drowsy. I was thinking about how we were soon going to visit Grandmother. Her white island was one of my favorite places. The scent of her pipe was in my nostrils.

Then I could smell the scent of sun-warmed skin. A body lay before me, stretched out in the fork of a bough. A girl's body with round hips and young breasts. I reached out a hand and stroked her soft belly. Orseola smiled at me. She took my hand and brought it to her breast. I was excited. I leaned forward to take it in my mouth.

I forced myself awake at that moment, which required great effort. My heart was racing and I sat up with the world spinning around me so intensely I had to hold on to the tree trunk to keep from falling. Aurelo was asleep in his bough fork, and I knew that it was his dream I had seen. His gaze and his hands had been on my body. It was extremely distressing to see myself in the dream of another, through the eyes of another. I did not know what was real and what was not, everything was blurred, like the fog that covers Goveli for several days, sometimes weeks, in the winter. I sank my teeth into a branch. The bark tasted like dust, the green wood inside was acrid and bitter. This was reality. This was truth.

Careful not to wake Aurelo, I climbed into a larger tree, and from there back into the city and to our hometree. Mother was there, sitting in the main room and feeding Oera mashed mango. Obare was playing with his bark boat. Sunlight filtered in through the window. The room smelled of sour milk and overripe fruit. I was on my guard against everything. Anything might be a delusion, someone else's dream. I tried to think of things that only Orseola could know, such as where her first tooth was hidden, and where she stole her first ever fruit, and the last person she had fought with. But how could I know that these memories were real?

125

"Mother. When did you begin to weave dreams?"

Mother licked the spoon before hanging it up on the wall, and put Oera down on the floor. She crawled over to Obare and made a grab for his boat.

"I had just become a woman," Mother replied in a pleasant tone, and stretched until her back cracked. She had been working at the Queen's court for most of the night. "A little older than you. My mother tested me, as our kinswomen have always been tested. She had me sit by the bed of a sleeper, and asked me what I saw." As she gazed out of the window I knew it was not the swaying branches she was looking at, but a far-off memory. "It was a great ocean and a small boat. I could not see who was in the boat. My skills were very weak, to begin with."

"How did you learn to weave?" My head was pounding. I could not rid myself of the image of that hand before me, that foreign hand, touching my breast.

Mother tutted and stood up. "You know what your grandmother is like. She couldn't teach the craft as a master to her apprentice, oh no. She had me discover everything myself. Learn the hard way. I lost years through her method. You won't have to. If your time comes, I will train you myself; you won't have to make all the same mistakes I did."

She looked at me properly for the first time since I came in. "Have you seen something?"

I nodded. She stiffened and tilted her head to one side.

"So young . . . Did it frighten you?"

I nodded again. Dared not meet her gaze. Afraid that she could read from my eyes what I had seen, the shameful thing. I had been taught from a young age that the worst thing a dreamweaver could do was enter the dream of another unbidden.

She smiled. "That is understandable." She came to me and drew me close. "I haven't had time to prepare you. I couldn't have guessed that the dreams would come to you so soon. But it does make me happy that you have the gift, I must say. I have always hoped that one of you girls would carry it. Now I can pass on the lore." She gave me a quick stroke on the cheek. "We begin tonight. I have no work to do, so meet me on the roof when the little ones are asleep."

I was relieved. Now Mother would teach me. She would show me how to distinguish between dreams and reality. I did not want to jump out of the window again. Or suddenly see myself from the outside. It had been a terrifying experience.

ω

But Mother and I spoke different languages when we spoke of dreams. I did not understand her, and she did not understand me. She sat me down by Father's pillow while he was sleeping, and showed me how to tune in to his dream, and weave in a new element. But I found it difficult to do what she showed me. It felt all wrong—unnatural. When I did it my own way, she became furious, smacked my fingers and hissed, "Respect!" so loudly that Father woke up. Then she flung out her hands. "If you don't do as I say, what is the point of me teaching you anything?" she snapped, and disappeared out through the door. The hanging bridge creaked under her weight as she paced away from the hometree. But I wanted her to teach me. I wanted her to show me how to hold reality close and keep foreign dreams at bay, but when I asked

127

her about it she did not understand what I meant. I always did as she said, and followed her movements, and watched with a sigh as the dreams slowly faded away. But Mother was pleased with me, nodded and corrected some tiny detail. It was as if she could not see what I saw. As if the colors and energy of a dream were hidden from her. For me a dream starts as an overwhelming sensation, then come the images, and I see what the person is dreaming about as if I were really there. The feeling is often so intense that I carry it with me for several days. If it is a bad dream, filled with terrors, then I go around in horror and fear and cannot shake it off. Yet even when the dreams are not unpleasant, the burden is heavy. It was heaviest when I was a child and defenseless against all the anxiety, longing and pain of the dreamers.

We were bickering more and more often. She wanted an obedient student and daughter. And I wanted to be obedient, but was too desperate for knowledge that she could not give me. I loved her with ireful fervor and, though I did what she asked of me, it became harder and harder. I had difficulty sleeping, afraid of what dreams might force themselves upon me. I began to sneak out at night, and climb to solitary trees on the outskirts of the city to get as far away from the dreamers as I possibly could. I became hollow-eyed and weak from lack of sleep, I lost my appetite. I no longer played with Aurelo. I missed his companionship; the hole he left behind was as though someone had scooped out my core with a spoon. But I could not rid myself of his dream. His version of me. Though I knew that nobody can control their dreams.

One night, Mother and I were sitting in the dark by Father's pillow, she on her dreamweaving stool and I on my cushion, and I failed at the simplest of tasks: to introduce a fish into Father's dream. Or some rain. Or climbing. I had done it before, and more difficult things besides: escaping from a storm, preparing a meal, an encounter that ends in tears. But this time I was so tired, and so frightened, that nothing would work for me. My hands were shaking and I was fighting to hold back the tears.

Eventually Mother lowered her hands and leaned back. She looked at me and sighed. I let the last fragments of Father's dream slip out of my reach, wither away and disperse.

"It's time I took you to my mother," she said shortly, and stood up.

We set sail the following day.

ω

Mother packed for the journey: clothes, dried fish and drinking water. More than was required for a one-day journey. But on the ocean one must always be prepared for storms. Gifts for Grandmother: dreamsnares made by my aunts out of horsehair and human hair, pearls and dried berries.

We rarely visited Grandmother, and the few times we did, it was with the whole family. Mother and Grandmother did not get along. I did not know why. I knew only that Mother sometimes got the notion that she needed to visit her mother, and then she took all us children with her. To show us off, or as a shield? This time Mother and I sailed alone. The boat felt empty. Mother barely spoke to me. She sighed as she loaded the boat, and again when she untied its mooring from the boat tree and poled us out of the delta.

As soon as we emerged onto open water, the light was sharp. My eyes were accustomed to only seeing the sun filtered through leaves and branches. I sat at the fore and squinted. Even the air was different. Light. Salty. There are several islands outside Goveli, and when you first catch sight of them in the haze of the sun they appear to be no more than shadows, specters in the blue. Then they begin to loom increasingly clearly, high and rocky. So unlike our leafy delta. On the larger islands are small villages; on the smaller ones, just houses scattered like driftwood on the shore. The people live not in trees but in houses built of stone. I wondered how they could sleep without the wind's lullaby in the treetops. The island people were different. They saw the world differently from us.

Grandmother lived alone on the farthermost island. Her little house was halfway up a steep slope above a beach of smooth pebbles. We reached the island in the evening when the sun was at its lowest western point. Grandmother's island is called Aspris. It means "the white island." It has no trees, only some low bushes and grass where Grandmother grazes her small herd of goats. When we came to land, the goats were standing on the highest ridge of the rocks and staring down at us. White and black and brown-horned heads against a pale-blue sky. I was a little afraid of them. They were nothing like our Bark. They were wild and dangerous and nameless.

Grandmother was standing high on the sloped shore and waiting while we dragged the boat in. She was even smaller than I remembered her, hunched and white haired, dressed in some shapeless black garment. It was difficult to believe that this woman, no larger than a child, had given birth to four daughters and a son. Mother respectfully knelt to kiss her bare foot, revealing no expression. Grandmother held out a bowl of water from the island's spring and Mother drank before passing the bowl to me. The water was delicious and completely different from what we had at home. Then we were each given a piece of hard goat's cheese. Nobody had said a single word. Grandmother barely looked at her daughter. But she inspected me carefully. The sun disappeared and, with it, the shadows. The cheese was salty and delicious, while Grandmother's gaze felt harsh on my skin.

"Are you teaching her?"

Grandmother spoke to her daughter without taking her eyes off me. Mother nodded.

"She is clever. Only her handling is a little clumsy, but she sees clearly."

"Sees clearly." Grandmother scoffed. "Why have you brought her here?" Her words were short and hard. Mother shifted her weight from one foot to the other.

"May we come in, sit down? I have brought gifts from Laela and Imjanda. We . . ."

Grandmother ignored her. "Do they enter you? The dreams?"

It took a heartbeat before I realized she was talking to me.

"Yes."

"Can you distinguish between dreams and reality?"

Mother gave me a sharp look. I had never dared speak to her about any of this. I had hoped she would guess, understand. I quickly shook my head.

"Of course you can, Orseola." Mother was impatient. "You see the dreams very clearly. It is only that you don't do as I say."

Grandmother sighed. "Come. Let us eat."

ᛒ

Grandmother made up a bed on the floor for me. Mother got the sleeping mat and Grandmother took a blanket and a mat for herself and lay on the beach beneath the stars. I lay for a long time and listened to the sound of Mother's steady breathing. Grandmother's house was very small. Hundreds of dreamsnares hung from the ceiling, made of bulrush and horsehair, feathers and pearls, bone fragments and nuts. Some were slowly spinning and jingling. I could not sleep. I missed the swaying of the trees. The stillness was making my skin crawl.

I carefully slid out from under my blanket. The door did not creak when I opened it. Outside was a starry night and a new moon. I could see the dark lump of Grandmother on the beach. I walked over the rattling pebbles toward her and sat on the corner of her mat.

"What do you do with the dreams you capture?"

Grandmother stayed silent. The ocean whispered to itself out in the night. I was not sure whether she was awake. Then a shoulder moved under the blanket.

"You understand why I live out here?"

I thought for a moment. Nobody had ever spoken of it. Grandmother was of the delta folk, like us. I did not know how long she had lived on the island. What could make someone leave the trees and fruits and the city? What could make me choose solitude?

"The dreams. You are escaping the dreams."

Grandmother sat up. She withdrew a pipe from the folds in her robe and stuffed it carefully. The leaves were fresh and sweet smelling; Mother had brought a whole bag with her. Once the smoke was billowing in abundance, Grandmother took a long and pensive puff.

"They wouldn't leave me in peace. Even after I stopped dreamweaving and passed the craft down to your mother, the dreams came to me in droves. I had to go as far away from other people as possible." She absentmindedly offered me the pipe and I shook my head. "I have the dreamsnares to capture any dreams that have lost their way."

"But then what do you do with them?"

Grandmother looked at me. Her eyes shone in the starlight.

"I drown them," she said shortly.

"Your own too?"

"I stopped dreaming a long time ago."

"How do you do it?"

"That you must learn for yourself. This is what your mother found so hard to understand: the lore of dreams cannot be learned. We see them in our own ways. They affect us all differently. Your mother, she is clever. Well regarded. But her way is precise. Practical. You and I . . ." She picked a leaf off her tongue. "The dreams come to us, whether we like it or not. Isn't that right?" I nodded and she took a long puff on her pipe. "Tell me. What has happened?"

I told her about the flying dream and the others. In the darkness I was not afraid. I knew that Grandmother would not judge me. That she had experienced similar, or worse. I explained my fear, and how difficult it had become to know for sure what was reality and what was dream. She nodded, her face expressing neither surprise nor alarm.

"You and I, we feel the dreams inside us. You must be careful not to let them in too much. They can begin to take possession of your being. Erase your boundaries. Do not worry, there are ways to protect yourself. But it takes time and work. You have been struck early, much younger than I was. It is inexcusable to enter the dream of another unbidden. You know that?"

I nodded. It was one of the first things Mother taught me.

"What happens to us is not unlike that. It is involuntary, but still not permissible. Do not speak of it to anybody."

She sat quietly awhile. It was chilly at the sea's edge and I was shivering. She snapped out of her musings and covered me with her blanket. It was rough and smelled of goat.

"Sleep, Orseola. Lie down here with me and dream, and I will weave you an explanation. Most of it you will only understand later, when you are older. But it will stay within you, to arise as needed." She smiled, and the smile transformed her face so that she no longer looked like my grandmother. "Nobody forgets a dream I weave for them."

"But Grandmother, you do not weave anymore, Grandmother," I said, repeating the word so as to anchor her here with me and make this wild and dangerous persona disappear. She chuckled and became my grandmother once more.

"For my own blood I can break my abstinence. Come, lay your head here on my lap. Tomorrow I will teach you to plait dreamsnares. They can afford you some relief while you are in training."

I lay down with my head on Grandmother's bony thigh and the blanket over me. My ears were filled with the sound of the ocean's swell, almost like the whisper of wind through leaves. The smoke from Grandmother's pipe filled my nostrils. And I dreamed.

It was a dream woven with artistry. It was nothing like the dreams my mother wove for me. It was much more vivid and powerful, starker than anything Mother made. During this one night I learned more about dreams and dreamweaving than from all of Mother's instructions put together. It spoke directly to that place inside me where I saw and touched dreams. Some of it I did not understand until later, when I had learned more about dreamweaving and my abilities had developed.

Some of it I do not understand to this day.

ꞵ

The day I left Terasu was one of the first clear days after the rains. The air in Goveli was filled with the sound of birds exulting in the warm sun and their drying feathers. For several moons we had been mainly shut up inside, with the rain as constant company, drumming against the roof and leaves. The little ones squabbled and fought. Father escaped often to his workshop to work on instruments, whether commissioned or not, late into the night. Mother and I had stopped arguing. We stayed silent instead. Silent through daily life and its chores, silent through her continuing instruction in dreamweaving. Not that I was learning anything from her anymore. We both knew it but refused to acknowledge it. So we wove dreams for Father or the few clients who braved the rain and the slippery hanging bridges to come and request Mother's services. And though I did as she asked, it was unthinking and lifeless. Mother had hoped that dreamweaving would bring us closer together. But instead it was driving us apart.

I had hung dreamsnares above my bed. Mother looked at them with dagger eyes and tight lips, but said nothing. The snares held some dreams at bay, but could not hold back the strongest ones. So I practiced. Many nights I lay awake in my bed and struggled

135

to stand my ground. To cling tight to who I was, to the boundaries that defined me, and to strengthen them against the unrelenting barrage of dreams trying to make their way in. I was growing stronger. Grandmother had given me a talisman, a necklace of seeds that I wore around my neck day and night. When I did not know what was real and what was someone else's dream, my fingers sought the necklace. I recognized the shape of each seed. If the necklace was not there, or the seeds were the wrong shape or size, I knew that I was in a dream. I had learned how to creep out of dreams as well. It worked best with the simple ones, the minor ones. Nightmares were worse.

That night I had stayed awake listening to the wind in the trees and the absence of rain. Finally the rains were over. Finally I could leave this house, venture out among the trees again.

I packed a bundle of belongings. Bound my stool to my back. Looked at my sleeping family. My husband. My children. I crept out without waking them. Ran barefoot over the bridges. My heart was hammering in my chest—would they discover my flight? The sound of steps behind me. I turned around. There stood my eldest daughter with her angry eyes. I could not let her suspect anything.

"I have a client," I said. "Go home to bed."

She did not obey. She never obeyed. She opened her mouth to scream, to expose me. I became furiously angry. I lashed out before she could make a sound. Lifted her over the rail of the bridge. She was heavy and struggled in my arms, her breath warm on my neck. She was writhing soundlessly, the unholy necklace she wore scratching at my cheeks. I pried her loose from me and sent her sailing downward. The water enveloped her. She left no trace.

I groped around my neck—nothing there, no seeds. I had to get away, get out, this was not true. I had to continue my escape before anyone else woke up. The trees grasped at me with branches like fingers. I stumbled and fell down into the water, my feet touched the surface, I used all my might, more than ever before, grappled for a stronghold, got a grip, clawed my way out of the dream before the water enveloped me.

I sat up and staggered outside. Vomited over the veranda rail. Stood outside and breathed. The morning birds had already awoken. Soon the others would be awake too.

I crept into my parents' room. Mother was sleeping, motionless but with a wrinkle between her eyebrows. Her rib cage was lifting up and down with steady breaths. One of her hands twitched slightly in her sleep.

She had thrown me in the water. She had wanted to run away from us all. I could still feel her turmoil inside me.

A dream is not the same as a wish, I tried to remind myself. People cannot control their dreams.

I could still feel the disgust she had felt, seeing myself through her eyes, standing there on the bridge. She must truly despise me. I was a disappointment to her. I could not even manage the simplest of tasks.

I reached out and took hold of her dream. It had never been easier. I had only just been inside it, and all its scents and sensations were still in me. I let sadness flood into Mother's dream, I channeled all the sadness I was feeling into her like a giant tidal wave. She shuddered and whimpered softly. Father sighed heavily in his sleep. She should grieve for killing me, her own daughter. I wove in an image of me with delta clay all over my body and dripping-wet hair. My eyes were accusatory. I opened my arms out to her.

You can give a dreamer feelings, visions and experiences. But you cannot control how they will react.

Mother did not respond to my embrace.

In anger, I wrapped my arms around Mother and flung us both down into the sea, letting her nose and mouth fill with water. If she could not love me, she would learn to fear me!

Mother's body was jerking and writhing in her bed.

Her dream self was fighting for freedom. Then she stopped all resistance.

Mother lay motionless in bed.

I lunged forward and shook her body. It was lifeless, cold. I called her name, and Father sat up, half asleep and uncomprehending. I was crying. I slapped her repeatedly in the face.

One gasping breath. Then another. She jerked, sat up in bed, eyes wide open. Glared at me. I could never have imagined such horror as was present at that moment in her eyes, and in my heart.

"She wove me a dream," whispered Mother to Father, who was clutching her hands in concern. "Unbidden."

Father froze. They both looked at me. I got up quickly, wanting to run away. Away from the awful, unthinkable thing I had done. But by that point Mother had come to and she was faster than I. She jumped up and grabbed me by the wrist. Hard. I had grown nearly as tall as her, but she was still stronger. I could not get away.

Without a word Mother dragged me outside. Father followed after with the little ones in his arms and on his shoulders. I stopped struggling and let myself be taken. Over bridges, one after another, straight into the heart of the city. A gentle breeze rustled in the leaves. The wood in the bridges was still damp after the seemingly endless days of rain. It smelled of wet wood and decay, like it always did after the rains. Many families were already awake, and curious eyes followed our movements. I heard the bridges creaking behind us where people followed to see what was happening.

Mother dragged me directly to the Queen's tree. She stopped on the great platform before the tree.

"I bring with me an accused criminal, and demand the Queen's ruling," she said in a loud voice.

"What crime has been committed?" asked one of the two guards standing in front of the steps that led up to the Queen's residence.

"Dishonor to dreams," Mother said loudly. One of the guards turned around at once and climbed up the steps.

"Think what you are doing," said Father in a low voice.

"She has to learn," said Mother resolutely. "She is a plant that needs pruning. Her gift is great, but it brings with it great responsibility. I cannot have a criminal as my apprentice."

Nothing about me being her daughter. She saw me as no more than a troublesome student who had failed.

"Forgive me, Mother," I whispered. "I did not know that you could . . . that it was possible to harm someone in a dream."

She was still holding me in a firm grip, but did not look at me. "Maybe not. But you knew that you mustn't enter another's dream unbidden. That you mustn't weave without the dreamer knowing. It was the first thing I taught you. It is the most essential pillar of our craft. If we went into dreams against people's wills, we would soon be suspected and feared—persecuted."

The hatred she had felt toward me in the dream was still clinging to me. I was a disappointment. I was burning with contempt for her, and for myself. It was like a heat in my body, a fever with no outlet. I began to tremble.

The Queen descended the stairs, accompanied by two guards and two maidservants. I had never seen her so close up before. She was older than Mother, with white in her hair and lines around her eyes. We must have awoken her. She turned to Mother. A servant handed her an obsidian knife, the one she always carried when she dealt justice, to cut truth from lie and right from wrong.

"What is the crime?"

"My daughter, a dreamweaver in training, entered my dream unbidden, Your Grace," replied Mother. "It is the greatest transgression of our craft. She must be judged accordingly."

"As her mother, it is your right to impose punishment," said the Queen pensively. One of the guards fetched an ornately carved chair for her to sit on.

"It is truth," Mother nodded. "But this is a grave crime, which could damage the reputation of our craft irrevocably. I wish for the punishment to be public."

The shame. I needed to get away. I could not bear everybody's eyes on me. I tried to twist out of Mother's grip, but she held me firmly.

"Very good. Then I shall punish in your stead, as a mother would her child." The Queen turned to me. I could not look at her. I could not take my eyes off the knife, the dark, gleaming blade.

"For your crime, not against your craft but against your parents, I sentence you to one whole moon as the lowest of the low. You

140

are to carry out all tasks whosoever may ask of you. Empty the latrines. Gut fish. Slaughter goats. You shall be everybody's child, so that you might learn to respect your own parents."

Mother exhaled heavily and let go of my hand. It occurred to me, much later, that she feared the Queen would mete out a punishment befitting a craft defiler, not a disobedient child. What I had done could have led to much worse punishment.

But shame was raging through my body. Such powerlessness. All I could see was that Mother loathed and despised me. That all the love I felt for her was coldly refused. And now everybody would see my shame, everybody would find out what I had done. At the same time, I was furious. How could Mother be so cold? How could she disgrace me this way? I wanted to see her feel something, anything at all!

The knife in the Queen's hand was calling to me. Enticing me.

Before anybody could react, I lurched forward and grabbed the black blade. Slipped through the arms that grappled after me. Stuck the knife deep, all the way to the hilt, into the soft trunk of the Queen's tree.

All sounds around me went silent. I saw gaping mouths, black eyes. People were screaming, but I could not hear what. Everything happened slowly, so slowly. The fever was released from my body. I was empty, completely empty. A frenzy of movement everywhere, hands pulling out the knife, arms protecting the Queen, hands gripping me. In the middle of all this frenzy there was one person as calm as I was.

Mother.

Her arms hung loosely by her sides. She looked me in the eye, just once. The only thing I could read in her eyes was despair.

Without hearing what was being said, I knew what would happen. To harm a tree, with knowledge and intent, was the worst thing anyone could do. And this was the Queen's tree I had stabbed. Exile or death.

The Queen spoke. Mother fell to her knees. She kissed the Queen's feet. She spoke and spoke, I could see her lips continuing to move. I no longer cared about anything. Whatever happened, happened.

Mother must have been begging for my life. Someone threw a tunic over my head. Took me away, down stairs and ladders. To the boat tree. I was dumped in a boat. Some bags were thrown in after me. A water bottle. The rope was cut. The boat was pushed out to sea.

I could no longer see Mother or Father. Only gaping mouths up among the branches. A stone came flying. I turned to look in the direction it had come from and thought I saw the snub nose of my old friend Aurelo.

I lay on my back in the boat and let the tide carry me out to the open sea.

ϖ

The worst part is that I surrendered voluntarily. It is my bitterest memory. Everything could have been so different. I have only myself to blame.

I let the boat drift past all the known islands. I could have rowed to Aspris. The way there was easy. Grandmother would have taken me in until the exile was lifted. Or I could have lived on the island with her, shared her simple life and grown old there.

But I did not want to inflict my dreams on her. I already knew

142

how they would be. What they would contain. How could I tell her that I had intruded on a dream? Tried to kill my own mother?

I knew that they had packed food and water for me. I did not care. I lay on the bottom of the boat and let myself scorch in the sun until my skin peeled and my lips cracked. The waves swayed me like the tree branches used to. It is the same wind, I thought. Same wind as home.

I no longer had a home. My family wanted nothing to do with me. My life was meaningless.

I lay that way for a long time. But my body was weak and refused to die. It crawled up to seek out the water. I drank, ate, looked around.

There was nothing to be seen except the ocean, brilliant with sunlight. No islands. No sandy shores.

Never had I been so far from home. There were no other people. No voices or sounds except that of the water lapping against my boat. And something else was different. I realized that while I dozed in the boat, I could sleep undisturbed.

I was too far away from anybody to be affected by their dreams.

I drank some more. Decided not to die, at least not yet. Stowed away my shameful memories and searched for a fishing line. There are always some in Terasu boats. Fishing lines and hooks and knives.

The knife was not black obsidian, but a simple flint blade.

I got a bite on the second day.

ᛒ

Sometimes I think back to those days on the ocean as the simplest in my life. Not the best. I was never truly free of the shame and

143

guilt. I had left behind the dreams of others, but neither were my own pleasant. Yet everything was so simple out at sea. Survival. That was all I thought about. I split open one of the sacks to make a shelter from the sun. I ate raw fish. Sometimes sea turtles bumped against the side of the boat. I could catch the smaller ones by hand and haul them into the boat. I drained their blood when the water had run out. One day it rained and I could drink the water that collected at the bottom of the boat. The nuts and dried fruits I had been given lasted a long time.

I did not drift for long. A handful of days only. When I caught sight of the ship, I was still strong. Not desperate. Mostly curious about who it was. It was an immense ship. The kind we did not have in Terasu. I had never seen anything so big built by human hands. It must fit a great many people, I thought.

I could have let them sail by. If it had been nighttime I would have. For I would have seen their dreams. And I would have known.

I raised my hand and waved. Somebody up on deck waved back. Movements. Several heads appeared over the railing.

A call. A language I did not understand. I called back.

"May I come aboard?"

Voices, calls. All incomprehensible. But then: a ladder was lowered. I maneuvered my boat in closer with an oar. Grabbed the ladder and climbed up.

I am choosing life, I thought, and left my little boat behind me, floating away alone on the waves, full of fish scales and turtle corpses.

Hands pulled me up over the railing. Many men. Hard eyes,

rough arms, shining steel. I had only seen steel knives at the Queen's ceremonies. In Terasu we were ignorant of the secrets of steel. Suddenly I was afraid.

A man dressed in expensive garments approached me. Inspected me carefully. Smiled. He laid an arm on my shoulders, and spoke words I did not understand. His voice was warm and smooth. The others held back. This was the man who made the decisions. He stroked a finger lightly over my dry lips. Spoke quietly in my ear. He led me through a door, leaving the armed men behind us. Inside was dim and my eyes saw nothing, burned as they were by the sun. His hands drew me farther in, gently. A bed. I relaxed. He could see that I was tired, he could see that I needed to rest. I sank down on the bed. It was so soft, after those nights spent on the bottom of the boat.

"Water," I said to the man. "I am so thirsty." I made a gesture like drinking. He nodded. He understood.

He leaned over me, pushed me down on the bed and with a single movement he forced himself inside me.

He did not let me drink until the next day.

ᚹ

It is incredible how strong is the desire to live. Even when you wish for death, your body fights to continue breathing, eating, sleeping. Loving. Not that I know, for I have never truly loved anyone. But my body has often betrayed me when I have wanted to die.

ᚹ

The first night aboard I realized where I had ended up: in the clutches of the god of the underworld. The smiling man dreamed

145

horrific things. I had never experienced anything like it before. I had no dreamsnares to protect me.

He kept me in the little cabin for weeks. I never saw daylight. Dreams and reality bled into one another. I knew what he was capable of. I saw his fears, his appetites, his desires and deeds. I saw his plans. It all seeped into me and I struggled against the visions night and day as I became enveloped in his blood-soaked mind. When he took me, which he often did, I had no energy to fight back. I did not even know if what was happening was real, or one of his twisted desires. I did not always know whether it was him or one of the other men.

We sailed for many days and nights.

Through his dreams I understood who he was. I learned words of his language.

He never spoke to me. He had no name. I became so absorbed by him that I lost myself.

At times, lying among the stench of the unemptied chamber pot, and the smells of sea and tar and fish and bodily fluids, I knew that I wanted to die. But all wit abandoned me, until all I knew were his wishes. His orders.

A sound came that was different from the others. It was not the lapping of water against the side of the ship. It was not the wind's swift flutter in the sails or the creaking of wet rope. It was the sounds of many different birds.

I propped myself up on my elbows. We must be near land.

A little later the door to the cabin opened. Bright light streamed in and I turned to look. A man came in. It was not him. The man said something to me, and I understood.

"Up."

146

I wanted to obey, but my body was so unused to moving—to obeying the commands of my own mind instead of his. The man came to the bed with an expression of disgust and pulled me up. Pulled me out of the door, outside on the deck.

At first I could not see anything. The light was sharp and merciless on my eyes, so accustomed to darkness. The scraping of boots hurrying toward the deck. Voices were calling, and this time I could understand some of the words. The air was filled with the screeches of birds, and the smell of honey and conifer trees. When my eyes adjusted, I could see that we were sailing past islands where the vegetation was nothing like ours back home. The sun looked the same, but its heat was different. Drier. Lighter.

Somebody crouched down next to me. I thought for a confused moment that it was to offer me support. Then I felt something around my wrists. Rope. My hands were twisted behind me and tied tight. As if I were a threat that needed taming. My heart was pounding.

Then I saw him. He came walking over the deck, dressed in sea blue and silver. He stopped for a short while and spoke to the man next to him. I understood one of the words.

Ocean.

Then he carried on walking. I was worth no more of his time. There were jobs to be done. He was already talking with one of the other men, something about rope.

The man by my side pushed me up to the railing. Grabbed hold of me to lift me up.

Death awaited me down there in the ocean. My body was putting up a fight. It did not want to die. Not even broken and defiled as it was. I hissed and writhed. The man swore.

My mouth stopped on a word. I called out.

"Anji!"

I had heard the word in his dreams. I knew it was a word full of power. It incorporated all of his desires and fears.

He stopped talking. He took a few steps and stopped in front of us. He tore me out of the other man's grip, grabbed hold of my chin and turned my face toward his.

"Speak."

The smile was gone.

I groped desperately among the few words I knew. I had to make him understand what I could do. What I could offer him.

"Dreams. I give."

A stream of words, none of which I understood. The grip on my chin hardened.

"Sleep. I give. Dreams."

He quieted. Looked me in the eye. It was the first time I saw straight into the eye of the man inflicting all of this on me. I could only hope. Wish. Something glinted in his eye. Maybe curiosity, maybe greed.

He glanced to the side, briefly, considering. He said something quickly to the man who had tied me up, of which I did not understand a single word. He strode away over the deck and disappeared in among the men. I was pushed into a corner and lay there, forgotten, while we sailed farther with the ship full of men working frantically. I saw relief in them, and expectancy. We were close to the end of our journey, and they would soon be home. They were thinking of their women awaiting them. They were not thinking of me.

The sun made its way across the sky. I lay still. I watched everything. I waited.

ω

By nightfall I could sense that we had come very near to dry land. The ship dropped its anchor in a small bay. They probably wanted to sail into port during daylight. I had one night to prove my worth. Otherwise I would be drowned before daybreak. Nobody wanted proof of what had happened on board to follow them home.

When all the ropes were lashed, a man came and loosened my ties. I was led in through another door, to a large cabin lit by many candles and lamps. The smiling man was sitting by a table and finishing his evening meal. The smell of cooked fish reminded my stomach that they had not given me anything to eat that day. He looked up when I came in. Smiled. Gestured for me to approach.

"Come."

I walked on unsteady legs. Placed myself at the other side of the table.

He gestured to show that I may eat what was left. Laughed and said something to my guard; I understood the words "strong" and "full." Maybe he thought that I needed my strength. I stuffed my mouth with bread crusts, fish guts and a slug of wine while I furtively followed his movements around the room. He went out to piss, came in again, washed his hands in a basin. Got help from the guard to take off his boots. He undressed, exhibiting no shame in letting me see him naked. Only smiled at me mischievously. Like a child. As if he had not been taking me in the most degrading way night after night. I wiped my greasy fingers on the tablecloth. He had put on a nightshirt and looked at me as if to ask, "What now?"

I pointed at the bed.

"Sleep." He laughed and lay down. "Dream. What?"

He did not understand me at first. Then he raised his eyebrows.

"Can I choose?"

I nodded.

"Flying!" He explained something very quickly, and I gestured to him to speak slowly. He stretched out his arms and explained more clearly. I understood that his favorite dreams were the ones in which he flew. High above everybody else. I had been so frightened that he would ask for something I did not know that I could not weave. But a flying dream was the first thing I saw when my powers arose. And I had already entered one of his flying dreams during my time on the ship. I knew what they were usually like. At once I became calm. I could do this.

The guard sat down on a stool by the door. He was staring at me. I was clearly such a great threat that I could not be left alone with the man. I blew out all the candles and lamps, but the guard prevented me from blowing out the last. He had to be able to see what the dangerous little girl was doing. I smiled to myself and knelt by the pillow.

I waited. The guard waited. The ship around us was creaking and cracking. I heard distant voices and calls. The candle flame flickered. The taste of wine lingered in my mouth.

The man in the bed was asleep.

It had been a long time since I had woven a dream. It did not matter. I leaned forward and began to weave.

I made him take off from the roof of the palace where he lived. I had often seen it in his dreams. Men and women, whose faces I had learned to recognize, were running around below him. I made them stretch out their hands toward him, grasping in the air and calling. Begging him to come down. But he soared triumphantly, higher and higher, over the palace, above them all. He was free. He glided over a garden, swooped down to a hill. At the foot of the hill, construction was taking place, and men were everywhere with timber and tools and blocks of stone. In the middle of the building works there glittered a spring, dark and enticing. It was enclosed by a high wall. I let him dive down to the spring, to see that all was as it should be. Then he flew upward again, higher and higher until everything and everyone was below him and he alone reigned over all the eye could see.

It was not a difficult dream. I only used images I had already seen from him. But I knew that it was good. It was full of precisely the sensations this man was hungry for. When it was finished, I leaned back on my heels and let him carry on sleeping. He would remember it when he awoke. And he would let me live.

I could have killed him right there. I could have let him plunge to the ground and break his neck. But I had not yet understood the extent of his wickedness. I did not know everything he was capable of—or what my life would be like in his hands.

I was afraid. But not for the right reasons.

Had I harmed him they would have killed me, immediately. And I wanted to live, then.

Now I wish I had chosen death. His, and mine.

The guard was snoring in his corner. I waited.

Dawn came.

ᛗ

I was given water and oils to wash myself with. A strange garment of saffron-yellow silk was laid out for me, along with shoes of soft leather. Undoubtedly they had been bought, or stolen, during their

151

travels. Maybe to give to the women who were waiting back home, or to sell. At home, I had never worn anything other than barkcloth against my skin. He put three rows of shining pearls around my neck with his own hands.

My seed necklace was hidden under my clothes. It was the only thing I had left from Terasu. It was the last thing I had that could help me distinguish madness from reality.

I was worth something now. I was something he could use. Use for something other than to satisfy his immediate appetites. As soon as he awoke, his manner toward me was completely changed. I could see him evaluating, weighing up. Determining how he could best use me, make the most of my abilities. He tried to question me, but I did not have enough words and could not understand his questions. He looked impatient, but then nodded to himself. Seemed to decide on something. Adjusted my hair, took a step backward. Looked displeased. Searched through a coffer at the foot of the bed, found a comb of gold-shining metal that he stuck in my hair. He smiled. Now I was satisfactory. Now I looked expensive enough.

I was given a cup of wine to drink and the best food a ship at the end of a long voyage could provide. Then I was left alone in his cabin while the ship sailed past the last islands. From the round window, I could see a port glide into view. Many ships, big and small, crowded at docks and piers. The port town had a myriad of flat houses, a little like those on the islands outside Goveli. Fields extended beyond the town, sloping up to hills farther north. Here and there the fields were broken up by small groves of trees. None of the trees were like the ones at home.

I had traveled very far. I felt no fear, nor anything else. My insides were hollow of feelings, or at least of my own. All the feelings, images and nightmares of the dreamers flickered past in a whirlwind of impressions. There were people sleeping in the port town as well, and their dreams sought me out like mosquitoes to flesh. My hand felt for the necklace of seeds, and I stroked them with my thumb, one by one. Over and over again. In Goveli it had only been occasional dreams that had seeped into me. I do not know why it was different in this foreign land, perhaps because the dream landscape was so foreign to me. Perhaps because all of my protective walls lay in ruins after what he had done to me. Perhaps because I was no longer sure who I was, and what I had become in his hands.

I no longer feared death, nor anything that might befall my body. All I felt was oncoming madness. Not even that frightened me. It was as if I had no feelings, and yet I fought to stay strong. Mostly out of curiosity for how long I could endure.

We came to shore just shy of the docks, and small boats began to transfer men and goods to land. My thumb followed the sharp edges of the seeds. The gentle scratch, the pain, held me fast to the present and to my body, while feelings of agitation, hunger, fear and impotence glided past. I saw a woman at a party where the guests had no faces. I saw a man chasing a laughing young woman through dark, gleaming lanes. A man grappling with a fish, bigger than himself, its scales glittering, moss green and hibiscus red. The fish's big, cold eyes stared right into my own.

My thumb followed the contours of the seeds.

The door to the cabin opened and he entered. He bowed quickly and gestured to me to follow him. I picked up the saffron-yellow garment and walked slowly out into the sunshine.

153

Wordlessly he helped me down a rope ladder and into a boat, where some sailors received me. Without speaking, they rowed me to land. I sat on a chest, with bags and bundles by my feet. One package among others.

I was helped up at the quay by more strong hands. I stood there while the boat was unloaded. Some men oversaw the unpacking of the cargo while the boat returned to the ship to fetch more. A curious crowd had gathered at the end of the quay; they were pointing in wonder. Their skin was a different color from mine, and their hair was dark and straight. They were also all at least a head shorter than me. "The palace," I heard them whisper. "Ohaddin."

I avoided eye contact. I stood tall and looked out to sea. There, somewhere beyond the waves, was my home. But they had cast me out. I was no longer welcome.

My thumb followed the contours of the seeds.

GARAI

For a long time, the new Garai has kept me safe and kept my master satisfied. He has been growing ever darker inside, and ever harder to please. Sometimes he uses violence. This is new. Yet the physical violence is easier to bear in silence than when he digs his way into my innermost being, penetrating my very soul. It is difficult to defend myself from this. Years have passed, and I—the real Garai—have been lying in wait. I visit the spring as often as I can, to kneel outside the locked door and listen to its life force flow. Sometimes I come across Kabira there. She looks away and ignores me. She ignores her own heartache too.

Her sons are growing. Korin is approaching the threshold to manhood. The boys are cold toward their mother, and I know this causes her untold torture and heartache. She hides behind a mask of indifference.

ॼ

Yet something has happened. Something for which I have been waiting several years. As ever, we were not informed beforehand. I was sitting in the great hall recently one morning, busy drawing a flower. Kabira was copying verse out onto a decorative scroll. Winter had come and the hall was cold, despite several fire pots burning. Orseola was with us that morning after spending a sleepless night weaving dreams for the Sovereign. She was sitting with some strange handicraft in her lap—a round circle she had woven with the bulrush I saw her picking from the lakeside the previous day. Now and then she pulled a strand of hair from her dark head and wove it into the work. I still cannot get used to her presence. For so many years it was the wife and I alone; when Orseola arrived, she upset the balance. My master does not even lie with her, and the Sovereign showers her with expensive gifts in thanks for the dreams she gives him. She learned our tongue quickly, but does not pronounce the words quite like we do. She rarely speaks. I saw her in a tree in the garden, in the very highest branches. I continued walking and pretended not to notice. But it reminded me of how young she is. Younger than I was when I came here. A child, on the brink of womanhood. I have tried to be more pleasant toward her since then, though it is not easy. She says that she sees our dreams, and laughs as though it were a joke. I do not believe it is.

What does she see in my dreams? Does she see me flying over the Meirem Desert? Does she see me dancing with my sisters under the light of the moon? Does she see me running with bleeding feet on my eternally fruitless hunt through a desert of sharp stones?

The doors to the dairahesi were unlocked with a clatter. All three of us looked up from our tasks. Two guards entered, followed by servants carrying a chest and several parcels. Finally a woman entered: a young, black-haired beauty. I imagine Kabira would have resembled her fifteen years ago. She was dressed in a yellow jacket with pink embroidery—not exceptionally masterfully done, but of sound quality. She wore many trinkets around her arms and feet. Almost like a bride. But not quite. She came to a halt on one of the bloodsnail-red carpets and looked on, arms loose at her sides, while the servants, under the guards' supervision, rushed into one of the empty rooms, where they put down the chest and began to unpack the parcels. Estegi was among them. Somebody fetched bolsters, cushions and lamps for the newcomer's room.

The guards did not speak to us. Kabira put down her brush pen and clasped her hands across her belly. Her face gave nothing away. I turned my back to them and continued to draw. I knew what this meant, but I did not know how to feel about it. Joy—I was free! Fear—now I had no excuse to put off my destiny.

I continued my illustration. Behind me the scurrying steps of sandal-clad feet padded to and fro across the stone floor. The guards' orders were brief. Then the doors to the dairahesi were closed and locked once more. The flower on the paper before me looked completely deformed and not in the least like the model in the vase on the table. I would have to do it again.

Kabira got up slowly. I peeked over my shoulder into the room. The black-haired woman was still standing there, with Estegi awaiting instruction by the door. Orseola had gone back to her work. She looked as though she were listening to music, to a melody only she could hear. Kabira circled the newcomer.

"She appears in good health. That is good. How old are you, girl?"

"Nineteen," she answered in a whisper.

Kabira took hold of her chin. "Open your mouth."

The girl did as she was told, but the look she gave Kabira did not go unnoticed by any of us.

"All teeth remaining. It is a good age."

Kabira let go of the newcomer's chin and wiped her hands on her gown, as though distracted. As though it were incidental.

"Did he buy you?"

The black-haired girl shook her head and lifted her chin, very slightly.

"I am a gift from my father. He wanted to curry favor with the Vizier."

"Then you must do your father proud. Estegi! Fetch two ornamental combs from my jewelry box."

Estegi bowed and hurried away to Kabira's quarters. I slowly rolled up my drawing. Two combs are more than one. Anything was better than being slave-sold.

The girl seemed to want to go to her own room, but without a word and barely even a movement Kabira prevented her from doing so. Estegi returned with the combs. Kabira quickly and expertly set the girl's hair up with two copper combs, just as she had done to mine.

"Wear these."

Then my master's wife swept out of the hall without another word. The girl remained motionless a moment, confused, and looked at me and Orseola. When nobody said anything, she pursed her lips and puffed out her chest.

"My name is Meriba," she announced to no one in particular. Then she went into her room, anklets and bracelets jingling, and shut the door behind her.

ᛒ

I have mainly kept to my room since. There is no reason for me to go out. My master no longer sends for me. He sends for Meriba instead. I catalog my plants, but it is difficult to complete the work because my master no longer gives me paper or ink. I am writing this on the back of a discarded drawing. It is the last paper I have.

The food they bring me is very simple. Only now do I understand the privileges my master afforded me because I was his favorite. Now he has a new favorite. I do not care that the food is simple; I push aside all meat and fish and eat only vegetables, rice and lentils. Nothing else appeals. The only thing I truly miss is paper.

I do not open the window shutters. I am feeling sensitive to the sharp light, and keep my lamps lit night and day instead. Kabira knocks on my door sometimes. She thinks I am unhappy. Estegi comes with fried weja, candied almonds and sweet rice cakes. Everything I once ate so insatiably. The food comes from Kabira's personal table. As wife, she still enjoys a heightened status and respect. But I do not touch the food. Kabira is mistaken. I need no solace.

I am not unhappy. There is no space inside me for unhappiness. I am shedding my skin. Beneath this old skin is one even older. It is thick and hardy. It shall endure. It has scars along the wrists— one for each offering. I have whittled myself a staff and I have dried herbs. There are some I could give my master to induce a heavy slumber. Then I could take the keys. Go out to the spring one night. Unlock the doors, one by one. Under the full moon, so shall it be. With the power of this place flowing through me, with an offering to the veins of the earth—blood for blood—there are no walls that can stop the old Garai from emerging.

But my master no longer comes to me. And everywhere there are guards.

Garai shall not be hindered. One day she shall find a way. I have buried the new Garai. I no longer need her. Finally I am only myself.

Praise the earth and the life force that I could still find my true self! I was not lost forever. It is a wonder, after all these years.

Garai, desert's daughter
Garai of the blood
Garai of the life force
Garai of the song
Garai the vengeful

Meriba is her master's darling. Her quarters are filled with flowers, vases, paintings, golden lamps and candlesticks. Her bed is overflowing with cushions, animal hides and silk-embroidered sheets. I always accepted Iskan's gifts with an expression of gratitude, because that was what he expected. But I never understood the point of all of these things; just objects with no purpose. Meriba loves the objects. She lives for them. She arranges flowers, changes her jewelry several times a day, rotates the colors of her clothes according to the season, blackens her eyes with charcoal and paints her little mouth red. In her master's eyes she is irresistibly beautiful.

She does no work. She sits on the largest and most beautiful bloodsnail-red cushion with her hands idle in her lap, watching what we are doing through half-closed eyelids. She is constantly surrounded by a flock of servants, rearranging cushions and lamps, fetching food and drink—which Meriba then barely touches—furs when she is cold, and incense according to her whims. Estegi is not among these servants. Meriba said at once that she did not want to have to look at her ugly face. Meriba must have only pretty young girls to whisper and giggle with.

We were sitting together in this way recently one evening. I have started leaving my room now. My skin has shed—I am ready. It is still winter and cold winds blow, so we rarely go out to the garden. The cold does not bother me, but the same rules apply to everyone in the dairahesi. Meriba does not want to go out, so we all sit inside. She was in a bad mood, which must mean that she had quarreled with her master, or that he had denied her something she wanted. She had her girls light several fire pots but was soon displeased with their fumes.

"This one is too close!" she screamed to one of her servants. "I have sensitive skin; it cannot stand being scorched so!" She gave the girl a smack with her sandal. "Don't just stand there, move it!"

The girls rushed around, their eyes wide with fear. Orseola, who was dozing on several large cushions, opened one eye. She had been weaving for the Sovereign for several nights in succession. He suffers from nightmares otherwise—dark and unrelenting, they drag him down into an abject and nameless terror, or so Estegi told me. She gossips with the servants in the royal palace and can often tell us a thing or two. Orseola pulled her silk shawl over her face and turned her back to us. She never seems to be able to sleep properly. Meriba ignores her for the most part, seeing as she cannot fathom Orseola's place in the hierarchy. Seeing Orseola move from the corner of her eye, she snapped at her irritatedly.

"Retire to your own chamber! It is distasteful to sleep in company."

"At home," said Orseola in a deep voice, still facing the wall, "nobody sleeps alone. Others always close."

"You are not with your savages now," Meriba snarled. "You are in Karenokoi. Here people do not sleep on the floor."

Orseola turned to Meriba. Her eyes opened wide in that special way, as though she is looking at someone standing right behind you. "The white man comes again tonight. He will eat your face before he pulls out your hair."

Meriba paled and closed her mouth. Orseola got up, gathering her cushions and shawls. She bowed to Kabira and gave me a slight nod before disappearing into her room.

Meriba sat quietly awhile, breathing heavily. The rain was beating against the window shutters and the fire pots were spitting. I was poring over a scroll I had found in the little library about the history of Karenokoi. I wanted to learn more about Anji; if there was anything written about it or the other sources of power. At home in the clan all such knowledge was passed down the generations through story and song. I am starting to recall them more and more clearly every day since I left the new Garai behind. One of them goes like this:

Sanuel by the rocks
On one ancient leg
Beyond the shore
The great lake around
It speaks the truth
Bestows the power
Offer your red
Blood for blood bidden
Taste the life force
Sap of the earth

I wonder if this is the first time anyone has written this song down—bound it to paper. The thought fills me with a sudden unease. Certain things should not be written so that just anybody can access their secrets. Maybe I should strike it out. But nobody here knows where Sanuel is. Or which is the greatest lake. These are names and truths only we in the clan understand. So I will let it remain, but I must be more careful in the future.

Kabira was sitting and writing a letter at a low table some servants brought to her. I did not know who she was writing to; perhaps she had family or friends beyond these walls. I have never seen anyone pay her a visit except her sons. Meriba was picking anxiously at the sleeves of her jacket. Kabira's brush pen was scratching against the paper. My scroll was rustling as I read. Meriba's many bangles were clinking gently.

There was a rattle at the main door. It was unlocked and opened and in stepped Iskan. I believe it was the first time he had visited the great hall of the dairahesi. All three of us fell at once to our knees before him, foreheads to the ground. I stole a glance at him, as it had been a while since last I saw him. His beard and hair were as well groomed as ever. Jacket deep blue, trousers white as snow. Fingers heavy with rings of different metals. He looked around and smiled.

"How pleasantly you live." He stepped forward to the table where Kabira had been sitting and peeked at her letter. "Does it please my wife to write?" Kabira took that as permission to rise to sitting. Her face expressed no sentiment.

"To my cousin Neika, husband. You met her once. She has recently become a grandmother for the first time."

"So young? She cannot be much older than you, wife."

163

"Her daughter was married at a tender age," replied Kabira.

"And you were not so young when Korin was born." Iskan picked up Kabira's pen and twirled it wistfully between his fingers. "Well, will you not show your husband a little hospitality?"

Kabira snapped her fingers and Estegi hurried forth to receive her bidding. Then Kabira personally laid some large cushions by the table for Iskan to sit on and set her writing materials aside. Iskan snapped his fingers at me and Meriba and we sat up again. Meriba's face was a storm of confusion and concern. If her master had not come to take her away and gratify his lust with her, then why had he come? Kabira was the mistress this time and she never lost composure. She ordered for the fire pot to be carried nearer to Iskan and for several lamps to be lit. When Estegi came with wine and fruit and cakes, Kabira filled her husband's drinking bowl herself.

"Thank you, wife." He sipped the wine. "You keep a good vintage. I shall be sure to send you more."

Kabira bowed her head.

"And we shall send a cask to your cousin's daughter as well. A fitting gift, would you not agree? With a child in the house she is bound to receive many visitors wishing to extend their congratulations, and she must have something to offer them." He smiled at Kabira and for a brief moment something flashed in her eyes. Confusion? Fear? Hope? She looked down and I saw no more.

Iskan turned to me. "Come and taste, little savage. Even if you are not so little anymore."

I obeyed at once and went to sit to his right. He shook his hand free from his sleeve, reached for a piece of melon and placed it between my lips. Then he seemed truly to look at me for the first time. "Why, you have slimmed. Your cheeks have lost their roundness!" He smiled. "Have you sulked yourself thin, my savage?"

I did not know what I should answer. I had lost the new Garai's ability to find the right words to please him. I did as Kabira did: bowed my neck and looked down. Iskan took it as confirmation. He stroked my arm.

"Now, now, I will be sure to visit you again soon." I clenched my teeth as hard as I could. In the corner of my eye I could see Meriba glaring venomously in my direction. She looked like a kawol whose prey had been snatched by vultures. "In the meantime, is there anything I can do that may offer a little solace?"

I did not look up. "Paper, Master. If it please you."

He laughed softly. "Ever humble." The final word was clearly directed at Meriba. "So be it." He waved Estegi over and whispered something in her ear. She bowed and left the hall.

Iskan took another sip of wine and leaned back, surveying his surroundings with relish. "It is truly pleasant here. You women certainly know about all this decorating business. Flowers and so forth. My servants do not understand such things."

"It is Meriba, Master," I said. "What you see was created by her hand."

He ignored my interjection. "Wife, some more wine. And then can you not recite something for us? You were skilled in it, once."

Kabira was mistress of herself once more. With an expressionless face, she poured more wine and got to her feet. She stood quietly for a moment and gazed into the quiet shadows of the hall. Meriba was sitting a little farther away, on her pile of pillows and furs. Iskan had not asked her to join his table. I could see her battling with herself to keep her feelings under control, but they were all reflected on her face. Anger, jealousy, hatred—and fear.

Kabira chose one of the ancient love elegies that evening. What inspired her to do so, I cannot say. Maybe Iskan's sentimental tone. Maybe an entirely different reason, known only to her. It was an epic poem about two young people who fall in love on first meeting, and fight against countless setbacks and obstacles to be able to meet a second time. It ends with them both dying, each on their own side of a wall, without ever having met again. It is very moving. I have never known such love. I have felt desire, both in the clan and on occasions with Iskan. I have loved my sisters and my mother. But a love one is willing to die for? I wonder if such love exists anywhere other than in poems.

When Kabira was finished, Iskan looked pensive. Then he thanked her courteously and patted me on the cheek before leaving the hall. He had not uttered a single word to Meriba. Yet I had the feeling that this whole evening was a display for her eyes. A lesson she must learn. A threat: without my favor, you are nothing. You have nothing.

Meriba has understood. Now she despises Kabira and me. Kabira ranks above her, so she cannot take revenge on her. I, on the other hand, am lower than she, and pose no danger.

She set fire to my herbarium while I was bathing. All my years of work were destroyed. All the pressed flowers, the pictures and notes. Only the private notes are left now—the secret, hidden ones. When I came back to my room, there was nothing but charred remains in the fire pot. Next to it Estegi sat crying. Her clothes were sooty and her hands covered in black.

"I tried to save them, Garai. I tried, but she wouldn't let me in until everything was ablaze."

I turned her hands over to look at her palms. They were burned. I fetched water to wash them carefully, then smeared them with aloe. Estegi sobbed but said nothing more. Inside me I could feel something break loose, something that had been stuck for a long time. Far too long.

ω

Afterward I went out into the garden. I was given permission, seeing as Meriba was still out of favor. Two guards followed after, but then allowed me to roam freely. It was a cold day without rain, yet everything was wet. I walked to the small grove of zismil trees that grow near Anji's hill. I know the uses of the tree's resin, its leaves, its nuts and roots. I do not need notes to know this. The knowledge within me cannot be destroyed.

I lay on my back beneath the trees. Nobody was watching me. The garden was silent. The birds were sleeping with their heads tucked under fog-dampened wings. The insects were seeking shelter in the moss and bark. The earth was moist beneath my jacket. I plunged my fingers into the wet earth, feeling twigs and leaves crumble apart. There was a powerful odor of life and decay. I shut my eyes. I heard water gently dripping from the branches of the trees. Mist crept slowly over my cheekbones, my eyelids. A barely perceptible breeze rustled through the crowns of the zismil trees. My breathing was calm and even. There was a pulsing murmur in my blood. I surrendered my body. I was completely

167

free. Nothing was tying me to this place. My spirit became light and I started to rise into the air. First I saw my body way down on the ground, then it became obscured by the canopy below me. I saw the ocean in the south, Areko in the east. The fields and spice plantations in the south and west. Paths like narrow ribbons streaking across the green landscape. A flock of geese stained the sky with their black bodies, and I followed them northward as they flew. Mountains, lakes, rivers below us. The wind beneath our wings. I veered off to the east and left the geese behind. In search of my sisters, certain I would find them. They drew me toward them like beacons. I traveled far, I saw everything, and the sources of power all over the earth were burning like torches below me. Mountains, springs, rivers, lakes. The very arteries of the earth. I found my sisters, one by one. Different lives they lived, both good and bad. There was only one I could not find. The littlest. The youngest. Guera, with her skinny arms. She was nowhere to be found.

I returned to my body as I felt somebody shaking it. I opened my eyes to see the two guards bending over me. They reeked of sweat and their expressions were stern. Each had a dagger in his belt. All of a sudden, with the deftness of a kawol, I snatched one of their daggers. Rolling out of reach, I made an incision in my left arm before they could stop me. I let the blood trickle down into the roots of the zismil trees. Roots extending deep into the earth. For this is the uniqueness of the zismil: it can grow even in arid parts because its roots find water hidden far below the surface. Water that other plants cannot reach. The crowns of the trees swayed as they accepted my offering, and as the guards dragged me away, I could feel my blood conversing with the roots, and I could feel the roots carrying my blood into the depths of

168

the earth, to the primeval origin of their power. Far below, where springs also source their flow.

Anji has tasted me now. The life force is reaching out to me. The zismil trees have become my sacred offering grounds. I go there when I can, and the trees whisper me truths and imbue me with strength. I dress only in brown now. I do not wash my hair. Everybody avoids me, even Kabira. Meriba believes that she broke my sanity. Little does she know that in truth she set me free. The only thing I have left now is these notes, and the paper Iskan gave me when Meriba was briefly out of favor.

She is his favorite again now—he summoned her once more and then presented her with a hair ornament containing threads of black pearls and ivory. Now he has traveled away; there is war in the East again and the Sovereign has sent him to deal with it. Two moons have passed since he left. The Sovereign's sons cannot have succeeded in subduing those who must be subdued, or slaughtering those who must be slaughtered—I do not know which. More and more of my old life is coming back to me now: I fast on the sacred days, sing the sacred songs and dance the sacred dances. Some must be danced at night, but I cannot be outside under open sky as I ought to be, so I dance in my room instead. This morning Kabira took me to one side.

"Garai." It is not often that my name passes her lips. She looked at me with a serious expression. On her hands I noticed the first appearance of age spots. They are subtle, but reveal the years that have passed. How long have I been here? Sonan, Kabira's youngest, was born soon after I arrived. Now he is already nine years old. It is difficult to fathom that so much time has passed. It means that I, too, am no longer young.

That is good. An old wisewoman is more powerful than a young one. The older I grow, the more my knowledge deepens.

"Garai, do you hear me? You must cease with this. Meriba will tell Iskan of your transformation the moment he returns."

I looked up, perplexed.

"He will not stand for it. Do you understand? A madwoman in his dairahesi and household."

"Madwoman?"

She shook her head impatiently. "You sing at all hours of the day and night, in some unintelligible tongue. You do not bathe. And I hear frightening noises from your chamber in the middle of the night. If it is a new moon on his return, be on your guard. Do you understand?" She turned and walked away, with her dark head held high. I turned to face Orseola, who was sitting mending her sandals.

"A madwoman?"

"Not all know wisdom when they see it," she said, and bit off a thread. "Nor evil." She sighed. "The Sovereign Prince is very sick again. I believe it is because the Vizier is away. He does something to the Sovereign before he goes away. Then the Sovereign is weak and sick and cannot make decisions without him. Many bad dreams." She shuddered. "They stick."

"The water," I said to myself, but Orseola pricked up her ears. Her dark eyes widened.

"Yes, in the water. The Sovereign drinks the spring water for health. The Vizier adds something?"

"The moon is waning. He does not need to add anything."

"Mysteries. Only mysteries." Orseola got up, exasperated, and turned on her heel.

"Wait." I held up a hand. "It is the water itself that is harmful. The spring, the sacred spring behind the locked door." I pointed out into the garden. "It is sometimes harmful and sometimes good. It is a source of power. The Vizier uses the water to do his bidding."

"The Sovereign must be warned!" Orseola looked horrified.

I looked at her and shook my head.

"You cannot. You are still but a dreamweaver: a slave. The Sovereign would ask Iskan, and put his back against the wall. With the power of the spring's water, he could render you harmless in the blink of an eye." I saw her questioning expression. "Kill you. He has been the Sovereign's Vizier for a very long time, and he has corrupted him in body and mind. The Sovereign would never take your word over that of his adviser. And you would gain nothing but your own death."

I could see that she was considering it; that death was not an entirely unwelcome outcome.

"But do not worry. The Vizier will not kill the Sovereign. He wants him here so that he has someone whose strings he can pull. He wants to be the one to stand in the shadows and make everybody dance to his tune."

ω

Iskan is still away and Meriba is pregnant. She is even more demanding now: special dishes at ridiculous hours, oils to massage into her swelling belly. Her moods are dreadful and all the servants are afraid of her. She is hoping for a son, of course. It would heighten her rank and place. Kabira's sons will always take precedence over sons born to concubines, but all sons raise a man's status, regardless of who may bear them. And they can fulfill important functions in the plots and intrigues of the palace.

Kabira is keeping a careful watch on Meriba's changing figure. I often catch her eyeing Meriba's belly with a thoughtful expression. Is she really so threatened by the idea that Meriba may have a son? As wife, her position is safe, although she and Iskan rarely seem to have contact these days.

It is all the same to me, in any case. The goings-on of the dairahesi are no longer my concern. Because every day I am moving further and deeper into my old self. The trees are answering my call. They bend their branches toward me as I approach. The life force throbs beneath my skin now, and my scars shine white as snow.

ᴡ

Early yesterday morning Iskan returned. There was a clamor of horses and men as they rode into the stables in the west. Meriba wandered impatiently from window to window and waited for her master to call for her, but the day passed and no word came. She went into her room often to change her clothes and jewelry, only to continue her pacing. I have not seen her on her feet that much since she fell pregnant.

Orseola was sitting alone in a corner, muttering to herself. Sometimes the dreams overwhelm her. I have started boiling her a brew of sowane and aulium. It delivers her into a deep and dreamless sleep. But I cannot help her when she is awake and plagued by everybody else's lingering dreams. She has tried to describe it to me. She says that sometimes she wanders around in the Sovereign's dreams for days after seeing them. Or in ours.

172

And if there is a servant who was up through the night and sleeps during the day, she has trouble ridding herself of her dreams too. Her dreamsnares afford some relief, but Ohaddin is filled with dreamers. The snares cannot capture every dream. I suggested once that she should tattoo a dreamsnare on her forehead, but she only let out a desperate laugh.

"And do what with the dreams it catches? Carry them with me, forever?"

Instead, she wears the dreamsnares—around her neck, under her clothes—but they are always too few.

ω

Iskan came to us late the same evening. It is summer now, and the shutters were open to the balmy night. Kabira was playing the role of wife and gave orders for a great dish of iced fruits and pitchers of chilled tea. Our lamps flickered in the draft from the windows as Iskan stepped in.

He aged while he was away. He limped slightly on his left leg, and his left hand was bound with bandages. His hair had grayed a little and the lines around his mouth had deepened. It is because he has not had access to the spring, I thought. He goes into decline as soon as he is denied Anji's power. I looked in his eyes and saw that all-seeing gaze, the one that spears straight into my soul. He had already drunk water from the spring. And the moon is waning.

He was in good humor; he had Kabira serve him tea and even ate some of the fruit.

"What a grueling winter it has been," he said, licking his fingers. "However, I have obtained what I desired. Now all the

173

vassal states from Areko to the Maiko Desert swear allegiance to Ohaddin, and pay taxes to the Sovereign's coffer. Karenokoi is no longer a minor realm. Thanks to me, the Sovereign Prince now has dominion over the greatest realm that has ever existed. Soon none shall remain who can challenge us." He smiled widely. "The campaign reaped more fruits, besides. In Harrera there was a man with vast knowledge. Of great things, dark and dense. It is mine now. It is contained in my library. And in Koiama I came upon stones from their holy mountain that still possess immense power. I shall have them built into the wall around Ohaddin. Our palace shall be impenetrable, should the districts ever revolt." He fed himself candied almonds.

I thought of all the people of Renka who lived outside Ohaddin. In Areko and in the provinces. What protection would they have against the wrath and vengefulness of the eastern districts? But I said nothing.

"Meriba, my flower, come to me," said Iskan, beckoning to her. "How—"

He stopped short when he noticed her stomach. She was seven moons through and already large.

"I certainly have been away a long time," he said slowly. "The flower is already bearing fruit. Come."

Meriba glided timidly over to her master. He laid a hand on her belly and she blushed most becomingly. Kabira looked away, her hands clenched hard on her lap. Iskan made a soft sound, not quite a sigh but thereabouts. Meriba shuddered. He removed his hand.

"Follow me." He got up and went over to the door. "We shall take a little walk in the garden, you and I."

Confused but still blushing, she followed her master. The doors closed behind them with a bang, and the lamp flames flickered. Kabira jumped to her feet, rushed over to a window and stared out into the darkness. Soon voices drifted to us from the garden: Meriba's nervous giggle, Iskan's deep tones. It was a very still night. I joined Kabira where she stood. Not much could be seen out there in the dark; Iskan had taken no torches with him. The outlines of the trees and bushes were drawn sharp in the moonlight.

Then came the sound. The one I have learned to listen for. It was perfectly clear in the still night: a lock being turned, a heavy metal door being opened. Kabira turned sharply away from the window.

"It cannot be prevented," she said to herself, wringing her hands. "There is nothing I can do. No."

I rarely see Kabira upset. She rushed to her quarters and closed the door behind her.

Orseola was with the Sovereign, so I was left alone, spying out into the moonlit night. It was quiet again. No wind blew. Suddenly the canopies of the zismil trees began to shake violently. The rustling sound was unmistakable. They were trying to tell me something, and though my blood sang in response, I did not understand the message.

ω

This morning I was awoken by a prolonged scream. It was Meriba. The labor had begun. Far too early. I took what I thought might be necessary from my herbs and concoctions. Estegi was already waiting for me outside Meriba's room. No midwives or old ladies bothered to witness this time—it was not a wife giving birth to an heir, but a mere concubine and her bastard. When we went in, I saw, to my surprise, Kabira standing by Meriba's bed, among all the vases, painted screens and pottery. Her skin was very pale and the lines around her mouth were deep.

"She has long been suffering already, in silence," she said shortly. "Her strength is waning."

I could see that she was right. Meriba's eyes were sunken deep in her skull and her skin lay taut over her cheeks. Her breathing was shallow and strained. I pulled the cover to one side and pressed her belly gently. All signs were bad.

Then she opened her eyes and I gasped. Her eyes were completely black—nothing around the irises at all. A chasm was opening inside her. I looked at Kabira, who first pressed her lips together, and then blurted out, as though involuntarily: "This is what he does. If the child is a girl."

In that moment many things became clear: why Kabira had only sons, and why she never answered directly when asked how many times she had been pregnant; what happened on Meriba and Iskan's walk to the spring last night.

Hatred raged through me, violent and corrosive. To misuse the powers of the earth in such a way! To have arbitrary reign over life and strength. To eliminate girls from one's lineage and family, as though they were worthless. To pervert that which should be used for good!

ω

I did all I could for Meriba. She was nearly senseless with pain and unable to speak; what I gave her did not afford her much relief.

But the labor did not last much longer. The child was small, and eventually she emerged in a flood of blood and water. I held her in my hands as her tiny lungs fought for breath. Everything about the little body was perfect: the fingers and tiny fingernails, the bent legs, the soft soles of her feet. Eyelids like petals.

It is the worst thing I have ever had to witness. She wanted to live, but she was too small. I laid her at her mother's breast, where she took her final breath. I looked away. Out through the window. Never have I felt so powerless.

Meriba did not live to see more. The dark water was tearing her apart from the inside, making her shake and shudder and writhe. A horrific death. Kabira, Estegi and I sat by her bed until the last moment. Kabira held one hand and I held the other. I mumbled prayers to the earth to receive her body and bestow it with new life. They have different beliefs here in Karenokoi, but as a wisewoman it is my duty to escort the dying to the other side. And we have shared the same man, Meriba and I. That is a bond that cannot be unmade.

When eventually she left her pain-racked body we sat silently awhile. The sun was shining through the window and children's voices could be heard from the garden. Kabira's sons were playing outside. I closed Meriba's midnight-black eyes. Estegi straightened the covers around the two bodies. Kabira lit three candles. I cannot say I mourn for Meriba. But I mourn for her daughter. The girl whose father chose to forsake her life. Her little body barely made a bump under the sheet. The hair on her crown was thick and black.

We left the room. Kabira sent Estegi away to pass on the message of the deaths, and ordered tea and a soup to fortify us.

We ate together in the small shaderoom. She had ordered a soup with vegetables and mushrooms, and I was grateful for the lack of meat.

When I had finished eating, I looked at Kabira.

"You survived."

Kabira stared for a long time into the red-painted bowl in front of her.

"Thrice." She was quiet. "I believe I survived because I grew up with Anji's water. I had developed a tolerance, though I never drank it when it was oaki. My body was accustomed to its power."

"Is that why you were worried about her pregnancy?"

Kabira nodded slowly. "Though I did not know that it would kill her."

The doors to the hall swung open and Iskan came storming in. Without a word, he stomped away to Meriba's room. He stayed only briefly before coming out again. We clasped our hands and looked at him in silence. He stared at us.

"She is dead!"

"It can hardly come as a surprise," answered Kabira. I was amazed by her courage. Iskan had a wild look in his eyes, almost as black as Meriba's had been.

"This was not my intention. You!" He pointed at me. "You murdered her with your poisons! You envied her, you always have!"

"Did you give her Anji's water, Iskan?" Kabira's eyes were burning. "If so, it was you who murdered her, not Garai!"

"Quiet, woman!" Iskan smacked her across the mouth. "Guard!" He pointed at me. "Thirty lashes!"

My punishment was enforced at once. There, in the hall, the guard tried to pull off my jacket but I stopped him. I took it off myself, and the shirt underneath. I folded them neatly and laid them on a cushion. Then I bent forward.

I bled anew with every lash. Each one an offering. Thirty new scars, and I dedicated them all to Anji, and Meriba, and the newborn girl, and all of Kabira's daughters, and to my sisters.

If he had truly believed it was I who killed Meriba, he would have killed me as well. He knew who was at fault. Yet he refused to bear the blame.

ᴡ

He has four new concubines now. Young, beautiful, easy to control. I cannot tell the difference between them. They are remarkably interchangeable, as was his intention. He does not want to get attached to anyone again. Because I could see in his eyes that he was attached to Meriba, as much as it is possible for him to be attached to anyone. One of them is already pregnant. I think he will let her have the baby, regardless of its sex.

Kabira is changed. She is brooding over something. I do not know what it is, but I am concerned for her. She has a darkness inside her that I cannot reach. We do not speak of such things, but we seek out each other's company more and more. Orseola keeps to herself, but Estegi, Kabira and I sit together once more, to paint, draw, write and drink tea. I am also brooding. Because now I am intent on more than just an offering. Now I crave more than just vengeance. I am going to set Anji free, though I do not know how it might be done.

KABIRA

One night I was awoken by Estegi with long-awaited news: the Vizier's mother was dying. As Iskan's wife, it was my duty to keep vigil by the deathbed, so I was escorted by two guards, with Estegi in tow, out through the golden lattice doors of the dairahesi. It was the first time since the erection of the new palace that I was permitted access to the residence Iskan had built for his mother. Where she had raised my sons and kept them from me. Raised them to take after their father, especially the eldest son. They were all asleep and I had given orders not to wake them. Not yet.

We passed through large but sparsely furnished chambers. One, with floors of pink and white marble and many red-lacquered columns, was empty but for an altar on which incense and candles were burning. The floor before the altar was sprinkled with rose petals. I presumed it was in honor of the memory of Iskan's father.

The old woman did not know that her husband was killed at the hand of their own son.

Our steps echoed as we hastened from room to room. As Estegi led the way, it occurred to me that she must have been here before. She, a lowly servant, moved with more freedom around the palace than I, wife of the Vizier. I watched her long, skeletal shadow glide across the floor, and for a moment I was struck with a white-hot blaze of envy. Like a flash of moonlight on Anji's water. Then I returned to feeling nothing at all.

The old woman was lying in a chamber filled with shadows and flickering flames. Formal mourners were sitting by her feet. Their faces were painted white already and they rang brass bells and sang the wailing songs that guide the soul along the right path when it leaves the body. On the bedside there were dishes and bowls filled with everything that Izani ak Oshime-chi would need for her final journey. Gold and silver coins. Incense, tobacco and wine. Seven shells for the seven fishermen. Gazing at these objects, my thoughts turned to my own parents, and how they had died without these gifts. And my siblings, who had no mourners to help them on their way.

Izani was lying propped up on a mountain of silk pillows. The curtains around her bed were open but still she was in darkness. Estegi knelt by the door. Slowly, with dignified steps, I came to my mother-in-law's side.

She did not notice me at first. Her thin lips twitched nervously, as though trying to form words or take deep breaths. Her sunken eyes were darting here and there. Her hands lay motionless on the bedcover. I leaned forward and looked her straight in the eye.

"Here I am, Mother dear." I suffused the words with all the venom I could muster, but spoke quietly enough that the wailing women could not hear me. "I am here to ensure you receive the final farewell you deserve."

Her wandering gaze focused on me and her hands continued to twitch.

"Iskan. Iskan."

"He is not here. He is in Areko. I have sent word, but I am afraid that he will not make it in time. The message may be delayed." I smiled. It was a smile I had learned from Iskan himself. "But we can speak of Iskan, if it please you, Mother dear."

"Yes. My son. My fine son." Her breathing came intermittently. She was anxious, but not afraid—not yet.

"I have many stories to tell about him. Would it please you to hear? Let me start from the beginning. Let me tell you about all the lives your beloved, precious son has taken."

She took a deep breath and tried to speak, but I did not allow her an opportunity. I revealed everything. All the blood on Iskan's hands. I started from the beginning and omitted no detail. I came in close to the dying woman's face, and mercilessly named every poor soul whose death I knew of. In each case I could provide proof and explained in detail the connections. At first she did not believe me. She pressed her lips together and looked away. But she could not close her ears. She could not shut me out. By the time I came to tell of how Iskan murdered his own father, and how he had spoken of it afterward, the sun was rising. She emitted a terrible scream, and I clasped her hand and gestured to the mourners to carry on singing, for the inevitable end was approaching.

"Liar," she wheezed. "Give me something to drink."

"Are you thirsty?" I whispered in her ear. "Are you wearied by the thought of your son's misdeeds?" I lifted an empty bowl from the adjacent table and held it to her lips.

"Here, drink deep of this cool water. Let it soothe you, just as you soothed me when I was pining for my sons. When I was weeping for the daughters Iskan killed. I hope it affords you the same consolation you gave me."

The mourners were ringing their bells, the day was dawning

and still Izani lived. I began to fear that Iskan would indeed make it to her bedside before she left her body. I had bribed the messenger with a piece of jewelry so that he would not make haste. It was a great risk. I chose not to think about what Iskan would do with me if he discovered what I had done.

I recounted all the evil deeds Iskan had committed, and perhaps embellished my knowledge with a little conjecture. Izani was writhing like a worm, the sour putridity of death on her breath, and yet her spirit refused to surrender. She wanted to see her son. I could not allow this to happen. She must not reveal what I had been saying, and I did not intend to allow her a moment of peace before she died.

"He never performs offerings to the spirit of his father," I whispered, my lips tight against her ear. "He does not honor his father's memory. And neither will he trouble himself with yours." I smiled, knowing that though she could not see it, she could hear it in my voice. "But a good wife honors the memory of her deceased mother-in-law. She makes offerings on the correct days. She ensures that the spirit does not wander empty-handed and starving among the dead. How fortunate you are to have such an obliging daughter-in-law. One that will show you the same love and respect that you have shown her. I will give you precisely what you deserve: you who have taken my sons from me; who have filled their minds and hearts with lies about me, their own mother."

The final look she gave me was full of terror. I dug my long nails deep into her dry, defenseless palm. For one moment it seemed as though I could see her death, and it was close. I gathered all my strength to draw it nearer, my ears filling with a murmuring thrum. Perhaps a little oaki remained inside me after all.

"Under my watch, you shall be forgotten before one moon has passed."

She whimpered, and her will gave way to mine, and she took her final breath.

ᚦ

Iskan arrived shortly thereafter. He sat for a long time on the other side of his mother's bed, with his head pressed against her breast. I was still holding her hand as it grew cold. She would know that I was there. Her spirit would not forget.

I felt a glimmer of hope in that moment. A possibility, albeit a slight one. I had been ruminating over my plan for a long time. Several years had passed since the death of Meriba. The new concubines were filling the dairahesi with their children—both boys and girls. Yet I had to remain patient. I had only one chance. If I failed there would not be a second. I was already old—relegated into the shadows, forgotten. This was my final opportunity to step forward and claim a morsel of happiness before I faded away and disappeared into nothing.

I took the first step that day, by Izani's deathbed. I reached across the cover and took hold of Iskan's hand. My other hand was still clutching Izani's claw.

"Iskan ak Honta-che. Grand Vizier of Karenokoi and all its vassal states. Right hand and succor of the Sovereign Prince. My husband. Permit me to comfort you through this trying time, I who know you better than anyone."

Iskan looked up at me. His eyes were bloodshot, and for a brief moment I was surprised that he was capable of grief. However, this was not the suffering of a loving son for his deceased mother.

It was the pain of a man who had lost the only person who shared his vision of himself: infallible, flawless, constantly held back and misunderstood by those around him.

"Thank you, wife," he said simply, and squeezed my hand.

Then, as always, he was blind to the depths of my hatred. He was so full of himself that he was incapable of comprehending the effect of his actions on other people. I was his wife. I had been quiet and obedient for many years. My loyalty to him was evident.

Of course, hate was not the only thing I felt for him. I had fought hard to smother any other feelings and leave space for loathing alone. Yet I had loved him once. An echo remained that could never be silenced. I had always loathed myself for it, but at that moment I pardoned myself. Without that echo I would not have been able to do what needed to be done.

I released the dead woman and led my husband outside while the mourners emitted their final wails and rang their bells so that all in the afterworld would hear that a new soul was on its way.

I took Iskan to my chambers. I had had Estegi make them as pleasant as possible, and provide all of Iskan's favorite delicacies, and a pipe to smoke after eating. I made sure he was sitting comfortably, in prime place, and ordered a young maidservant to fan him to alleviate the heat that lingered despite the sun already lowering in the sky.

Iskan drank the wine, and then sat with a confused expression on his face like a little boy. His hair had grayed around the temples, and, though he remained a fine-looking man, he had bitter lines around his eyes, which I saw as the marks of Anji, and he could no longer be considered handsome.

"What a great loss for a man to have no living parents," he said. I bowed my head so that he might not see my face.

"So it is, Iskan-che. Perhaps a man can find solace in his sons on a day such as this?"

Iskan smiled at me. "You truly do know me well, Kabira-cho. Have them sent for."

I had not seen them for many moons. The proposal had been for my own sake, and I had forewarned their servant so they were dressed and ready to offer their father words of grief and condolences.

I was seized by the heart at their entrance. Korin was a young man, broad shouldered and handsome, already dressed in white for mourning. He bowed to me formally with his hand to his forehead before giving his father a heartfelt embrace and kissing him on both cheeks. Enon was a mirror image of his elder brother, but with a downier beard and shoulders more slender. He gave me a reticent smile and kissed me on both cheeks. I inhaled deeply his scent of rose water and sweat, and greedily stored its memory in my heart.

Little Sonan was no longer little either. At fourteen years old he had just received a sword and horse of his own. He took after his two elder brothers in most ways, but he reminded me most of my own brother, Tihe. They both laughed easily and inspired laughter from all in their company. Sonan was loved by all: from servants to honored guests, from cooks in Iskan's kitchen to the Sovereign Prince himself.

He did not know whether he should follow the example of Korin or Enon, so after he had bowed he stood before me awkwardly, uncertain what to do. I gestured to him to embrace his father. My arms longed to wrap around his thin neck and press his bony shoulders into my body, but I knew that Korin would scold him if he allowed this to happen. Enon could do as he wished. He was old enough.

All three young men bore signs of grief and tears on their cheeks. Their grandmother had been like a mother to them. She had raised them when I could not. She had overseen their wet nurses and their teachers, and taught them to be men. Men like their father. They sat in conversation with him now, speaking about the departed, drinking to her soul. Even Sonan was allowed to drink wine and soon his cheeks flushed. When his two elder brothers were deeply engrossed in conversation with Iskan, he drew closer to me.

"Cho?"

"Yes, my son?"

Every time I was allowed to say the words my heart would beat a little faster.

He swirled the bowl in his hand and did not meet my gaze. I waited, though I wanted nothing more than to take him in my arms and hold him to my breast.

"Now that Izani-chi is gone . . ." He paused. "May I visit your chambers? Should it be a great inconvenience?"

Had the crone not been dead already, I would have strangled her with my bare hands then and there. I had to wait a moment until my voice was steady and calm enough to respond. Sonan looked up at me, his eyes large and apprehensive. He was the most sensitive of my sons. He must have had a difficult time under Izani's reign. He was not like his brothers, nor his father.

"Sonan. My son. You are, and always have been, welcome in my chambers, whensoever you wish."

I took hold of his hands and looked him in the eye. "I would never turn you away from my door. I would never see it as an inconvenience to entertain my beloved children in my residence."

I spoke quietly, so that Iskan could not hear. Sonan looked at me with surprise and relief. I could see that he was thinking of all the lies Izani had filled him with since birth. Undoubtedly that his mother did not love him, nor want anything to do with him. He was too well brought up to pronounce them out loud. Izani was the only mother he had ever known. There was no way for me to erase the past fourteen years that separated us. Yet perhaps there was still a possibility to claim at least one of my sons as my own. He held my hands awkwardly in his, which had already grown large and broad.

Korin gave us a suspicious look and I lowered my head at once. I had to play the role of subservient wife. He looked at Sonan's hands in mine and furrowed his brow. He stood up.

"We will leave you now, Father. And you are right. I will consider taking a wife." There was a certain coldness to his voice and I glanced in surprise at Iskan, whose mouth was drawn into a disapproving line.

Korin bowed to me briefly. "Sonan."

My youngest son got up reluctantly and released my hands. I dared not say anything, nor remind him to visit me, afraid that Korin or Iskan would forbid him. Korin left the room with Sonan in tow. Enon shrugged his shoulders apologetically, kissed his father on the cheeks, and gave me a hasty kiss before he left. A faint scent of rose water lingered behind.

Iskan sat, still with furrowed brow, and glared at the wall. My well-considered plan would not work if his mood did not brighten. I sat before him, carefully removed his shoes and began to massage his feet. It repulsed me to touch him. To feel his skin against mine. It was an abomination that he could sit there, alive and well before me, when he was responsible for the deaths of so many.

"Iskan-che, what is weighing on your mind?"

"Korin. He goes against his father's express desire." Iskan sighed and leaned back, stretching his foot forward to give me better access. "I wish for him to marry the daughter of Eraban ak Usti-chu."

"The Sovereign Prince of Amdurabi?"

Iskan scoffed. "So he called himself, yes, but in reality he was no more than a governor to the true Sovereign Prince of all Karenokoi. In any case, he died last moon."

"Was he not here as a guest last moon?" I laid Iskan's foot carefully in my lap. He smiled widely at me.

"Indeed. He must have eaten something that did not agree with him, because he traveled home quite ashen and died soon thereafter. There were no traces of poison."

I revealed no hint that I understood what Iskan had done. "And now you wish for Korin to marry his daughter?"

"His eldest daughter, yes. He never sired sons, and the eldest daughter is Enon's age and sole heiress to Amdurabi. If Korin married her, he would become Governor, and Amdurabi would become a district of Karenokoi, just as Baklat and Nernai already have. Since I have come to power, the landmass of the realm of Karenokoi has tripled, and its riches likewise. Amdurabi is now vulnerable; with merely a female heiress, anybody could take power by force. However, it is in Karenokoi's interest that Amdurabi is stable. Armies in the vicinity would be a threat to our security as well. And we are dependent on their rice and wheat, as Karenokoi produces mostly spices now. On my advice, our economy has had a great boost thanks to the spice trade." He sighed, lifted down one foot and stretched out the other for me to massage. "But it leaves us vulnerable when it comes to food provisions. The laborers have started to complain since I had the Sovereign issue a decree that their own growing plots should be planted with etse. I have no time for a revolt right now, so I must ensure there is sufficient food to keep them quiet."

"But Korin does not wish to wed the daughter of Eraban? Is she homely, or disfigured in some way?"

The furrow returned to Iskan's brow. "Not at all. Not the most beautiful of women, but not disfigured, and there is no stain on her honor. I may well have chosen her for him, even without the whole district as dowry. However, he has the notion that he wishes to marry someone of his own choosing. And the only things he has in mind are soft, round breasts and a pretty face!" Iskan took a big swig of wine. He had drunk a lot already, which was just fine. I hurried to fetch more wine and filled his bowl before continuing to massage him.

"You chose your own wife."

Iskan laughed. "Yes, and certainly not for your beauty. Just like Eraban's daughter, you came with a dowry. Korin must realize that he can have succulent flesh as well. Marriages are arranged for other purposes."

His words stung. I had believed that he loved me, once. I had believed that he found me beautiful.

"You are a wise man. Korin ought to heed his father's words."

Iskan sighed. "He has always been stubborn and filled with his own ideas. Enon is easier to steer."

"Perhaps you might sweeten the proposition?" I lifted his foot down from my lap and sat up straight on a cushion. "Seek out the five most beautiful women in the land and let Korin choose himself some concubines. As a wedding gift."

It is not easy for me to admit that I spoke these words. That I gambled away these girls' lives and Korin's life in such a facile manner. My life was worth so little to me at the time that I did not value others' particularly highly either.

Iskan smiled and raised his cup to me. "Kabira, a little of my wisdom has rubbed off on you. So shall it be, on my honor. And the power and might of Karenokoi shall grow, and thereby so shall mine."

He was in good humor again. His feeling of well-being made him look at me a little differently that evening, and I had ensured that his head and judgment were powerfully influenced by wine. I drank too. I needed a little inebriation to be able to go through with my plan. I was afraid. Yet there was another feeling at play: loneliness. It was so long since I had been touched. I had loved this man once. Once, I had desired him.

The necessary task was not as difficult as I had expected.

I had known Iskan a long time. I knew what he liked. I gave him the right mix of meekness and compliance, of girlish admiration and timidity. Iskan's only weakness was flattery. He never tired of hearing about his own excellence. I got him where I wanted him.

I got him between my legs. I got his seed in my belly.

ᛒ

I knew it was a girl. Everything about the pregnancy felt like the ones Iskan aborted when Anji showed him that I was carrying girls. I was terrified that he would discover I was with child. I had to be able to keep my daughter. I had to have something of my own. Someone to love. Someone who was mine alone. The thought of a daughter was born in me when Meriba lay dying. I had been biding my time ever since. Waiting for Izani to die. As long as she lived, I could not put my plan into action.

It was easier to hide my pregnancy than I had thought. Iskan was probably ashamed that he had allowed me to seduce him. Me, an ugly old woman, when he had so many beautiful concubines to call to his bed. I had thought that perhaps he . . . I do not know. I was foolish enough to believe that something might have changed. Yet he continued to avoid me. He had never been in the habit of visiting my chambers, so I kept myself there, and stayed quiet. Izani was no longer there to spy on me and betray me to her son. The sunlight hours had grown long by the time I finally dared venture out into the garden, on the days when I knew for certain that Iskan was not in the palace. I never set foot in the great halls of the dairahesi. I sewed clothes for my little one, and carefully hid them. I read and transcribed poetry. I painted. Yet after a while it was not enough. At times, when I knew most of the dairahesi to be elsewhere, I mustered the courage to visit the little library, and began to read the scrolls therein. It was mostly the classics, which I had read many times before, but they kept me occupied for a time. Once I had plowed through the stock, a desire awoke in me for more. It was as if the girl in my womb, who was now kicking and prodding inside, craved more than just physical nourishment from me. She wanted knowledge.

I knew that Iskan kept a large private library. That is where he stored the scrolls he gathered from all corners of the earth, including in scripts he could not read, simply to deprive others of the possibility of gaining access to the knowledge they contained. I suddenly found myself hungering for scriptures like a woman starved.

The only person to visit me in my self-inflicted confinement was Sonan. True to his word, he visited on occasion. Not as often as I would have liked, not even as often as he himself wanted, but whenever he could sneak away from the watchful eyes of Iskan and Korin. Korin was to wed the daughter of the Governor of Amdurabi. He took four concubines, each more beautiful than the last. Both he and Iskan were occupied with the preparations, and now and then Sonan was able to slip unseen into my chambers. Apart from Iskan, my sons were the only men allowed in the dairahesi.

Sonan suspected nothing about my condition, young and naive as he was. I dressed in loose-fitting jackets, and he had no experience of pregnancy. We would often sit at my best table, which I always made sure was laden with all his favorite treats. It was a pity that I could not bake or prepare any of it myself, but I gave the servants detailed instruction of precisely how everything should be done. It was such a joy to be able to sit across from my youngest son, free from watchful eyes, free from Izani's sharp comments and disapproval. Nobody made any attempt to come between us and I was able to gaze to my heart's content at his beautiful eyes, his soft chin, his quick smile. I could take his hand if I wanted to—hold it, feel his warm skin against mine.

There was a certain reservation about him after fourteen

years of separation. He was pleasant and respectful in his way, but there was no immediate closeness between us. Izani had filled him with too many lies about me, and his father and elder brother had made him too uncertain of his own capabilities and instincts. He wanted to believe that I was a loving mother, but he did not dare. Not at first. And, though it was difficult, I let things develop in their own time. We spoke about everything imaginable simply and comfortably while the moons passed and my belly grew. We spoke of his love of riding and hunting, and how he did not enjoy combat practice. About how difficult he found it to learn texts by heart, as his teacher demanded, but that he was good at writing script and copying paintings. He enjoyed swimming and rowing in the lake and he had several good friends among the royal court of the Sovereign Prince.

"I am very fond of reading," I said one day when the worst of the summer heat had finally passed. We were sitting in my shaderoom, where he had just eaten his fill of fried weja. Birds were singing outside and two lost butterflies were fluttering about the room. Sonan followed their movement with his gaze, enchanted. "I have already read through everything in our library."

"Father has a great big library in Serenity House," replied Sonan, brushing away a little sugar from his lower lip. I leaned forward and stroked away the last of it, and he gave me a surprised but warm look that made my heart sing. "I could bring you some scrolls."

"That should be a great pleasure, my son, but I do not want you to displease your father for my sake."

Sonan made a dismissive gesture. "He and Korin have traveled to Amdurabi. The wedding is to take place there, because Father says it is important that the people see Korin and Hánai together so they know who their new ruler is."

"Hánai, is that her name?"

Sonan nodded. I had not heard her name before. To everyone she was just the daughter of the Governor, not a person with a name of her own.

"So it means that nobody will notice if I bring you some scrolls. What would you most like to read, Mother?"

ᚹ

Suddenly a whole world was opened up to me. Sonan brought me as many scrolls as I wished. I read and read. He described the shelves to me, and slowly I formed an image of Iskan's library. I learned how he ordered his scrolls: where he kept the historical works, the location of the texts on medicine, and where he hid the most secret works—the ones about sources of power, like Anji, around the world. These scrolls were few, and several were in scripts I did not know, and the descriptions in them were often meandering and cumbersome. They were intended to confuse the uninitiated. Yet, with patience, I was able to decipher and understand a good deal of it. It was as if the child inside me helped at times. She turned, and I immediately understood something that was previously unintelligible. She kicked at my rib, and patterns emerged and took shape before my eyes. She was of Iskan's seed and Iskan was infused with the power of Anji. Perhaps some of that power lived also in the child I was carrying.

I rarely moved beyond my quarters, and yet I traveled the world over. In some texts I followed voyagers across vast oceans to the far North and East and South. Then I studied expert accounts of the functions of the body, and sailed through the human bloodstream. I flew among stars in the sky, swam with fish in the sea, followed the crops of the changing seasons along with tillers of the soil. I sat with monarchs on thrones and criminals in dungeons. I grappled with foreign gods, watched the world being created, and mused over what was good and correct, and the nature of truth, and argued over ethics with the oldest master teachers.

It would have been the best time in my life, were I not living in constant fear of being discovered.

ᛟ

One morning, when the heat had passed and the winds blew cold around the palace, I was sitting by the first fire pot of autumn and reading. It was a scroll Sonan had brought me the previous day, and it came from the secret section of Iskan's library. It was the first text I had encountered that spoke of Anji. It was ancient and written in code, with mysterious symbols. Iskan had added his own notes to the text in an attempt to interpret it, with Anji's help, but had not got far. Anji clearly did not want to assist him in everything. I knew that if only I could get access to her water under the waxing moon I would be able to read what was contained therein as easily as if it were written in my own tongue. I could just about discern some patterns; when the girl in my womb kicked, a thread of meaning glinted among the symbols. I saw a snake, an apple, a five-petaled rose.

"You should be careful." Startled, I dropped the scroll I was holding with a thud. Garai was sitting cross-legged on a silk cushion on the other side of the fire pot. I had been so absorbed in the text that I had not heard her enter. I attempted to pull my jacket down over my swelling belly, but it was futile. Garai's sharp eyes had not missed a thing.

I picked up the scroll to make sure it did not get damaged. Then I leaned back, folded my hands demonstratively over my belly and met her gaze with defiance. Those pale eyes, they always frightened me a little. I could not get used to them.

"How far are you?" asked Garai. I did not respond, and the chains on her comb jingled slightly as she tilted her head to one side. Her pale skin was flushed pink from the heat of the coals. She was so thin that her collarbones stuck out sharply from the neckline of her jacket in the dancing glow of the embers. I remember precisely how she was dressed, in a dove-gray jacket without embroidery or embellishment, with loose trousers in a lighter shade of gray. She wore no ornament but the comb in her hair. Around her mouth were wrinkles I had not noticed before, and the skin around her eyes showed many lines, as thin as spider legs. Time was catching up with her too. However, unlike other women, Garai did not seem to resist; she welcomed it.

She sighed and inspected my belly. "Not many moons left, I should think. Two, maybe? And nobody knows about it?"

I pursed my lips. "What do you take me for, a mere concubine? I have been exceedingly prudent."

"And Iskan has been staying in Amdurabi recently. Good. But if he discovers your pregnancy now and chooses to abort the girl it will take its toll on you. It makes no difference how accustomed you are to oaki water. You are too far through. And too old."

"Hence he shall never know."

"What will you do when she is born?"

I hesitated. Looked down at my hands, where the first dark

flecks were beginning to spread—a sign that I was no longer young. My plan had been my secret; I had been thinking on it and honing it for such a long time. Yet Garai could reveal it to Iskan right now if she so chose. It did not matter if I told her.

"How did you guess?" I asked, to buy some time.

"You keep to your quarters. You meet no one but your son. I know that you spent the night with Iskan after his mother's death. It was not difficult to deduce."

"Does anyone else know about this?"

"Orseola. But not because I said anything to her. She has seen it in your dreams."

Orseola. She was incalculable. Dangerous. I did not understand her and one could never guess what she would say or do. "And the others?"

Now it was Garai's turn to scoff. "They do not care about you at all. For them you may as well be a painted screen, as long as you do not benefit from their master's favor. All they care about is their rank and order of preference, and who is Iskan's current favorite." Sadness came over her expression. "It is not their fault. They have nothing else in their lives. Three of them cannot even read. How are they supposed to fill their empty days?"

"Now that Izani is no longer here to watch over me, I mean to present the girl as a son."

Garai raised her eyebrows. She sat quietly for a very long time and observed me. Then she gazed down at the embers. I clasped my hands, hard. Tried to fill my mind with the crackling sounds of the coal, the shutters rattling in the wind, the solitary screech of a bird in the sky outside. The child in my belly was tucked up and still. Waiting.

"We must be very careful. I can be her nurse, so nobody from outside need enter. Do you plan to breastfeed personally?"

I nodded. My fingers were digging into my palms. I held my breath.

"Good. That will reduce the risks. We must simply never give him a reason to doubt. I will speak with Orseola. She is our weak point, but there is a chance that she will go along with us." She smiled a sour smile and stood up.

I held out my hand. Tried to regain control over the situation.

"Why are you helping me?"

Garai blinked those disconcertingly pale eyes.

"I am not helping you. I am helping her." She pointed at my belly. "You have made a choice. She has not."

When she left, I had to lie down awhile. The girl was kicking downward, against my most tender innards, and I wondered what I had done.

In my dream Lehan came to me. She said nothing. She only looked at me, and then pushed me with both hands, and I fell and fell.

ω

The girl was born one moon later. Iskan had returned from Amdurabi but did not come to my chambers. I had stayed quiet and still like a mouse afraid of being discovered by a cat. I did not call on the servants and had Estegi and Garai tend to me. Estegi knew about the child. She massaged my swollen feet every evening, she rubbed my bulging belly with almond oil and kept me company in the sleepless nights when the baby's kicks kept me awake. When the birth started, and the contractions made me gasp for air and pant in pain, I wanted to hear her read aloud from the latest scroll Sonan had brought me from the library. I knew I could trust Estegi not to tell anybody about the forbidden texts, and she had a pleasant voice, deep and soft. But she could not read.

"Fetch Garai," I hissed between the pains. Estegi bowed and hurried away. It was interminably long before she returned and I lay there fighting against the scream that was desperate to come out. No one must hear that a child was born in my bedchamber that night.

They came sneaking in so quietly that I did not even notice them enter until they were standing beside the carpet I was crouched on. Garai's eyes glistened in the lamp light.

"We were nearly discovered," she whispered. "One of the concubines woke up. I hope nobody notices that my bed is empty."

There was no room for fear among all the pain. "Read," I gasped, and pointed at the scroll.

Garai went over to the table and examined it with interest. "Where did you get this?"

I waved my hands in anger. Another dagger pierced my belly and made it impossible for me to speak. Estegi answered for me.

"They are from the Vizier's library. Her son brings them for her."

Garai nodded slowly. She unrolled the scroll and started to read in a quiet voice. This one was about the sacred plants of Elian and their uses. Estegi crouched beside me.

"Come. Walk with me."

Supported on her arm, I began to pace around the chamber. I did not hear much of Garai's recitation, but her voice gave a rhythm to my wandering and my feet followed the plant names across the floor. Blackleaf, water root, skull bonnet, tripoint shine, erreberry, wolf paw, winterhem, a name for every ache. I clutched Estegi's bony hand and she took all of my weight on her hard hip when I needed to rest.

It was after midnight when I got on all fours and bore down. Since I had given birth to three sons already my daughter slipped out quickly and almost without strain on my part, in a gush of water, blood and mucus. Garai delivered her, and Estegi dried her off as I rolled onto my back. The umbilical cord was still connecting us when I held her to my breast. Dark eyes, wrinkled red skin. She was alive, she was breathing, and she was completely quiet. The only thing to be heard in the chamber was the breathing of three women. Estegi and Garai either side of me looked on as the girl found her way to my breast. She suckled, and the night was dark around us, and the enormity of what I had just done found its way to my heart with full force. I looked at Garai. She was smiling the brightest smile I had ever seen cross her lips.

"She is perfect, Kabira. Just perfect." She saw my concern, but it did not dampen her joy. "She is strong. There is a reason that she is here, I can feel it. Can you? Hear her speak with the earth, with the life force!"

I listened and heard the soft sucking from the child's mouth, panting with endeavor. She was outside me now, not inside. Her body was warm and solid against mine. She had a smell like all babies do, and at the same time one altogether her own. It was rich and dark, like earth and leaves and water. Like Anji.

I could not hear what Garai heard, but I understood what she meant. This girl was firmly anchored in the world. In this place. Perhaps I had some of Anji's water in my body when it was creating hers. Perhaps Iskan's seed had carried the spring's water, good and dark. She was of us both, and of Anji and Ohaddin.

"Her name is Esiko," I whispered. "Iskan may name her what he will, but her name is Esiko. After my mother."

"Is she to be his son?" asked Estegi in a strangely wistful tone.

"She shall be his youngest and most beloved son," Garai answered in my stead, as though it were a prophecy. I kissed Esiko's downy little head. For that one night she was mine and mine alone. She stopped suckling, shut her eyes and fell straight to sleep in a way none of her brothers ever had. She was entirely her own person, even then.

SULANI

B y the time they captured me I had already single-handedly destroyed hundreds of enemy soldiers. First with arrows dipped in winemussel poison. When that ran out, with bludgeon and blade. They bound me, and after beating me bloody they took me to the army encampment. There must have been at least five hundred tents. In them slept the commanders. Sometimes two by two. The number of foot soldiers was far greater. They had heavily armed fighters: curved, shining swords; helmets; breastplates and leg guards. The arms were often unprotected. Not many bowmen. Good horses, also with armor around their heads and flanks. All in perfect order and strictly disciplined. The soldiers I killed only made up a fraction of the army's forces. It would not stop their advance. Yet my victory was great. I held the army back long enough to give the river folk time to pack up their belongings and escape downstream.

I thanked the River spirit for the victory she bestowed on me.

I was pushed through the mud to the captain's tent. In the shadows incense was burning. Many burn sweet-smelling substances to mask the smell of death and corpses from the field. The captain stood by a table covered in papers and maps, toying with the handle of a dagger. A man of medium height, not quite young, but with a smooth, expressionless face. Broad shoulders and a certain muscle mass—the type that comes from a lot of riding and sports. Not from any genuine fight for survival. A weak chin, covered by a meager beard.

Beside him, on a pillow, sat a little boy of around ten years old.

"Are you the one who led the attacks against my forces?" asked the captain without looking at me. "Who destroyed the bridges on our way, who stole our equipment in the night, who killed our messengers and scouts?"

He took a step toward me. He had left the dagger on the table. There were no guards in the tent. I could snap his neck with my bare hands. The boy would scream but it would already be too late. I shifted my weight from one foot to the other. Prepared myself.

"Where are the others?" The captain advanced on me. "You have slain hundreds of my men over the last few days." He leaned forward and eyeballed me. "What I do not understand is why you have put up such a resistance. I thought that this part of Jaferi was almost uninhabited?"

I shifted all of my weight onto one foot. My hands were ready. Dry mud and blood fell to the floor as I stretched my fingers in preparation.

He saw the minute movement and shook his head.

"No. You will not do that," he said, and smiled. It was the smile of someone who had killed before. Someone who had enjoyed it. Then he did something to me. With his eyes. They pierced me. It hurt terribly. Far more than the wounds inflicted by steel earlier that day. When the pain became too great, I collapsed on the mats that covered the tent floor.

The child tilted his head to one side and watched as his father broke every bone in my body.

I did not scream. The child did not scream. The captain stood with his hands stretched over me and carried out his work with concentration and precision. All that could be heard in the tent were my groans and the sounds of the camp drifting in from outside. Stomping boots, horses' whinnies, the clatter of weapons and tools.

Only when I lay broken and half dead by his feet did the captain lower his hands. He turned to the child.

"Look you, Orano, this is how I handle my enemies. What do you think we should do with the scum now? Leave him by the riverbank, so that the others may see what we do to those who attempt to resist us?"

The child leaned over me. My vision was blurred and I saw only a light oval coming toward me.

"It's a woman," said the child's voice.

The captain leaned forward. He was quiet for a long while.

"You have sharp eyes, my son. Do you see anything else?"

"Yes, Father, can't you? She is filled with the power."

"The river." The captain sounded surprised. "There must be more to it than I had suspected. Clever boy."

The forms leaning over me disappeared. Then the man appeared sitting on his haunches beside me, holding something up to my lips. "Drink."

My jaw was crushed so that I could not even drink if I wanted to. He poured some water into my mouth and waited, unmoving. After a moment he gave me more. That time I could swallow. The pain slowly lessened.

"You see," said the man, speaking not to me but to the child, "Anji's water heals her faster than I have seen it heal anybody before."

"It is because the power already flows through her," said the child. "Her river and Anji are akin."

"Akin, but not the same." I was drifting out of consciousness and barely heard his last words. "I would very much like to learn more of this power, but it is too great and difficult to dominate. There may be more like her: river warriors imbued with the power of the water. The river must be destroyed."

ω

When I awoke, I did not know whether it was morning or night. The tent was as dimly lit as when I had arrived. I was lying on my side with my cheek against the soft mat. My mouth was dry. My body no longer ached. I stretched out one arm, then the other. When I sat up, I could feel something heavy around my neck. I brought my fingers to my collarbone and found a solid metal collar encasing my throat. From there ran a thin metal chain that was attached securely to an iron ring in the ground.

Something moved in the tent. I was not alone. I immediately retreated until I was pressed up against the canvas wall of the tent.

"Why are you dressed like a man?" asked a high-pitched voice.

It was the child. He was sitting on a mountain of red and blue cushions. Next to him were a lamp and a table covered in rolls of paper. He was watching me without fear, without any expression on his little face at all. His hair was short and dark, his eyes nearly black in the dim light. His father and the guards were nowhere to be seen.

"Why are you dressed like a man?"

I gestured at my clothes and shook my head. If I could lure the child closer, I could frighten the captain into letting me go. Or take revenge by killing his child. Revenge for forcing my people to flee. Revenge for destroying their home. My home. I was the River Warrior. Vengeance was mine to exact.

The child inspected me carefully. "You are right. Your clothes are neither those of a man nor a woman. You haven't cut your hair. When I first saw you, I thought that all savages wore their hair long." He leaned forward. "And full of mussel and snail shells."

I held his gaze. Tried to coax him to come closer. But he did not move.

"You are the only one, aren't you? You are the only one who does this."

I nodded. The shells in my hair rattled.

There were bones of wading birds in there too. And otter teeth. I raised my hand and beckoned him over, but he shook his head, still solemn.

"No. You are dangerous. I can see that. Very dangerous." He leaned his head to one side. "Almost as dangerous as my father." The child nodded. "You have seen it too. Because you have the same power inside you. The same as my father and I. He can choose whether to use it or not. This I cannot do."

He looked down at the mat, was quiet a moment, then returned to me.

"Yet you fight in battle like a man. Why? You needn't. You could stay home embroidering and playing the cinna if you wanted."

"Then who would protect my people? My River?" The words scratched my throat. I could not remember the last time I had spoken.

"The men, of course."

"Why them and not me?"

The boy sat quietly for a long while, and, for the first time, I saw his expression change. He chewed thoughtfully on his lower lip and seemed concerned. Even worried.

"They are stronger?"

"I have killed hundreds of your father's strong men."

"But you are different. You are . . ." He could not find the right word.

"I am the River Warrior. I have dedicated my life to the River. She has bestowed her life force on me. She does not care what I have between my legs."

The boy blushed and turned away. I huddled into my corner and leaned my forehead on my knees. I must find a way to escape. Escape or die—once I had exacted my revenge.

A little later the captain came into the tent in traveling attire. He walked over to his son.

"Has she said anything yet?"

The boy gave me a quick glance.

"No, Father. I wonder whether she is a mute. Or has taken a vow of silence."

"How very irritating. I could force her to talk, but we do not have the time. We must disempower this river as soon as possible. I have sent for Sonan. He is to meet us at the source. My maps indicate that it lies some days' travel eastward."

"How will you disempower the river, Father?"

"Sonan is bringing my scriptures," answered the captain as he gathered a few things in the tent. "I am certain the answer will be contained therein."

Written words—as if they could disempower my mighty River! And he wanted to travel upriver. Good. That would give my people plenty of time to get away in their canoes. I smiled to myself. The man seemed to sense this. He came over to me.

"I believe the savage will be of help. When the time is right."

His words made my heart stop for a brief moment. I was one with the River. But perhaps torture could drive her secrets out of me. I did not know how the River could be killed, but perhaps I knew something else that could be of use to him.

I had to die. It was the only answer. It was the only way to save the River. But again, it was as if he could see inside me and read my thoughts.

"I have postponed your death far into the future. It is no longer yours to decide over."

This man had crushed every bone in my body without touching me. I did not doubt he could decide my death.

ʊ

We traveled east with a diminished army. The captain, his son, his commanding officers and fifty or so men. Around half of them were on horseback; the rest were on foot. Bringing up the rear were a few mares laden with the captain's tent and supplies. I was chained to the saddle of the last horse. An addition to the spoils of war. I could hardly see the captain and his son where they rode, tightly surrounded by their entourage.

The water I had been given to drink was potent indeed and had healed all my wounds. Not even the River water had such fast-acting healing properties. We were traversing my land. This was where I had lived and worked and played since Onna first tempted me into her mud hut with that bowl of salt fish and fresh bread, so many years ago. Copperless and starved, I had been wandering the village for several days, stealing food where I could. But Onna gave me food, and then a home. Without asking for payment. Without asking for anything in return.

The bushes and trees opened up and we walked along the slope of the first hill. The River was to our left, too far away to hear. But ever since I became the River Warrior I had been able to sense her presence, however far I wandered. The ground was good. Firm and resilient underfoot, easy to walk on. I walked straight-backed as is befitting of the River folk. I considered myself to be one of them, though I came to them late.

Onna told me later that she originally thought I was much younger than I was on account of my skinny legs. When I ventured through her door, enticed by that first bowl of salt fish, I was given hot food—clam soup, blackberry and nut pie and beer her neighbor had brewed. I devoured it hurriedly, convinced that she would ask for something in return. Nobody had given me anything for free in my years of wandering. Never.

There was always a price. I did not believe it was my young flesh she was after. She was an old woman. I thought she must be one of those wisewomen. Maybe she wanted my young eyesight. Or my memories. Maybe she was taking them as I was eating, without my knowledge.

"Take them," I said. "Take them all."

She screwed up her watery eyes and peered at me. Then she gave me more pie and said nothing. I searched my mind carefully and found all my memories still there, entire and clear as the day they were created. The morning when I came in after staying overnight in the pigsty. The sow had given birth, and I had to make sure she did not roll over onto her new piglets. Inside our hut it was quiet. No fire in the hearth. No breakfast. Mother and Father were lying in their beds, already stiff. Little brother in his crib with his back arched in pain, also stiff. The disease that had snuffed them out was visible in the blisters on their hands and faces.

All the huts in the village. Full of silence and death. I alone, in the pigsty, was spared.

I rubbed my eyes with my palms. The memories would not leave. Nothing could rid me of them.

"Take them," I screamed. "Take them. I cannot bear them any longer!"

Onna was quiet and her eyes were kind.

Sometimes I wished I had never met such kindness. I told Onna that, in my darkest moments. I struck her for saving me. I cursed her, spat on her, clawed at her face. She would always repay me with even more persistent love.

The River gave me Onna. The River gave me a home, a people. Then she gave me her very essence. And in the end she took it all away.

I was treated like an animal on the journey. I was given plenty of water to drink but it was noticeably not River water. Had I been given that I could have torn my shackles clean off. When we pitched camp in the evenings, I was given bread to eat. I was used to fasting and this fare suited me fine. The men left me alone and did not bother me much—just a little taunting in jest. Spat on the ground before me as they passed. They found me frightening and repulsive. A woman taller and stronger than them was not something they could tolerate.

One day a solitary rider arrived from the South. The scouts

had heard word of his arrival, so he was given free passage through to the captain. We set up camp for the night shortly after, earlier than usual. I paid close attention to the organization of the troops. There were always three scouts when we were on the move, one ahead, one behind, and one to the south. At night armed guards kept watch in three shifts. Two men guarded the horses, provisions and me. At night I was chained by my hands and feet so I could not run away. The locks and chains were of good quality. Removing them was not an option. But they allowed me a certain mobility, and if I could just sneak away or overpower the guards, I could get out. I had no interest in running away. But I did want to kill the captain.

The guards were well trained and gave me no opportunity. They did not sleep at their posts, they hardly spoke to each other and were constantly alert. These were men who were under tight control. I never heard them talk about their leader. Not a word. Nor did they ever complain.

The next day we started early, while the dew was still on the grass. Its wetness refreshed my feet. We had come up high among the hills now. I heard the white herons call. The white herons are the guardians of the Lake of Sorrow. It is said that their feathers bestow good luck and fortune. But I know there is no such thing as luck.

They were a sign that the lake was near. It is a sacred place. A place one must not approach indifferently or without cause.

As the men leading the horses drove on, we soon came over the final crest that revealed the clear, cold water of the Lake of Sorrow. It is not a large lake, but it is deep, and none know what its depths may conceal. None save the herons. The tops of the mountains beyond the lake were dazzling white against the clear spring sky. The sky was never so boundless and clear in the valley below.

To our left was the River. The captain ordered his men to set up camp, his voice echoing in the stillness over the lake. The herons on the far side of the water lifted their heads to observe us. The captain himself came riding over to me. His jacket was as blue as the sky. His eyes as cold as the water. Without a word he untied my chain from the packhorse's saddle and rode away with it in his hand. His steed was a sprightly one and I stumbled and fell. Three other horses were accompanying his, but I could not see their riders; I had to keep my eyes on the ground beneath my feet. He steered straight ahead to the point where the River flowed out from the lake. He should do it now, at once, and not waste time.

I collapsed to the ground when he reined in his horse. Men dismounted. Boots stamped around me. Then a hand appeared and pulled my head up by the hair.

"I thought I would need you to disempower the river," said the captain. "Now that does not appear to be necessary." He was squatting beside me and leaning over me. He lowered his voice. "I have scriptures, you see. I have gathered knowledge from all corners of the earth. My son brought the most important one here to me. It tells of places like your river. I know more about the earth's sources of power than anybody. Most people believe they are no more than legends and tales from the olden days. But I know that they are absolutely real. And you know it too." He laughed quietly with his face close to mine. His eyes were large and his pupils covered his irises nearly completely. The River inside me was fighting against the power inside him.

"Soon they shall be just that: legends and tales. For I have discovered the key to their undoing and I mean to eradicate them, one by one. What do you imagine might be necessary to strip a place of its power, little warrior?"

I moistened my lips, not in preparation to answer, but rather to buy time. My hands were free. I pretended to fall down to the ground. When he moved his hand to get a better grip of my hair, I lunged at him. My hands closed around his throat. I have strong hands. River-strong. I squeezed with all of my might.

The captain smiled. "No," he said, and my grip immediately loosened. Someone was there at once with a sword to my throat. The captain released me and stood up.

"Bring her here," he said over his shoulder. The swordsman took hold of my shirt and dragged me across the ground to the River's shore. She was not large at her source. Several small streams from these mountains and hills fed into her flow, but the Lake of Sorrow was her greatest supply. It was the origin of her power, though the same power did not live within the lake itself.

They stood there, the captain and his little son—a boy with the same weak chin as his father. The swordsman threw me down by the captain's feet. My neck was bleeding and stinging where the sword had pierced my skin. The blood dripped slowly on the ground by my River. She was singing. My blood sang in response. Around me men were standing on sacred ground bearing arms and steel.

"All that is needed," said the captain quietly to himself, "is a foreign oaki. Then the river is no longer itself. Fortunately, I have precisely the thing."

He untied a wineskin from his belt and shook it. "There is enough left. Good."

He removed the stopper and poured its contents, which looked like clear water, into the River.

The herons took flight at once with a collective shriek; dozens of giant birds' wings beat the air. I leaped into the water. He let go of my chain and let me fall. The water engulfed me. The water I had swum in and drunk from so many times. But now it was not the same. This was normal, ice-cold river water. The River, my mother, my everything, was no longer there. Without a struggle or farewell, the spirit of the River had disappeared.

Without her I was nothing, and had no protection. Everything flooded into me at once and my world was enveloped in darkness.

ω

Black. Convulsions in my body. Head heavy, filled with blood. The smell of horses in my nostrils. Mouth dry, lips cracked.

Bound to the back of a horse. Army sounds around me: boots, the clatter of weapons. I opened my eyes to the sight of a brown horse's flank, glimpses of grass, dust thrown up by thousands of pairs of feet. I shut my eyes again, and let the darkness take me.

ω

Water. Clear and cold and commonplace. I tried to drink, but most of it spilled. As I tried to lift my head, a hand supported me. I drank more. Tried to open my eyes; it was difficult. Saw nothing; was I blind? The water bowl was taken away. My head

215

was lowered to the ground, the sound of light steps walking away. I lay there blinking. After a while I could discern a gleam of light. I still had my eyesight. I lay on the ground in a tent without lamps, but a little light seeped in from outside, maybe moonlight. It was night. I moved my arms, they were free. Around my throat I could still feel the collar and chain. My body was frail. All the strength the River had given me had disappeared. The protection also. I could not hear her murmur inside me, only the beat of my own human heart. And my breathing, shallow and weak.

The quick steps returned and a small figure appeared in the tent. It was the child. He crouched down next to me and handed me a bowl. I was able to sit up by then, so I held the bowl in my own hands, and drank. Wiped my mouth with the back of my hand. He handed me a piece of bread. I took it and twisted it in my hands. It smelled of salt and sweat.

"Why am I alive?"

The child did not answer straightaway.

"I don't know." His voice was pensive. "I thought he would drown you in the river. But he had you fished out after watching you struggle for a long time. You looked dead. But Sonan said that your heart was beating. So Father ordered that you be lashed to a horse and taken along."

"Where?"

"Home to Ohaddin."

"Southward."

"Mm." He inspected me carefully. "You no longer have the power inside you. How does it feel?"

I did not want to answer or even think about it. I tore off a piece of bread and stuffed it in my mouth. My eyes had grown accustomed to the darkness. Now that I could see better I saw that this was the captain's personal tent. I saw the child's dark eyes sparkle in the sparse light, and white teeth in his half-open mouth as he watched my movements carefully.

"Why did you come to these parts?"

"Father needed more money. He has emptied his coffers with the expansion of the palace in Ohaddin and taxes can't be raised any higher. He says he hasn't the time for a laborer uprising." The boy yawned and I wondered how late it was. And where the captain was. "There is woodland here with timber we do not have in Karenokoi. We took over some minor realms north of Karenokoi, to ensure their loyalty and to prevent them attacking when Father is occupied with other business. Then we marched to these lands, which we were told were uninhabited. We will ship the timber southward on the river to the sea, and then ship it farther and sell where it fetches a good price. There is a silver mine here too. People appeared and fought back when we struck, so Father killed them. They were in the way."

It was my River folk he spoke of. When the enemy attacked, we defended ourselves. But when the attack proved to be insurmountable, I ordered the survivors to flee and continued the fight alone.

"So it was all for silver and gold? Your father is a greedy man." I swallowed the last piece of bread. Licked the flour from my fingers. It tasted salty.

"Yes, he is." The child produced some dried fruits from a pocket and handed them to me absentmindedly. I chewed on the hard morsels. "But not for silver or gold. He wants to rule. The silver and gold helps him to do that."

"Who does he want to rule over?"

"Everything. Everyone."

ϖ

The child had curled up under a blanket on the other side of the tent and gone to sleep. I ran my fingers along the length of my chain. Pulled it until I felt resistance. Then crept quietly, on all fours, holding the taut chain until I came to one of the tent poles. The chain was locked, and the lock was robust. The chain was too. I could have sawn off the tent pole, if I only had a tool to do so.

The tent flap was lifted and more moonlight streamed in. I froze. I had not heard a thing. My formerly sharp senses were blunted and feeble. The captain made a quiet sound as he stepped into the tent.

"The little warrior is certainly alive." He let the tent flap fall and took a few steps into the tent. He lit an oil lamp, without haste, without worrying about turning his back to me. He was in no hurry. Once the lamp was lit, he poured something into a bowl and sat down on a cushion. As he sipped the contents of the bowl, he looked at me for the first time. His mouth was hidden behind the rim of the bowl. He studied me carefully, as if he had all the time in the world.

I began to back into my corner.

"I have been wondering why I spared your life." He stroked his bearded chin. The child under the blanket stirred, disturbed by the sound of his voice.

"I am a conqueror. I conquer areas, resources, populations. People and their minds. Do you know why I have the most disciplined army of the last hundred years? They fear me, little warrior, just as you fear me now."

I shrank my head down between my shoulders.

"You did not fear me before. But you were mistaken, were you not? Everyone should fear me. Most do not know why, yet fear me anyway." He stretched and yawned, suddenly bored. "It is almost too easy. I take what I want. Perhaps I shall see to it that my name receives the appendage 'the Conqueror.'"

He stood up and walked toward me. I tried to press myself into the ground, to make myself invisible. I have never been as afraid as I was in that moment. The River's power had abandoned me, and stripped me of my defenses. All the sensations I was previously able to hold back now filled me with such force that I could barely breathe. I did not fight back when he tore off my trousers.

When he was finished, he wiped himself off on my clothes. I shrank away with my arms around my head. Everything smelled of him.

Before he extinguished the lamp, I saw a movement in the corner of my eye, where I peeked out between my arms. It was the child turning away and pulling the cover over his head.

ᚹ

After that the captain changed his manner toward me. He enjoyed subjecting me to ultimate humiliation. He used my blood for dark arts I know nothing about. I do not want to know.

The child sometimes fetched water and bread for me at night.

"What is your name?" he whispered once after his father was finished with me and had fallen asleep. He was sitting a little way from me, on account of the smell. I ate quickly, greedily. Before someone discovered us and took my bread from me.

"Sulani."

The child hesitated a moment. I glanced at him. He was chewing his lip.

"My name is Orano."

I had heard his name. His father used it. Yet he hesitated before pronouncing it.

"Where is your mother, Orano?"

"At home, in Ohaddin. In the dairahesi where women ought to be." He tossed his head. "I accompany my father into battle now. I am old enough. He teaches me everything. I am the youngest, but he loves me the most."

"What has your mother taught you?"

"Other things," answered Orano evasively. "Less important things."

"More food."

He searched his pockets and found something. Held out a hand filled with nuts.

I grabbed hold of his wrist and pulled him toward me. The nuts fell with a soft clatter on the floor. I held his slender body against my filthy clothes, and saw a contortion in his usually expressionless face. I twisted his slender wrists, hard. He did not scream.

"Scream for your father so he can watch you die."

"He will kill you."

"But first I will have my revenge. He will witness your death, and know that the fault is his to bear. He will never be the same."

These last words I whispered straight into the little brat's face. I moved my hands around his throat.

"Scream then! Call for your father!"

"No," he said, just as his father had said when I had my fingers around his throat. But this time it was not imbued with the same dark power that had suppressed my strength. This was only a word, but was still more than a mere refusal.

"No," he said again. "You will not kill me."

It was simply a fact. I squeezed harder. His eyes bulged, but he did not fight back.

His face grew darker and darker. I opened my own mouth to scream and wake the captain. To get my revenge before he killed me.

Time stopped. There was nothing but the child's rapid pulse against my palm, my breath, the heat of the little body against mine.

I let go and pushed him away. The warrior was gone for good. I recoiled and pressed my face against the mat. Only Sulani was left.

Orano crawled away from me. I heard small scrabbling sounds.

A hand reached out and tipped the scavenged nuts into a little pile before me.

ω

We arrived in Ohaddin at dusk. The army stopped outside a high wall and only the captain and his closest men rode in through the gate. I was once again chained to a packhorse led by a guard. On the other side of the wall there was a muddle of houses of a sort I had never seen before, with flat roofs. Lanterns hung by the doors, and lamplight shone through the windows and formed pools on the streets. I could hear voices of adults and children, the bleating of goats and the cackling of some sort of tame bird. The air smelled of smoke and food and muck. I had never seen such a large city before, and, despite my fatigue, I forced myself to look around. I had to know where they had taken me.

We came to another wall, where a smaller gate was opened for the captain. Here most of his entourage diverged and only the captain and his sons rode through. The guard leading my horse gave it a smack on the rump so that it continued through the gate on its own. It was received on the other side by a guard, with a shaved head and dressed entirely in blue, who led it farther without a word.

We found ourselves in a walled park. I could not see how big it was in the half-light. In the east stood a small cluster of large red buildings with columns and several stories. In the west was a group of smaller but equally extravagant buildings. Between them spanned a garden. I could not see much of the vegetation in the growing darkness, but I could hear the sound of running water, birdsong and wind rustling through dry leaves. From the buildings in the east I could hear music and laughter; from the ones in the west no sounds came, though the windows were illuminated. When the horse stopped by a veranda and hung its head low, I stopped and hung my head low as well.

The horse would be led to a stall in a warm stable. Fed, maybe brushed.

I did not know what was to become of me.

Two new guards, also with shaved heads—one short and stocky and the other tall and bearded—came out through a golden doorway. The stocky one did the lock that attached my chain to the horse's saddle and took the lock in his hand. He led me up onto the veranda and through the doorway, with the tall guard behind us. He closed and locked the doors. I was in the captain's palace in Ohaddin.

I was taken along a long passage with many doors and arches to an open courtyard with a pond. In the courtyard there was a staircase that led upward. The guard led me up the stairs. I did not see people anywhere or hear any sounds apart from the clink of my own chain.

We came to another golden entrance. The guard unlocked it and walked toward me. I backed away. He tutted impatiently, grabbed my neck ring and unlocked that too. Then he gave me a little push so that I stumbled in through the doors. They were locked behind me. I was in the captain's dairahesi.

I found myself in a hall with a high ceiling. In the middle of the room there was a fountain as white as the herons of the Lake of Sorrow. Windows on two sides were open to the night air. The hall was brightly lit by both candles and lamps, and the floor was laid with thick carpets. Around the two low dark-wood tables there were masses of large pillows, and on the pillows there sat women. At one table all the women were young, with long black hair, jackets in bright colors and masses of jewelry. They looked confusingly similar; I could not even figure out how many of them there were. On their table lay embroidery, cards, dice, and dishes of fruit and other good things to eat. Around them children of different ages were playing.

Around the other table sat three women. One was old, with gray-streaked dark hair and an old woman's wrinkled hands. Her attire was expensive but much simpler than that of the young women. The second woman's hair was extremely fair. Her trousers and jacket were plain and brown. She did not wear any jewelry either, other than a comb in her white hair. Her skin was of a different color from mine and that of the dark-haired woman; it shifted between brown and red. The last woman had darker skin than anyone I had ever seen, her hair was curly and her eyes were round. It was very difficult to say how old she was, but the look in her eyes told me she was older than I. In her ears and around her throat there hung strange woven objects with pearls and snail shells in the threads.

"What is that!" cried one of the young women. "Where did it come from?" She covered her mouth with her hand in reaction to my stench.

"Do not be ridiculous," said the old woman sourly. "Iskan must have brought her here. I heard from the servants that he was expected tonight."

The white-haired woman turned to her. "That means that Orano has also come home." The old woman smiled, and from her smile I understood that she was Orano's mother.

"I have had his favorite dishes prepared." She was about to say something else but was interrupted by one of the young women.

"Is she just going to stand there? Surely they do not suppose that she lives here? I refuse to sleep in the same chamber as her!"

"You wish to defy your master's wishes?" said the dark-haired woman in a deep voice. "You wish to send word to him: I do not want to live with your newest woman? Is he to give you your own chamber then, Aberra?"

It became very quiet around the young women's table. The white-haired woman smirked. Finally another of the young women stood up, one with many bands around her ankles and arms.

"Well, I am certainly glad I have my own chamber. I shall retire now. My master is sure to call upon me tonight." She left the hall through a small door and several of the others made faces behind her back.

"She should be careful," said the one they called Aberra. "She has been the favorite for a long time now. He is bound to change his mind soon."

"Maybe to this one," said one of the others with a nod in my direction. They laughed. But the old woman looked at me thoughtfully.

"What shall we do with her?" she said quietly to the white-haired woman.

The walls around them began to distort before my eyes. I felt myself swaying back and forth. It had been a long time since I had eaten or drunk anything.

Then a woman emerged from a shadowy corner and glided soundlessly over to me. A pair of strong arms supported me just as I was about to fall. I caught sight of a large nose, hair in an austere plait, a full mouth. Then everything went black.

ᴡ

I woke up. Everything was soft. A bed, cushions, silk against my skin. Somebody was holding a bowl of water to my mouth, but it was not Orano. They were not the hands of a child; they were broad and strong. Darkness came and went as I slipped in and out of consciousness. My body did not want to be awake. Sleep became an escape. Those hands were there feeding me soup, soft food, bitter-tasting concoctions. Sometimes I could feel the hands wandering over my body, washing wounds, applying dressings. Always with the same tenderness. I kept my eyes closed even when I was awake.

Sometimes I was sent to him as well. He had his way with me. Afterward there were more parts of me to wash. More wounds to tend to. I kept my eyes closed. I was there behind them, but he could not see me.

Then a day passed without him, then two, then more. I opened my eyes and saw sunlight. A grated window, cabinets, chests, carpets, pillows. A bird was singing in a tree outside: a lark. My body did not ache as much. I sat up in bed. There was a door; it was closed. When I tried to stand up, my legs did not want to carry me, and I sank back down with a groan. The door opened at once and she entered, the one with the nose and the soft hands.

She was by my side immediately, helping me into a comfortable position. She tended to my latest affliction, where he had cut me in the corner of my mouth.

"Can you eat?"

I tongued at the sores inside my mouth. Opened it tentatively, grimaced and shook my head.

"Do you want to bathe? Drink?" Her voice was husky. I liked it.

I nodded. She smiled a crooked smile. "Good. Then we will bathe you first. Wait a moment."

I did not move while she was away, and stayed leaning back against a cushion. The sun streaming in through the window grate warmed my legs. I was naked but I refused to look at my body. I have always carried my scars with pride. They were proof that I had fought well. But these injuries had not been inflicted in battle.

She returned with a large blue garment and wrapped it around me. Then she led me, slowly and patiently, out of the room, through the large hall with the fountain—where several pairs of curious eyes followed us but nobody spoke—out through another door and down a staircase. The last door opened into a room filled with steam. She helped me into a basin of hot water, and I groaned as it scorched my many wounds and sores. Then the pain was replaced by pleasure. My companion rolled up her trouser legs and waded into the water, where she began washing my body and hair with something that lathered and smelled good. Sometimes, she touched places he had touched and my first instinct was to recoil. But these were kind hands that wished me well. Eventually I was able to rid myself of the image of the man on top of me, inside me, and simply accept her care.

It took a lot of scrubbing to clean away everything that clung to me. When I was bedridden, she had washed me with rags, but that method was limited. My hair needed a lot of scrubbing; it was matted and full of dried-in unmentionable things. She had to cut a lot out with scissors. She removed my snail shells and bird bones without a word. They belonged to the warrior, and that was no longer who I was.

Afterward she dried me carefully, and rubbed sharp-smelling salves on my sores. I stood still, passive, and let it all happen. Then when she had finished and wrapped me up in another garment, I opened my mouth to speak for the first time.

"Your name?"

She looked down at the floor, as though she had suddenly become shy.

"Estegi."

"Sulani."

She looked up. "I know." When I looked confused, she added: "Orano told his mother about you. We know a little about who you are."

"And you? You are a . . ." I did not know what word I should use. All of this, from the golden doorways to the food, the bath, the smells, sounds, it was all so foreign to me. "Wife?"

She snickered. "I am a servant. I have served in the Vizier's dairahesi since I was a child. Before that I served his mother."

"Thank you."

She understood what I meant and looked at me solemnly. She bound the cloth around my breast with care. Gave the knot a little pat. Her hands were not old but neither were they young. She was older than I, but by how much I could not say. On an impulse I took hold of one of her hands, felt the bony back of her hand against my palm, pulled it to my lips and kissed it.

Estegi stopped. Looked at me as my lips rested on her skin. A blush rose from her neck up to her cheeks. She withdrew her hand abruptly. Perhaps I had done something wrong. I lowered my hands and did not move until she had opened the door and led me up the stairs again.

When night fell, I thought about her name. Estegi. It was similar to my own.

ω

The captain did not like me being clean and smelling good. His interest waned after I had bathed. He sent for me, but not every night, and his perversions diminished. My sores healed.

I kept to myself. The other women, with their handicrafts and clothes, their gossip and concerts in the garden, did not want to know me, and nor I them. The eldest, who I later learned was the First Wife, Kabira, rarely seemed to be in the dairahesi. The white-haired one, Garai, I saw sometimes walking in the garden. Orseola, the dark-skinned one, was often in the Sovereign's palace at night and slept through the days.

It was Estegi who kept me company. She always had a lot to do—she was Kabira's personal servant and she kept her busy—but as soon as she had a spare moment, she would come to my room. She brought me food. She helped me to train up the strength in my arms and legs when my injuries had healed and I was able to move again. She supported me as we walked through the garden and she pointed out all its wonders.

But she was the greatest wonder of all.

She gathered together all the fragments that remained of me. Of my body. Of my very being. With her tender care she sewed me up into a whole person again. As whole as a person like me can be. Ever since those first walks in the gardens of Ohaddin she has been my strength. Everyone has always seen me as the strong one, the protector. The one who keeps others safe. But for me Estegi was the only safety this world had ever offered.

KABIRA

A new darkness had entered Iskan. He was drinking from Anji's dark water with increasing frequency. Those brown eyes, once so beautiful, had blackened to the extent that his pupils and irises appeared to merge. On the surface he was calm and composed as always, but darkness was brewing beneath the veneer. He used it in ways I never knew possible. Estegi told me and Garai about what he had done to Sulani, and her appearance afterward. Estegi had difficulty finding the words to describe it; she faltered, gestured, then gave up, and looked at us with wide, helpless eyes. There was nothing we could do. Nothing we dared do, for nobody wanted to attract Iskan's attention. He must have been facing hindrances in the world outside Ohaddin of which we knew nothing, but which were darkening his mind. Something was causing him to drink of the oaki ever more frequently. The dairahesi was a closed world of its own and very little knowledge of the outer world reached us. Sonan was married to a daughter of one of the Sovereign's most trusted men. I was pleased, because both Korin and Enon had been married to governors' daughters in other districts where they now lived and wielded power, and they came very seldom to Ohaddin. Despite Sonan and his wife living within the palatial grounds of Ohaddin, I seldom saw him either. He had a son of his own, and duties that his father imposed on him. He had become a grown man with very little time for his mother.

The only one who was not afraid of Iskan during these dark times was Esiko. She resided with me but scarcely spent time in my chambers. For the most part she was her father's shadow and followed him wherever he went: on excursions from Ohaddin, overseeing trade, advising the aging and feeble Sovereign, on his visits to Anji. He kept no secrets from her. Though she kept many from me.

Once I entered my chamber after bathing and found her dressed in one of Garai's old jackets, one I had given her when she first arrived and was Iskan's favorite. It was pale blue with elaborate embroidery and did not suit Esiko at all—the color was entirely wrong for her skin and hair. It was the first time I had seen her in women's clothes and I froze in the doorway. She had hung some of my jewelry around her thin wrists and neck. Esiko met my gaze in the mirror, unconcerned.

"What are you doing?" I asked, making an effort to keep my voice calm.

"I wanted to know what it felt like to be a woman," she replied, and swung her arms around thoughtfully. "It's difficult to move in this stiff cloth."

"One grows accustomed," I replied, and quickly stepped in and closed the door. I could not risk somebody seeing her.

She let the armlets fall to the floor with a clatter and crawled out of the jacket as quick as a polecat. "Lucky I don't have to."

Her naked rib cage was still completely flat, with no signs of breasts forming. Her hips were narrow without a hint of roundness. Every day I studied her body and searched for signs that she was becoming a woman. I knew that I must have a plan for when it happened. How would I conceal it from Iskan? How could I save my child? Yet I could not bring myself to dwell on it. I wanted to keep her with me forever, as my secret daughter, and I refused to acknowledge to myself or to Garai that time was marching mercilessly on and we were getting ever closer to the day when her body would betray us.

ꚳ

I stood on the wall and watched them ride out into the dawn. Iskan had permitted me to leave the dairahesi for the first time since he had brought me to Ohaddin from Areko, over twenty years previous. Esiko stood by my side. My three sons were riding at the head of the army, on three midnight-black stallions. Banners were flapping in the biting wind. I leaned against the rough battlements of the wall. As the sun came up, its sharp rays met armor on the chests of both man and beast. I saw three strong men in the prime of life, and at the same time I saw three little boys riding away from their mother.

They had ridden into battle before, but never so far away. Iskan had explained to Esiko, who then explained to me, that a new power had risen in the Northwest. Elian had risen against Karenokoi's authority and begun to encroach upon the vassal states along its border. They had taken over two states, Baklat and Nernai, which, according to Esiko, were crucial for Karenokoi's economy. They provided the grain for the entire realm. Spices were now the only crop farmed in Renka and the districts surrounding Ohaddin, and they were its source of gold. Gold, but no bread or rice. The prices of food had soared. Now other district governors were looking to the Northwest, either in fear of invasion by Elian, or beginning to see a glimmer of opportunity.

232

Iskan was no popular leader. For he was the true leader now, and everybody knew it. The Sovereign Prince was a confused old man. All strength had drained from him since the death of his sons. He no longer emerged from his chambers. He was very old, and the succession to the throne was unclear—who was next in line with the Sovereign's sons dead? One of his illegitimate sons? None of them had dared stand up against Iskan. Everyone knew the consequence of open mutiny: instant death.

Though Esiko did not speak of it, I learned from Estegi that the principal cause for the uprising in Elian was the slave trade. Slaves were a further export commodity that Iskan had introduced into the trade of Karenokoi. He was inspired by Harrera, where he had bought Garai so long ago. Selling young women was profitable, and he needed more gold for his perpetual expansion. Iskan wanted to appropriate as many sources of power as possible, in order to destroy them. He was plagued by the fear that somebody else would master prophecy and death as he had, and then use it against him. On the Vizier's command, young women were kidnapped away from poor villages in Karenokoi and its vassal states, and other nearby realms besides. The girls were then sold to traders in Karenokoi and beyond. It had gone so far that mothers in certain regions where the slave scouts were most rife, such as Elian, disfigured their daughters by shaving their heads, cutting or burning their faces, pulling out their teeth. Anything to try to keep them safe. Those born with a cleft lip or birthmarks were seen as blessed. They were safe.

Iskan claimed to have had no choice but to send his sons out to head the troops. Naturally he could not go because he was too old. Too important. But he was encountering problems with the population. They despised him from the pit of their starving stomachs. He could not quell them with the threat of death, for they were already staring death in the face. For a long time he had managed to keep them subdued with the cult that he had built up around the Sovereign Prince, as a sort of infallible forefather for them to revere. But they had not seen the Sovereign for several years. Everyone knew who ruled, and an uprising was on the horizon. Iskan did not want to kill more people than he had to: people were labor and therefore necessary for the crucial spice plantations. He had tried to replace some who had died in the last great famine with slaves brought in from Harrera, but to no avail. Now he was trying to inspire cooperation by presenting Elian as their true common enemy: Karenokoi is under attack—we must all unite in the fight against the invaders! Esiko told me that he was working hard to manipulate the people's outlook on the war. I do not know how successful were his attempts. All I knew was that my sons were a part of his campaign.

It seemed that Iskan no longer trusted anyone but his sons, and scarcely even them. The previous night, Sonan had told me that Iskan was becoming perversely suspicious even of Korin. He had accused him of withholding resources in Amdurabi.

"What plans do you have for the gold?" Iskan had asked. "To enlist your own soldiers, perhaps? To march against whose armies? I am warning you. You cannot revolt against me, do you understand? Nobody can, but especially not you!"

Korin had stood with bowed head and tight fists and assured his father that the gold was to feed the population and nothing more. That he was a good and obedient son, who wanted to obey his father's wishes in all ways. However, he humbly entreated that he may stay home in Amdurabi and not take part in the campaign against Elian. Hánai, his wife, was pregnant again, and he really ought—

"Ought to what?" Iskan had mocked him. "Hold her hand while she is bearing down? I am sure I know your real motives. Do not worry. You shall go to battle with honor. I hereby name you commanding officer of the campaign."

Korin thanked his father for this great honor, but when Iskan turned away, Korin's eyes were filled with hate. Korin was a middle-aged man already, and deeply resented taking orders from his father as if he were a boy, and not a governor in his own right with six children and a seventh on the way. He did not care about his people any more than Iskan did, but he was not as far removed from reality as his father. If Amdurabi's population revolted against their governor there would be little he could do. If he left his district, the situation would be even more uncertain.

Sonan and I conversed late that night, with Esiko by her brother's side, drinking in every word. Despite her closeness to her father I knew we could talk freely in her company. She had never betrayed me or us to her father. She simply stored everything he told her, and everything I told her, in her little head, her face like an expressionless mask. I never knew what she was thinking, and sometimes I wanted to shake her until she let me in, allowed me to see her true self. I could never get truly close to Sonan either—the distance Izani had created between us when he was little was too great—yet Esiko was supposed to have been mine from the beginning.

Sonan was afraid. He had not said so—no young man would say it to his mother the evening before leaving for battle. Despite his age, he had never fought in a war before. He was recently married, with a little daughter, and had no desire to leave his hearth and home. Yet he did everything that his father and brothers ordered him to do.

"I am no warrior, Mother," he said quietly as Estegi was clearing up after our meal. "Neither am I a leader. Father has appointed me as leader of a mercenary band of mounted archers from Tane. These are tough men, Mother. Seasoned in battle, masters of their art. They despise me and my inexperience. I do not blame them."

"You can learn a lot from those archers," said Esiko. "You are fond of archery, aren't you? There's no one who can shoot from horseback like the riders of Tane."

Sonan mumbled something unintelligible in answer and shortly after stood up to go. I wanted to hold on to him, but could not think of a reason to make him stay. He leaned forward and kissed my cheeks.

"If anything should happen to me . . . I know that your influence is limited, but try to take care of my wife and daughter. Seeing as I have no sons, I know that my family are of little interest to Father."

"Do not say such things, my son," I said, and pulled him fiercely to my breast, holding him more tightly than ever before. I held him as I had wished I could when he was little and at the mercy of Izani's cruelty. "You shall return to us all, whole and well."

"I will ensure they have all they need," said Esiko calmly to her brother. "You need not ride out with a heavy heart."

Sonan gently released himself from my grip. He clapped his youngest sibling on the back. "I know I can rely on you, Orano. And you have Father's ear. Live well, little brother."

"And you, brother."

They kissed each other warmly on the cheeks. Esiko and Sonan had always got on well.

Sonan gave me a final hasty kiss. "I must go. My wife promised to stay awake to see me and I do not want to make her wait. Live well, esteemed mother."

He left, and we were alone. I hid my face in my hands. Though I was distraught that Iskan sent all three of them away together, I hoped that Korin and Enon would keep an eye on their younger brother.

"Father is sending a supply of Anji's good water to protect them," said Esiko to me, and yawned. She started extinguishing the oil lamps, one by one. Estegi had been sent to bed. I looked up and watched Esiko's figure in the increasing gloom. Her hips were beginning to grow a soft roundness now; it could not be mistaken. Her budding breasts could be hidden under stiff silk jackets, but the hips . . . And her entire face had started to take on an altogether more feminine form. Soon our secret would not be concealable from anybody. I still did not know how we would protect her.

"That is good. Then they are safe," I said, my mind still fully occupied with my raw yearning for Sonan.

Esiko paused with an extinguished lamp in one hand. She looked at me with eyes that suddenly appeared much older than the girl before me.

"Anji's power is bound to this district, to Renka," she said. "It diminishes the farther away the water travels, and with every other source of power it passes. Father knows this, but sometimes I believe he forgets."

I stood up abruptly.

237

"Have you seen something? Answer, girl!"

"I have seen many things in Anji's water. Never have I seen my brothers' deaths reflected there."

"What does that mean?" My voice was trembling.

"It means that wherever and whenever they should fall, Mother, it shall not be here."

ω

I was reminded of her words as my children rode away from me that morning. They did not know that I was standing on the wall and watching their departure, and none of them turned around. They were too soon obscured by the houses beyond the wall, but I lingered as the sun was rising. I could hear additional commanders from Ohaddin joining their small troop. The foot soldiers were waiting outside the city. I heard the city gates being opened to the sound of fanfares and jubilant calls when the soldiers saw their leader riding out. Korin was well liked, or more so than his father at least. I looked toward the Halim mountains in the northwest, and their undulating peaks that marked the army's destination. They were planning to reach the pass between the highest mountains as soon as the following day.

When I turned around to go, Esiko grabbed my hand in a most uncharacteristic gesture.

"You have me, Mother," she said, and squeezed my hand. "I will stay by your side until their return."

I withdrew my hand from hers and groped my way to the staircase where the guards of the dairahesi were waiting for us. My feet and hands had to show me the way; my eyes were blinded with tears.

Several weeks later, the messengers started to come. Esiko brought with her reports from Sovereign House, where she sat by Iskan's side every day and listened in on all of his meetings and negotiations. The first reports told of the arrival of Karenokoi's troops at Baklat, where they were met with tough opposition. The enemy forces were larger than expected because the local population chose to fight on the side of Elian. Such was Iskan's unpopularity.

Iskan tried to recruit more soldiers to send as reinforcements, but, as Esiko recounted, nobody accepted the call to arms. She only came to our quarters in the evenings. She said that so much happened in Sovereign House that she did not want to miss a thing. She looked tired, with dark shadows under her eyes, and she let me fuss over her.

"He is sending orders and counterorders several times a day," she said. "It is soon full moon. He is waiting to see what Anji will tell him then. I have never seen Father this way before. It worries him that the battles are being fought so far away from Renka."

"From Anji, you mean. But if the enemy was overpowering his forces, could he not simply order them to retreat?"

"Have you ever seen Father withdraw from anything? Admit defeat? You who never leave these quarters, what do you know of war! Of strategy!"

I looked at her, astonished. "As a woman, as the Vizier's wife, I am not permitted to leave Beauty's House. You know that." I attempted to change the subject. "You are exhausted, little one. You should not spend so much time in Sovereign House."

"I am Father's right hand," said Esiko. "He cannot do without me now that my elder brothers are away."

A shiver went along my spine. My father's right hand. That is what Iskan said when first I met him. My arms dropped limply at my sides. I looked at Esiko. She had her father's weak chin. His marked brows and thin nose. In many ways she was a mirror image of Iskan, which helped to conceal her sex. Yet, unlike her father, she very seldom smiled.

"I'm going to bed now, Mother. Make sure I am woken at dawn, and tell the servants to bring me breakfast in my bed. I am going directly to Father's house when I rise."

And off she went, leaving me alone with my musings and fears.

CLARÁS

I used to work down at the port. I received several men every night. The poorest of the seamen, the ones who couldn't afford a beautiful woman, or even a normal one. Only a handsome face fetches a handsome price. Nobody wanted to attend to these men. Not even me. You never knew if they could pay. They were old and reeking, and missing fingers and teeth. When the rich man came, in fine clothes and with good-smelling oils in his hair, and wanted to buy a night with me, nobody could believe it. Least of all me.

But he didn't want the choice ones; the beautiful ones. He was drawn to the ugly and disfigured. Like me.

One night wasn't enough for him. He wanted to own me.

The other girls in the pleasure house were jealous. They dressed up in their finery and tried to entice the man into buying them instead. But it was me he bid for. I thought my life would become easier. No more nights receiving man after man. Never again worrying about food or clothes or a roof over my head. I sent the money he bought me for to my parents. Then I followed him, with no more belongings than the clothes on my back.

He took me to Ohaddin: the capital. I had never been there before. I had never left the sea before. The palace grounds were the size of the whole port town. The houses were tall, the roofs high, the gardens fragrant. Never could I have imagined such a place.

I strained my neck as I was brought through the entrance of the dairahesi. I couldn't see the sea.

The golden doors were locked behind me. I ran over to a window and looked out. I saw roofs and trees and green fields beyond. But couldn't so much as smell a hint of the sea.

I was one of the last to come to the dairahesi. But I was the first who decided to escape.

ꚙ

I came to Ohaddin late one summer, soon after the war in which the man's three eldest sons were killed. I think that is why he was drawn to me—he wanted someone to degrade. The dairahesi was full of the smells of incense that the wife burned in memory of her sons. I hardly saw her at that time. When I caught glimpses of her, she would walk slowly and uncertainly, as if she didn't know where she was. Always supported by her youngest son, Orano. Her face was like parchment. An old, broken woman.

The women in the dairahesi ignored me. They didn't want to see my disfigured face. They were afraid that if they were pregnant and looked at me their children would be deformed like me. The only ones who spoke to me and seemed not to care about my cloven lip were the servant girl Estegi and the dark woman they called Orseola. She was much older than I, but still we became something similar to friends.

Time in the dairahesi was slow. Like syrup. As a child, I worked for my family, for our very survival. With my father and brother in the boat, day in, day out. I set fishing lines and nets, took fish out of the net, cleaned them. Dived for mussels and oysters. Hunted big fish with a harpoon. I was useful, a part of our vital web. In work it didn't matter what I looked like. But in the dairahesi there was nothing to do. My hands lay idle on my lap. I dried up slowly, and withered.

242

ϖ

It was early autumn when I discovered I was with child. I decided at once that this child would not be born in captivity. It would not be his child: only mine. And it was my duty to give it a life worth living.

ϖ

One night I dreamed that I sat at the fore of a fishing boat with the wind in my hair. The air smelled salty. The boat below me was very small, but sleek and strong, with gray-green sails. As soon as I woke up, I searched for Orseola.

I found her by the pond in the courtyard, where she was sitting and dunking her dreamsnares in the water. She called it drowning dreams. Who knows what she meant.

"Was it you who showed me the boat?"

Orseola shook her head. Her arms were dark with moisture. She didn't look up, but her hands had stopped working.

"No. But I saw it. Most beautiful dream I have seen here." Her voice was quiet and emotionless. Then she looked at me and raised her eyebrows. "The taste of freedom will stay with me all day."

That was her way. She changed mood from one moment to the next. Unpredictable as a summer storm.

"The boat will be mine," I said. "I'll name it *Naondel*."

"Where will you sail? Home, little stickleback?"

"Yes." I waited until she looked at me again. "Home to the sea. You know that the house where I grew up is no longer my home."

Orseola shook her head. "No dowry, little stickleback. What a tragic story. Ach, ach, so sad. Forced to sell your body. The only one of us who came here of her own free will."

Bitter words rose in my throat, but I gritted my teeth. "Wherever the sea is, there is my home."

She turned away and gathered her pile of dreamsnares. The pearls and bones glimmered wet and cleaned.

"You can find me a boat," I said. "Search through the dreams that come to you. Somebody must own a gray fishing boat, small and sturdy, with a slender hull and gray-green sail. I know it. *Naondel* showed herself to me because she should be mine."

"Can you sail far in such a boat?" asked Orseola, still looking away.

"As far as you like as long as you have food and water."

"There is a land beyond the southern sea," she said. "Terasu. There may be some still who live there. Who may have forgiven me by now."

I looked at her. She was unpredictable. But she had greater freedom than the others in the dairahesi. She left Beauty's House sometimes and was allowed to move around the Sovereign's palace. And as I had asked her to search for a boat, she was already party to my plan. I wanted to escape. No point in denying it.

"Can we get protection there?"

She gave no reply. Something had happened in her homeland, that much I knew. But I didn't know what, nor what awaited her there.

I looked up at the patch of blue sky above us. A single cloud drifted slowly past. One that promised calm weather and sun. I turned to Orseola, and bound my fate to hers.

"We can sail there. But you have to help me find the boat. She exists somewhere. You can search through dreams from the coast."

Orseola removed her hands from her face. Shrugged her shoulders. As if the whole idea were of no interest to her. "But how to get to the coast? How to get out?"

"We can worry about that later. First we need a boat."

Days passed. The child inside me was growing. The man knew; he told me it was a daughter and that he would allow her to live. His words didn't matter. He wasn't the one who would decide this child's fate—I was.

ω

Orseola came to me a little later. I had just returned from the man's bed.

"Have you found the boat?" I asked.

"No. But I have seen another dream. Sulani and Estegi are planning their escape."

She looked at me.

I shook my head.

"No. They are creatures of the land. They know nothing of the sea, of storms, of watery depths and sails."

"Sulani knows water," Orseola objected. "Rivers. And she is strong, her soul means to shine and she will let nothing stand in her way."

"Neither will I."

"Estegi can move more freely than we. She is only a servant; she is not watched. She can gather supplies."

"I don't trust them."

"You do not trust me either," said Orseola. "But you need me. And we also need a warrior and a spy."

I thought about what she had said. I listened inwardly. And I came to the conclusion that she was right. A warrior and a spy would make it easier to escape.

So Orseola brought them to my room one evening. Sulani sat down on a cushion close inside the door. From the first moment she was the one to keep guard and protect us. Estegi brought tea and fruit. She always treated me as equal to the others. I liked her for that. I wondered why she wanted to flee. She was not imprisoned here, not in the same way we were.

I made them swear an oath first. An oath not to reveal our plan of escape to anybody. They swore without protest. Sulani on her river. Orseola on the memory of her mother. Estegi on her secret. I looked at her. Tried to guess what she might be hiding. She was always so calm. She seemed so secure and certain.

I swore on my unborn child.

We spoke in low voices. Orseola explained. Sulani questioned and challenged. She started to outline a plan and made a list of necessary items. I added the things the others seemed not to know about: rope, sails, shelter from rain and sea. Sulani knew a lot about drying and preserving food. Estegi knew even more. We agreed to begin setting aside all the food we were given that could be preserved. We couldn't take it directly from the store, else it would be discovered, but we could take it from our own portions. Estegi knew of an unused, forgotten storeroom where we could keep it all.

When they had left, I sat by my window and stared out toward the sea. My room faced west, but if I pressed my face against the grate, on clear days I could just about see a shimmer far off in the south. That night the wind set in from the south and I could feel the breath of the sea on my skin.

Soon, I whispered, to the sea and to my child. Soon.

I wondered which of the women would betray us. The thought didn't worry me. That is the way of people: unreliable, dishonest. Not like animals. Animals are neither good nor wicked, only themselves.

But I had a plan. I was doing something, for myself and for the child. That was all that mattered. To have something to work toward. The fish in my belly swished its tail.

ʊ

We, the oath-sworn, had gathered in the bathing room on the ground floor to talk undisturbed. Nobody was there, the hot and cold baths were empty and shone in the light of our lamps, but still I was afraid that somebody might hear.

"We must fight our way free," I whispered. "With weapons."

Sulani scoffed. "None of you know how to wield weapons. And we have none, besides. It is too dangerous. Too risky."

"Are you not a warrior?" I asked.

"Was. I was a warrior." She looked at me darkly. "You three do not know how to wield weapons." Estegi laid a hand on her arm and spoke to her in soothing tones. As one does to a seal that has become tangled in a fishing net. Estegi's hand rested on her sinewy arm for a long time. I looked at them.

Then I looked away.

"There are not many guards," I whispered. "At night there are only two. We lure them in somehow, then strike them unconscious. We don't need weapons for that."

"But if we do not succeed, they will raise the alert at once," objected Sulani.

"If they were sleeping, I could come up from the servants' quarters and steal the keys," said Estegi. "To open the doors and let you all out and lock up behind you, so as no one would even know you were awake."

"Orseola can give them dreams," I whispered.

"I cannot make them sleep," said Orseola.

"No, but you can give them dreams when they sleep. If they fall asleep at their post. Before the night of the escape. Dreams that give them . . ."

I searched for an idea of something that could help us. "Dreams that are so beautiful that they want to return to them and carry on sleeping. When they are asleep, you give them such sweet dreams that they don't want to wake when we take the keys and leave."

"It will not work. How can we trust that they will sleep deeply enough? That they will sleep at all? We cannot wait, night after night, in the hope that this will happen." Sulani leaned carefully against the wall and grimaced. The man had hurt her badly, again. Estegi leaped to her feet at once to fetch a cushion and make Sulani comfortable. Then she picked up one of the bottles that stood in the niche that ran around the bathing pools, and poured a little of the sharp-smelling oil into her hands. Then she began to massage Sulani's feet. Sulani muttered something in protest but let her continue. Then Estegi spoke. Which she seldom did.

"I think we should make them sleep. With a drink. Garai could surely make one for us."

"No!" I raised my voice. "The more we are, the worse our chances."

"We could dig a tunnel," Sulani proposed. "From here, from the baths. At night there is no one here to see what we are doing."

"That would take years!" I threw up my arms in exasperation. "I need to leave this place before my child is born."

I left the others, frustrated, and returned to my room. It had been a mistake to invite new people into my plan. We couldn't even agree on how we would escape.

ᚹ

One day we were all herded out of the palace together. We were given no warning about what was about to happen. After the autumn, when Karenokoi had suffered such defeat, we were given less and less information about what was happening outside Ohaddin. I believe that the wife and Garai knew. But they rarely spoke to us. They went out first, warmly dressed in quilted jackets and piles of shawls. Orano walked by Kabira's side. Mother and son were both dressed in bright white to signify their grief for the dead sons. Estegi and the other servants were carrying parasols and cushions and baskets of food. The rest of us walked behind, out into the garden. The air was cold and the sky was high. It was early winter. My first in the palace. From the animal park in the southeast came the roar of unknown animals and the screech of foreign birds. I wished I could visit the animals there. To afford them a little comfort in their imprisonment. Maybe even set them free.

A stage had been built in the south part of the garden, by the edge of the pond, but it was empty. The guards led us to a platform that was screened off from the outside world by garishly painted screens. We sat down on the cushions the servants were setting out. Next to the wife there was a fire pot, and thick animal hides were spread over her legs. Some of the children were whining and being shushed by their mothers. I pulled my hands into my

249

sleeves, away from the cold wind that was sweeping in from the mountains in the northwest.

We waited.

The Sovereign's women came with their children. The Sovereign's wife, an old white-haired lady, bent with age, arrived on a palanquin. Her daughters and grandchildren gathered around her, all wrapped up in expensive animal hides. Then a low hubbub could be heard from the other side of the painted screen as the rest of the court took their seats. The stage was still empty. I wondered whether a traveling theater company or musicians would appear. Nobody seemed to know. The servants were carrying around dishes with food and hot wine with honey. I took a bowl and warmed my cold fingers on it. I hadn't been cold since falling pregnant, apart from my fingers. Orano and Kabira sat in front of me. I couldn't hear what they were speaking about, but the wife asked her son something and he shrugged his shoulders. He would soon be a young man. I wondered how long he would be allowed to roam freely in the dairahesi. As the man's only surviving son, he had taken on a new role. He would surely be married off soon.

Not that this was any of my concern. I would soon be far away from here.

Then quiet fell over the murmuring crowd. Men were led onto the stage. They were naked, and their backs and legs were bloody from whip lashes. I understood at once what was about to happen. I did not want to be there. But guards surrounded our platform—there was no way out.

There were five men in total. One of them hardly more than a boy. He couldn't walk unaided and had to be dragged onto the stage by guards. These guards bore no resemblance to the ones who guarded the dairahesi. They had helmets and swords. They showed no mercy. Five sticks were soon raised on the edge of the stage. The men were bound tightly to them. The boy was barely conscious by this point.

The man appeared on the stage. He was dressed in a long, blue quilted cloak and high black boots, with a fur hat against the cold. He was as impeccably dressed and groomed as always, but his movements no longer had the control I was used to seeing. He paced the stage without looking at the men behind him.

He spoke but I didn't listen to his words. I did not want to hear—or see. Words reached me anyway: Traitors. Everyone is against me. Betrayed us. Blood on their hands. No secrets from me. Confessed.

The wounds the men bore could have made absolutely anybody confess, I thought.

Punishment. Death. A thousand small deaths. A warning to you all.

Orano shuddered. The wife said something, he stood up, she held him back. He looked as if he wanted to rush up onto the stage. His father looked at him and made an angry gesture. Slowly the boy sank down next to his mother.

Five men with white-painted, clean-shaven faces and heads entered the stage. The man disappeared out of sight, probably to join the rest of the court. The white-painted executioners carried blades with an unusual curve. Before I had time to look away, they began. One executioner per prisoner. With the knives they began to carve the meat from their bodies. Slice by slice. A thousand small deaths.

The men were screaming. Not loudly. Quiet, confused groans. One of them spoke. Pleaded his innocence. That he had done nothing, nothing at all.

I did not look. But I could not shut out the screams. Mothers hid their youngest children in their shawls. The older ones looked on, in horror and fascination. The servants brought around plates with sweet things and more honeyed wine. I sat and stared hard down into the bowl in my hands.

We sat there all day. A thousand small deaths takes a long time.

Sometimes I looked at Kabira and Orano. They were quiet at first, but then the wife started speaking more and more urgently to her son. He mostly just shook his head. Between some of the prisoners' screams I heard a few words.

"Will even this not make you understand?"

"Father would never harm me. Never!" Orano had stood up and was leaning over his mother. His face was very pale and his hands were shaking. He didn't look at the stage.

"He would consider it betrayal," said Kabira. She extended her hands toward Orano but he shied away.

"You are wrong! I am his only heir, I have committed no crime." His voice was shrill. He sounded like he was trying to convince himself.

After a while he sank back down onto the cushions next to his mother.

"I cannot lose you too. You are all I have left." Kabira turned to face her son. She was crying. I had never seen her express either joy or sorrow before that. Her bony hand grasped for her son's. He withdrew his and turned away. After a while she lowered her hand. The tears continued to run down her cheeks. Then she pulled a shawl over her head and I could no longer see her face.

It was evening by the time the last of the prisoners' moans had died out. From the corner of my eye I saw the men being taken down from the stakes. The man came up on stage again. He was standing taller now. His eyes were burning.

"Justice has been done!" he cried. "Those who have betrayed their Sovereign and their realm have received their due punishments! Let us celebrate. Music!"

While the musicians were making their way onto the stage, still slippery with blood, we women and children were taken back to our golden cage.

A shark eats when it is hungry. Sometimes it kills more than it needs, but that is its instinct. It does not torment its prey unnecessarily. Nature is cruel, they say, but never have I seen such cruelty in nature as I saw that day in Ohaddin.

ω

We were very rarely allowed to go out in the garden after the executions. The man's twisted suspicions had grown and he had increased the number of guards. I had planned for us to escape by climbing over the wall, but soon I realized that this was impossible. The man wanted to know where we were at all times. He suspected conspiracies and dangers around every corner. The stench of death and decay was closing in around him. His eyes were nearly entirely black now, only a little white around the iris. He still visited me, though my belly had begun to grow. It was as if he relished the unspeakable things he did with me—did to me—even more now that I was pregnant.

One sunny winter's day I went out to the little pond in the courtyard. I wanted to see some sky, and breathe some fresh air.

Maybe smell the scent of the sea. I missed the garden more than I thought I would.

The window shutters to the wife's residence stood open above me. I sat on the little bench by the pond and squinted in the sunlight.

"You told him?"

The wife's voice drifted out through the open shutters. Piercing and panicked.

Orano answered her. "Yes, Mother. And you were wrong. He did not reject me." The boy's voice was shrill with indignation.

"He will punish me! He will consider me guilty of high treason! Oh, do you understand nothing?"

"You are wrong, Mother." Orano tried to calm her down. But his voice was not calm, it was darting up and down like a swallow. "I explained that you so wanted to provide him with another son. That you did not understand the consequences of your actions."

The wife did not reply.

"He is not angry with you. Not . . . really."

"On Lehan's soul. He is going to take his revenge, but he knows how to bide his time. You are so blinded by Anji that you cannot see your father clearly, Esiko."

Why did Kabira call her son by a girl's name?

"You are wrong, Mother! I am nothing like him. And do not blame Anji!"

"No, the fault is mine for showing him the spring, once upon a time. I told him of her secrets. And now you are becoming as deranged by her power as he is!"

254

"I am not deranged," Orano—or Esiko—screeched. "And Father has not rejected me, so see how wrong you are!"

"Can you continue to be his son?" There was a challenge in the wife's voice.

We both had to wait for an answer.

"Outwardly. For a while. But I will keep to our quarters. He was . . . upset. I cannot go to Anji without him again." Orano said this last part hesitantly. Softly.

"That is one good thing in all of this at least."

"Anji is a part of me! Neither you nor Father can keep us apart!"

A door slammed.

A sob was heard. Just one.

Nothing else could be heard. I waited a moment. Then I came inside.

ᚹ

Orseola found *Naondel* on a midwinter's night when the cold, dry winds were sweeping over Ohaddin from the north. She woke me in the middle of the night. Her eyes were shining.

"I have found her!"

"Where?" I sat up, ready to rush out at once.

"A fisherman in Shukurin has her. He is ready to sell her if the price is right, I believe."

The boat. We had the boat! I stopped thinking about how we would escape the dairahesi. Now, instead, I was plagued day and night by thoughts of the buying price. I valued everything in the dairahesi with my eyes. Could it be stolen? Would anybody notice? Could it be sold? Kabira had eyes like a sea eagle. A girl had stolen from the dairahesi, and therefore from the man, some years before I came, Orseola told me. She had been executed, naturally, and the wife had been careful with inventory ever since. *Naondel*'s buying price was all around us, many times over, but there was no way for us to get hold of it. The wife and Garai had a lot of jewelry they had been given by the man, but Orseola and I owned almost nothing.

ʊ

The man was out on yet another of his expeditions. He was searching for something. Estegi said she had heard him say that he only needed two things: power over death, and an heir. I didn't care. Everything was calmer when he was away. I could be in peace. I was hungrier than before; the child inside me wanted its portion. But I still kept back as much as we could dry and save. Estegi pilfered a little from the stores. Our supplies were growing slowly but surely.

What we were lacking was money. And time.

It was not yet spring, but we had to leave during the pre-summer forward winds. That is what I had decided. I should still be carrying the child inside me by then. We hadn't long.

"Can we not just take the boat?" whispered Sulani one night in Orseola's room, where we had started to meet. Orseola rarely slept at night anyway.

"It's in Shukurin now," I answered. "It's two days' travel there by foot. We've not that much time. One night only. Come morning light, his guards and soldiers will come to find us before we've got halfway. But if we can get *Naondel* sailed up along the river to Ameka, the town west of Ohaddin, then we can reach it before dawn. And I don't believe they will search for us on the river."

"I do not want to steal," said Estegi. "My cousin can bring our money to Shukurin and sail it to Ameka."

"Attempting to steal a boat is risky. It might be there, or not. It might be locked, maybe with a chain. Someone might discover and pursue us." Sulani sighed. "Oh well. So we must buy it. But we cannot get that kind of money together."

"I can sell my jewelry." Orseola was lying on her back on her bed and staring up at the dreamsnares spinning slowly around on their threads.

"What jewelry?" I had never seen her wear anything other than dreamsnares.

"The ones the Sovereign gave me in thanks. For the dreams I have woven." She rolled onto her stomach and pulled out a jewelry box from under her bed. Estegi, Sulani and I leaned forward. When Orseola lifted the lid, all three of us gasped. The box was filled with hair chains of silver and gold, arm bands, finger rings, ankle chains and many other ornaments. Everything in silver or gold and set with many precious stones.

"Could you not have mentioned this before?" Sulani's voice was quiet and full of menace.

"Dead things of metal." Orseola shrugged her shoulders. "I forgot I had them."

ᴡ

The man's absence made it easier for Estegi to sell the jewelry. She was no saleswoman, she did not know how to haggle. She had never visited the bazaars outside the palace walls before. She was swindled. Still, we made enough for *Naondel*. We dared not sell everything; it attracted watchful eyes and questions. But an anklet

257

and a few hair chains were enough to buy an old fishing boat. Then we sent Estegi to ask her cousin to buy it from the fisherman and sail it up to Ameka. The night I learned through Estegi's whispers that she had succeeded in the task was the best of my life since I had left my father and mother's little mortar house by the sea.

I had begun to grow heavy and was finding it more and more difficult to move. I knew that we had no time to lose. The child could not be born in Ohaddin. *Naondel* was our way out. Freedom was close. But then Iona came to the dairahesi. Her arrival changed everything.

IONA

I, Daera, chronicle this account on Iona's behalf, as she can no longer do it herself. This is Iona's story, from before she came to Ohaddin.

T he island smelled of honey. The scent reached Iona long before she could clearly distinguish the island through the heat haze. She was surprised. She had been prepared for many eventualities, but had not imagined that the island would have a fragrance of its own. As the boat neared land, its origin was revealed. The black rocks were dotted with delicate flowers. The island looked hard and uninviting in the distance. It consisted of rocks reminiscent of giant, slanted lizard scales with razor-sharp edges. But between these scales grew hardy wee flowers in pink, yellow, purple and white. They were the source of the scent. She took it as a good omen.

She undressed before stepping on land, as Alinda had instructed her. The oarsman sat with his back to her. If he turned around it would be punishable by death. But he did not concern her in the least. Was he old or young? Fair or dark? Haggard or handsome? It did not matter. As she removed her coat and gold-embroidered slippers, her silken dress and underclothes, it was not the gaze of men that occupied her thoughts.

Mild breezes brushed her skin like fine silk; they served as sufficient clothing for her. She climbed out of the boat with a single step and knocked on the thwart as a signal to the oarsman. She did not look back when she heard the creaking of the oars.

She had no need to see the boat grow smaller and smaller and disappear into the distance. She knew what was happening. She knew the oarsman was rowing away, never to return. She was concerned only with what lay before her.

The island was the size of a large pasture, rounded like a small hill, where no trees or bushes grew. At its highest point stood the small temple. The sky was a brilliant blue, holding the island in a tender embrace. Alinda was right, thought Iona: it is beautiful. She stood there awhile with her feet in the cool water, feeling the stones roll under her soles. There was no other place on earth she would rather be. It was a wondrous sensation. To know that one has found her place.

She took her time walking up to the temple. She wanted to prolong each moment. Sea-snatchers flew all around her like bolts of silver lightning. The air was filled with their shrill cries. They made their nests on the roof of the temple as they had done for hundreds of years. They had seen girls like her come to the island throughout the ages, consumed with their mission. The birds had never seen any of the girls leave.

Iona would be the first.

The rocks hurt her feet, but she thought nothing of it. Soon pain would cease to matter, she thought, and was filled with a joy so intense it made her quite dizzy. To think that all this had been granted to her! A butterfly fluttered past, lemon-yellow wings with edges tinged as black as grief. She was surprised to see it this far from the mainland, but then she understood that the flowers provided nourishment for it and its kind, and they in turn became food for the birds who fertilized the flowers with their droppings. The perfect cycle of life and death. Another good omen. Never had she felt the presence of the cycle so profoundly. Never had she encountered such a feeling of holiness.

She climbed the last part up to the temple that awaited her, and her alone. It was small and gray, built with a type of stone not unlike the black island rocks. To one ignorant of its existence it would be easy to sail past. This was intentional. Here only the anointed may come. On the ground around the temple was a circle of white shards that, according to the beliefs of Iona's people, represented an unbroken protective ring around the heart. She had been told of the circle but it was a different thing to see it with her own eyes. A shiver went along her spine as she carefully stepped over the white splinters and on toward the temple.

The door was colored eggshell blue but the paint had flaked to reveal the bare gray wood underneath. She wrinkled her forehead, perplexed and incensed that disrepair could be permitted in this holy place. She took a deep breath and stepped inside.

It was a bare little room. In one corner stood a table with a little velvet-dressed altar laid with the athame, the stone, and the bread, in the form of some dry ears of wheat. Two windows, one on each side of the house, let light in through windowpanes of real glass, but the glass was so flyspecked and dingy that it was difficult to see through. The floor was bare. There were no traces of the previous anointees.

Iona had expected something different. Something . . . more. She thought about the temple back home, with all its grand chambers and halls. All the gold, the silk cloths, the carved red wood, the fragrances of incense and costly oils. Wax candles in every room. And Alinda's residence. Even the chamber where she received pilgrims had thick mats of blue and gold on its floor, and walls embellished with painted frescoes of The Eternal Cycle. One of them depicted this very island, with the temple on its summit, and a bloody sea foaming against the rocks.

Iona reflected that the artist had forgotten about the flowers.

She went in. The floor was cold beneath her feet. She walked forward to the altar table and touched the ears of wheat. They crumbled apart. They must have been very old. The athame's blade was blunt. Only the stone looked as it always had, gray and smooth with a light band around it, dissecting a lighter circle in its center. In the temple back home the stones were polished until they were perfectly even and smooth, and often oiled until they shone. It was clear that the only polishing this stone had received was from the ocean itself. She thought to herself, contrarily, that it was more beautiful than all the temple stones, because it was pure unto itself.

There, too, it smelled of honey. She saw no signs of the previous anointee. Iona reemerged, knowing that her most important task was at hand. The sun was high in the sky, and it warmed her neck and back as she searched among the rocks along the shore. First she walked around the entire island, focusing on the rocky crevices along the waterfront. Then she widened her search to the shallow water surrounding the land. It was turquoise and clear, free from seaweed, and though she could see far, she found nothing other than sea urchins and mussels. When night came and the sun sank down in streaks and banks of rose, purple and gold, she was still empty-handed.

With the darkness came the cold. She was above things like cold and pain now. This was what she had been taught. She went into the temple and lay down on the floor. It was as cold as ice.

She tried to hear Alinda's voice inside her. What would she have advised now? "This is a holy place. Not a place for the body, but for the mind. Think, Iona. What is required of you?"

At once she knew, and her mind became calm. She sat up and prayed.

So passed the first night.

ω

The dawn was magnificent. Iona's joints were stiff from the night of cold discomfort, but to see the sun rise, to see day conquer night yet again, restored hope and warmth within her. She resumed her searching at once. Carefully, without stepping on a single sea urchin, she waded out until she came to deeper water and could start swimming. It was one of the first things she had had to learn as the anointee: to swim, for this very purpose. The waters around the Matheli Peninsula were warm and the seabed was sandy. Alinda used to hold her up by the belly and speak to her in her soft, silky voice. She had been so proud of Iona when she took her first strokes on her own. Iona had been proud of herself. After that she took every opportunity to swim and dive. Just as she took every opportunity to practice all the skills her anointment required.

How strange that she was finally here. In the very time and place all her schooling had centered around. That the last ten years of her life had been preparing for. This was the end.

She dived in. The sea enveloped her and shut out all sounds. She opened her eyes.

The water was clearer than in Matheli. She could see to the bottom. Small fish caught the light as they swam by. Salt stung her eyes, but she forced herself to keep them open. She swept her eyes across the ocean floor below. Stones, sand, rocks, sea urchins. How would she ever find what she sought?

This was her mission. Failure was unthinkable. She said a prayer—not one of Alinda's, but a prayer of her own making; imbued with a feeling rather than a prayer of prepared words. Then she came up for air, and dived down again. Spying, scouting. Stones, sand, sea urchins, fish. Came back up for air. Continued, stroke after stroke.

A white glint in a crack in the rocks caught her attention. When she had to come up for air, she did not open her eyes at all above the water's surface, so as not to be blinded by the sun. She dived back down. Opened her eyes. There, in a crack among rocks newly disturbed, something shone white. She swam down and stretched out her hands. The skull was stuck fast in the crack and she had to pry it loose. The rocky edges were sharp and ripped open a gash on her wrist. She felt no pain, but saw her red blood seep through the skull's empty eye sockets.

Blood. Blood attracted predators. She lifted her gaze, and for the first time looked out through the sea instead of down to the bottom. It was never-ending. She could see far, until eventually everything disappeared into dark, unfathomable depths. Depths that could conceal absolutely anything. Absolutely anything might be drawn here by the smell of her blood.

She was gripped by an unexpected and all-consuming fear. She gasped and got a mouth and lungful of sea water. She had to get away, at once. She kicked herself upward with several strong strokes and burst through the surface, coughing for air. At any moment something could grab hold of her, drag her down underwater, sink teeth and claws into her defenseless flesh. She kicked gracelessly to shore, scraped her belly on the sharp rocks, scratched a knee on a sea urchin—there must be more and more blood filling the water, she had to get up, away, she had to escape. Coughing and trembling, she staggered onto land. She could not stay by the water's edge, she must go farther, into the temple, as far from the sea as she possibly could. Only when the door slammed shut behind her did she dare stop, and her breathing slowed.

She held the skull wedged under one arm. She laid it carefully down on the velvet, next to the athame, stone and wheat. Then she mustered the courage to peek out of the window.

The ocean spanned huge and glittering around the island. Nothing other than the waves broke the surface. Nothing could be seen to move out there except birds. It was difficult to say for sure, as the windowpanes were so dirty. Long she stood and gazed. Then she went to the other window and continued to stare. She did not go outside.

As the sun began to sink toward the horizon, Iona sat on the floor, examining her wounds. None of them was especially deep, but she knew that they could start to smart and fester if she did not wash them. Yet she had nothing to wash or bind them with. Nothing like that would be found here. This was not a place for living: it was a place for dying. She had believed that she was prepared for her death, but on that day she saw that her certainty had been false, her confidence an illusion. She covered her face with her hands in shame. How could she disappoint Alinda so? Disappoint all of Matheli, all the faith the people had vested in her? To be the offering, that others might live and thrive and reproduce. Her role in The Eternal Cycle was clear: her death, for their life.

She sat and prayed. But she came upon no answer, not in the received prayers, not inside herself. Only when the colors of the sunset filled the dirty windowpanes did a thought occur to her. Something she had been taught. Not from Alinda, not in Matheli, but at home on the farm. She had so few memories from there. Milk warm from the cow. The scent of cut grass. Red poppies in her hands. A song, an embrace, a few words. And then a piece of advice, uttered by someone aged—not her mother, she believed, but someone even older. Father's mother? A near-toothless mouth telling her how to clean wounds if nothing else was at hand.

She sat up straight. There were no bowls in the temple. No vessels at all. Nothing that could serve her purpose. Except the skull.

She stood up and walked over to the altar. The skull was entirely smooth and clean. It had been lying in the water for a long time and small fish and crabs had polished away the tiniest last fragments of flesh. All the teeth remained in the jaws. The skull was surprisingly small. Either she had been a slight one, Iona's predecessor, or very young. She had been sent to the island when Alinda was still a child. Many years of plenty had followed the offering, so they had not had reason to send another anointee for a long time. Therefore Iona was permitted to reside in Matheli for ten whole years.

Iona wondered what her name had been.

Suddenly it struck her: she had never heard their names. Her predecessors were all of them nameless girls. How soon would it be before her own name was forgotten?

"Forgive me," she whispered to the girl's skull.

She squatted and held the skull between her thighs. She had

not drunk anything since leaving the mainland. On the island one had to fast. There was nothing to eat, nothing to drink. But she had not relieved herself since she arrived—the thought had not even occurred to her—and she was able to fill the skull halfway. She braved her way outside the temple door and carefully cleaned the sores on her stomach, thighs and legs, feet and toes with her own urine. It stung, which was good. It meant it was cleaning the wounds.

She knew that she should wash the skull, but she could not bring herself to leave the temple and go down to the sea. She laid the skull beside her on the floor, huddled up next to it and felt a little less alone.

So passed Iona's second day on the island.

ᛒ

The next morning the wind was up. Gray cloud banks chased each other across the sky. She was very cold, and nearly delirious with thirst. The salt water she had swallowed the day before had only worsened her thirst. She knew what she must do next: shatter the skull against the rocks, with help from the stone and blade, and spread the shards in a white circle around the temple so that her predecessor might be reunited with her sisters. Just as she had done with the skull of her predecessor before her. Just as the next girl would do with Iona's skull when she came here. That was the rite, that was the code. That was how she had been taught. If she did not fulfil this, one of the most important parts of her destiny, what was all her learning worth? What was her life worth?

Yet she could not bring herself to do it. Not just yet. The skull was her only company. Her only vessel. She had already defiled it with urine. That must be taboo. So what would it matter if she did not then fulfill her task immediately. She would do it, a little later.

She sat on the floor and watched the sun rise through the dirty eastern window, and suddenly the sight of the dingy glass filled her with a sanctimonious rage. She took the skull with her down to the sea, not caring whether there was something hiding in the depths, waiting to seize her as soon she set foot in the water. That was why she was there after all. She filled the skull with water, carried it up to the temple and leaned it against the wall so that no water spilled. Then she went to the altar, removed the stone, wheat and athame and turned the velvet cushion upside down. She was lucky, for the velvet cloth was attached to the bottom of the wood only with small tacks, which were easy to pick out with the blade. Only when she had gotten halfway through the row of tacks did she realize what she was doing. She was desecrating an altar. She dropped the athame to the floor. It was abhorrent. How could she?

She gazed out of the window, at the bare floor, the undecorated altar, the paint that had flaked off the door. The whole temple had been desecrated through unconcern and neglect.

She picked up the athame, removed the last tacks, and unfurled the velvet cloth. She laughed out loud.

"Well, aren't we lucky," she said to the skull.

The cloth was folded several times and was more than four times larger than the cushion itself. She could even wrap herself up in it at night. But first she would give the temple the devotion it deserved.

With the water in the skull and the velvet cloth she cleaned and polished the windows as well as she could. Then she washed the cloth and laid it out to dry on the rocks by the temple. It lay like a giant red flag shining in the sun. If anyone from Matheli came sailing past to see whether the offering had been fulfilled, they would see what she had done from far away.

She opened the temple door and climbed on it to get up to the roof. As she struggled to her feet, her hunger and thirst made the world spin around her, and she had to sit down. Once the dizziness had subsided, she stayed standing a moment and just looked. The ocean was sparkling, and infinite in every direction. There were no other islands to be seen. She was alone in the world, alone with her fate. Until that moment she had been too focused to see what was around her. Nothing had been of any importance but the temple and her tasks. She turned her attention to the roof.

She had hoped that a depression somewhere might have collected water from the recent rains. None had. She fought back tears. A sea-snatcher dived past her, very close, and landed in its nest. Suddenly she saw that camouflaged against the gray roof were dozens of nests filled with eggs.

The birds fought back, swooping at her with beak and claw. She did not take all the eggs from the same nest. She sucked them raw, sitting on the roof among the angry birds and falling feathers. They tasted wonderful.

The eggs made her strong again. There were mussels in the sea, and sea urchins, if she could catch them without hurting her hands. But she was not ready to enter the water again. She no longer knew if she was ready to die. She sat with the skull in her arms on the lee side of the temple, waiting for the velvet cloth to dry.

The skull looked at her with its empty eye sockets and Iona went back to wondering what her name might have been. It felt important that she had a name, that she was a person. She had never named anything before, not even one of the temple hounds. Now she could give her predecessor a name, and therefore an identity as someone more than just the offering, the chosen one, the skull. It was difficult. She did not know how names were chosen. She tried to invent an original name, but it felt ridiculous. She ran her fingers along the jaws of the skull, along the smooth surface of the cheekbones.

She was so fragile and small. And so dead. She had entered into death long before Iona. As had Iona's sister, about whom she remembered nothing but her name.

"Mizra," she said, and Mizra smiled at her with her bared teeth.

So passed Iona's third day on the island.

ʊ

The wind continued for several days. The surf crashed against the island in a steady rhythm, like the beating of a heart. There were no more birds' eggs. She could not catch the birds themselves. The salty meat of mussels only worsened her thirst. There was no rain on the horizon.

She wrapped herself up in the velvet and went down to the beach with Mizra and the athame.

She had come here to die. But now she was slowly perishing of hunger and thirst—a prolonged death wholly unlike the one she had been prepared for. When she had found Mizra, she had started to fear the monster. Now she welcomed it. She wanted to die as Mizra had: a quick, honorable and meaningful death.

Looking into the empty eye sockets, Iona hoped with all her heart that that truly had been the nature of Mizra's death.

She raised the athame. At first the blunt blade did nothing more than scratch her palm. It is difficult to consciously hurt oneself. She made contact and pressed firmly until the skin yielded and red blood trickled forth. She squeezed as much as she could into the sea.

"Here I am!" she cried into the wind. "Come and take me!"

She licked the last drops from her palm. She hoped that the blood would be bait enough. She had surely bled more when she had been swimming and found Mizra, yet that had lured nothing out from the deep. Perhaps what was needed was a purposeful offering. She did not know. Alinda had never said anything about it. In her stories the chosen one came to the temple island, performed the proper rites with the remains of her predecessor, and then her death arose from the sea.

Could it be because she had not smashed Mizra, and therefore the circle was incomplete? Iona still could not bring herself to do it. She had named her. Mizra was hers now. She no longer belonged to the island. They belonged to each other.

Iona gazed out to sea. She pulled a corner of the cloth over her head to shelter her eyes from the glare of the water. There, far off on the horizon, she could see a dark speck. The first thing that had broken the uniformity since the day she arrived.

She sat down with Mizra in her lap and the athame in her hand, and waited for her monster.

ᴖ

He came in a boat. He did not look as she had imagined. He was not a giant, with teeth longer than she was tall, and talons as sharp as scythes. He was an ordinary man, in clothes of silk, and with gold on his chest. He did not even appear to bear any weapons. His boat was small, with a single sail and a canvas stretched over the bow.

She sat motionless and waited for him. Once he had reached the island he cast his anchor, jumped into the water and waded the last way into land, dragging the boat with a rope before mooring it to a rock.

When she saw his eyes, she knew her time had come. They did not belong to a human, nor an animal. They were nearly wholly black; they were the eyes of a monster. She stood up and let the cloth fall to the ground. She bared her breasts and let the athame fall with a clanging sound against the rocks. Alinda had not given her any words with which to meet her death.

"Greetings," she said.

He looked her up and down. She understood then that this monster needed neither talons nor teeth. He was equally dangerous without them. She could see hunger in his eyes, a hunger that no offering in the world could satisfy.

"Well met," he replied, and smiled. He was neither old nor young, beautiful nor ugly, yet his smile was that of a primeval predatory beast.

He did nothing, however. He did not approach her, he raised no weapon, he did nothing to enact the offering.

It filled her with uncertainty. She did not want to wait any longer. She bent down and picked up the athame, took a step forward and handed it to him.

272

"Here. Do it quickly."

She closed her eyes. She was not so brave that she could meet her death with eyes open. Hunger and thirst were making it difficult for her to stand upright any longer. Soon her legs gave way.

Arms caught her and laid her down on the soft velvet. When she opened her eyes, her gaze met his. His eyes were dark and, if possible, even more filled with hunger. Yet he made no attack.

"Wait," he said and disappeared from sight. She shut her eyes again. Against one of her hips, hidden under the velvet, she could feel the lump made by Mizra. She was giving her strength to endure whatever might come.

Soon a shadow fell over her. "Here," said the voice, but she could no longer keep her eyes open. What good would it serve? Something pressed against her lips. She parted them, and cool, fresh water trickled into her mouth. She coughed, then drank, long and deep.

He gave her bread, but she could not eat much. She was so tired. He moved to and fro between the boat and the temple, carrying something. Then carrying her. She clung to the velvet, and to Mizra inside it. He laid her on the temple floor, but this time there was something between her and the floor, something warm and soft. He pulled the velvet over her.

She slept.

When she awoke, she was given more to drink. She ate something, maybe fish. And something else sweet and juicy: some fruit. She slept. He did not touch her.

ᚹ

When she awoke, the monster was crouching by the door and

273

looking at her. She sat up and drank more water. She was naked: there was no point in hiding her body. He had already seen it. It belonged to him.

The eyes of the hungry one were shining. Iona tried to suppress her fear. She tried to keep her heartbeat as steady as the tide. She tried to meet her fate with pride and strength, as Alinda had taught her. She had diverged from the path, broken the circle, but it had reclaimed her and sent her fate in a form she could never have imagined, yet which now seemed inevitable.

"Do you feel better now?" He got up and stood before her, as a tower obscuring the light.

"Yes. Thank you." She understood why he had helped her to convalesce. An exhausted prey was no challenge. She was glad. She did not want to be weak.

"Have you been here long?" He turned to look out of the window.

"How long have I been sleeping?"

"A day and a night."

"Then I have been here for . . . I do not know exactly. Many days."

"Without food or drink?" He shaded his eyes with his hand and looked out over the sea, as if he were searching for something. Her search was over. This was what she had been waiting for.

"I ate birds' eggs and mussels."

"In my land there are tales of your creed. That you sacrifice virgins to a beast on a barren island in the middle of nothingness. I did not believe it was true."

"I am committing myself to The Eternal Cycle," she said. He laughed.

"I mean no offense. But you do understand that there is no monster? That the girls come here and slowly starve to death?" He looked up at the temple. "But still there is a presence . . . an energy. It drew me here. I am interested in sources of power, you see. All the stories I hear about springs with the power to heal, about mountains that bestow wisdom, about rituals that grant eternal life"—he looked at her askance—"I must investigate. Most are untrue, or contain fragments of what was once true. Some, however . . ." He looked distracted, as though dreaming. "Some turn out to be true. And I see to it that I make the true sources my own. Else I destroy them, so that nobody else may utilize their power."

"You make mountains your own?" She tried to understand what he meant.

"If need be. An area can be conquered. Streams can be staunched. Knowledge can be recorded and removed. Objects . . . I have a library full of scrolls containing knowledge the rest of the world could not dream of."

"What are you doing here?"

She could not help but ask, though she knew the answer. He was here to take her life. He could deny that he—the monster—existed all he wanted. She recognized a monster when she saw one.

"I have sailed a small fleet of ships east from my land in search of more sources of power. The spring from whence I draw my power is not sufficient. I have discovered vulnerabilities." He tensed his jaws a moment and was quiet. Iona waited. He turned to look out of the window, to gather himself before continuing. "We sailed to Matheli to learn more of your creed. I received confirmation and moreover was told that a fresh girl had just been sent here to die. I left my ships in Matheli, so as not to attract attention, and sailed here alone." He smiled at her, baring all of his white teeth. "And I found you."

His fangs were visible as he bent over Iona. She exposed her neck, like prey. Yet he began groping at his trousers, his hands fumbling with the drawstring. His breathing became heavy and his eyes misted over. He took out his member; it was engorged. She understood at once what he wanted, and it was not her death.

"No!" she screamed, and crawled back onto the sleeping mat. "You must not defile me, must not sully the offering!"

He was down on his knees, already between her legs, groaning and panting.

"There is nothing to make an offering to," he said. She thought of her people and the drought of recent years and knew he was wrong. She kicked and tried to clamp her thighs together, but he pried them apart with his strong legs. He was the monster, everything a monster should be, and yet it was wrong, this was not how it should be.

"You are supposed to kill me!" she screamed. He sneered, saliva dripping onto her belly.

"If you insist. Afterward."

He was ruining everything—this was the moment she had been waiting for her whole life and he was taking it away from her.

"No!" she screamed, and fought all the more wildly. He pushed her, hard, and as she fell backward her hand found Mizra's skull under the cloth and a new strength flowed through her.

He recoiled, gasping.

"What was that?"

Her fingers found their way underneath the cloth to the smooth bone, into Mizra's eye sockets. She became completely calm. The monster receded and before her there was but a man with a slackened member.

"You do not touch me," she said. It was not a command, but a certainty. He retreated farther, until his back was pressed against the far wall.

He nodded. Looked at the lump under the cloth: Mizra. "Such power."

"Go now."

He left her.

Iona wrapped the velvet cloth around her and bound Mizra in a fold at her hip. The athame lay on the floor next to her, perhaps because he had thought to use it when he was finished with her. She tucked it into the cloth at her waist, and wrapped the stone from the altar into the hem. She looked around her. Now all that was left was the sleeping mat, his wineskin, and the little altar table. A bare room that had seen so much suffering. Then she stepped out into the sunshine and closed the flaking door behind her. The man was nowhere to be seen. With one hand on Mizra she walked around the temple, inside the white circle. She wondered whether he had spoken the truth. Had all the chosen ones starved to death? All those girls before her? Or had their monsters come? The crack in the ocean floor where she had found Mizra—was it natural or ripped open by some unspeakable horror? Had Mizra's death been a part of The Eternal Cycle, or meaningless?

Death is always meaningless, whispered Mizra between her fingers. Iona contemplated this. Perhaps it was. Or perhaps Alinda was right. Yet she knew one thing for certain: she did not intend to die of thirst and starvation on this island.

She went down to the boat. He was sitting in the stern and securing the load.

"Take me away from here," she said, with her fingers in Mizra's eyes. He looked up. She could not read his expression.

"Now?"

She nodded. She let him help her up into the boat. She sat there as he gathered his belongings from the temple and lashed his bundle onto the boat. She stared out to sea. It was clear blue. Her mother's eyes were the same color, Iona suddenly remembered.

When he pulled up the anchor and she looked at him, she knew that the monster had not disappeared. It was only biding its time. Without Mizra she would be utterly defenseless.

Coiling the wet chain into the boat, he addressed her suddenly.

"Your name?"

"Iona. And yours?"

"Iskan."

That was the name of her monster. And he possessed her death.

CLARÁS

One morning I had gotten up early. Spring was coming, and I sat by my window watching birds fly. A swan flew past on heavy wings. Starlings ran about below my window, pecking at worms. I saw no sea birds, but I could make out the sea as a far-off shimmer. A southerly breeze carried with it the smell of salt and seaweed. The man had been away for a long time on his travels. We had assembled a good deal of provisions. Very soon it would be time to leave. I had decided how we would escape, despite Sulani's protests. We would gather in the great hall at night and lure the guards in, perhaps by breaking something, or some other way of attracting their attention without waking the other women. Two of us would wait hidden in the shadows with heavy objects. We would then catch the guards unawares, strike them unconscious, take their keys and escape. The guards had never met resistance from the women of the dairahesi before, so they would not be prepared for it. If we succeeded in surprising them, it would not be difficult for three women to strike down two men. Estegi would be waiting outside the doors with the provisions. We would take all we needed and run, under cover of darkness. *Naondel* awaited us. The ocean awaited me. We had to set off on our voyage when the northeast winds began to blow. They would take us to Terasu in ten days, or a little longer. There were islands along the way where we could stop for supplies. But it was still half a moon before the right winds would come.

So we waited.

And the man returned.

It was Estegi who brought the news. Garai and I were sitting by the little pond in the courtyard. More than anybody, it was probably Garai who most missed the freedom to visit the Garden of Eternal Serenity when she wished. She was sitting with one hand in the water and looked to be listening with concentration. I was sitting on a bench facing the sun and the southerly winds. Estegi came out through the archway, knelt and bowed, first to Garai, then to me.

"The Vizier of Karenokoi wishes to assemble his entire household in the great hall," she said. I shuddered. I had forgotten about him. *Naondel* had been filling my thoughts so much that I had almost forgotten why we must flee.

"When did he return?" asked Garai. Her long white hair hung like a shawl over her slender shoulders. She had been bought, as had I. I knew that. But she had been sold against her will.

It was not really my will—to sell my body, to come here—but at least I made the decision.

"Yesterday night, my lady." Estegi hesitated. "He did not come alone."

She and Garai exchanged glances. Was Estegi the one who would betray us? She was close to the wife and to Garai, but also to Sulani. They shared a different closeness.

We went in and up to the great hall. The fountain was flowing. Women and children had gathered. Then a door was opened and in walked the wife and her daughter, Esiko. They sat down on some cushions slightly away from the rest of us.

We waited.

He liked making us wait. Our time was his to waste. He never had to enter an empty room if he did not want to. We must always be available to him.

The children ran around playing while the women drank tea and chattered. If any child came too close to me, with my deformed lip, their mother would call them anxiously back to her. Orseola sat beside me with an absent expression and said nothing. I saw Sulani, straight-backed as always, with Estegi not far behind. Garai greeted Kabira, but they didn't speak.

The golden doors were opened by a guard and in came the man. Behind him there followed a young girl. She was short, barely reaching his shoulders, and her hair, as black as the night sky, fell down to her ankles. She was dressed in an ankle-length dress of fiery red, straight and without embroidery. On one hip she had a large lump: was she deformed? No, the lump moved freely under the cloth, so it was an object. Her eyes were large in her pointed little face.

She was very young.

Younger than I was when my father told me to leave.

The man stood in front of us and smiled. Shark teeth.

"I have traveled long, but finally I have found what I sought." He presented the girl, without touching her. "A second wife. She will provide me with many sons, and secure my position. I married her yesterday when we arrived at Ohaddin."

The girl looked at him with an expression I couldn't interpret.

I looked at Esiko. Her face was pale and her hands were shaking. Next to me Orseola made a strange noise. She was looking straight at the girl, her mouth half open and her upper

281

lip shining with sweat. I laid a hand on hers, to stop her from speaking. From drawing attention to herself. The more the man forgot we existed, the better.

"First Wife."

Kabira stood up and came to her husband, bowed deeply and awaited orders.

"See to it that Iona has all she needs. Give some of your chambers over to her. A suitable wardrobe. Jewelry." He waved his hand dismissively. "All such things."

"Yes, my lord," the old woman replied, and bowed deeply. I had never seen her so subservient toward the man before. It must have been on account of the daughter. Because he had let her live, and he had not punished his wife. Not yet.

Perhaps this was a form of punishment.

Without another word he turned and left the dairahesi. Flustered mutters spread at once among the concubines. A new wife! Nobody could have predicted that.

"She is but a child!" said Orseola beside me. "But a child!"

It was true. She looked barely old enough to have started bleeding.

"When we flee . . . he will only fill our places with younger and younger girls."

I shushed her, but she took no notice. Nobody seemed to be listening to what she said; everybody was talking over each other.

"He must be stopped!" Orseola was shaking so hard that I could feel her trembles. "He must be stopped!"

"He holds death in his hand," I said, and followed Iona with my gaze. Kabira showed the girl to her residence. Forced to give up her own rooms and her own comfort: what a humiliation for a woman like her. "You have said so yourself. There is nothing the likes of us can do. Only save ourselves, if we can."

"He may hold death," whispered Orseola, "but I hold dreams."

ᚤ

Estegi brought up the problem of sails one night soon after.

"We are going to need sails," she said, when we had gathered down by the bathing pools again. We who would flee. Estegi had said little about our escape once we had succeeded in buying *Naondel*. The boat was awaiting us in an abandoned boathouse in Ameka. Estegi had even been there to make sure it was true. I was used to seeing her as a servant: the one who fetched us tea and sweets, emptied chamber pots or sold jewelry on our behalf at the bazaar. Not the one who came up with ideas.

"Has *Naondel* no sails?"

She shook her head. "No. My cousin had to borrow one from the fisherman to sail it upriver, but he needed it back."

"What does the fisherman know of the buyers of the boat?" asked Sulani, ever the strategist.

"He believes it was for my cousin."

"And your cousin? What does he believe?"

"He believes I have a lover." Estegi blushed. "And that we are running away together." She flashed a quick glance at Sulani.

"We need sails," I said. "Terasu is far. Rowing is too slow. Too difficult. For the likes of you, that is."

"Sails," said Orseola. "We have a boat, but no sails."

Sulani looked at me. "What makes a good sail?"

"Strong, light. Sail makers are highly respected artisans. A difficult craft. I can fix a decent net, but I'm no sail maker."

Estegi leaned forward. "Do you know what makes a good sail, then? How it feels, how it moves?"

I nodded.

"Good. Then I can sew it." She leaned back and clasped her hands on her lap. Sulani looked at her for a long time, then smiled.

"We have nothing to sew it with," Orseola objected, and I laughed.

"Cloth is about the only thing we do have in this golden cage! Don't you see what surrounds us? Silk! Silk pillows, silk curtains, silk in our clothes. We have as much hard-wearing, feather-light silk as anyone could ever wish for."

"The pillows are too small," said Estegi immediately, rubbing her fingers together, as though warming up to start sewing already. "But the curtains are good. And maybe we can request whole rolls of fabric, to sew new jackets with."

"We mustn't ask anything of him now, you know that," I said.

"But we know someone who can," Orseola put in. We looked at each other.

"We can't let her in on the plan," I objected. "How can we make her request it without telling her the truth?"

"If I may make a suggestion," Estegi said. She had stood up and was standing next to Sulani, still with her head bowed respectfully, and yet as more than a mere servant. She was one of us now. "We can try simply asking. She is helpful and anxious to please."

"We need silk," I said. "Without sails *Naondel* is a bird with clipped wings. I will go to her tomorrow."

ᚹ

I sent Estegi with a message: might I visit the new wife to pay my respects? The answer came quickly: enter. So I bathed and washed myself thoroughly, and used sweet-scented oils to mask the smell of fish and seaweed that always clung to me. I stuck the comb in my clean hair, walked through the great hall and down the corridor to the private quarters, where I knocked on the door to what was now Iona's residence.

Estegi opened it and I stepped in. Then stopped. Her room was so unlike any other I had seen in the dairahesi. The stone floor was bare. There were no painted screens or great vases. The window shutters were open to the spring sun. There was a simple altar against the far wall, with a knife, a piece of bread and a stone placed upon it. Iona was sitting on a cushion holding something in her lap. Something white, with empty eye sockets: a skull. Opposite Iona sat Garai. She looked up and frowned.

"Why do you disturb us, Clarás?"

"She is my guest, priestess," replied Iona. Garai was none too pleased but turned back to Iona, and to the skull.

I came forward and sat next to Garai. With her there I could not make my request.

"It is an unfathomably powerful object you have in your possession. With its help you could free yourself from your master." Garai did not seem to be able to take her eyes off the skull.

"He is not my master," replied Iona seriously. "He is my monster and he possesses my death."

Garai remained silent. Then she bowed to Iona and left the room in haste.

I waited for Iona to address me. She was a wife. I was a mere concubine. Newest and lowest in ranks.

Iona was silent. She looked at me pleasantly but without interest.

A cat came padding in from another room and stepped straight into my lap. It purred as I stroked its soft ears. The skull in Iona's lap stared at me with its black holes.

Life and death.

"Was there something you wanted?" Finally she broke the silence. Finally I could speak.

"You have the Vizier's ear. Could you request fabric from him?" It was all I could say. Without wit or eloquence.

"What sort of fabric?" Iona ran her fingertips across the jagged teeth of the skull. It was a very small skull. Maybe a child's.

"Silk. We don't get any more of it. We who are not the Vizier's favorite, like you."

I could sense Estegi squirm behind me, embarrassed by my clumsy manner. But Iona looked at me with a friendly and steady gaze. Then she turned her head, as though listening to something. She nodded slightly.

"I was given a great deal of silk cloth to decorate my rooms, but I prefer to keep them simple. Estegi, fetch the rolls from my bedchamber."

Estegi bowed and disappeared through a door. I could not take my eyes off the skull.

"Who is that?"

Iona smiled, a shy smile that lit up her face.

"Mizra. My friend and predecessor. She sacrificed her life to the monster. I am awaiting my turn."

"You wish to die?" I laid a hand on my belly. Felt the fish inside me flapping and kicking.

"To maintain The Eternal Cycle. Of life and death." She rested one hand on Mizra, like a bonnet. "It is my purpose. I have no other."

"All of us must die," I said. "Why die before the spirits of your ancestors summon you?"

"I do not recognize the spirits of the dead," Iona replied. "The Eternal Cycle demands the sacrifice of a few to bestow well-being on the many."

"My purpose is to take care of this child," I said, and showed my belly. Iona nodded.

"It is good to have a purpose. Then you know that all decisions that help to fulfill it are the right ones."

Estegi came in holding several rolls of silk cloth in shimmering colors, some thin gauze and others coarse raw silk. More than enough for our sails. I thanked Iona with the finest words I could think of and bowed again and again. She lifted the skull to her cheek.

"Mizra tells me it is important that you obtain these cloths. Choose the gray-green, it is the least visible against the ocean."

I stumbled out with Estegi following after. We looked at each other. She shook her head.

"I have not said a word!" she whispered. "You must believe me!"

The ocean. *Naondel.* She knew something, but what? And was she the one who would betray us? She seemed to be on the man's side. She was not afraid of him.

And he was a man to be feared.

ʊ

He still came to me sometimes. Iona was clearly not enough to satisfy his lust. Or perhaps he chose not to defile her with the things he did to me. He visited Sulani also. I saw the marks on her face and body. She never complained. Estegi nursed her wounds and swellings with light, tender hands.

Sometimes I looked at them and wished that someone would touch me in that way. Sometimes, after the man had used me, I wished that nobody would touch me at all.

ᛒ

We had everything we needed for our escape. Estegi was quick with the needle and thread, and the sail was soon completed. The days approaching the night of our escape ran together like grains of sand.

I had decided that we would flee five days after the last full moon of spring. That is when the wind begins to blow from the south, but it is not yet too hot. The sail was waiting, ready, under my bed. Everything was ready. Our small but sufficient supplies were waiting in the forgotten storeroom. My belly was round and I was slow, but when I felt the child's strong kicks, they inspired strength in me too. It was the night before the full moon.

It was the night when everything went wrong.

ᛒ

I was woken by the need to relieve my bladder. This was happening more and more often since the child had grown big. Once I had finished using the chamber pot, I heard steps coming from the great hall. I opened the door and followed the sound.

Orseola was standing there looking down into the fountain. She was often brought back to the dairahesi at night, after weaving dreams for the Sovereign Prince. Through the lattice

288

doors I saw the silhouette of a guard in the darkness. Only one that night.

I walked over to her. She did not look up at me. She was staring down into the water.

"One must never harm a dreamer," she said, so quietly I had to lean forward to hear. "Mother said so, and often. Never harm." She fell to her knees before the fountain and leaned her forehead against the cool marble font. "He wanted to fly," she whispered. "So I let him fly. I took all the memories I could find of high places, wind on his face and stormy seas. I wove better than ever, little stickleback. His eyes watered in the wind. Thick clouds wetted his skin. He did not know he was not awake. I ruffled his eagle feathers in the wind, it whistled in his ears, strong gusts tossed him here and there until he did not know what was up and what was down." She gripped my shoulder. "She is so young! She is a child! He must be stopped, little stickleback, somebody must stop him! Else he will bring younger and younger girls here once we have left!"

"Who are you talking about? And which girl?"

She laughed, loud and shrill, and it echoed in the empty hall. The guard turned around.

"Back to your chambers," he said in his half-man's voice. "Now."

"I was summoned by the Sovereign," whispered Orseola, her face close to mine. "I cannot get to him, our enemy, but I can harm him through the Sovereign! If he has no one whose strings to pull, who is he then? Where is his power?"

"Orseola, what have you done?" I whispered. Her grip on my shoulder was strong.

"He fell, little stickleback," she hissed. I heard the guard rattling the keys and I started shaking Orseola, trying to shake the madness out of her.

"What have you done?"

"I found all his fears, little starfish. Every one, and I tied them into his dream, and finally I tied in the memory of his mother dying in terrible agony when he was a boy. With my most beautiful knot I tied it. His dream-self faltered, once, twice, the third time it did not righten again. I blasted him with his own fear of death. He fell like a stone!" She was breathing in violent gasps. I heard rattling at the doors, the guard unlocked them and came in. His steps echoed on the stone floor. Had I been prepared, we could have taken him by surprise there and then—the perfect opportunity! But it was too early. I needed Sulani with me. I had nothing to strike with. But at least I knew that our plan would work. Especially if we were lucky and there was only one guard on the night of our escape.

Orseola whimpered, loudly now. "He will wake no more, little fish! Never, never more."

I jumped to my feet. The guard was in front of us. "Her mind is darkened. I'm trying to get her to her bed."

Without a word I took Orseola by the hand and together the guard and I dragged her to her own bed. She offered no resistance. The guard reluctantly left us, with orders to go to bed as soon as she had calmed down. Even then my eyes were searching for something heavy, something to strike him on the head with. But no, it was the wrong night. I would see to it that we were prepared for the next time.

"The greatest taboo," mumbled Orseola. "Banishment is too good for one such as me. No, no. My birth tree must be cut down. Burned. No shoots left to sprout. I have violated everything. Mother, Mother, forgive me, MOTHER!"

She screamed and raged until finally I had to leave her alone, filled with a profound horror.

If what she said was true, if the Sovereign was dead, what would the man do then?

ɯ

Orseola had killed the Sovereign Prince. But she had done it so skillfully that nobody suspected her. She had been his dreamweaver for several years, and few even knew what it was that she did. They believed she was his concubine, a favorite the Vizier loaned out. If their passionate embrace had been more than an old man's heart could handle, whose fault was that? No one's. He had fallen asleep peacefully in his own bed. He had already outlived all of his contemporaries. No one in Karenokoi had ever reached such old age. He had joined the ranks of his ancestors, belatedly.

But the Vizier had held the Sovereign's death in his hand. He must have known that somebody had taken it from him. I didn't fully understand this, but it was how Estegi explained it to me. She had been there since she was a little girl and knew more about Ohaddin and the intrigues of the palace than any of the rest of us oath-sworn.

He had been suspicious of everybody since his sons had died. When Esiko turned out to be a girl, his persecution mania was further fueled. Now that the Sovereign had died without his consent, without his knowledge, he seemed to lose his mind. He raised the number of guards all over. They were no longer eunuchs, as we were used to. They were soldiers, heavily armed with hard faces and scarred hands. They guarded all the doors and windows in the various buildings of the palace. It was entirely impossible for us to put our plan into action. Our escape route was blocked.

We had *Naondel*. We had food and sails. But we no longer had the possibility of escape.

KABIRA

My sons were dead.

Following the death of the Sovereign Prince, Iskan had all of his male relatives executed, convinced that there were some who coveted the throne. Including the children. And those still suckling at their mothers' breasts. And any woman who might be suspected of carrying the Sovereign's child. There were no public executions. But we, the residents of Ohaddin, heard the screams on that horrific day when the slaughter occurred. The screams of children, cut off abruptly. The screams of mothers, never-ending. I felt nothing when I heard them.

My sons were dead.

The next day smoke lay thickly over the Garden of Eternal Serenity, over the golden roof of the palace, over the whole of Ohaddin. He had the bodies burned on one of the hills north of the city. They would receive no burial. They would be obliterated, not united in eternal life with their ancestors.

That day Ohaddin was shrouded in smoke and deathly silence. Nobody spoke. The thick smoke silenced even the birds.

My sons were dead.

Orseola went crazy that day. She had always been unstable, but now she raged in a mania beyond reaching. The guards of the dairahesi bound her to her bed so that she could not harm herself, and Garai forced soothing concoctions into her.

I suspected I knew the cause of her suffering.

My sons were dead.

ᚹ

Iskan came to me after the Day of the Burning Bodies. He had not visited me in a long time, not since Esiko told him the truth about her. Esiko was with me when he entered my chambers without warning. I fell to my knees at once and bowed down to the floor. After a moment's hesitation Esiko followed my example. She had not yet grown accustomed to behaving as a meek woman must. She was wearing women's clothes, on her father's decree, but her hair was still short and I could not reconcile myself with the sight of her dressed as a girl. She was changed. She was timid, and did not leave our chambers. I was glad to keep her close. As close as possible. Anything, so long as I did not lose this last child. Esiko sat and waited for her father to summon her and accept her as his confidant, his closest adviser, once again.

He had not summoned her since he had discovered the truth.

"Rise." I peered up at Iskan. It was Esiko he was addressing, not me. She was crouching and looking expectantly up at her father. He grimaced with disgust.

"What a monstrosity. Such short hair, and why do you wear no hair chains? Ten, to show that you are of the house of Che. Do not show yourself in public until your hair has grown."

Esiko appeared as though he had spat in her face. He turned to me. Looking into his entirely black eyes was like seeing into the land of the dead. I thought that perhaps if I looked long enough I would start to hear the wails of his victims.

"Is she a woman in all ways? Between her legs?"

"Yes," I said. "Naturally." They were the first words I had said to Iskan since he had killed my sons.

He scoffed. "Who knows what harm it has done her to grow up as a boy. It will be a long time before Iona can provide me with sons. Anji has shown it. However, Iona holds something of far greater value to me. As soon as I take possession of it, no one will be able to get the better of me again. Until then I must strengthen my standing. I shall see to it that I eradicate the final opposition. None shall remain who might threaten me. Misfortunes do occur. I realized that when the Sovereign died. Now that he is dead I must reign in his stead." He smiled. There was no joy or warmth in his smile. "The conspirators had not counted on that. They gave me the throne as a tidy gift. However, I need someone by my side. Esiko shall be married off as soon as she is presentable. I am going to great lengths to find a good candidate. Someone who can take over from Korin. Someone who is entirely loyal to me."

"But I am loyal, Father!" Esiko burst out. I took a deep breath. She must not displease him. He was capable of absolutely anything. She was no longer his son. But Esiko did not understand that.

"I have served you well, you have listened to my counsel, I know all about your dominion. I know all about Anji! Father, I beg of you, let me visit the spring again. Let me prove my worth."

Iskan turned to her, slowly. Studied her carefully, expressing no emotion.

"You have lied to your father and lord. Do not speak to me of loyalty. Do not speak to me at all. Count yourself lucky that you are still alive. It is only because you have a function to fulfil. You are to be married." He looked at her, expressionless. I thought about how she used to ride on his shoulders. When she was a little boy.

He turned and left. Esiko remained motionless, her eyes filled with tears. I had not seen her cry since she was four years old.

"We can expect nothing more," I said. "Marriage is every woman's destiny. Perhaps he will find someone who does not live too far away. Then we can see each other often." The mere thought of not being able to see Esiko every day filled me with panic.

Esiko turned to me. "I expect more!" she screamed. "This is your fault. In all my fourteen years I have learned to expect more. I am son of the Vizier! And now you want me to be like you. A woman. One who wants nothing, knows nothing, does nothing!"

Then she spat on the floor before me and stormed into her own chamber.

ω

Anji had granted her power to Iskan. Anji had aided him in all of the dreadful crimes he had committed. Anji had stolen my daughter from the very beginning; while Esiko was still inside me, the force of the spring flowed through her veins. My daughter had always listened more to the spring than to me. Anji could command Iskan indefinitely. He would take my daughter or he would kill her. I could not let these things happen.

There must be a way to strip Iskan of his power.

Without it he would be an ordinary man. An old man. His grip on Esiko would loosen. She would finally see him for what he was and then she would be mine. As I had initially believed she would be, that evening when I took Iskan into my bed for the last time.

ω

I was awoken that night by the smell of smoke.

At first I thought it was the lingering smell of burned bodies torturing me. Then I opened my eyes and saw a blazing red glow dance across the walls of my chamber. I rushed up and over to the window.

The Palace of Tranquility was in flames. The building that housed all the Sovereign's concubines and daughters who had survived the massacre.

Esiko rushed past me and out through the door. I pulled on a jacket and followed quickly behind. The dairahesi was filled with a clamor of voices, movement, fear.

Esiko was running toward the lattice doors before the stairs. A single guard was standing there, one of the new ones, recruited from the army. She addressed him by name.

"Barado. Brother-in-arms. Open this door."

He shook his head. "Sorry, little sister. The Vizier's orders are not to be contradicted."

"Where is the Vizier?"

"Nobody knows." He could not conceal his worry.

"Who is leading the firefighting, Barado?"

Esiko continued to use his name. To remind him of the bond they were bound by.

"I don't know, Ora— . . . little sister. Most of the guards are there fighting it now."

Outwardly she was still Orano, Iskan's son, but the guards of the dairahesi had seen her as Esiko, in women's clothes, and they knew the truth. I do not know what Iskan had told them. Perhaps nothing. He was not required to explain himself to anyone.

"Somebody must lead the effort, Barado. You know that.

It requires a commander. It was not long ago we were in battle together," said Esiko earnestly. She was not pleading. She was decided, collected: a leader. "We flexed our bows side by side. Everybody who is able must help to quell the fire. You too. I will lead the effort, if you all will follow me. And if the worst should happen, if the fire spreads, surely you do not want to bear the responsibility for all the Vizier's women being burned alive?"

Just as the Sovereign's women and children were being burned alive at this very moment, I thought. I looked at my daughter. She stood straight and tall before the guard, and he looked at her. Without another word he produced the key and unlocked the door. Only then did I see how Esiko was dressed, in her old Orano clothes. Blue jacket, white trousers, high boots.

She turned to me.

"Mother, if the fire threatens this house I want you to lead all the women and children to safety."

I nodded.

She disappeared down the steps without another word.

I looked around. The great hall was deserted.

I slipped out through the lattice doors without hesitation. Unescorted, for the first time since this palace was built. As I was running down the steps and out into the garden, I was reminded of my vision following Lehan's death. My vision of this house, of the women who now lived there. I had known nothing of them at the time. Now they were my only companionship and had been for all the years of my confinement. Esiko had entrusted their lives to me.

I did not care whether they lived or died.

GARAI

I have long been preparing for the blood moon. The stars have shown me that it is close at hand. Mother taught me to read the signs. It is the time when the moon's power is at its strongest, and she draws the life force of the earth toward her. It rises to the surface and all offerings at this time are more potent than ever. I can feel it in my entire being. My very bones sing of the life force. I have not had the opportunity to walk among the zismil trees in a long time; Iskan has forbidden us from going outside after all that has happened. Nevertheless, I can feel it when night falls. If I dance the moon dance it is as if the zismil roots extend from my own feet, and I can extend them down into the depths of the earth, below the mountains, and I feel the life force simmer and seethe. My roots find their way into the deepest origins of this source of power. She is calling to me. As I sit and write this, in the light of a single candle, the call grows ever stronger. It seems I do not only feel it in my body, but I hear it also, as a great clamor. The air in my room thickens, it must be the life force filling the very air! It smells of . . . smoke?

I just got up and looked out of my window, and it is smoke. And the noise is of people screaming. The Palace of Tranquility is in flames.

And the spring is calling to me.

I once took a knife from our evening meal, hid it and thoroughly sharpened it so that the blade is now as keen as Mother's offering dagger, though not of obsidian. I shall take it now. This is my chance. If I find just one open door, I shall go to the spring and make one more offering—a great one. An offering made under the blood moon to a source of power as strong as the one bound here in Ohaddin—this will transform me into a priestess as powerful and wise as Mother. Or more still. There is no time to lose. I am taking my notes with me. This could be the offering I never return from, in which case I do not want anyone to be able to find my papers. I am dressing warmly to face the night. I am ready.

CLARÁS

Estegi woke me. I had been deep asleep, and it took me a long time to swim up to the surface. She stood leaning over me with a lamp in her hand.

"The Palace of Tranquility is burning," she said. "The doors are unlocked."

I sat up. "Can we escape? Now, tonight?"

She nodded. "I will wake Sulani." She left my room without a sound.

As I rushed to dress, I thought of Orseola. I knew that she would be a burden. Something that needed dragging along, that could weigh us down to the bottom and sink us. But sometimes burdens are necessary. Nets would float away without weights. Besides, she had helped me to find *Naondel*.

I lashed the bundled sails onto my back with a thin rope. Sulani came in, fully dressed and grim faced. Behind her came Estegi, who quickly packed items in a bag: lamps, oil, tinder boxes. Sulani had several rolls of rope around her waist and over her shoulders. Good. They had listened to what I said. I saw something else in her hand, something shining and sharp.

I pointed. "A weapon?"

She held out a long knife. "Estegi smuggled it for me. A warrior does not go into battle unarmed."

Suddenly I was glad I was not fleeing alone.

"We can go down the stairs," said Estegi quietly. "First via the storeroom. And then?"

She looked at me and at Sulani.

I didn't know how she would get us beyond the palace grounds. After our plan to surprise the guards I hadn't come up with another. Sulani stuck the knife into her belt.

"Over the pagoda roof of the spring. From there we can get to the wall. We have rope. We can lower ourselves down."

I laid my hands protectively over my belly.

"I will help you," she said. "There is no other way. The gates are too heavily guarded. Are you shod?"

I didn't understand what she meant.

"We will need to cover a long distance quickly and under cover of darkness. You cannot go barefoot; it is too great a risk."

I showed the sandals on my feet. Estegi showed hers. Sulani nodded in approval. She had woven her hair into small, tight plaits and bound them back so they would not disturb her. I wore only my copper comb in my hair. Estegi had covered hers in a blue scarf.

"Orseola?" Sulani asked.

"We must take her with us." We left my room and went out into the great hall. Several other concubines were gathered there, some with tiny babes in their arms. They stood in front of the windows. The fire's glow reflected in their eyes. They didn't look at us. I rushed into Orseola's room. She was sitting cross-legged on the bed.

"Away, away, away," she mumbled in a monotone. I found her sandals and straightened her legs. She let me put them on her, passively, the whole time muttering, "Away, away, away." I dressed her in a quilted jacket and bound her jewelry box to her back. Sulani stuck her head in.

"Can you manage with her?"

I nodded and led Orseola out of the room. She saw the flames through the window and stopped. "Dreamsnares," she said suddenly, very clearly. Estegi rushed into her room, then soon returned and showed us her bag.

Sulani took the lead. I followed behind with Orseola on my arm, and Estegi came last. Nobody spoke to us as we left the great hall for the corridor beyond. It was dark. The smell of smoke was unmistakable.

"Crackle, crackle," said Orseola. "The dreams go up in smoke."

Sulani pushed against the main door. It swung open. She peeked down the stairs and motioned for us to follow. I took one final look behind. The other women were still standing by the windows. The fountain was quiet. The air was heavy with smoke. I followed the others down the steps. Held my breath as we walked. I was afraid that Orseola would draw attention to us. I thought about what the guards would do. What the man would do. For so long I had been thinking about the escape, dreaming and planning. It was hard to believe that it was truly happening.

We reached the lower floor. Estegi led us through corridors I had never walked before. They were narrow, twisting and dark. The servants' quarters. We met no one. They were all presumably busy fighting the fire.

Estegi opened a door and told us to wait. After a while she returned with two sacks. From one she took out filled waterskins. We bound them around our hips; I tied Orseola's tight. Sulani heaved the sack up onto her back, but then Orseola chuckled.

"The battle horse becomes the pack mule."

Sulani looked at her. "It is true. I cannot fight while heavily laden."

Without a word Estegi handed her little bag to Sulani and took the heavy sack.

We continued through a small door out into the garden. Now the smell of smoke was even more intense. The Palace of Tranquility was like a flaming torch. It would burn to the ground. Figures were running between the trees with buckets from the stream, lakes and fountains. Voices were shouting, both women's and men's.

We crouched low and ran. The trees' shadows hid us. Bushes scratched my legs. I had to pull Orseola along with me. She was slowing me down, but Sulani waited. She ran ahead, constantly vigilant, held up a hand, made us wait, then hurried on. I followed after as though blind. I felt just as helpless, putting my trust in this almost entirely unknown woman, as a blind person trusting their guide.

We came to the building with the pagoda roof in the northern part of the garden. The door to it stood open. I heard voices. Sulani gestured to us to wait as she crept forward. I dragged Orseola with me up against the wall of the building. Estegi released the heavy sack. Crumbs of soot fluttered down like snowflakes.

"It's Kabira and Esiko," whispered Sulani when she returned to us. "And Garai is with them."

"What shall we do?" I whispered. I looked up at the pagoda roof. The lowest edge could just about be reached, if someone helped me. My belly was weighing me down. I was already out of breath. If we started climbing now they would hear us. "Should we wait?"

"An opportunity like this will never come again." Sulani's forehead was deeply creased. "We must away tonight."

"I'll go in," said Estegi. "I know them. If I speak with them they will not hinder us." She didn't sound as certain as her words. Sulani looked at her a moment, then nodded.

"We will wait here."

Estegi disappeared through the open door.

KABIRA

I reached Serenity House without being seen. All the guards were rushing around carrying water or saving what could still be saved from the Palace of Tranquility. The palace doors were open. I did not know where the library was, only that it was located on the ground floor. I tried many doors, some locked, some that opened into empty chambers. My steps echoed on the marble floor. My heart was racing. I did not even know for what purpose I sought the library. To search through the secret scriptures in hope of finding something to save Esiko? Or else rescue the most valuable in case the fire spread? Find something that could strip Iskan of his power, once and for all?

I do not know.

The farthermost door was locked, and I knew at once it must be the right one. Esiko had told me where Iskan safeguarded the keys: in a box in his bedchamber. On the upper floor.

I went back through the corridor and found the staircase. I dried my sweaty palms on my trousers before starting up the stairs. Then I heard noises: clanking and thuds. They were coming from upstairs. I hesitated—did I dare go farther? The moment I stopped a figure appeared on the stairs before me. A man in leather mail had his back to me and was dragging something heavy.

I slipped down the steps and hid behind an open door. I could glimpse the bottom of the staircase through the gap between door and frame. I heard a groan and several heavy thuds, and then I saw a brief flash of a guard, dragging a weighty sack behind him.

A looter taking advantage of the prevailing chaos. He was brave, and stupid. Iskan would find him, no matter where he tried to hide.

Then it occurred to me that he would find me too. With Anji's help, no one could hide from him.

As soon as the guard had disappeared out of the front door, I hurried upstairs. Iskan's quarters dominated the entire upper floor: a series of chambers that at first glance appeared sparsely, almost humbly, furnished. I, however, knew the value of the few scattered vases. I recognized the true price of those ancient painted screens. He had an art collection worthy of a Sovereign, but when value is not displayed in glittering gold or jewels, few would realize what riches he hid there.

I suspected that the guard had pilfered simple things such as silver candlesticks and other inexpensive items. I rushed through the chambers, afraid that the box with the key had gone into the plundering guard's hefty sack. But when I came to Iskan's bedchamber I saw it at once on a low table by his bed: a plain wooden box.

In the box was a single key.

I was soon downstairs and inside the library. Esiko and Sonan had described it to me in detail. It was not difficult to find the shelves with the most secret scrolls. The ones that contained all the hidden knowledge. The knowledge that Iskan wanted to keep for himself. I scanned over the scrolls, trying to decide which I needed most, when a scraping, metallic noise cut through the din of the fire.

I rushed to a window that looked out on the garden and burning building. It appeared that the fire had spread to the Temple of

Learning adjacent. Between the Sovereign's palace and Serenity House was the prison Iskan had built for Anji. The noise I had heard was the sound of the door to the prison. I could not see it from my window, but I was entirely certain. Someone had just opened it.

When I looked around, I found a leather satchel and packed the most valuable scrolls into it. The ones I knew that not even Iskan could decipher, including some that told of sources of power. I knew that he had made no copies. He was too suspicious for that. I pushed in as many as possible, though I could hear the paper crumple and tear. I was not thinking about their preservation—then. I was thinking about flames and burning paper and vengeance. But most of all I was thinking about Anji.

ω

Several people ran past me as I rushed through the Garden of Eternal Serenity on the way to the spring. Nobody hindered me; everybody was occupied with quelling the fire, escaping the fire, helping the injured. I ran as well, so they might think I was participating in the same effort. As I was approaching the wall around Anji, I saw that the door was open. I continued to run until I reached the door and quickly slipped inside.

It had been so long since I had been in her presence. I stopped in front of the door and took a deep breath. She smelled like she always had. Moisture, soil, rotting leaves. Yet the surrounding walls Iskan had built had made the smell concentrated and almost stale. And what walls they were: gold relief patterns with images of mountains and wild animals. The floor was marble mosaic. Several burning torches hung around the chamber, and the golden walls reflected their glow. I saw now that the pagoda roof had an aperture at the top, covered by a grate. Iskan had presumably recognized that he could not keep Anji apart from the moon if he wanted to read the future in her water, which of course he did. Once inside, the light from the blaze was less visible, and paled almost into nothing under the intense light of the full moon.

At the edge of the spring sat Esiko, with one hand in the water. I walked slowly over to her. Stopped and, for the first time in over thirty-five years, looked down into Anji's black water.

It was like looking down into a well of bereavements.

Suddenly everything rushed over me like a tidal wave. Mother, Father, my siblings whose faces had slipped from my memory and become lost. My three strong, beautiful sons. All those who had died at Iskan's hand, with Anji's help. I fell to my knees, weighed down by a sorrow so oppressive I could no longer stand. I wept as I had not wept since Iskan took Korin away from me. My tears disturbed the surface of the water. Esiko sat still beside me and said nothing. When I had finished weeping, without a word she passed me a silver ladle. I filled it with water and drank.

Anji's power flooded through me. It was like silver gushing through my veins, like intoxicating wine, like the sap of youth. I could feel years of youth returning to me. The sensation was stronger than I remembered from the times when I used to drink the full-moon water. I sat up straight and took a deep breath.

"It is the blood moon," said Esiko, and pointed up through the grate-covered aperture. The moon above us was red like wine. Red like blood. "I have never experienced it before. Something is happening with Anji's water. She is showing me the future more clearly than ever."

I turned my gaze toward the surface again. I saw the red moon reflected. I saw my face, and my daughter's. I saw us slipping away from each other. Farther and farther, until a vast ocean lay between us. I saw women from the dairahesi working side by side. Other images drifted past, distorted and difficult to understand. Threat, great destruction. Germination, something new. Then I saw a much clearer image: Esiko on the Sovereign's throne, with all of Karenokoi at her feet.

I shuddered and turned to look at her.

"It is difficult for you to interpret Anji's images," she said softly, with a tone I had not heard her use with me since she was very little. "For me it is mostly very clear."

I was consumed with fear. Would Anji pull Esiko into darkness and madness as she had done with Iskan? Would she murder and poison just as he had to achieve her ends?

"Esiko, promise me that you will not drink the dark water, the oaki, promise me!" I leaned forward and grasped her hands. "This spring has led only to suffering and death. It must be walled in so that no one may ever come to it again!"

Esiko stood up straight and the softness disappeared from her posture and tone. "I am not my father, Mother. I would use the spring correctly. As she is intended to be used. You should see yourself now, after only one ladle of her water you have regained years of youth! You look strong and healthy. What is wrong with that?"

"There is nothing wrong with aging," I said, and before I could stop myself, I continued. "I wish I could age faster, that I might die and be released from my suffering, and forget about everybody whom I have loved and who has been taken from me. But Iskan will not allow me to die, because he likes to see me suffer. Have you already forgotten your brothers, Esiko? Have you forgotten how they loved and doted on you, their youngest brother?"

"Their deaths were not the fault of Anji, Mother." Esiko crossed her arms and turned away from me.

"Were they not? Iskan capitalized on her power, that is true, the fault is his. But the spring is the source of his arrogance." I turned my face up to the red moon to stop more tears from flowing. "You should have had sisters, do you know that, Esiko? Many sisters. But Iskan stole them from me, aided by Anji's power. He murdered them all. That is why I hid your sex and had you be my son, Esiko. To keep you."

"It's not true!" said Esiko. "Stop it, Mother!"

"Look down into the spring," I urged her. "See for yourself."

"No! Your lies are too shameless. I will not sully Anji with them."

"Look!" I implored, and tried to force her head down toward the surface. "See if I am lying!"

My death. Suddenly something touched it. Held it in an iron-hard grip. Did not draw it closer, but did not release it either. It felt as if someone were holding my heart in their hands.

I gasped for air. Esiko's eyes met mine, first hard, then defiant.

"Impossible," I gasped. "The water is not oaki now."

"I have grown up with Anji's water in my veins. I have played at her edge, read the future in the water of every full moon. I can do things that no one else can. Not even Father."

At that moment someone entered through the open door. Esiko released my death and we both stood up abruptly.

It was Garai. Her long hair shone like white fire in the moonlight. Suddenly I was reminded of the world beyond Anji, of screams and shouts, the crackling fire. Might we be trapped here? Surrounded by fire? I was not concerned for my own sake, but Esiko . . .

"How does it look?" I asked. "The fire?"

311

"Starting to come under control," Garai replied shortly. She rolled up her left sleeve and inspected her arm carefully. There was a row of scars on the inside of her arm, most of them silvery and difficult to see in the dim light, but one was darker than the others.

"Good," said Esiko, more to Garai than to me. "I gave orders that all the guards and servants must help put it out."

That was why the buildings were so empty of people. A thought struck me.

"Where is Iskan?"

Esiko looked away. "He is at the Palace of Tranquility."

"It was he who started the fire," I said, and looked at my daughter, but she did not respond. That was confirmation enough.

Garai approached the spring, knelt and drank a sip of water directly from her cupped hand. I turned to face Esiko again.

"Do you not see? Iskan is mad, afflicted by the madness of the life force. He is willing to do whatever it takes, kill as many as it takes, to reach his ends. Surely you have seen the truth in Anji, Esiko, my only daughter?"

She was quiet for a moment. "When you first met Father, what was he like?"

"Self-obsessed. Willing to do whatever was necessary to get what he wanted. He thought that everybody was against him, and that he was superior to everybody else."

"There, you see!" She turned to me, her eyes beseeching. "He has always been that way! But that is not I, Mother, can you not see that? I am not Father."

I wanted to hold out my arms and embrace my daughter—my beautiful, strong, wise daughter. Yet all I could feel was the grip she had held on my death.

312

Now it was I who turned away. Then I saw someone. Estegi glided in through the door like a shadow and walked straight over to me. She did not bow. She stood tall and looked me in the eye.

"I have delivered two of your children. I have served you. I have kept your secrets as my own. Do you trust me?"

Taken aback, I regarded Estegi the servant. Estegi the woman. She did not look like herself under the glow of the moon.

"I trust no one, Estegi. But I trust you no less than my daughter or Garai." As I said their names I realized that they were the only people in the world who meant anything to me. I glanced at Garai. She had a blade in her hand, held against her bared left arm, and stood muttering something to herself. Only then did I understand that she was my only ally against Iskan, against the dairahesi, against the world. More than Esiko, who had always been closer to her father than to me.

Garai and Estegi, the two who had always stood by my side.

Estegi contemplated my answer and then nodded.

"Good enough for us," she said. Then she turned to Esiko. "Will you not shout for help? Will you not call the guards, no matter what you see?"

Esiko turned to me, to Garai and to Estegi. "Have I ever before? Who do you take me for?"

Estegi quickly turned and left. Soon she returned with three other women. Sulani, Clarás and Orseola. They were all carrying sacks, rope and bundles. I could not prevent myself from laughing.

"What a sorry sight! What do you think you are doing?"

Sulani stiffened. She approached and stood tall above me.

"We are leaving this cursed place," she said through gritted teeth. "We have had enough of being treated like animals."

"You will not get far." I shook my head. "How could four solitary women evade Iskan's power and madness?"

"We have a plan." Sulani pointed at something in her belt. I looked.

"A knife stolen from the kitchen? That is your plan? Your weapon?"

"What do you know of our plan?" Sulani did not take her eyes off me. "What do you know about what we can do? What we are capable of?"

"Sulani." In Estegi's mouth the name became an entreaty. A gentle caress. The word alone made Sulani step aside. Estegi looked at me, still with the eyes of a free woman. She used my name as though we were equals. "Kabira, we have long prepared for this escape. We have a boat."

Clarás made a move to stop her, but Estegi shook her head. "Kabira is just as imprisoned as we. And Garai too." She raised her voice to include Garai, who was now kneeling and chanting, blade in hand. "Perhaps you do not see the cage as we see it, Kabira. But it exists. And you can be free."

"Free?" I laughed, and even I could hear how bitter and wounded my laughter sounded. "Free? There is no freedom, Estegi. Not for me. Not from what keeps me captive."

"Yes there is, Kabira." She laid her hand on my arm. "Freedom is possible, even for you."

I shook my head. Shook off her hand. Turned away, toward the spring where Garai was kneeling, and rubbed my cheeks with my sleeves.

Garai slashed at her skin with the blade. A dark streak welled up. Blood dripped down into Anji's water.

And Anji responded.

CLARÁS

We all felt it. Whether we had drunk the spring water or not. A torrent of energy rushed toward us, engulfed us, flooded into us. Orseola was thrown backward. I caught her before she fell. It was like a storm, like a great wave gushing down over our heads, drowning us in its power, and leaving us flapping and gasping like fish on the shore.

None of us were the same after that. I could feel it inside me—the force that had taken possession of me. I could see everything as though with new eyes. I saw what power there was in the spring's water, saw it as plainly as seeing that blood is red. When I looked at the other women, I could see that the same energy had entered into all of them, in different ways.

Garai stood up. To my eyes, she was now lit up from within. She placed the knife in her belt and looked straight at me.

"I am coming with you. There is nothing left for me here now."

"We don't have the food supply for more people," I said.

"I can fast. Where are you journeying to?" She walked toward me. Her steps resounded with the echo of the energy surge we had all felt. With my new eyes I could see the energy glowing inside her like a second heart. She had truly acquired all the power of a priestess. Behind her Kabira and Esiko continued to speak in low voices. Sulani looked at Garai skeptically.

"You are old. It is a long journey."

Garai laughed. I believe it was the first time since I had come

315

to Ohaddin that I had heard laughter free from bitterness. "I can survive without food or water far longer than you can, warrior. I know more about the powers of water and earth than you do, Clarás. And I know more about healing and birthing than Estegi." She pointed at my belly. "I can help you."

"It is true," said Estegi. When I looked at her, I saw that her hands appeared to be glowing. Hands deft at crafting and making. "She knows more about healing than anyone. She can aid us in sickness. The way is long."

I yielded. "So be it. You can bear my burdens, priestess. We have a boat in Ameka, one night's westward march."

"And the voyage, where is it to?"

"To my land," said Orseola. She was completely calm now. I could see the glowing energy as a blanket around all that gnawed and ripped at her insides. "To Terasu, the giant trees and the island of the mangrove swamps."

Garai seemed delighted. "Sources of power I am yet to discover, yet to make offerings to! We must leave without delay."

"You do not give the orders, old woman," said Sulani. I saw the new energy, this gift from the spring, glow as new strength in her arms and legs. "I am the one who—"

She stopped. There, in the open doorway, stood a slender young girl with her hair wrapped around her like a cloak.

Iona.

"I heard my monster calling for me," she said slowly. Everyone froze.

She was the one. She was the one who would betray us. The man's new wife. The child bride.

As soon as she caught sight of Garai, she lifted one hand to shield her eyes as though from a bright light. Then she bowed low before her.

"Priestess."

"Offering," responded Garai, and bowed in return.

"We must go at once," hissed Sulani. "Who knows what she heard? Who knows what she will tell him? Anybody could turn up here." She pointed up at the grate-covered aperture in the ceiling. "That is our best means of escape. But how can we remove the grate?"

"I heard everything," said Iona in her girlish voice. "I heard it all."

Sulani turned around. The knife glinted in her hand. She only managed a few steps toward Iona before she was hurled backward. With my new vision I could see a power in Iona. But it was different from ours. It throbbed, dark and dangerous, and emanated from an object she held wrapped up at her hip.

"Mizra will not let you harm me," said Iona. "Nobody can harm me. Not before the proper offering has been performed."

Estegi raised her hands. "None of us will harm any other. Sulani." Her voice contained a warning.

"Iona," said Garai. "Will you come with us?"

"Oh, no." Iona shook her head. "My fate lies here with my monster." A flicker of hesitation. Something faltered. "But . . . I thought he was here. That he was calling to me. I thought the time had come."

"The time has come, little wife."

There he was, standing in the doorway. We had waited too long. I cursed them all internally. They had slowed me down. Had I been alone, I would have already been on my way.

Had I been alone, I would never have found *Naondel*.

"Look what we have here," he said slowly as he entered. As he approached us, he stepped into the moonlight. I found it hard to look at him with my new sight. A dark power was glowing red and black throughout his entire body. There was little human left about him.

I had to cover my eyes from the terrible light. His white trousers were black with soot. His hands and face likewise. Behind him raged the roar of the inferno, but quieter now. It was coming under control. "A little gathering. A midnight gathering." His voice was drawling and smug.

Nobody spoke.

"What sort of intrigues are you plotting now? Conspiracy, betrayal—there is always someone." He shook his head. "Imagine if you all burned to death in the great fire." He looked at us thoughtfully. "All together. You rushed out to help and a burning roof came crashing down on top of you. Yes, so it was." He sighed. "It will be an inconvenience to replace you all in one go. Costly. And yet, so it is."

Esiko stood up. She walked over to him.

"Father." She held her hands outstretched with her palms facing upward. "I have been here the whole time. They took refuge here, for fear of the blaze." She gestured to all of us. "These women are not even friends, Father. They barely converse with one another."

"Esiko." He said the name uncertainly. It was still unfamiliar on his tongue. "My daughter."

Esiko bowed her neck humbly.

"When have I ever put my faith in the words of women? If

they are not all planning some wickedness together, then at least some of them are individually. Or if they are not doing so yet, they soon will." He shrugged his shoulders. "I am tired of them anyhow. It may be a boon to get some fresh blood into the dairahesi."

"Permit me to lead Mother to safety first," Esiko said quickly, without looking at us.

"Kabira." He turned to his first wife, the old woman. "If anyone is plotting wickedness against me it is she. Anji knows." He spoke in a gentle hush. "Anji has shown me everything." Kabira stood watching her daughter. Something was passing between them. I don't know what. Kabira turned and looked away, her arms hanging limply. She was a woman who had lost hope a long time ago.

The man turned to Iona. Swift as a hungry shark.

"You. Are you part of the conspiracy? Will you murder me as I sleep in your arms?"

"You possess my death." Iona looked at him, unafraid.

"I possess you. The time has come."

Iona hesitated.

"The monster summoned me," she mumbled, to convince herself. She moved the fabric at her hip, unwrapped a bundle and produced an object. The skull. The one I had seen when I visited her room. That was the source of the dark energy streaming out from her. She held it up for all to see.

"My predecessor. My protector. Her name is Mizra."

GARAI

I bowed to the skull, the offering, the priestess. She had offered more than I ever had, and in death had gone beyond where I ever could. Her power was greater than I could have imagined. Greater even than that of the spring.

CLARÁS

I ona laid Mizra on the ground. Unbuttoned her jacket with unhurried, dignified movements. Exposed her throat.

Now she was powerless. Helpless.

"I am ready. The circle shall be completed. Life and death, one and the same."

The man laughed, took a few steps toward Iona and began to untie his trousers. She shook her head violently.

"You know that you cannot desecrate the offering by defiling my body," said Iona.

SULANI

She had stood up to him, that girl. So small—how had she succeeded in opposing him with his desires and threats and violence? I looked at her. Skinny limbs, black hair like a torrent of rain over her shoulders. Iskan before her, full of the pulsating dark power. How could she withstand it?

She pressed her back up against the wall. We were all standing around her, and we all looked on, but none of us intervened. Not even I. Though my arms were throbbing with their newfound strength, and though I had a knife in my belt. This has filled me with shame ever since. We were many, and he was one, yet his power over us was so great that we dared not do anything. For several years he had owned us, and controlled every aspect of our lives. My body had not forgotten the pain he had inflicted on it. He shall kill us all, I thought, and there is nothing we can do to stop him.

CLARÁS

The man licked his lips. "Little bird, you know I never cared about your sacrifice. However, I do have a great interest in your body." He exposed his member and I heard Esiko gasp.

"Father, not here."

He did not respond.

I laid my hands across my belly. We were so close to succeeding, to escaping, and now he would kill us all. I was convinced of it. So what did it matter what he did to Iona's body first?

It was nothing he had not already done to the rest of us. I looked around. Could I steal away without anybody noticing?

Iona reached for the skull, but the man kicked it out of reach. Kabira bent down and picked it up. She held it in one hand, in wonder. The man ignored her.

Iona flattened her back harder against the wall, looking around wildly, all composure gone. "I would rather die!"

The man tutted and wrapped his hand around her throat. "How obsessed you are with your own death." Then he let go, laughed, reclothed his member and brought out a dagger. "Here." He handed the dagger to her. "I can take you afterward just as well. Yet somehow I highly doubt your desire to die would remain were the decision your own."

Iona stared at the blade as if she could not understand how it had gotten into her hand.

"I was waiting for death. I was ready for it. I have been trained for death my entire life. The monster and the offering, that is the foundation the circle is built upon." She laughed. Looked straight at Iskan. She no longer appeared dainty and slight. All of a sudden she seemed to tower above the man.

"The story of the monster and the offering has another possible ending," she said. She held Iskan's dagger in a steady hand. She touched the tip to her throat. Pressed it against the exposed skin. Iskan smiled that smile we all knew too well.

"Not for me." He lifted his hands and held them out toward her. "For a monster one death is as good as another."

"One death is as good as another," repeated Iona. "So be it."

She turned the dagger lightning-quick and thrust it deep into his chest.

In the same moment Kabira threw the skull into the spring.

Esiko screamed.

KABIRA

When I picked the skull up from the ground and felt its extraordinary power in my hand, I understood what I must do. For Esiko's sake. I looked at her, my beloved daughter, all I had left in the world, and my eyes blurred with tears, knowing that she would despise me. Knowing that to save her I would have to lose her forever.

"I love you," I whispered, but nobody heard, save Anji and the skull.

As Iona thrust the blade into Iskan's breast I turned and cast the skull into the water.

I can still hear Esiko's scream. At first I believed it was due to seeing her father injured, then due to seeing what I had done. But she collapsed to the ground, her face contorted in pain.

"It burns!" she screamed. "Father, help me!"

GARAI

The spring was dying. It was seething and simmering in its opulent prison of marble and gold. It was the best outcome. To imprison such life force is wrong. It goes against all natural harmony. But I could feel its death throes course through my own body, and the pain was excruciating. It was only thanks to the new power inside me that I could withstand it.

Esiko had lived all her life with the power of the spring inside her. Hers was a struggle between life and death.

KABIRA

I rushed to my daughter where she lay on the ground. Despite her pain, she recoiled from me.

"Don't touch me!" she gasped. "Don't touch me! Be gone! I never want to see you again! You have killed her, you have—" She arched her body in pain like a bowstring. "You have taken away from me the thing I love most! Go!"

I stepped back. I knew this would happen. Nevertheless, the sense of loss was so piercing that I could hardly breathe.

Everyone I had ever loved. I would lose them all. And the fault, once again, was mine to bear.

CLARÁS

F ool," said the man. "I have been most careful to protect my own death. You cannot reach it with a mere dagger." But he was sweating. He groaned. Maybe Iona couldn't reach his death, but she had caused him pain and injury. He glared at Iona with eyes as dark as a bottomless chasm. She cowered, flailed her arms helplessly, and suddenly fell backward with a scream.

"He is drawing her death nearer," whispered Garai suddenly in my ear. "Now is the time."

At first I didn't understand what she meant. But then the child inside me kicked. Run away. Run away.

The man was groaning with a cavernous rattling sound. He was conscious, but barely.

There was no time to talk. No time to make plans. We had to get away, away from the man, away from his control. Before he drew all of our deaths closer. Sulani and Estegi were holding sacks and rope, Orseola and Garai pulled Iona along with them. I took Kabira by the hand and pulled her along with me.

We left the man and daughter behind us, lying at the side of the dead spring.

SULANI

It was for Estegi's sake that I decided to flee. Everything I have done since meeting her has been for her sake. She wanted us to join forces with Clarás and Orseola: I did as she asked. Then she wanted to include Garai and Kabira, and she did not want to leave Iona behind. Her wish was my command.

On her say-so I lifted the others up onto that pagoda roof in Ohaddin, and helped them escape from the wrath of the captain. They were practically weightless; my arms were stronger than ever before. Not even Iona's barely conscious body caused me strain. It was as if the life force from the River were rushing through my veins once more. Though it was not the same. This power was distinct. It smacked of something different. It commanded me in a different way. I was no longer an agent, an avenger. I was only myself: Sulani.

Why had I not picked up the blade and plunged it deeper inside him? When the last woman was up—Clarás, with her heavy belly—I looked around. I could have run back and killed him. He could claim whatever he liked about his death, enough stabs and he would be done for.

There was no one to be seen. I was only a few steps from the door.

"Sulani." Estegi's face appeared over the edge of the roof. She reached out her hand. I took it, felt its softness, the short fingers, the bony wrist. With her help I hoisted myself up until I got a hold on the edge of the roof and swung up onto it.

We walked, crouching, across the roof. I glanced eastward. The Palace of Tranquility was no more than a smoking pile of debris. The fire that had spread to the Temple of Learning was under control. At the roof's edge I stopped and scanned our surroundings. We were directly above the outside wall that enclosed the palace. Heavily manned. The guards had barely even left their posts to help with the firefighting.

I did not like the thought of escaping along this wall. I had neither planned for it nor mapped out the route. I knew that the captain's men were well trained and hardy. Terror had made them become so.

"Wait here," I said. "Keep quiet and still."

Estegi nodded. I swung down onto the wall. How glorious to be able to move again—to run, sneak, and dodge. I located the first patrol with ease, came upon one of the guards from behind and slit his throat before my presence was even noticed. The other had no time to so much as draw his sword before he too was silenced. No other guards could be seen on this stretch of wall but I was not familiar with their routines or patrols. Perhaps another patrol was soon on its way. Perhaps they had a system of regular signals to confirm all was well. I pulled off one of their helmets and stuck it under my arm. Then I peered down over the wall, to see what lay outside. It was dark below, but I could make out small houses built up against the wall. That was good. It meant alleys we could hide in. I ran back along the wall and whistled quietly up to the pagoda roof. Estegi threw down one end of the rope I had left there, and I fastened it to a ring in the wall. They slid down, one by one. A simple escape with Estegi. That was all I wanted. She had accumulated one wing-clipped woman after another. That was her way. She could not turn her back on someone in need. When she came sliding down the rope, a little clumsily, I caught her in my arms, and for one brief moment I held her close. I breathed in her warmth and scent, then released her to catch Iona, who was being lowered down by Garai. Iona was conscious now, but very weak.

"Is everything well?" I asked.

"My death," she wheezed. "He has brought it so close, it is snapping at my heels." She smiled a crooked little smile. "And now I no longer welcome it like a stray dog."

Garai untied the rope and jumped down without it. I led them part of the way along the wall, but not all the way to the dead guards. I retied the rope and fed it down toward the roof of a little house below us.

"Now is the greatest challenge. If we can reach the city without being discovered, we can head west under cover of darkness. Quickly and quietly now."

Garai descended first, without making a sound. She was lithe and strong for her age. She helped the others down while I kept a lookout. Kabira was clumsy and slow and made a lot of noise as she came down the rope. She fell the last part of the way. I looked around. Held the blade in readiness as Estegi went down to the roof, followed by Clarás.

Orseola looked at them. Without a word she pointed east along the wall. Moonlight flashed on approaching spearheads. I beckoned to her to climb down. They did not seem to have discovered us yet, or if they had, they were without bows. I hoped that Estegi would understand that she must take the others with her and move on immediately. Iona could not manage the descent on her own. I set her down. Her little body buckled into a gray lump, barely discernible in the shadows. I quickly put on the helmet and ran to meet the guards. They must not discover Iona, or the rope. Or sound the alarm.

They probably did not believe their eyes at first. There were three of them, and they simply stood there awaiting my arrival. They thought I was one of them, on my way with a message. The black of the night worked in my favor. I was already in close range when one of them raised his spear in doubt. His grip was weak, and I easily tore the spear from his hands, turned it around and pierced his heart. He bent double with a howl. The guard on the right launched at me with his spear, but the third guard was forced to hold back as the top of the wall was too narrow for three men. I kicked the spear to the side and brought out my knife. It was short, I had no range, yet he had no chance to draw his sword before I stuck the knife in his throat. He fell to his knees at once, but the first guard remained standing, the spear still protruding from his wound. The third guard at the back charged at me with a roar. I groped for my knife but could not get it. I dived at his legs and managed to bring him to the ground with all this new strength—my old strength, once so familiar, which I had thought was lost forever. His heavy kit limited his movement. Before he could get back on his feet, I crawled from under his legs, spun around and jumped on his back. His chain mail did not stop me knocking the wind out of him. I tore the sword from his hand and thrust it in his unprotected neck.

Then I slit the throat of the first guard as well. Out of mercy.

I took off my helmet, pulled the knife from the other guard's throat and gave it a quick wipe on his trousers. The sword was good, but would be impossible to hide during our escape. One of them had a dagger, much longer and better than my knife. I stuck both knife and dagger into the waist of my trousers, and ran.

Iona was waiting exactly where I had left her. I lifted her up on my back and she wrapped her arms around my neck. I swung down from the top of the wall holding the rope in both hands. Carrying Iona made it harder to climb, but only slightly. Soon I reached the roof of one of the houses below and looked around. Nobody in sight.

Good. Estegi had had the good sense to take the others with her and move on.

I let the rope dangle and walked across the roof. I readjusted Iona on my back, held onto her legs and jumped down from the roof and into the narrow alley that ran along the front side of the house.

I felt a hand on my arm. I spun around, both blades at the ready.

"Shh," came Estegi's husky voice. "Over here."

She led me through a labyrinth of alleyways where I would surely have got lost. The moon was obscured by clouds and the darkness had intensified. I had never been in the city beyond the palace before, but Estegi had been there often on errands for the dairahesi. She led me to a doorway where the others were waiting, quiet as mice. Without a word we continued through the city. Now it was Estegi's turn to lead us, Estegi who knew what to do.

Ohaddin had no city walls—the captain had not gone to the trouble of defending anything other than the palace—so it was easy for us to escape unseen. Naturally we encountered some nocturnal wanderers: drunken men, errand boys, bakers already on their way to their shops to begin the morning's bread. But if anyone tried to speak to us, Estegi simply looked at them and held up her palms, the words died on their lips and they left us in peace. It was as if they could no longer see us, or they no longer cared. In this way, we passed through the city and onto the highway leading westward from Ohaddin to Ameka, the town that serves as a trading point for the great Sakanui River. Goods imported from overseas are transported along the river to the capital.

Dawn was already approaching and we had only just emerged from Ohaddin. Iona was hanging on my back, but this did not cause me difficulty. What did slow us down was Kabira, whose fall had left her with a hurt foot and a limp, despite Garai's support.

"We have to take a different route," I said when we had all stopped for a short moment to rest.

Orseola was staring into the darkness. "There is a path. Southward. A goat trail. Not often used."

"How do you know?" I was suspicious. As far as I knew, Orseola had not moved around beyond the walls of Ohaddin any more than the rest of us, apart from Estegi and perhaps Kabira in her youth.

"I have seen it in their dreams," said Orseola. "This whole landscape is etched on my mind like a map." She sounded bitter. "I never asked for it. I do not want to carry it with me wherever I go. Just give me trees and I would be happy."

We soon found the path and began to follow it. Our progress became more laborious. We tripped over roots and stones. Orseola went first and warned us of all hindrances to come. She stopped by a spring in a grove of bao trees. Everybody drank, and so did I. Fresh water was on my mind. We had several waterskins with us

331

to fill from the river before we reached the sea, but would they be enough for the voyage? There were three more in our party than we had originally planned for. The food would certainly run out, but one can survive a long time without food. Water is another matter.

We were stumbling in the darkness, which very soon began to fade into light. After that our steps were more visible, but then so were we—to guards and soldiers and spies. Or the captain himself.

But he had lost the spring water, and without it he could not heal himself as easily as before. Though Iona had not succeeded in slaying him, he was severely wounded.

Wounded animals fight back the hardest.

As the sun's first rays were creeping over the horizon, behind us we heard the sound of hoofbeats along the road to the north. We crouched behind some bushes and waited. Morning birds were singing. From the west came the sound of goats bleating. When nothing broke the peace, we eventually emerged and continued walking. Orseola came behind me and I went back in the lead. Iona was breathing heavily on my neck. This landscape was foreign to me, with unfamiliar valleys and heights. I longed for the dense brushwood of my riverbanks instead of these mostly open, newly sown fields. At times the path ran through a grove of bao or etse trees, but trees did not mean safety. Soldiers and spies could be hiding in there just as easily as we could.

We saw some people, but only laborers sowing the land. At one point two young boys came running toward us, chasing their herd of goats and frolicking kids. They stopped and gawked at us. We truly were a bizarre troop of women, some with more expensive clothes and jewelry than they had ever seen in their lives, others modestly dressed. Garai was barefoot. Furthermore, I was carrying a semiconscious woman on my back.

One boy stared, unafraid, straight at Kabira, who was wearing the finest clothing.

"What's her ladyship doing here?" he asked, picking his nose. He had dirty bare feet and was wearing a shirt and trousers of undyed linen.

Kabira stared at him.

"Did your mother teach you nothing? How dare you speak before you are spoken to—to an unknown woman, superior to you in age and rank?"

The boy just stood there with his mouth open.

"Answer me, boy!"

"Dunno, milady," he mumbled.

"Shockingly impudent behavior. It is not for you, goatherd, to ask me anything. It is not for you, or you—" she turned to the second boy—"to even recall that you ever saw us. Understood?"

They nodded and mumbled in the affirmative, then ran off after their goats as fast as their skinny legs could carry them. The jingle of the little goat bells disappeared into the distance along the path in front of us.

"The gift of words and lies," said Clarás, looking at Kabira's mouth.

"What do you mean?" I asked.

"The life force of the spring has bestowed something on each of us," said Clarás. "Haven't you noticed? Though the spring be dead, it lives on in us. You have been given strength in your limbs; Garai, the sacred powers of a priestess; Estegi, the ability to create

333

with her hands; Orseola, a calm energy that helps her control the dreams. And I can see everything."

Estegi caught sight of the blood on my clothes. We had not stopped since the sun had come up, and in the darkness she had not seen it.

"Sulani! You are hurt!" She came over to me and examined my body with fretting hands.

"I am not hurt. The blood is not mine."

"But . . . " She dropped her hands to her sides. Looked me in the eye. Then looked away.

I turned around and readjusted Iona on my back. Gritted my teeth, hard, and continued to walk.

ᴡ

First I recognized the scent of the Sakanui River. It did not smell like my River, but I inhaled it deeply anyhow. We saw more and more people in the fields, and sometimes we passed someone on the path, but when Kabira spoke to them they seemed to forget immediately that they had seen us at all. When the roofs of Ameka ahead of us first came into view, so too did the first soldiers. It was still morning, but the sun had risen a fair way above the horizon.

We sat down in a dell and conferred. It was decided that we could not risk entering Ameka all together. Clarás could sail and Estegi knew where the boat was kept, so they two would go and sail it south along the river and find us on the bank. I wanted to wait until we were under cover of darkness, but Clarás insisted on sailing that same day.

"They would never suspect that we have a boat," she said, and gazed impatiently at Ameka.

Estegi nodded. "I believe he has sent most of the soldiers northward, where Sulani is from, and eastward, where Garai is from. We must travel as far away as possible before he realizes his mistake."

"If Esiko doesn't reveal our plan, that is. She heard everything."

"My daughter will not betray us," said Kabira, "do not even think it." At once I felt a sense of calm flow into me. Of course she would not. We were entirely safe.

"Stop," said Clarás quietly, and Kabira flinched. The calm in me disappeared.

Clarás and Estegi gathered the ropes and sails and disappeared farther along the path. Garai was sitting bent over Iona, both hands on her forehead, muttering something inaudible. Then she looked up at me.

"Her death is very near now. There is nothing I can do."

"We are not leaving her here," I said. In my mind's eye I saw her once again thrusting the dagger into the captain's chest. She had done what I had not been able to do.

"I did not mean that either," said Garai. "But now we must bind her to your back. She cannot hold on any longer."

We bound Iona to my back with one of Kabira's shawls, then proceeded to diverge from the path and head through the rolling fields heading southwest. We passed groups of laborers, so emaciated they resembled slaves. All this fertile soil, and nothing to eat. Only spices for trade. Most had not the strength to trouble themselves about us, but if anyone looked at us, once Kabira had spoken to them, they immediately looked away.

Kabira could not hurry her steps, especially through the fields, and was slowing us down. I wanted to reach the larger spice plantation farther south. There we could be hidden from curious eyes. The sun was burning my neck and, though Iona was a light burden, I was dripping with sweat. When we finally reached the trees, I was as grateful for shade as I was for their protection.

"We are too close to Ohaddin," I said. "I would rather continue our trek but it is best that we wait for the boat here. We can only hope that Clarás and Estegi come quickly."

As always when I say Estegi's name, I felt a sudden burst of warmth in my heart. Then I remembered her expression when she realized why I had blood on my clothes.

I had just laid Iona down under a tree when the soldiers came.

CLARÁS

The scent of the river brought tears to my eyes. It was nothing like the smell of the ocean, and yet it was water. Free, flowing water. Estegi and I decided to walk through the town without trying to hide. Before we reached the houses, I removed the slave comb from my hair and hid it. Estegi was dressed as a servant. Nobody was suspicious. My clothes were simple; I could have passed for the daughter or wife of a merchant. Estegi had to carry the sails and ropes, or else it would have seemed strange.

Estegi led me through the streets and I looked at the people we passed. People with jobs, errands, lives. Soon I too would have such things. I would give these things to my child.

The boathouse lay on the southern edge of the town. Estegi's cousin had said that we could simply come and take it. But when we reached what we believed to be the right boathouse, it was locked. The only thing to do was go in via the water. Without a moment's hesitation I took off my jacket and dived in.

Swimming in water! Muddy, sweet river water, but water all the same. My dry skin soaked in the moisture. Below the surface I opened my eyes and my hair swirled before my eyes like seaweed. I swam underwater until I saw her keel, and I knew it was her: *Naondel*. A strong, fine keel. Healthy wood. I surfaced by her side, like a whale calf to its mother. Pressed my cheek against her. Breathed in the scent of wet wood. She had been polished with oil and hemp. That was a sign of good craftsmanship.

Reluctantly, I climbed up and opened the gate out to the river.

As I stepped into *Naondel*, she took my weight like an old friend. She had no equipment, not even oars. She had a single mast for a square sail. She was around thirty feet long and wide, with an angular stern. Not made for sailing on the open sea, but she would do for our voyage to Terasu. In the absence of oars, I had to push her out and then along the length of the boathouse to the pier where Estegi was waiting.

Just as she had thrown aboard the rolls of rope and the heap of sails, a man appeared and spoke to us.

"Hello there."

A beardless man had appeared behind Estegi. He was a little older than I, his face was sea worn and his body well worked.

Estegi turned around at once and bowed low to the man.

"We are readying the boat." She used no title of respect, yet her words were most respectful.

"You stole it."

"Not at all." She turned up her palms. "The boat belongs to my cousin. Freeman Wadi. He has bought it but wants us to prepare it and sail it to Shukurin."

"How can a servant have a freeman as cousin?" The man peered suspiciously at Estegi. Her words had not succeeded in calming his suspicions. Without drawing attention to myself, I began to organize the things on deck.

"My parents disowned me," she said, looking at the ground. "But my cousin has always been good to me."

I looked at Estegi, and wondered if this were true.

She was still standing with up-facing palms and I could feel a power flowing from her. The gift of the spring. The man hohummed and then looked at *Naondel*.

"You need help with the rigging?" Without awaiting an answer, he stepped aboard. Together we hoisted the sail. I was glad of his help, as it had been a good while since I had handled rigging. We thanked him profusely afterward, offering a portion of our food provisions as a gift, but he declined. He stood by the boathouse and watched us sail away. With my hand on the helm I felt a deep sense of calm. We were on our way. I had a boat. But Estegi's words lingered with me.

"Did they really disown you? Your parents?"

She nodded.

"I had to leave my home 'cause there was no money for a dowry. Is that what happened to you?"

She shook her head. "No. It was when I was very little. I am not—" She stopped. She did not want to continue. So I let her be. Some things are better left unsaid.

SULANI

There were seven of them. They outnumbered us. On horseback, heavily armed. I had my dagger and knife, so I could kill two or three, maybe more, but not before they had a chance to harm the other women. Or capture them, capture all of us. Back to the cage. Back to him. The captain, the man, the monster, the Vizier: Iskan.

Soon they had us surrounded. Iona was lying on the ground, up against the trunk of a tree. Orseola was crouching by her side, with one hand on the trunk, muttering something. Garai stood tall by my side, not cowering nor hiding. But what could she do to help me?

The leader of the soldiers, a young man with a chestnut beard and heavy gauntlets, turned to Kabira.

"Kabira ak Malik-cho. Your husband demands your presence in Ohaddin at once."

Kabira looked disdainfully at the man on the horse. "Tell my husband, the Vizier of Karenokoi, that his wife was nowhere to be found."

The soldier's eyes flickered. His gaze swept across us. He gathered his reins to turn his horse and his men did the same.

But then he shuddered and furrowed his brow. "You are to follow us. At once." He gave a signal to his men and three of them sheathed their swords and dismounted.

The soldiers had been on the lookout for us. It was not as easy to make them forget that they had seen us as it had been with strangers.

Orseola's mumbling became more and more urgent. The treetops were whispering and rustling in the wind. Dead leaves crumbled beneath the soldiers' boots as they stepped toward us. One of them was advancing on Iona. The other two on Kabira, Garai and me.

Garai held her hands out to one of them.

"No," she said, and he stopped. With his mouth half open and his weapon held high, he became as though petrified, with only his eyes still moving.

I drew the dagger I had taken from the soldier on the wall and attacked the other soldier. He was unprepared, and I thrust my weapon into his eye. He was killed instantly. The leader, still on horseback, let out a shout and started advancing toward me, with the three remaining mounted soldiers close behind.

The rustling in the trees was growing ever louder, and it merged with Orseola's muttering. I pushed Kabira to the ground and passed my knife to Garai, narrowly dodging the leader's horse. My dagger afforded me little reach, so I dived to the side and slit the throat of the soldier who was standing over Iona. I took his sword and spun around.

The leader's horse whinnied and reared. One of the mounted soldiers started screaming and flailing his hands in front of his face. The horses whinnied, bucked and reared, trying to throw their riders.

Everywhere was teeming with insects. On the horses, on the soldiers' armor and uncovered faces. Crawling, stinging, biting, thrumming. Beetles, ants, spiders, cockroaches, centipedes; all called forth from rotten stumps, tree trunks and dark, moist holes of the earth. The men and horses became frantic. They screamed and thrashed around, and their swords fell clattering to the ground. Only the man Garai had frozen stood stock-still as beetles and cockroaches crawled over his open eyes, in his hair and ears, over his entire body until he was blanketed with a black, living thrum. Then he fell onto his back. Spasmed a few times. Then lay still once more.

Not a single insect touched us women.

The soldiers had lost all control over their mounts, and the horses bolted through the trees. We heard the hoofbeats fade into the distance. Then all was quiet, but for the creeping, crawling sound of millions upon millions of scuttling insects.

I looked at Orseola. She smiled at me.

"Trees can talk to one another," she said. "Only most have forgotten. I helped them remember. They can also call forth insects, when dangers threaten. They did very well." She patted the tree trunk and the insects began to crawl back into their holes and hiding places.

Garai had caught one of the fallen soldiers' horses by the bridle and was whispering to it gently. Its ears were pressed backward and its eyes were rolling but it remained, trembling, as she spoke.

"Keep a hold of him," she said to me. "I will catch another."

I did as she said. Held the horse and stroked his neck and spoke to him.

Kabira sat cross-legged next to Iona, who lay unmoving on the ground under the tree. Orseola stretched out beside them and went to sleep. Nobody spoke.

We did not know how much time we had.

We had no choice but to wait.

After a long while Garai returned with a brown war horse. He was following her willingly though she did not hold his reins.

"We will send the horses to the north," she said. "They could easily have carried four women away. It may serve to mislead our pursuers. For a while."

"We can only hope," sneered Kabira.

I looked at Garai. "How do we make the horses walk north?"

She patted the brown stallion, who nuzzled her cheek. "Not walk. Gallop. And leave clear tracks behind."

Garai beckoned to the horse I was holding and he started walking toward her at once. She removed both their saddles and saddlebags, then stood between them and spoke quietly. Both animals bowed their heads to the white-haired woman, and flicked their ears toward her. She touched their muzzles and brows, and gently stroked over their eyes. The brown stallion neighed and tossed his head. Then he galloped away, closely followed by the other horse, and they disappeared at full speed.

I lifted up one saddle, carried it down to the river and flung it in as far as I could. Garai brought down the other and did the same. We sat down next to Iona and waited.

CLARÁS

S he took to the river beautifully. The water was dazzling. The helm was smooth. The halyard creaked as the wind filled the sails and we traveled downstream at a good pace, aided by both wind and current. It was like the old days. It was just as I had dreamed. We weren't safe yet—we were far from safety—but my heart was singing, and as full as *Naondel's* sails. Even if they found us now, even if I was stabbed with a sword, pierced by an arrow, I would die free. And they would never take me alive, that I swore to myself. The child in my belly was not flapping or kicking, but neither was it sleeping. I could feel it inside me, rocking in rhythm with the sway of the boat, in awe of all these new wonders. All these miracles.

Estegi sat at the fore and did not take her gaze off the east bank. Her eyes were searching through each grove of trees. I looked only forward. Southward. Seaward. It was so close now. I could taste it on my tongue. My skin was tingling and prickling with expectancy. Soon. Soon we would be there.

"There they are!" called Estegi urgently. "I see them! Stop!"

Reluctantly, I steered inland. *Naondel* was responsive to my every command. I hauled in the sail. She drifted to shore with barely a sound. I cast the anchor as Sulani waded out to meet the boat. She held it as the others quickly climbed aboard without a word. Estegi leaned out and laid her hand on Sulani's, and their eyes met. For a moment Sulani's face lit up, became beautiful, like the sunrise over the sea. Then it returned to normal just as suddenly.

Garai held the boat while Sulani waded back and fetched Iona. She lifted her gently into it. Her face was pale. Her eyes were closed.

"Is she dead?" Estegi bent over the girl and tucked an empty sack under her head.

"No." Garai climbed aboard, last of all, and sat beside Iona. She stroked her forehead. "But she does not have long left."

I reached for the halyard to hoist the sail again. Garai raised a hand to stop me.

"Wait. Come."

I picked up Estegi's small bag of provisions and stumbled under its weight. Then I crouched down on the deck with the others.

I could see it all plainly. It was the power from the skull that had kept her alive for so long. It was holding her death at bay. But this power had diminished to no more than a pulsing little speck deep behind her forehead. Almost totally gone. The spring's life force was in all of us in different ways: in hands, arms, eyes, heart, and mouth. In Iona it was all but extinguished.

When it died, she would die too.

Suddenly she opened her eyes.

"Sisters," she said, her voice weak but clear.

Then she shut her eyes. Inside her there flickered a weak blue glow.

Garai pulled out her knife. Held it over Iona's breast, over her heart, the tip pointing down.

Estegi held up her hands. "No! You mustn't!"

"It is to save her. You must trust me," she said to Estegi, who slowly lowered her hands.

Garai looked us in the eye, one by one. "Do you trust me?"

We nodded. We had no choice: trust one another, else be done for.

Garai lowered the knife's tip slowly toward Iona's breast. Barely touched the pallid skin.

"I offer you," she said loudly. She passed the knife to Estegi.

"I offer you," said Estegi, and brought the blade with trembling hands toward the girl's heart, as if about to stab her. After her, Orseola took it. "I offer you."

We all took the knife and brought it to her breast and said the words. My turn came last. The handle was warm from the hands of the other women.

"I offer you."

The flame of the life force flickered one last time. Something passed from Iona into all of us. A small part of her power. A memory of what she had been. A gift from the spring, or a gift from herself.

Iona's chest did not rise and fall any longer.

Nobody spoke.

The water lapped gently at *Naondel*'s hull. Estegi wept quietly. Sulani laid a hand on her shoulder. Kabira cleared her throat.

"She is not lost," I said. The others looked at me. I eyed the knife in my hand. "Something of her remains in each of us now. Each of us who held the knife."

Garai nodded slowly. "Clarás is right. Therefore we all carry a part of one another inside us. That was Iona's intention. We are forever bound now, like sisters. Whatsoever shall happen to one of us, shall happen to us all." She looked down at the dead girl. "You are free now. No one's offering any longer."

She caressed Iona's face, from the forehead down to the chin.

When she removed her hand the face was that of another. Same hair, same fair skin, similar shapes of nose and mouth. But it was completely changed. The cheeks had become rosy. The lips were fuller. The girl opened up her eyes. They were brown.

She sat up and looked at us.

"My monsters," she said. When she smiled, dimples appeared in her cheeks.

She gazed out to sea. Shut her eyes and inhaled deeply.

"What strong lungs I have!" she said, and opened her eyes again with a giggle. She held her hands up to her face. "What fine hands!" She ran her hands all over her body, exploring and feeling. "How beautiful I am!" She smiled, and her smile was irresistible.

"I shall name myself. That will be my first deed in this new body." She sat quietly awhile, concentrated. "My name is Daera."

ʊ

As *Naondel* sailed southward along the Sakanui, Daera sat at the fore with the wind in her hair. It wasn't immediately noticeable, but slowly the bonds of our sisterhood were growing. Woman to woman. With Iona's strength and name in our hearts. Each with a share of her darkness and courage.

I had had a brother, but no sisters. Now I suddenly had six. I looked at them closely with my hand resting on the helm of *Naondel*. All I could see of Daera was her back and flying hair. She was laughing into the wind. Sulani sat straight-backed with head held high, examining the eastern shore. Her chin was sharp, her arms powerful under the embroidered jacket. Estegi sat by Sulani's feet, with head bent over sacks and supplies, sorting and ordering. She trusted us: me to steer us, Sulani to protect us. Orseola lay on the bottom of the boat with her head on a sack and eyes shut. I do not believe she was sleeping. I believe she was seeing dreams, but not her own.

Garai and Kabira sat side by side: two old women with deep lines in their faces. One head of shining white hair, one dark and streaked with silver. They reminded me somehow of sea turtles, ancient and wise. I saw now that Kabira was carrying a burden, something large and bulky. How had I not seen it before?

"What have you there, sister?" I asked.

Kabira turned to look at me. I had not used her family name, Cho. I had spoken to her without being spoken to first.

"Sister." She observed me contemplatively. "I had sisters, once, Clarás." She showed the bundle in her lap. "These are the most secret archives from his library. Some of which he has not even deciphered himself."

"Perhaps our fate is of no interest to Iskan, but he will want to reclaim those." Garai spoke without anger or complaint.

Kabira looked at her.

"With their help he could reawaken Anji. Or find new ways to enslave people."

Garai nodded but did not speak.

Kabira thought awhile. "Sisters. So it is." She raised her voice so that all on the vessel could hear.

"My sisters. I have stolen from Iskan. Knowledge—dangerous knowledge with which he could regain his power. Hurt others

348

anew. These are scrolls he will regain at any cost." She lifted the bundle from her knee. "They may not appear as much from the outside, but inside there is much that is yet hidden even from me, but about which I intend to learn. Perhaps this knowledge can be of help to us and others. However, it could be very dangerous if it falls into the wrong hands. What do you think I—we—should do with it?"

"Destroy it," said Sulani at once. "So that no one else may learn about it. Some things should never be recorded, and learned only by those who have no need for written words to understand them."

Garai nodded. "I agree, sister Sulani. In part. I also believe that some things are best kept nowhere but in human hearts. But Iskan stole this wisdom from others. Have we the right to destroy their teachings?"

"He is already searching for them." Orseola sat up. "Not for us, but for them. I see it in his dreams."

"You can see his dreams? From here?" Garai leaned toward her.

"Yes." Orseola frowned. "I could not see his dreams for many years. He shielded himself with the power of the spring. But now he is naked. I can see far now. I can weave dreams from afar. Farther than I had thought possible."

"Can you send him a dream? A dream to deceive him? Into sending the soldiers in the wrong direction? Perhaps a dream that we rode northward?"

Orseola smiled. "Yes." She shut her eyes, and her hands began to dance before her face. I kept an eye on the sails and watery depths. The sun was high above our heads. On the east bank of the river spanned newly sown fields, and the calls of the laborers came drifting across the water. Nobody paid us any attention. A mild wind rustled in the rushes along the riverbanks. We were getting closer and closer to the ocean.

Orseola opened her eyes. "He is going to search in the north," she said.

"How can you be sure?" Sulani said with a frown, before adding: "Sister." She seemed just as surprised to hear the word come out of her mouth as Kabira had.

"How can you be sure that you can swing a sword? Slay a warrior?" Orseola lay down again and shut her eyes, content as a cat in the sunshine. "No need to destroy the texts. You have my word, sister."

And so it was decided. Nobody protested. I don't even know if Daera heard our conversation. She was lying on her belly at the fore, staring across the cloudy river water. She followed the flight of the dragonflies and water striders with her gaze. She looked at everything as though it were new, and created just for her. I felt a vague envy, which soon disappeared. I turned my face to the sun and adjusted the helm slightly, and felt *Naondel* respond.

DAERA

Now is the time for my story, finally it is time! I remember crystal-clear that day on the river when I was born. Everything is etched in my memory: the shadows of the trees on the riverbank, the river's scent of mud and rot, how smoothly *Naondel* flew through the water. I remember every blade of grass; though Kabira says it is impossible, that is how it feels! Everything was so miraculous, so incredible, but nothing more so than my own body. I had a body that was all mine! It was not destined to be an offering. It was not someone else's to possess. It was mine alone, and as I sat at the ship's fore, I was fully engaged in the sensations of living in this, my very own body. My hands were soft and flawless. My heartbeat steady and even. In my mouth my teeth rested against each other. My eyes could see, my ears could hear. I had more than I could have ever wished for. I ran my fingertips over the soft skin of my neck and a shudder of pleasure spread through my body. I could feel pleasure! I laughed and turned around to look at my sisters, the ones who had made me. So beautiful, so fragile, so strong. I fell to my knees beside Estegi and grasped her hands.

"Thank you, my sister, for showing me trust," I said, and kissed the backs of her hands. They felt harsh and hardened in my soft, dainty ones as I caressed her calloused palms. Estegi blushed and mumbled a thank-you. I looked up at Sulani, who was piercing me with jealous eyes, but I laid my chin on her knee anyhow and smiled up at her. "Thank you my sister, for protecting me with your

351

strength." She gave a quick nod, and then looked away, out toward the shore. She was watching over us. I felt safe in her company. I crept down next to Orseola on the deck and whispered in her ear, catching her thick locks of hair in my mouth. "Thank you, my sister, for confusing our pursuers." She turned to face me and rubbed her nose against mine. I got up and went to the helm of the boat, where I bent over Clarás, who was sitting with her swollen belly and the ship's helm in her hand. "Thank you, my sister, for steering us true," I said. Clarás smiled at me with her deep-gray eyes and I could feel her smile reach all the way inside me.

"I have not steered us true yet, little sister."

"But I know that you will!" I swung around and skipped over to Kabira and Garai, who were sitting mid-ship like two little birds, observing all that was happening around them.

"Thank you, my sister, for slaying the spring. For choosing us." Kabira looked at me with a fathomless sorrow in her eyes. My heart ached for her, for all she had suffered. My instincts told me to fall to my knees, and I lay my head on her belly. "I can be your daughter, if you like," I whispered. Her knees were hard and bony beneath me, but then she placed her two warm, wrinkled hands in my hair.

"That should be fine," she said, but her voice sounded thick. I looked up at her weathered face, and at Garai's.

"You have much inside you, Daera," said Garai, and I laughed because it was the first time someone had pronounced my name and it was unbelievably beautiful!

"Thank you, my sister," I began, but then I choked up and it was difficult to get the last words out. "For creating me. For delivering me."

She smiled, a smile that was both austere and warm, and laid her hands on top of Kabira's. Four hands upon my head. Like a blessing.

ѡ

We anchored before we reached the ocean. It was evening, with blue shadows and twilit birdsong, and it was all so beautiful that my heart could hardly bear it all. Between us and the sea lay the port town of Shukurin. Estegi had said it was not really a town, rather a trading point connecting river and sea. Sulani did not want us to sail through during daylight. We would wait until the first hour of dawn, when few were awake, and slip past unnoticed. That was the plan. We hid *Naondel* among the rushes, for this close to the ocean the river was full of boats of various types.

Clarás lay down at once in *Naondel* to sleep. She was pale cheeked and Estegi was fussing around her to make her as comfortable as possible. Observing the round belly under her jacket, I saw something push against the skin from the inside. A foot or a head. An entirely new person was waiting inside there. Someone new, like me.

When she was finished with Clarás, Estegi filled a waterskin with fresh river water. Sulani helped her, and occasionally their hands brushed against one another, as though by accident, and they exchanged glances. Their glances made me tingle inside, tickling at places I did not even know existed in my body. They had something between them. They shared something. I wanted that too.

Kabira and Garai also lay down to rest. I sat on the shore, gazed out across the dark river and saw the stars lighting up, one by one. Frogs were croaking in the reeds. Soon Orseola and Sulani were the only others awake, Orseola because she never liked to sleep when the others did, and Sulani because she was keeping watch. Restlessness fluttered through my body. The world was so beautiful, so new, I wanted to see and experience all that I could.

"I am going ashore," I said, and got up. Sulani shook her head, with that eternal wrinkle in her brow.

"That is not a good idea. Stay here."

But Orseola looked at me, and a little smile played at the corner of her lips. "Let her go, warrior. Some things cannot be confined."

So Sulani let me go, and I swam up to the riverbank and emerged from the rushes we were hidden in.

The sky was enormous above me. There were more stars than I could have imagined possible. A memory flashed through my mind—a different sky, above an island and ocean—and then it was gone. I wandered off along the path that ran between the riverbank and fields of budding okahara until I found a smooth slope. I lay on my back there and looked up at the vast blackness and felt myself disappear into it, and my cheeks were wet and my heart was aching for the beauty of it all, and because I could not fathom why I was receiving all these blessings.

I heard no steps. He moved so lightly and quietly that he tripped over my legs before I noticed his arrival. I sat up as he fell forward, and we looked at each other in the moonlight.

"Oh," he said. "Excuse me." His dark eyes were kind. His voice was gentle: no longer that of a child, though not quite yet a man. His hair fell across his eyes.

I smiled at him and saw that my smile made him bashful. He

rose to his knees and brushed the earth from his palms.

"What are you doing out here at night? It is dangerous."

"Nothing out here can harm me," I said, and leaned in toward him. I breathed in the scent of stables and sweat. I reached out my hand and stroked it over his arm. He took a deep breath but did not move. His skin was soft like silk, but warm and alive. I held my arm next to his and compared our skin: the color, the hairs, the veins underneath. I leaned my face forward and sniffed at his neck, behind his ears. Life! He smelled of life. My breath against his neck made him tremble. I wanted to feel the same. I sat astride him, pulled his face close to mine and kissed him. His lips were rough. I did not really know what to do, and neither did he, but it did not matter. We bumped noses and laughed, but then continued to kiss. He pulled me close into him. His shoulders were bony, his rib cage was hard. His body did not feel at all like mine. I peeled the shirt off his shoulders and explored his body with my hands. Slowly his kisses, his hands, his sex against mine, made me feel hot and weak and eager. I wanted it, I wanted to feel all of these new things.

With every movement we made together, more and more I claimed my body as my own. I wanted to know all about it, how it reacted, what it wanted. It was no offering, no one else's possession to decide over. It was mine and mine alone. To use as I wanted. It was like finding home, it was like falling among stars, it was everything and more.

Afterward I sat still awhile and felt the moist earth beneath my naked buttocks. He smelled different now. So did I. He was leaning on his elbow and looking at me in wonder.

"Are you for real? Or are you the spirit of the river?"

"For you I became flesh and blood tonight," I answered, and smiled.

When I had dressed and turned to go, he called after me, asked me my name, begged me to stay. I smiled into the night air as I continued walking.

"My name is Daera, and I stay for no one."

This, to me, was the most important event of our journey. Not the sudden storm that blew *Naondel* off course from Terasu and far off to the southwest. Not the hunger, nor thirst, nor our flirts with death. Not when Clarás's tears drew fish from the water so that we could eat our fill. Not how the bond of new sisterhood brought us closer together. Not even the storm that hurled us onto the rocks of the island of Menos, or our utter joy at finding ourselves safe, or the strength of the life force Garai and Clarás felt in the island, which made us realize we had found our new home. No, the most important thing was that night with the nameless boy, the night that brought me closer to life and far, far away from death.

KABIRA

I t is spring now. Our seventh on the island. Yesterday Sulani caught sight of the first trading vessel beyond the Teeth— the sharp rocks that protrude skyward from the water by the entrance to our port. Merchant sailors do not dare sail here when the sea is tempestuous. Sulani and Estegi waded out and met the little rowboat, and the ship waited behind. The tradesmen are not permitted to set foot on our mountainous island. No men are. Garai says it must be so. The source of power on this island forbids it. She says she has never felt such intensity of the life force before; not even Anji can compare to the island of Menos.

Sulani and Estegi bore the sacks of our purchases and set them down in the courtyard outside Knowledge House. It was a sunny afternoon and the stones were warm beneath my soles. One appreciates such things at my age.

Clarás went in to fetch a pillow for me and I sat on it by the door to Knowledge House. Estegi has decorated the door with wooden engravings; it is a masterpiece. Far below the beautiful surface the wood is scarred by fire. I ran my fingers along the burned wood. My fingertips were blackened by the soot, still loose, though three springs have passed since the men came to the island. The men whom Iskan sent after us. Three springs since they attempted to burn us alive. Three springs since we trapped and killed them all. They have no graves. We committed their bodies and their ship to the sea.

Estegi opened the sacks. Daera laughed as she picked out a

bundle of linen cloth, and Garai sniffed at packets of pods and seeds. Clarás's daughter, Iana, helped to lift the wares off the ground. Sulani carried in bags of salt, sugar and spices, and Orseola held up pot after pot of lamp oil. Estegi regarded me pensively and produced something from one of her sleeves. She sat on her haunches before me.

"They brought this with them also. It is for you. The tradesman said that he obtained it last autumn from another who sometimes swapped spices with the men who sail to Karenokoi."

It was a scroll letter, and though it was wrinkled and weathered, I immediately recognized my daughter's handwriting, and the signet that sealed the letter. It was the symbol of the Vizier.

All eyes were on me. Iana ran toward me and looked curiously at the roll of paper in my hand.

"What is it, Kabira? What have you got?"

Looking at her brown locks I thought, as I had many times before, that she had a little of my Esiko in her. They are half sisters. "Nothing, Iana. But tell me, what did you get from your mother?"

"Look!" she squealed with delight, holding up several skeins of golden-yellow yarn. "Mother says she'll knit me a sweater for winter!"

"How beautiful." I smiled at her. She is a most lovable child.

I read the letter alone, in the evening, once I had made sure that the others were sleeping. I lit a lamp and unfurled the scroll with trembling hands. It was stained and creased after its three-year journey. The letter was not long.

I sat awake for a long time after I read it. And I made a decision. The time had come to stop torturing the others. I had obliged them to write down all that happened in Karenokoi. Even Sulani and Orseola, who protested. Yet I had no alternative. As soon as we could afford to purchase paper, I felt the need to bind all that had happened into words. For I needed a bridge. A bridge to Esiko.

It is two springs since Clarás and her daughter came upon the bloodsnail colony on the island's southern side. This discovery was truly a blessing without equal. For the silk threads we dye with the bloodsnails bring us silver. And with the silver we can purchase such things as we need: salt, oil for food and lamps, rolls of paper and writing implements, fabric. Everything we had gone without for several springs. The first thing I sewed was a frock for Iana. When she was a baby, she simply went naked in warm weather and was wrapped up in rags or old sacks during winter. There was nothing else to clothe her in. Her childhood was characterized by lack.

Before Knowledge House was completed, we lived in a cavern beneath it, where it was dark and cold. But for the most part there was sufficient food to eat. Clarás taught us all how to harvest mussels and snails, how to fish with fishing lines, how to catch squids with hooks, find seabirds' nests and collect eggs—but always to leave one egg in each. Little Iana is already more skilled in these tasks than any of us. Water is her element and she moves through it like a seal—plump, swift and certain. I am too old to climb around hunting for birds' eggs, but on warm days I like to wade along the shores to harvest mussels. Garai is my companion, claiming that she is afraid I will fall and break a bone. "Such things are slow to heal for an old woman like you," she says, and insists on accompanying me. As though she is much younger than I. Old women, the two of us. We must entrust ourselves to the younger ones. I do not wade so often. I prefer not to take Garai away from her garden, which she started to cultivate as soon as Knowledge House was completed. She gathers seeds from the entire island and we obtain whatever else she needs from the tradesmen, if indeed it is obtainable. Garai is never truly at peace unless she is kneeling with her fingers deep in the soil, muttering about fertilizers and irrigation. I prefer simply to sit on the bench Sulani built in the south part of the garden and offer Garai sound advice, which she ignores. Yet I know she appreciates my company.

Sulani built Knowledge House. We very soon made the decision to stay, and not to voyage out on the ocean again in search of Terasu. The risk remained that we would be captured at sea, by pirates or Iskan's men. And *Naondel*, our beautiful boat, had crashed so brutally against the rocks that it was quite impossible to repair her. So we created a new home for ourselves. For all of us. Estegi and Orseola helped with the construction, but it was Sulani who, with arms full of Anji's strength, lifted and carried the great stones. She says she will build another house so that we may have one for sleeping and one for work. I think it is unnecessary, but Orseola nods. "To house those to come," she says, but she often says such strange things. Anji's power protects her mind, Clarás explained, otherwise our dreams would have driven her to madness long ago. Clarás can see such things. It is her gift. Orseola still cannot avoid our dreams, and in them she experiences all that we suffered in Karenokoi, over and over again. When we wake up and our dreams fade, she continues to live them, time and again. She bears a great burden, I understand that, yet I do not know how to help her. I have asked Clarás whether she might pose a danger. "She would never harm the child," was her response, and I had no choice but to be satisfied.

Sulani has built a little stable for her goats as well. The warmth of their bodies was a great joy when we lived in the underground cavern. It was always cold, however many fires we tended. Garai said it was because the life force is at its strongest down there. And, just like with Anji, it contains power for both darkness and light. It was thanks to this power that we were able to defeat Iskan's men. When they besieged us in Knowledge House, we went down into the cavern and hid Iana there. Garai spoke with the life force, committed a blood offering, and then we escaped along the mountainside through one of the paths running out from the cave. We were all overflowing with the life force then—even my arms were strong—and we hurled stones, enormous boulders, down onto the men. It was a cascade of rocks, and every last man was crushed to death.

Then Sulani used the rocks to build a wall around our house. For protection. But now Sulani must wait awhile before building anything new. Her belly is already large, and Garai says that she will give birth in the summer.

I must have been the only one surprised by her pregnancy. Garai, who cares for us all when we are sick, already knew. Orseola sees our dreams, so nothing can be hidden from her. Even Clarás seemed to have known. It was Daera who explained it to me, one evening as we sat alone and sewed. She was sewing a garment for a baby, and I had to ask about Sulani's condition. Daera looked up from her sewing, full of surprise.

"Estegi and Sulani have long been lovers, Kabira. You know that."

I scoffed. "And yet where I come from two women cannot beget children."

"But Estegi is no ordinary woman. Did you not know?"

I tried to hide my stupefaction. "You mean to tell me that she is a man? Garai has said that no man is permitted on the island."

Daera laughed. "No. She *is* a woman. In her heart, and that is where it counts. But her body is not really that of a woman. Or of a man. She has a little of both."

So Sulani is with child, and we will have another baby in our midst. I am looking forward to it. My time is limited. I cannot have much life remaining and it does not bother me. I have long welcomed death. I no longer seek death as an escape, but neither does it frighten me. I have seen enough. Done enough. Though it does make me happy that new life will be born on this island. New children who will be free in a way we sisters could never have imagined.

ω

We perform our tasks, and life here follows its natural course. It is hard work, but all is well. Garai sees to our nourishment and cures our ailments with her herbs and concoctions. Clarás and Iana do the fishing and the laundry. Estegi and Sulani take care of the goats, and gather wild plants for us to eat. Estegi manages our little kitchen and refuses to let anyone else prepare the food. Orseola soothes us when we are plagued with memories and haunted by night terrors. Daera dances and laughs and sings for us, sews clothes and paints beautiful pictures on the walls of Knowledge House, carves items from wood, helps Garai in the garden, and helps Sulani and Estegi gather berries and other good things to eat.

Only I have no purpose. The others scoff or laugh at me when I say so, each according to her nature. They call me Mother and say that I am the one who holds us all together. I do not believe this is necessary. The life force from Anji and Iona's offering is what bind us together. But I let them be. I devote my time to organizing and interpreting Iskan's secret scriptures, to writing down all that has happened, and encouraging the others to do the same. So that nothing is forgotten. This is what I have told them.

However, it is not the whole truth. It has also been to keep Esiko present with me. How I have worried about her. What did Iskan do with her after we escaped? What has her life become? Is she even alive?

Now I am holding her letter in my hands. Now I know. I shall write no reply. It is time I let go of my daughter.

ESIKO'S LETTER

Most esteemed mother, may your eyes remain sharp, your hands steady and your mind clear.

As I write this, I am sitting at a table in Serenity House. The sun is hanging low and shining through the large windows, and dust is flying like little lanterns in the golden light. By my elbow rests a bowl of wine and a dish of fried weja. The smell of them and their thin sprinkle of sugar sparkling in the sun make me think of the evenings we spent together in your chambers. They were quiet times, filled with soft shadows, sweet pastries and peace. With Father everything was quick, sharp, outlined with razor edges. You were the soft one. We had our secret and it bound us together. It felt as though you were holding me by threads of spider-spun silk wherever I went. Thus, thanks to your gift, I have enjoyed more freedom than you or any other woman in Ohaddin ever has. I will never forget. It is by virtue of this gift that I write to you now, Mother. There will be no other letter after this. For there is much I cannot forgive, and my gratitude for my freedom does not heal all wounds.

Most heinous of all is the loss of Anji.

Three years have passed since you murdered Anji. I feel the loss as a burning pain in my heart every day, the very moment I awake. You will never understand how it feels. You believe that you do, and I can well imagine your reaction as I write these words, scoffing and shrugging your shoulders, that irritating wrinkle that appears in your forehead, certain you know all there is to know about Anji because you grew up as her guardian and friend. Yet Anji was my twin; she was a part of me and I of her. She was with me since before I can remember. I cannot comprehend that she is gone. A part of me died with her, and I do not know how I shall bear it. Father does not understand my loss either; Anji has never meant the same to him as to me. And whatever he may think, she never spoke to him as she spoke unto me. I understood all she said effortlessly. She whispered it directly to my heart, my blood. She was a part of me from before I was born. Your experience cannot compare.

It is not only I who suffers, who feels the pain and loss of what once was. The whole of Renka has collapsed. No crops grow. There is nothing to harvest. I believe that the earth will recover, gradually—that is what I have deduced from reading Father's scrolls about other places that have lost their heart. For Anji was the very heart of Renka, and Father recast her as the heart of the entire realm of Karenokoi.

The laborers were the first to leave when they stopped receiving food and payment. They traveled eastward, for the most part, if they did not find work on trading ships. Some have become highwaymen and pirates.

The landowners remained the longest, reluctant to surrender their ancestral plantations and the graves of their forefathers. Yet now they too have left. The crop failures were so severe that they could not purchase food even with pure gold. And gold does not satisfy hunger. Where they are going and how they will survive is a mystery. Perhaps those who have collected enough gold and jewels can create a new life for themselves in other lands. Perhaps not. They may return when the earth is fertile once more. Who knows.

I am fully occupied with efforts to help the needy. On my orders, food from the Sovereign's repository has been shared out through the winter. I have brought in more supplies with what resources I have. However, little money remains after the war, and even less remains to purchase necessities. No one is willing to lend to Karenokoi after Father's expansions. I cannot raise taxes in the other districts, as the people are already living on their knees. I do not want to be hated and feared, as Father was. My people shall love and fear me.

The Sovereign's palace stands empty. I could inhabit it, but am content in my customary quarters. I have brought Sonan's wife and daughter here to live with me and I find the company does me good. I play with the child in the evenings. She shows great intelligence and her mother is a savvy woman who is already teaching her to read and write. Perhaps she will be my vizier when she comes of age. We make offerings in memory of Sonan, Mother, and of Korin and Enon. As long as I live, their spirits shall be honored and remembered. I hope this knowledge affords you some peace. I have also begun to burn incense and offer coins for the souls of my sisters. The ones to whom life was denied. Though I do not know how many they were, and though they are nameless, I honor them all through remembrance.

I make sure there are fresh flowers in the throne hall in Glory's Abode every day. The cult Father built up around the Sovereign is serving me well, and it is thanks to this that I am now able to govern Karenokoi. We are continuing to honor the spirit of the Sovereign on the day of his passing, and at harvest. We organize grand processions and share out alms and food for the poor. I grant all the servants, Sovereign's officials and laborers a day off so that they may honor and offer to the Sovereign, and to their own dead. In these ways I have taken the place of the Sovereign's eldest son.

There are some who oppose this. You can certainly guess who, though it matters little. Some men at the court. They say that I am not a man. Their talk does not worry me. I know so much more about Karenokoi than they do. I do not need Anji's oaki to keep them at bay, keep them calm and afraid. The soldiers love me. I have ridden into battle with them, fought by their side, proved myself worthy of their respect. They are loyal to me, even when the palace lapdogs start whimpering. I am sure to give the soldiers generous provisions and great respect, and to remind the palace lapdogs of such during the parades, when I ride out with my army instead of the courtiers.

I mean to govern this realm, and fortify the borders Father drew up for Karenokoi, and all the historians shall tell of Esiko, the first woman to rule Karenokoi. This is what Anji showed me before you killed her. I have decided to remain Esiko, though I could have called myself Orano. Yet as Esiko I act as Orano did, and am in all ways as Orano was. I will take a husband, someone with great wealth or perhaps an important position in one of the vassal states. In Nernai there is a governor's son, and I might make the Governor understand what an honor it would be for his son to wed the Vizier. For I am vizier now, I use the signet and enjoy the privileges of vizier, and all the vizier's servants and courtiers follow my orders. Though I have not killed my father for the position, as my father killed his, may his spirit rest in peace.

Father was enraged when you killed Anji, Mother, and all the more so when he discovered that you had stolen so many of his most secret scrolls. The injury Iona inflicted upon him kept him bedridden for a very long time. Once he was back on his feet and realized that Anji truly was dead, and that his library had been plundered, madness took him. I believe it was not long before he dispatched a ship to locate you all. I knew nothing of it, Mother, I swear. I believed all were loyal to me, but clearly some remained whom Father could bribe. I first heard of the expedition when we received news that it had failed. No survivors—how did you do it, Mother? I wonder about it sometimes. But then I see you all before me, gathered around Anji on that dreadful night, and I think of all that passed there and all that followed, and I wonder no more. Together you are capable of anything. You alone are capable of anything. You believe that I take after my father, but it is not so. Father has been driven by uncertainty and fear his whole life. Hence his need for Anji. You, however, were able to break free entirely by yourself. That is the strength I carry within me. That is how I know that I can survive without the spring, even though I grieve.

Yet Father cannot. When he found out that the men had failed to recover the stolen articles, his mind became definitively broken. He lost all hope of reawakening Anji, for that was the knowledge he believes is hidden in the stolen scrolls. He had not yet read them all, not solved all the mysteries, and neither had I, so I do not know whether what he says is true. Now he sits beside the lifeless water and mutters to himself. He even sleeps there. But Anji has been muted and does not respond. His mind is broken, he is like a babbling little child, and the years have suddenly caught up with him. His hair is white, his skin slack on his bowed body, his hands shake and all strength has deserted his limbs. I have stopped visiting him, because when he sees me he usually mistakes me for Izani, his mother. Sometimes he calls me Lehan and grabs for me with lustful hands. I have no wish to see him in this state.

He can no longer do any harm, Mother. Neither with the power of the life force nor with his own human hands. Nobody fears him any longer. I see to it that servants bring him food and that he has shelter from the elements, but that is all. I do not believe he will survive the next winter.

I thought you ought to know. You need not fear him or his vengeance. You can live out the rest of your life in safety and peace.

I know why you believed you must kill Anji, Mother. I understand your decision. Perhaps in your place I would have done the same—what do I know about having a daughter? All I know is that Anji was closer to me than you or Father ever were. I understand, but I cannot forgive.

Sometimes I believe that some of her life force lives in me still, and it is thanks to this that powerful men obey my orders. Perhaps the loyalty I inspire in my soldiers is a remnant of something that emanated from Anji as she died. Do you ever feel as though you received a gift from Anji?

No, do not answer. I do not want you to write to me. I do not want to know whether you are alive or dead, Mother. I want to retain my image of you on the island where you and the other women have made your new home, with the ocean winds in your hair, hoary and strong as the mountain itself. I know that you have survived. And now you know that I have too.

The glow of the fire pot has died down and an evening chill has crept in through the windows. A blackbird is singing outside. My eyes are heavy and my bed is calling. Tomorrow is another long working day for the Vizier of Karenokoi. There is so much to be done. I love it.

And I love you.

Farewell, Mother.

Esiko

DAERA

I am sitting and writing this high up in the mountain we call White Lady. Houses are good for rains and storms, but on a beautiful summer day such as this I want to feel the sun on my skin, and see Menos stretched out before me, and be dazzled by the glittering blue sea. After nigh fifty years, I am still overawed by the beauty of this island. Was there ever a more beautiful place? Mighty mountains reach for the sky, their slopes covered in olive trees and cypresses, and blanketed white with flowers in spring. I have walked every path along these mountains, and, though it is not my duty, I like to lead the goats out to pasture. I love the new novices; I love their laughter and their exuberance, and their very existence. Still, at times nothing can compare to aromatic thyme and rosemary under my feet and the screech of the koan birds as I tread these beloved paths yet again.

Iona was supposed to die on an island. It is a fitting destiny for me. My death is not far off now. I am the last who remains of we who sailed to Menos in *Naondel*. Orseola passed on last year, already an old woman. I will not reach such old age, but it does not matter to me. I have had a fine life. A real life! A life that came as a surprise and a gift. My bones will lie in the crypt with the others' someday. But I have asked them to bury my skull high on the mountain where I now sit. Then I will become Iona once more, and finally she will find peace.

After Estegi and Sulani passed away, Iana set out on a long

voyage to find their son, Taro, and give him word that his mothers were gone. When she returned, alone with a babe at her breast, she became the third Mother of our little abbey.

New novices arrive all the time. The rumors and whispers of an island only for women have spread around the world, perhaps from the fishermen and tradesmen who visit us. The stories have made their way to girls who have been beaten, persecuted, tortured. They have endured great dangers to find us. It is good that all we have built here will not fall and be forgotten. We have created something new, the likes of which exists nowhere else in this oft dark and troublesome world. Here the girls find peace, safety and knowledge. Here they learn that they are valuable and strong. Perhaps the ripples of change we spread from this island could one day subvert everything.

I will commit this text of mine to the Abbey's secret chronicles, where we safeguard the scriptures stolen from Ohaddin. May these be the final words written by the First Sisters of Menos. May this be the start of something new.

NAME LIST

This chronicle tells of Kabira of Ohaddin, Garai of the Meirem Desert, Estegi of Areko, Orseola of Terasu, Sulani of the River, Clarás of the sea, Iona of the sacred isle of Matheli, and Daera of Naondel. I, Kabira, have noted the following names, as they are important to our story.

Ohaddin
Esiko—Kabira's mother
Malik—Kabira's father
Tihe—brother
Lehan—sister
Agin—sister
Aikon—loyal old servant

Areko
Iskan ak Honta-che—son of the Vizier
Honta ak Lien-che—the Vizier
Izani ak Oshime-chi—Iskan's mother
Orlan—eldest son of the Sovereign Prince

Ohaddin, later
Korin—Iskan's first son
Enon—Iskan's second son
Sonan—Iskan's third son
Orano / Esiko—Iskan's fourth son/daughter
Meriba—concubine
Aberra—concubine

Amdurabi (district)
Eraban ak Usti-chu—district governor
Hánai ak Eraban-chu—daughter of Eraban

Terasu
Aurelo—boy
Oera—Orseola's sister
Obare—Orseola's brother

Menos
Iana and Taro—children

ACKNOWLEDGMENTS

Thank you, Nora Garusi and Anna Gullichsen, who gave me their houses so I could write undisturbed. There is a strong presence of Dönsby and Solhem in *Naondel*. Thanks to The Secret Badger Society and Ordmördarna for your help with all possible details in the manuscript. Thanks to the whole gang at Fantastisk podd, a wonderful and incredibly inspirational community to be a part of. Thanks to Nora Strömman, who quaked in terror along with me at a haunted house in Stockholm as I was rewriting Sulani's perspective. Thanks to Monika Fagerholm, who provided me with the inspirational exercises in Leros that helped me to find Iona. A big thank-you to Nene Ormes, who was *Naondel's* first reader and who helped steer me away from a lot of bad habits and slipups in style and form. What's more, you did it with tact, and with the right balance of praise and a firm hand. Thanks to Saara Tiuraniemi, who encouraged a text she had never read and provided insights that were of great help, and to my Finnish editor, Anna Warras, who helps me keep the faith when I have forgotten how. As always, thanks to my editor Sara Ehnholm Hielm, whom I follow through thick and thin, because without her I would not be the writer I am today. And thank you, Travis, for supporting, believing in, and discussing ideas with me. This book, like all the others, is just as much yours as it is mine.